HIGH HEAT

RICHARD CASTLE

HIGH HEAT

RICHARD CASTLE

👑 KINGSWELL

LOS ANGELES • NEW YORK

For information address Kingswell,
1101 Flower Street, Glendale, California 91201.

Editorial Director: Wendy Lefkon
Executive Editor: Laura Hopper
Cover designed by Alfred Sole

ISBN 978-1-4847-8150-0

Printed in the United States of America

To K.B.
For always and more

ONE

R*eykjavík*. The mere word sent shivers of ecstasy down Nikki Heat's spine.

Reykjavík. It was like a sumptuous gourmet meal, a fragrant bubble bath, and a shot of top-shelf tequila, joined in a way that the delights of each amplified the others.

Reykjavík. Say it loud and there's music playing. Say it soft and . . . Well, there was more loud than soft when it came to the very best parts of Reykjavík.

Yes, Reykjavík. To the uninformed—which included the entire world's population, save for one incredible man—it was the capital and main fishing port of the island nation of Iceland, a lonely chunk of volcanic rock in the North Atlantic, just south of the Arctic Circle.

To Heat, it was something else entirely. Something far less lonely and far more inviting.

Reykjavík was what her husband, the ruggedly handsome and world-famous magazine writer Jameson Rook, called where he had taken her on their honeymoon. He had chosen the name in the same spirit as the island's original Norse settlers, who dubbed their green, temperate new home *Snæland*—literally "snow land"—to deter Viking pillagers.

Rook wasn't looking to throw off the Vikings, of course. He was more concerned with *Us Weekly* and the gossip column of the *New York Ledger*, publications whose journalistic sensibilities often brought to mind plundering seafaring warriors.

To be clear, Reykjavík wasn't really Reykjavík, and it wasn't just one place. The newlyweds' Reykjavík turned out to be located on three different continents, in major cities and small towns, in the tropics and on the tundra.

Taken collectively, their tour of the various destinations had been like *Around the World in Eighty Days*, albeit not as lengthy. Jules Verne didn't have to contend with the New York Police Department's vacation policy. Then again, he also didn't have access to a rich friend's private jet, as Rook did.

Without having to bother with the inconveniences of commercial air travel, Rook had been able to show her the best of the hidden off-the-beaten-path gems he had discovered during his days as a foreign correspondent—every secret beach, locals-only restaurant, and little-known treasure you couldn't learn about in the guidebooks.

They had relished leisurely wine-and-cheese picnics in the Alps, laughing about nothing and everything, with the Jungfraujoch smiling down on them. They had sunbathed in the nude on the Amalfi Coast, safe in the knowledge that Rook knew spots the paparazzi didn't. They had meditated in a Tibetan pagoda, achieving an inner peace that was impossible to find when they were enjoined in the hectic pace of their daily lives.

And they had made love. Oh, how they made love. Heat was astonished at Rook's stamina and creativity, at how even now, years into their relationship, he had found new and inventive ways to take her to ever-greater heights, elevations of bliss that made the mighty Himalayas seem like lowly foothills. She had discovered a few new tricks for pleasing him as well. The phrase "let's go to Reykjavík"—or any of its various derivations—had taken on special meaning.

Suffice it to say the real Reykjavík was known for its unusual tectonic activity—and so was their version of it.

Heat hadn't thought getting married would change anything fundamental about their union. She thought they would throw a big party, take a nice trip, and things would continue more or less as they always had.

But Captain Nikki Heat, whose instincts as a detective were seldom wrong, had turned out to be mistaken in that assumption about her personal life. Getting married had lowered the last barriers between them, allowing for an intimacy like she had never experienced before. Heat had thought she was in love with Rook before their wedding. She recognized that was just a prolonged crush compared to what she felt now.

And if she sighed as she lay in bed and thumbed through pictures of their honeymoon, on an early Tuesday morning in October—more than a year since they had returned from Reykjavík—it was not because she was again thinking about her husband's magnificent ass. It was because the man who had made her the happiest woman on the planet was not around for a prework quickie.

Rook had been away on assignment since Sunday. The two-time Pulitzer Prize winner was writing a profile for *First Press* about Legs Kline, the billionaire businessman turned unexpected independent contender for the US presidency. Kline had seized on the general dissatisfaction with the main party candidates—the Democratic nominee, Senator Lindsy Gardner, was a librarian turned politician who was said to be too nice to be president; the Republican pick, Caleb Brown, was a take-no-prisoners lawmaker who was said to be too mean—and turned it into real momentum toward the White House.

Who is Legs Kline, really? That had been the question on the lips of the electorate ever since. Jameson Rook was the one journalist America trusted for a straight answer.

And now that the election was just three weeks off, the clock was ticking. Rook had been working day and night on the profile, to the detriment of Heat's love life. He had checked in the previous night from somewhere in the Midwest, where he had been visiting a Kline Industries fracking operation. Next it would be a smelting plant on the shores of Lake Erie and then a logging camp in the Rockies . . . or was it a liquid natural gas operation on the Gulf Coast?

She couldn't keep track. Rook had been vague about when he would return. All she knew was he would finish his tour of the Kline Industries facilities, then join the candidate on the campaign trail in the hopes of scoring a one-on-one interview. And that might take a while.

Just as she was about to let out another wistful sigh, her smartphone rang. She grabbed it off the nightstand where she kept it, its ringer always turned on high so it would awaken her from even the deepest sleep.

"Heat."

"Captain." It was the voice of Miguel Ochoa, the co-leader of her detective squad. "We got something at the precinct you really need to see. How soon can you be in?"

"On my way," Heat said, already swinging her feet to the floor.

"Is Rook with you?"

"No."

"Where is he?"

"I have no idea. Bismarck maybe."

"That's . . . Montana, right?"

"North Dakota, genius."

"Okay. Good enough."

She was about to hang up, but Ochoa added, "By the way, you eaten breakfast yet?"

"No."

"Good. Keep it that way."

The New York Police Department's Twentieth Precinct was not much to look at, unless you found visual splendor in unfinished paperwork, careworn steel office furniture, and time-stained carpeting.

Still, Nikki Heat loved it. She loved the way the way it hummed when there was a big case. She loved that so many of the people there had the brains and drive to pursue far more lucrative work but had chosen to protect and serve the people of New York City instead. She even loved the smell: all Old Spice, stale coffee, and determination.

The Two-Oh had been Nikki Heat's work home since she was a rookie so fresh out of the academy the ink on her diploma was still damp.

No one had given her much of a chance to survive more than a year or two back then. She wasn't some working-class kid who had spent her youth toughening herself on asphalt and glass shards, like so many of the rest of them. Everything about her—from her lack of bridge-and-tunnel accent to her flawless posture—screamed refinement. And police work wasn't refined.

In truth, the only reason her fellow officers paid her any attention at first was because it was rare to see a fashion-model-gorgeous brunette in a beat cop's uniform.

But they soon learned not to underestimate Nikki Heat. She quickly aced her sergeant's exam, and that was only the start. Heat was smart, hardworking, and devoted, a combination that earned her a spot as one of the NYPD's youngest detectives. Before long, she was a squad leader and a lieutenant.

Her latest promotion—one she had actually resisted for a time, so repulsed was she by bureaucracy—was to captain. And her experience over the past year with said bureaucracy made her hope her career would stay stalled where it was.

Ultimately, it was police work, not paperwork, that gave her satisfaction. As her management responsibilities grew—and, at times, threatened to overwhelm her—the only thing that continued to make her job worthwhile was that she was able to keep both feet in her precinct's investigations.

Which was why she made quick work of her trip to the precinct and then to the bull pen, where she found her detectives already assembled around a computer screen.

Sean Raley, the other detective squad co-leader, was the one in front of the keyboard. Ochoa was right behind him. Also on hand were detectives Daniel Rhymer and Randall Feller, who had helped Heat crack some of her biggest cases, and Detective Inez Aguinaldo, still considered the new kid even though she had a few years and some prominent investigations under her belt.

"What you got, Roach?" Heat asked, using the mash-up nickname for Raley and Ochoa.

"Some sick shit," Ochoa said. He turned to Raley. "You tell her, homes. I'm not sure I got the stomach for it."

"This video was sent to the precinct's main e-mail address earlier this morning," Raley said. "It was routed through an untraceable IP address. I've already spent a half hour trying to crack it and I can already tell I'm not going to get anywhere. Whoever did this must have learned their trade from the kiddie-porn guys. They're that good."

"Does the account have a name on it?" Heat asked.

"Yeah," Raley said. "It shows up as 'American ISIS.'"

Heat took a beat to absorb that information. She had been in numerous meetings where the NYPD's counterterrorism experts had warned about the threat from the Islamic State and the wannabe wackos who might claim to be its adherents. She had also been in meetings with Muslim clerics, teachers, and business leaders, who repeatedly reminded the NYPD brass that ISIS's version of Islam was a narrow-minded and deranged perversion of the religion as it was practiced by 1.5 billion peaceful people around the planet.

"Okay, let's see it," Heat said.

"I have to warn you, it's pretty graphic," Raley said.

Heat, who had solved crimes in which the victims had been found in every conceivable condition and at a wide range of temperatures—from frozen in suitcases to baked in pizza ovens—fixed Raley with a you-gotta-be-kidding-me glare.

"Okay, don't say I didn't warn you," he said, bringing his hands up for a second, then returning his finger to the mouse button and giving it a click. "Here goes."

The video was grainy and low quality, the kind that didn't seem to belong in an era when most people had eight megapixels on the phones in their pockets. It showed two men standing in a large open room, whose only structures were occasional support poles on a floor covered in prayer rugs.

The men had masks on their faces and sunglasses over their eyes. Every inch of their skin was covered. They wore sand-colored thobes on their bodies and turbans on their heads. Their hands were gloved.

Kneeling in front of them was a woman—a young woman, with a shapely, slender body. She was wearing jeans and a zip-up sweatshirt. Her head had been covered by a burlap bag with a black stripe running down one side. A few strands of blond hair protruded from the bag. Her hands had been bound behind her and may have been hog-tied to a similar binding on her ankles. Another rope was tied around her chest. It didn't seem like she could move.

The men seemed to be looking at someone just to the left of the camera, who must have nodded or given some kind of cue, instructing one of the men to begin speaking.

"We come to you in the name of Allah, the Real Truth, the Hearer, the Seer, the Benefactor, who the Prophet Muhammad, peace be upon him, has declared to be the One and Only God," the man on the left said. "We proclaim our loyalty to the Islamic State and to the caliphate founded by the great and visionary Abu Bakr al-Baghdadi. And we proclaim our fealty to Allah. May all we do please Him and serve Him."

"Allahu akbar," said the man on the right, who was holding something behind his back.

The men's voices had been distorted so they sounded muddled and mechanical, like Darth Vader at the bottom of a well.

"The devil United States of America and its devil military have attacked our lands and our people for many years, waging a modern-day crusade against our blessed religion and against all who exalt Almighty Allah," the one on the left said. "We have suffered under the imperialist thumb of the Yankee scum for too long. We have suffered as you rape our lands in your insatiable thirst for our oil. And today we say: no more!"

"Allahu akbar," the one on the right said.

"Now we are continuing the work of the great leader, Osama bin Laden, who first taught us we must take the fight to the enemy," the man on the left said. "We have joined the *jihad* that he declared but left unfinished when he was martyred at the hands of the pig enemy. And so we return to the place of his greatest triumph, here in the sin-blackened heart of America."

"Allahu akbar," the one on the right said again.

"There is no greater symbol of your ignorance than your lying puppet media, which only exists to spread the distorted propaganda of your Zionist government," the man on the left said. "And there is no greater sin than the way your people allow your women to shamefully expose their bodies and flaunt that which ought to be seen only by their husbands. And so we have chosen to execute this infidel female journalist with one mighty stroke."

He gripped the rope that had been tied around the woman's chest, lest she get any last-second notions about trying to roll out of the way.

"Allahu akbar," the man on the right said, before bringing a gleaming machete from behind his back, where he had been hiding it.

He held it high, brandishing it for a moment, then swung it with brutal force into the woman's neck.

Heat took in a sharp breath as the blade plunged into the woman's skin with a wet, meaty sound. The blow had been vicious—it just didn't have quite enough force behind it. The human neck is thick with muscles, bone, and sinew. It has been designed through millions of years of evolution to keep the neck firmly connected to the rest of the body, and it is not so easily severed.

The "one mighty stroke" turned into a series of desperate hacks, then eventually to a clumsy sawing motion. The victim surely would have slumped were it not for the masked man holding her up from behind. And she surely would have screamed, except her vocal cords had already been severed.

Instead, the man on the right just kept sawing in eerie silence, like he was attacking a particularly stubborn piece of brush with a branch saw, until the woman's head toppled off her neck. Heat watched in horror as it landed with a *thunk* on the carpeted floor, then rolled out of sight of the camera's lens.

At that moment, Heat thought nothing could be more shocking. Then the man on the left spoke again.

"This is only the beginning," he said. "We will soon seize another one of your journalists. It will be one of your most beloved writers, a man who represents the worst of your imperialist decadence.

"May it please Allah: our next victim will be Jameson Rook."

TWO

Every detective in the bull pen was now staring at their captain. Heat stood there, hoping her face didn't betray the heart-pounding turmoil the rest of her had suddenly been plunged into.

Jameson Rook. Did that masked lunatic really just say her husband's name?

She suddenly couldn't control her breathing. Heat had accepted that her own job came with its share of risk, and that some of that danger had a tendency to spill into Rook's life. Likewise, she had accepted that Rook's public profile made him a target for certain unsavory elements.

But normally that meant blind items on the gossip column and idiotic tweets from Internet trolls. Not machete-bearing masked terrorists.

This was beyond anything she had prepared herself for emotionally. It went to something she had learned from those counterterrorism briefings: ISIS didn't play by the same rules as everyone else. They didn't play by any rules at all. They turned women into sex slaves. They destroyed timeless masterworks of art. They burned captives alive. They had no concept of human dignity. They had no respect for human life. All they knew was brutality, violence, and destruction.

These men—and there had to be at least three, since there was someone behind that camera—would do whatever it took to get their hands on Rook, even if it meant martyring themselves. Especially if it meant martyring themselves. They wouldn't stop until Rook's head was the one bouncing on the floor.

Subconsciously, she brought her hand to her neck. People who study such things could have told her it was a classic gesture that signified feelings of vulnerability. The moment she realized she was doing it, she lowered her hand.

Too late.

"That's why I asked where Rook was," Ochoa said quietly. "I figured he'd be safe enough in Montana."

"North Dakota," Heat said distractedly.

"Whatever," Ochoa replied. "Don't worry, Captain. These guys can't get at him there. I don't think they even know North Dakota exists."

The other detectives weren't saying a word. They were all just looking at her, seeing how she'd react to the crisis. Ever since she became captain, Heat felt her life had been a series of tests. And she was not only taking them on her own behalf. She was taking them for her entire gender.

She was the first female captain in the history of the Twentieth Precinct. Some of the men who had come before her had been highly competent commanders who represented the best of what the shield was all about. Others had been careerist fools who had stumbled into the top spot by some combination of luck and the Peter Principle.

Heat knew she was being judged by a different standard. Maybe it shouldn't have been that way, there in the second decade of the twenty-first century. But Heat didn't confuse what should be with what was.

At that moment, her detectives were wondering: Would the boss keep her cool, assess the situation, and set the squad into action? *Like a man.* Or would she freak out and give in to her emotions? *Like a girl.*

Heat blinked twice. Then she got her priorities straight. She could worry about the case in a moment. Her husband's life came first.

"I have to make a phone call," was all she could say. Then she stumbled into her office and closed the door.

Her hands were shaking as she pressed the button to speed-dial Rook.

"Come on," she whispered fervently as the call connected. "Pick up."

There was no ring. The call went straight to voice mail.

"You've reached the personal mobile phone of Jameson Rook," her husband's smooth, sexy voice said. "Press one if you want to leave a message for my first Pulitzer Prize. Press two if—"

Heat jabbed her phone's pound button to shortcut directly to the leaving-a-message part, then waited what felt like an eternity for the beep to finish. Yet when it was through, signaling that she could begin talking, she realized she didn't even know what she wanted to say. Her mind had been racing too quickly to formulate anything coherent.

"Hey, it's me," she said, her voice sounding unusually tremulous and uncertain. "Look, it's really important. You have to call me as soon as you get this, okay? Like, immediately."

Heat let that linger for a second. It wasn't good enough. She had to impress upon him the danger he was in.

"If you don't get me for some reason, go directly to the police station in whatever city you're in. Tell them you need protection because there's been . . . there's been a credible threat against your life. And if you can't get to the police, at least find someone with a gun who can watch your back, and . . . Look, just call me, okay? I love you."

She ended the call and sagged against the wall. Then she turned and saw the blinds to her office were open. The entire squad could see her.

Very deliberately, she took a deep breath. Then another. She looked down at her blouse, which was crisply ironed and still tucked neatly into the flat waistband of her slacks. She brought her chin up and straightened her spine.

Then she opened the door of her office and returned to the bull pen.

"Play that video again," she said.

"Cap," Raley begin, "you sure you want to—"

"Play the fucking video, Rales," Heat said.

Time froze for a second. Nikki Heat almost never swore, and everyone in the precinct knew it. She fixed her detectives with a steely gaze and addressed them in a raised voice that had rediscovered its resolve.

"Let's not allow the sensationalism of this video to distract us," she said. "This is a murder investigation, people. Murder investigations are what we do here."

She pointed at the screen. "That video is our first piece of evidence. It's also the killers' first mistake. And I'm sure they've made others. I don't care about untraceable IP addresses. That video is laying down all the bread crumbs we need. We're going to follow the trail straight to those scumbags, and then we're going to put them away. Because that's what we do to bad guys here in the Two-Oh."

"Hell yeah," Feller hooted.

"We'll get 'em, Cap," Rhymer said.

Roach and Aguinaldo were nodding approvingly.

The video had knocked Heat off balance. But not for long. She had her legs back underneath her and her team assembled around her. And it was a group of detectives who were as good as any in the NYPD.

Those ISIS lunatics thought they were going to get Nikki Heat's husband.

Not if she got them first.

They watched the video again, this time with what Heat liked to call "beginner's eyes."

It was a way of thinking as much as it was a way of looking at evidence. Heat had long ago observed that veteran detectives often became jaded. Thinking they had seen it all before, they trusted in their experience to solve the crime and overlooked some of the small details that a nervous beginner, who made sure to take in everything, did not.

Heat put on her best beginner's eyes. She noticed the body language of the victim, who hadn't begged for her life—too proud. She noted that the man with the machete had swung the weapon with his left hand, making him unusual in Arab culture, which considered the left hand unclean and forced children to use their right. She saw the way the men on camera kept looking at someone off camera, probably the person who was in charge.

When the video ended, Heat instructed Raley to pause it, freezing the frame just before the screen went dark. The threat against Rook was now a thing she had put in its own box. Compartmentalizing was often the only way a cop could keep doing her job, and Nikki Heat was one of the best at it.

"Okay, first we need to identify our victim," Heat said. "We know she's a journalist, but New York City has a lot of those."

"Too many," Ochoa said, then immediately buttoned his mouth when Heat glared at him.

"Rales, can you give me an estimate of the victim's height?" Heat asked.

Raley, who wasn't known as the king of all surveillance media for nothing, said, "Way ahead of you."

He pointed toward the ceiling depicted in the video. It was white corkboard, with recessed fluorescent lighting fixtures. "Standard commercial fluorescent light bulbs are forty-eight inches long. All I had to do was take that known factor and use it to extrapolate the height of the victim. It got a little tricky, because the victim is kneeling. But assuming normal thigh-to-calf ratio, she is between five foot eight and five foot ten."

"Good work," Heat said.

She turned to Detective Feller, a streetwise city native, and said, "Head over to Missing Persons and see if anyone has recently called in a report about a white female under age forty, approximately five-nine. Start in the five boroughs but then go to the suburbs. Not many people on a journalist's salary can afford to live here. Look at Maplewood, Montclair, Poughkeepsie. You get the idea. Weed out the homeless, the runaways, and the drug addicts, and see if there's anyone left."

"Got it," Feller said.

"Opie," she said, looking at Rhymer, who brought his towheaded clean-cut looks and southern mountain twang with him from Roanoke, Virginia. "Call around to the major newspapers and magazines. Talk to the managing editors and see if they have anyone unaccounted for—maybe someone failed to show up for work or isn't answering her cell phone. But, for God's sake, don't tip them off as to what's going on. Just be as vague as possible."

"You betcha," Rhymer said.

"Oach," she said, and the short, powerfully built Miguel Ochoa stepped forward. "I want you to interface with Cooper McMains on the Counterterrorism Task Force. Let's get a line on any of the extremist groups in the city who might pull something like this. It's possible we're dealing with a new element. But if McMains thinks it's one of his frequent fliers who is suddenly escalating, let's start kicking down doors and looking for video equipment."

"And machetes," Ochoa said.

"Yes, and machetes."

"Rales," she said. She was now looking at the nattily dressed Irish American sitting at the computer. "I need a crime scene. There has to be *something* in that video that will help us identify where it was shot. Maybe there's a permit posted on the wall. Maybe there's a distinctive building we can see out the window. Just keep working it until you find something. We need a where if we're going to have any chance at coming up with a who."

"Yes, sir," Raley said.

Inez Aguinaldo, the only detective not yet tasked, shifted her weight. Heat had personally recruited the former military police-woman from the Southampton Village Police Department, out on the tip of Long Island, because Heat liked the woman's cool. Everything about Aguinaldo was buttoned-down and professional, much like the captain she now reported to.

"Aguinaldo," Heat said. "I haven't forgotten you. I'm just saving the best for last. I want you chasing down our odd sock."

When Heat used the phrase "odd sock," it was to refer to that one piece of evidence that didn't seem to fit with the others.

"Or in this case, it might actually be a different piece of clothing, which is why—no offense to the gentlemen here—I want a slightly more discriminating eye working it," Heat continued, then pointed to the lower left corner of the screen. "Rales, can you zoom in on that spot?"

Raley complied, enlarging what was otherwise just an empty spot on the floor.

"Can you sharpen it a bit for me?"

Raley played with the keyboard and mouse for a minute. Slowly, what had been a blurry, brightly colored blob in the corner gained resolution.

"Let me just isolate it a little more," Raley said. "And I've got one more filter I can pass it through."

With one last dramatic click, Raley brought the spot into focus. It was an exquisite silk scarf, one that looked altogether out of place on the floor of a jihadist's secret hideout.

"Give me two printouts of that," Heat said. "Aguinaldo, I want you to take this around to the department stores and boutiques. See if any-one can tell us more about it. This doesn't look like an everyday scarf to me. If we're lucky, it's some kind of limited-edition designer item only carried by one or two retailers, and we can start narrowing down who might have purchased it."

"Start at Saks," Feller volunteered. "If you go in the entrance at

Fifth and Fiftieth, the scarves are up on the second floor by the escalator, right next to women's outerwear."

Everyone in the bull pen was suddenly staring at Feller.

"What?" Feller said, defensively. "They got nice stuff there."

"He goes there to hit on the perfume girls when he's off duty," Rhymer explained.

"Might as well toss your line in the water where you know there's fish," Feller said, grinning. "I thought you country boys knew that."

"Okay, let's stay focused, people," Heat said, then turned back to Aguinaldo. "If any of the merchants give you a hard time about giving up customer info, let me know and we'll expedite a warrant. I'm sure Judge Simpson would do anything to help once he hears his favorite poker buddy is in trouble."

"You got it, Captain."

Heat walked over to a blank dry-erase board, grabbed a marker, and, in the spot where they usually attached a picture of the victim, instead drew a large question mark. Then she attached a picture of the scarf.

The murder board—where she and other detectives would keep track of leads and try to make connections between the evidence they posted there—had officially been started.

"All right. I want regular reports, people," Heat called as the detectives began to break up. "If you get a lead, for God's sake don't sit on it. I don't think I need to remind you, but time is not on our side here."

She also didn't need to remind them what was at stake.

Heat returned to her office, closed the door behind her, and tried Rook again.

Immediately she heard, "You've reached the personal mobile phone of Jameson Rook. Press one if—"

She hung up, then banged out a text message: CALL ME! 911!

The message disappeared into the cellular ether. Heat just stood there for a second, momentarily unsure what to do with herself. She looked over at her desk, which was mounded with CompStat reports, complaints about stop-and-frisk, vouchers in need of signing . . .

No. She couldn't face any of that right then. Heat was good at compartmentalizing, but she wasn't *that* good.

The case. The video. Her husband. That was all she could think about.

She needed a clear head and some fresh air. Or at least the best air New York could offer. That would help her work through the case again. The terrorists hadn't left her much to go on, but she still wanted to make sure she wasn't missing anything.

Before anyone could knock on her door and interrupt her with an overtime request, she fled toward the elevator, the one with half the NYPD shield on either side. Soon she was out on 82nd Street.

The crisp embrace of an October morning was there to greet her. A City of New York garbage truck was slowly working its way up the street, its crew making collections one and two bags at a time, a malodorous smell wafting behind it. A food cart vendor pushed past, heading in the direction of Columbus Avenue and the promise of greater foot traffic. A sidewalk oak tree—most of its leaves orange or yellow but a few of them still green—stirred in the breeze.

Heat sat on the steps to the precinct. A group like ISIS presented a unique challenge to even the best detective squad, because much like with an investigation into a random serial killer, the usual investigative paths—Had the victim received any threats? Who might have had motive to kill her? Was there a jealous husband, an angry boyfriend, a crazed neighbor?—weren't really available.

Yet unlike with a serial killer, in this case there was no profiling, no patterning, no textbook or behavioral expert to consult. Beyond the anachronistic interpretation of a fifteen-hundred-year-old religious text, there was no real explanation for their actions. Even if Rhymer or Feller did manage to identify the victim, asking why these terrorists had chosen to kill this particular journalist might yield no more results than asking why a shark had chosen to eat a particular fish.

Without even knowing what she was doing, Heat started walking in the direction of Columbus Avenue.

She passed a garbage truck making its pickup, then by an apartment building. There was construction on what promised to be a new hibachi place at the end of the block. On the other side of the mostly residential street there were brownstones.

These were all things she had seen a thousand times or more during her years in the Twentieth Precinct, such that she didn't notice them anymore. She could force herself to have beginner's eyes while on a case, but not while on a stroll up 82nd Street.

So she wasn't paying the slightest bit of attention to her surroundings when she suddenly saw something that made her stop in her tracks, something so shocking it was probably the only sight in the world that could have distracted her from the case that had become the most important of her life.

It was a homeless person, a woman, sitting on a bench under a bus shelter on the opposite side of the street. She was hunched over. There was a knit cap on her head. She appeared to be wearing most of the clothing she owned: two jackets and an untold number of sweaters and shirts underneath it. In front of her was a small wire-mesh shopping cart, likely stolen from a grocery store, which contained her worldly possessions.

Nothing about her should have been at all noteworthy, except Heat caught the entirety of the woman's face from a distance of roughly thirty yards. Their eyes locked for perhaps half a second.

It was all Heat needed. Human beings are part of the genus *homo*, a classification of bipedal primates that lack sharp teeth, claws, or any other defensive anatomy. For millions of years, people have relied, instead, on social interaction for their very survival. It has endowed the human brain with some exceptionally well-tuned equipment designed for the recognition and decoding of each other's facial structures, a talent we retain throughout our entire lives without the slightest bit of practice or training.

Even Alzheimer's patients, whose minds are muddled by a thick plaque that has robbed them of the names of their children, will still recognize their loved one's faces, and will brighten immediately—one could say reflexively—upon seeing them. The ability to recognize familiar faces is that powerful and hard-wired within.

That's why there was no doubt in Nikki Heat's mind during that half second. She knew exactly who it was. She knew because the face was so seared in her memory. She knew because it was nearly identical to the one she saw every time she looked in the mirror.

The homeless person on the bench was her mother.

A woman who had been dead for seventeen years.

THREE

The woman—might as well call her by her name: Cynthia Heat—broke eye contact first, looking down in her lap like she hadn't just been made.

Before she was Nikki's mother, she had been a spy, after all. And the first thing you do when you think your cover has been blown is pretend like it hasn't been, in the hopes that your mark doesn't register your mistake.

Nikki was just staring, too stunned to move. All the color had drained from her face. It wasn't wrong to say she looked like she had just seen a ghost, because to Nikki that's what Cynthia Heat was.

She had died in Nikki's arms. Hadn't she?

Her lifeblood had oozed out all over Nikki's shirt. Hadn't it?

Nikki had seen the knife sticking out her mother's back. Hadn't she?

The garbage truck rumbled in front of her, its diesel engine spewing exhaust, its air brakes announcing its halt with a sharp hiss. The noise broke Nikki out of her trance, and she started running up 82nd Street, in the direction of the bus shelter.

As soon as she was clear of the truck, she veered into the street, nearly getting run over by a speeding Uber driver. The car screeched to a halt just inches from Nikki's hip, its driver shouting curses in her direction.

Nikki didn't care. She didn't even break stride. She was hell-bent on reaching that bus shelter.

She couldn't see her mother anymore. The parked cars were obscuring her view of the bench.

"Mom!" she shouted. "Mom!"

Two cars, parallel parked so close to each other their bumpers were touching, blocked Nikki's path. She didn't go around but just leapt on top of them, using the combined bumpers like a step.

Once she landed on the other side, she could see the bus shelter clearly.

The bench was empty.

Nikki ran up to it. A man was leaning against the shelter, his face buried in that day's *Ledger*.

"Did you just see a woman sitting here?" Heat asked him frantically.

"Lady, there are eight million people in this city and half of them are women. Now, if she had looked like you, maybe—"

Heat ignored the rest. She looked down 82nd Street, but there was no way her mother could have covered the entire block in the amount of time since Nikki had seen her.

She turned her attention toward Columbus Avenue and took off at a sprint, nearly knocking over an old man taking his dog for a morning pee.

"Hey, watch it!" he yelled. His words bounced off Nikki's back.

She reached Columbus and looked left, then right. It was just a busy New York avenue in a vibrant residential part of the city. There was no hunched homeless woman. No overstuffed grocery cart.

No Cynthia.

Was it even possible for her to have gotten away? Nikki marked her mother's birthday every year—a ritual that usually ended with her getting good and righteously drunk—so she knew her mother would have recently turned sixty-six. It would have been a remarkably fast getaway for a woman well into her seventh decade, even one who was a former spy.

Nikki scanned up and down the block again. She looked high and low. She looked with beginner's eyes and veteran's eyes and everything in between.

But it didn't matter.

Her mother, one of the best spies the United States government ever had the honor to employ, had vanished just as quickly as she had appeared.

———

For the next twenty minutes, Nikki Heat scoured two full blocks of Columbus Avenue. She checked every possible nook, cranny, and hiding spot. Then she rechecked.

And yet, for all that effort, she came up just as empty as she had on first glance.

Finally, she began staggering back to the Two-Oh, her brain a blur of thoughts.

When her eyes had first fallen on the woman sitting on the bench, all the neurons and synapses dedicated to storing data about her mother's face had instantly fired. In those early nanoseconds, when it was all feeling and no thinking, Nikki had been absolutely sure about who she had seen.

Now her rational mind was kicking in. And it was throwing doubt into the equation. Her mother, alive . . . It was impossible, right?

Surely, it had just been the stress of the moment, the shock of the threat against Rook. The traumatized brain can play all kinds of tricks on itself. There were Native American religious rituals that involved dancing beyond exhaustion, which triggered hallucinations. Was this some version of that?

Or maybe it was some kind of regression in the stages of grief, like she was going back to square one: denial.

Or it was some bizarre form of substitution: Now that Rook, the man who had become her world, was being brought into peril, her psyche was retreating back to her mother, the woman who had been Nikki's world in childhood.

Or . . .

Get out of your head, Heat!

The thought hit her with a jolt. If she permitted herself, she could fall down into the alternate universe where her mother was still alive and she would never leave it. The obsession over solving her mother's murder had, at one point in her life, been all-consuming. She could too easily see herself becoming obsessed with this new fantasy.

And she couldn't allow that. Not with Rook in danger.

So she shoved that vision of her mother down deep, where she would deal with it another time. Or not at all.

She picked up her pace. By the time she made it back up to the bull pen, Ochoa was the only one left. He was standing in front of the flat-screen television that had been bolted into one of the corners.

"Bad news, Captain," he said.

"More?" Heat asked.

Ochoa tilted his head toward the TV, which was muted. "Afraid so. It looks like that video has been leaked to the media."

He pointed to the bottom-of-the-screen crawl on the local all-news station. TERRORIST GROUP CLAIMING ISIS TIES DECAPITATES NYC JOURNALIST IN BRUTAL VIDEO . . . BUNDLE UP! *FARMER'S ALMANAC* PREDICTS SNOWY WINTER FOR THE NORTHEAST . . . STOCKS MIXED ON— Heat looked back at Ochoa.

"They haven't actually *played* it, have they?" she asked.

"No. They've been congratulating themselves for their restraint. But you know it's going to be on the Internet any second, if it's not there already."

Heat shook her head. It would be an additional horror for the victim's family—not only losing their daughter or granddaughter or niece, but having her execution forever available on the Web for the entertainment of the sickos who would click it over and over again.

It was also a potentially negative development for her investigation. Once the video became readily available, there was always a possibility some attention-seeking lunatic would claim to be responsible. And without being able to hold back critical information from the public, it would be more difficult for her detectives to figure out if said lunatic was just playing them.

"Aren't you supposed to be working with McMains right now?" Heat asked.

"He's in a meeting," Ochoa said. "But I'm next on his agenda. Don't worry, Cap. We'll get this—Oh, hey! Legs Kline!"

Ochoa grabbed the remote off the wall, where it was attached with Velcro, and turned up the volume. The screen cut to the man who was improbably surging in the polls, threatening to turn the two-party system on its ear.

"You're not really thinking about voting for that guy, are you,

Oach? I think if he had his way we would have built a wall that kept your family from coming here."

"Nah, he's cool with us. He wants my people around so we can mow his lawn."

Ochoa continued: "Besides, did you hear about his private jet? It's this 737 with a *king-sized bed* in it. How cool is that? Talk about joining the mile-high club in style."

"And this makes him qualified to be president . . . how exactly?" Heat asked.

"Oh, I don't know. I'm actually voting for Lindsy Gardner. Baby got *back*!"

"So you're voting for a candidate because you like her ass?"

"It sounds kind of shallow when you put it that way. Let's just say I like her domestic policies."

Heat just shook her head.

"Anyhow, shhh, press conference time," Ochoa said. "If I weren't so devoted to Lindsy's, uh, domestic policies, I might vote for this guy just for the entertainment value. It's like watching *Beverly Hillbillies* reruns."

Heat rolled her eyes. The screen now read: LEGS KLINE/INDEPENDENT PRESIDENTIAL CANDIDATE/IN NYC FOR UNION SQUARE RALLY.

"Oh, jeez, he's here?" Heat said.

"Hey, not our problem. Union Square, that's the One-Three's mess."

Heat was paying attention despite herself. She knew Rook was supposed to be off somewhere, away from the candidate, visiting Kline Industries facilities. But she half hoped something about his schedule had changed and he had decided to join the candidate—and that he had decided to keep his phone off so he wouldn't be bothered by calls from his editor.

Maybe she'd catch a glimpse of him. Then she could call the Thirteenth Precinct and have him detained for his own safety.

The camera was now trained on a tall, angular man who stooped a little to compensate for his size. Michael Gregory Kline had grown to his adult height, six foot six, by the time he was a freshman in high school. The legend was that when he tried to go out for the football team, he was so skinny the coach cut him, declaring, "Sorry, son. You're just all legs."

The name had stuck. Its decidedly un-presidential folksiness might have been a disqualifying factor in a different era. But now it was a major drawing card for a candidate who was polling well with Americans tired of voting for candidates they deemed inauthentic and elitist.

They also liked his easy Texas charm and aw-shucks country boy humility. They liked his stories about how he flew a crop duster to help put himself through college, even though he barely fit in the cockpit. They liked his tales of steer-rasslin', varmint-huntin', and other activities that required dropping the "g" at the end of a gerund.

But he was also clearly no fool. He hadn't gone from struggling wildcatter's son to billionaire by accident. He had grown up riding the boom-or-bust cycle of the Texas oil industry and decided there had to be a better way. Shrewdly, over many years and many eighteen-hour workdays, he built an empire that took oil money made during prosperous times and plowed it into businesses that would still churn a profit when things were lean.

He grew his business prodigiously, reinvesting nearly every penny he made, barely taking a salary and continuing to live in a small 1920s Craftsman-style house just outside Dallas long after he should have moved to a bigger house and better neighborhood. He often talked about his meteoric rise, stressing that the simplicity of his management practices could be applied to government.

"You don't spend what you don't have," he said constantly.

Or: "If you invest in the future, you'll find you like what you have when you get there."

He was also way ahead of the curve when it came to matters like sustainability, recognizing years before most of his petroleum industry buddies that some of the notions being preached by the Sierra Club crowd—like harvesting natural resources in ways that didn't deplete them or looking for ways to use less energy and cut down on waste— not only made sense for the environment, but for the bottom line as well.

Kline had first come to public prominence when he wrote a best-selling business memoir entitled *It's Good to Be Good*. Long before

Google pioneered its "Don't Be Evil" corporate philosophy, Legs had promoted similar values within Kline Industries: the idea that you could make money *and* be a responsible corporate citizen. He was said to put incredible pressure on his managers to turn a profit, but also to do it the right way.

Heat knew Rook was trying to pry deeper into the Legs Kline rags-to-riches story. Was there a more calculating, ruthless side to Legs, a side that had spurned business partners and gouged out eyeballs on his way to the Forbes list? Was there rot beneath the gilding? Or had Legs Kline really perfected the art of making omelets without cracking any eggs?

"Well, hey there, everyone," Kline said to the journalists arrayed around him, smiling at them almost like he was surprised to see them. "Don't tell Lise, but I've spent the morning enjoying one of the seediest parts of New York City."

Lise was Kline's wife. The reporters around him seemed to draw in their collective breath. Was Legs Kline about to admit he had gone to a strip club? An off–Times Square peep show?

Then, with the timing of a seasoned comic, he said, "The bagels."

Everyone laughed. "Had three of them for breakfast this morning. Lise's been getting on me about my weight, so shhh, okay? But I will say, off the record, they were delicious. Can't get bagels like that in D.C., that's for sure. One more reason I don't trust Washington."

More laughter followed. Every Legs Kline press conference was like that: off the cuff, informal, like it had been thrown together at the last second. The insider talk was that Kline was going out of his way not to appear too slick or too organized. He also eschewed podiums or any apparatus that visually separated him from the People. These were the subtle acts of genius contrived by his media advisors so their candidate seemed thoroughly uncontrived.

"Mr. Kline, your Democratic opponent, Lindsy Gardner, was here last week," began a poofy-haired guy with a Channel 3 microphone cover. "She says you don't have the proper experience to be president, having never held elected office. How do you respond to that allegation?"

"Well, I certainly don't want to get on the bad side of Lindsy the

Librarian," Kline said, a smirk on his face. "Not sure I can afford the overdue fines."

Another round of chuckles rippled through the crowd. Poofy pressed on: "And your Republican challenger, Caleb Brown, says your economic plan will result in higher taxes for working-class Americans."

"Well, for starters, that's not true," Kline said. "But I have to admit, I'm surprised Mr. Brown even read my economic plan. I thought he was too busy picking the wings off House flies."

Chuckles abounded. He would be there all week. Try the salmon. And don't forget to tip your waiters and waitresses.

"Mr. Kline," interrupted a woman from CNN before Poofy could lob another softball. "By now you've surely heard about the gruesome ISIS-style video that was released this morning."

Kline instantly went solemn. "I did hear about that. I did," he said. "Haven't seen it yet. Don't think I want to. But I did hear about it."

The CNN woman pressed on: "You've made your stance on immigration from Muslim countries quite clear throughout this campaign. Would you—"

"Now hang on a second, young lady. Hang on," he interrupted, then shook his head.

"Look, I know that I'm running for office now, and that folks are thinkin' I'm goin' to start actin' in a certain way. And if I was a normal Washington politician, I know I'd be expected to use something like this to score what the pundits like to call 'political points.' Because you're right. I do worry about keeping Americans safe in this dangerous world of ours. I worry about that all the time. It's one of the biggest reasons I decided I wanted this job."

He swallowed hard, in a way that made his prominent Adam's apple bob up and down.

"But I have to tell you, there's a time and place for scorin' political points, and this isn't it. I think you know by now I'm not a Washington politician. I'm just a boy from Terrell, Texas. And in Terrell, when you hear about a family that's lost a loved one, you take your hat off, you bow your head, and you say a little prayer. I hope all of America is doing that right now for this poor woman and her family."

As if to emphasize the point, he hung his head extra low. From any other candidate, it would have seemed like political theater. But from Legs, it seemed genuine. That was what had made him so irresistible to the segment of voters that didn't care a whit about his lack of foreign policy experience or that he couldn't quite explain how a bill became a law.

The camera panned out at that point, to capture the entire press corps assembled around Legs. All of them, even Poofy, were taking a moment of somber silence.

Heat quickly scanned the mob of reporters. When she didn't see Rook, she left Ochoa standing by himself in front of the television.

She would be offering prayers for the victim's family, yes. But at the moment she had other prayers that were more pressing.

FOUR

Not ten minutes after the Legs Kline press conference broke up, Heat was in her office, sitting in an office chair that might as well have had spikes in it, for how jumpy she was.

She had tried Rook's mobile phone three more times. Still no answer.

When her desk phone finally rang, she practically lunged at it, not even bothering to look at the caller ID on the screen.

"Heat."

In return she heard not "hello" or "hi, it's so-and-so" but rather, "We have ourselves a situation."

Zach Hamner, the senior administrative aide to the NYPD's deputy commissioner for legal matters, seldom bothered with salutations, pleasantries, or introductions. He was known as "The Hammer" because it was how he was most often deployed by the people who gripped his handle. He was not only capable of making any precinct commander's life an unbearable hell, but he seemed to enjoy it. Heat had heard it said that The Hammer had all the warmth and compassion of a sea slug, but she thought that was unfair. To sea slugs.

In truth, Heat wouldn't have made it to captain without The Hammer working as her behind-the-scenes champion at One Police Plaza. He was, in that sense, her patron. The only problem was his ideas about patronage seemed to have been exclusively informed by Niccolò Machiavelli.

"What's up, Zach?"

"It's not what's up, it's what's going down," Hamner said in what, for him, passed as an attempt at sheer hilarity.

He paused for laughter. When it didn't come, he got down to

business by making his favorite pronouncement: "I've just come from the commissioner's office."

"Yeah. And?"

"He's seen the beheading video."

"Okay."

"He also just saw a stirring performance by presidential candidate Legs Kline. Were you watching by any chance?"

"I got to the part where he tried to recruit the reporters for a prayer circle, then walked away. What did I miss?"

"After he invoked God and Jesus Christ, he called on the lower power that is the NYPD."

"Oh?"

"He laid it at our feet pretty good, saying that it would only compound this tragedy if the detectives of this fair city couldn't solve the crime."

"Trust me, that—"

"He wasn't waving his pom-poms for us," The Hammer said, talking right over Heat's attempt at reassurance. "He was putting a target on our back. That little press conference ran on all the major networks. Everyone in New York City and in the outlying areas otherwise known as the United States of America saw him put us on the spot. You should be aware the commissioner considers this case the department's top priority."

"Well, Zach, I can promise you it's—"

"I'm not finished," Hamner interrupted again. "You'll know when I'm finished, because there will be a pause that indicates the end of a paragraph. Like this."

He left a second of airtime, then continued. "In the meantime, keep listening. The commissioner considers this our top priority, but not just because the perhaps-future commander in chief just put us in the crosshairs. It's also because the feds are swarming all over this one."

"The feds?"

"Did I stutter? Yes. The feds. They're claiming that as an act of quote-unquote 'domestic terrorism,' it falls under their jurisdiction. For now the commissioner's called bullshit on them, because it's just one murder. And murder is our deal. But I don't know how much longer he's going to be able to hold them off. They're threatening legal action."

"Well, I'll keep that—"

"Was there a pause? No. There wasn't. Because once again, I wasn't done. As I was about to say: the other thing that piqued the commissioner's interest was the threat against your boyfriend."

"Husband."

"Whatever. The commissioner asked me if I felt that would distract you or hamper your ability to dedicate your entire focus to this case. I told him, to the contrary, I thought it would give you every motivation to solve it. He wasn't convinced, but he said he'd give you a shot. So. What do you have so far? Come on. I need something to pass back up the ladder that shows you're on top of this thing."

"Well, we've determined the victim is between five foot eight and five foot ten," Heat said.

"That's great news if we're considering buying her a graduation gown, but I don't see how that helps us otherwise. What else do you got? Do we know who she is yet?"

"No."

"Do we know where she was killed?"

"No."

"Do we have anything that resembles a lead?"

Heat considered telling The Hammer about the scarf. But she could already hear him deriding her for sending one of her detectives on a shopping trip. There were some things she didn't want echoing around the hall of One PP. A little holdback with the higher-ups seemed prudent.

"I'll take that as a no," Hamner said. "Terrific. I'm glad my faith in you has been so well placed."

"Zach, I just—"

"Listen, in case you haven't figured it out yet, this is not a case. It's *the* case. That means we have resources here. Whatever you need. You want a helicopter? Done. You want a squadron of uniforms combing through trash cans in Central Park? Done. You want undercovers who look like skateboarders, techs who crack code written in Japanese, search warrants for the mayor's underwear drawer? It's done, done, and done.

"That's the good news. The bad news is, by my math, you've got less than twenty-four hours before the feds find some bullshit excuse to take it from us. So if I were you, I'd get cracking. We clear?"

Heat took a moment.

"Hello?" Hamner said. "Are we clear?"

"Are you at the end of a paragraph now?" Heat asked.

"Yeah. I am. Don't be a—"

"Good. So am I."

Then she hung up.

The sound of Heat slamming her desk phone receiver was still reverberating when her smartphone rang.

Thinking it might be The Hammer choosing a different mode of harassing her, she nearly picked it up and threw it across the room. Then she saw the screen read: MARGARET.

As mothers-in-law went, Margaret Rook was surely one of the more unusual. It wasn't just any mother-in-law who had once been called "one of the most magnetic stage presences in the history of the Great White Way" by Ben Brantley in the *New York Times*.

Now at an age she no longer allowed to be listed in press kits, she was considered one of Broadway's grande dames. Her star power alone could fill the Gershwin or the Palace. Even if all she was doing was making a cameo appearance, nostalgic audiences remembered how she once brought the house down singing the "Tits and Ass" song from *A Chorus Line*; or they recalled her evocative turn as Blanche DuBois in a celebrated revival of *A Streetcar Named Desire*.

She used Tony Awards as paperweights around the house and sometimes ordered her son about as if he were a part of the stage crew. She was also something of an unabashed cougar, bouncing from one younger man to the next even younger.

But underneath all the dramatics—and notwithstanding all of the silly flings—there was a mother who loved her son fiercely. There had been a lot of years, especially early on, when the high-paying roles hadn't come her way, when she had bounced from summer stock to off-off-off-Broadway theaters just to keep a roof over their heads. And for all the men who had come and gone, it was really just the two of them for the majority of his childhood. It had created a special, if sometimes complicated, bond between them.

The relationship between Margaret Rook and Nikki Heat was much more straightforward. Margaret recognized Nikki as the best thing to ever happen to her son, and she loved her accordingly.

"Hi, Mom," Nikki said, addressing her by the name that Margaret had absolutely insisted on after they returned from Reykjavík. At the time, Nikki had thought of it as a lovely gesture—in part because, up until this morning, she really had thought she had lost her own mother.

"Darling," Margaret said breathlessly. "I just saw the video and now I can't get Jameson on the phone. Please, please tell me he's standing in front of you right now."

"Sorry, Mom. I can't get him, either."

"Oh my God, do you know where he is?"

"I don't. He's out of town, working on a piece for *First Press*. That's really all I know."

"But you don't think . . . I mean, they couldn't . . . They don't . . . *have him*, do they? Those men?" Margaret asked, in a tone that was quickly climbing up the ladder toward hysteria.

"I don't know. I honestly don't know."

"My God, my God," she repeated. "I think I'm going to hyperventilate."

It was one of the rare times when Margaret Rook's off-stage theatrics were fully justified.

"I know exactly how you feel," Heat said. "I would have called you, but . . . Well, honestly, I was hoping you hadn't seen the video. Or at least that you wouldn't see it until we already had Jameson home."

"I'm afraid Jean Philippe is terribly clever with computers," Margaret declared.

Jean Philippe was her newest paramour, a man who was far closer in age to her son than anyone wanted to acknowledge. He was French, which meant he was gifted in the kitchen and—though no one wanted to hear Margaret talk about it—in other more *private* parts of the house as well.

"We heard about the threat on the news," Margaret continued. "And then Jean Philippe got on the computer. And then, oh my goodness, that poor, poor woman. And then to hear those . . . those *hooligans* say my son's name and to think about what they want to do to him, it was . . . It was the shock of my life, *the shock of my life*. I nearly fainted."

She hefted a groan that went high to low, like she was coming down an arpeggio. "Oh, would you listen to me go on? Me, me, me. How are *you* doing, darling?"

"I'm hanging in there. I've got a crime to solve, you know?"

"I know you do, kiddo. I know you do. And there's no one better in the world at that than you. That's the only thing that's keeping me going right now. My son may not be made of the stoutest stuff, but my daughter is tough as nails. I know those men won't get to Jameson as long as you're around."

"Thanks, Mom. We'll get him home safe. Don't worry."

They made promises they would contact each other as soon as they heard anything. Then they ended the call.

Heat reached out to a photo of her and Rook during one of those wonderful Reykjavík days. They had spent the morning sailboarding on the Mediterranean. In the afternoon, they had alternated between making love and dozing. At night, Rook had whisked her off to the opera—Teatro Real was doing *Madame Butterfly*. Then they barely made it back to the hotel before they were all over each other again.

The picture had been snapped just before a tired sun slipped beneath the western horizon, during the time photographers call "magic hour." They were enjoying a pre-show glass of wine at a rooftop bar. The entirety of Madrid was spread out below them, like it had been placed there just for their enjoyment. They were dressed for the opera, with Heat in a stunning floor-length Vera Wang with a plunging neckline and a daring slit up the side, and Rook, his hair carelessly tousled by the wind, in a flawlessly crisp bespoke white tuxedo that would have made James Bond tear apart his closet in jealousy.

Heat lifted the frame off her desk and traced her finger along Rook's lips, as if caressing the glass were the same as touching the man himself. He was *so* handsome, with his chiseled jawline, his strong chin, his knee-melting smile. She had never told him this—because Rook could be so insufferably vain—but the first time she ever saw him in person, after years of admiring his work from afar, her heart really did skip a beat. Even now, years after that first meeting, there were times when she kissed him and it was so exciting, it felt like it was all new.

She took a deep breath and, for a second, failed to hold off the terrible thought that kept assaulting her head: What if she had already kissed him for the last time? What if, right now, he was the one with the burlap bag over his head and his arms tied behind him, waiting in terror as these ISIS aspirants readied their video equipment so they could broadcast his execution? What if the only other person Nikki Heat had ever loved with her whole being also met a violent end?

The only thing that snapped her out of that horrific waking nightmare was a knock at her door. Heat quickly dabbed at both corners of her eyes, where she could already start to feel the tears forming. She was thankful she wasn't a cake-on-the-makeup kind of girl. Nothing to clump, run, or smear.

"Come in," she said.

The duty sergeant came in behind the opening door and stood just inside the frame.

"We got a call about a body," he said. "It's in a Dumpster behind a building on West 73rd Street. We got some uniforms heading there right now to secure the scene. They know not to touch anything. It's the girl from the video."

"What makes you think that?"

"Because," the sergeant said. "The caller stated he found a body. What he didn't find was the head."

FIVE

Heat grabbed the first pool car she could lay her hands on, then gave its gas pedal a vigorous exercising as she tore off toward West 73rd Street, her siren blasting and her lights flashing the whole way.

She pulled to a halt in front of a hydrant, leaving some NYPD-purchased rubber on the street, and snapped on a pair of blue nitrile gloves as she got out. Then she stopped herself.

Her ritual. She almost forgot. It was something she did before walking into every murder scene. It was that moment she took to re-center herself and honor the person who had been lost—to remember it was a life that had been precious to family, to friends, to colleagues, to a community.

And so Heat paused, just for a moment, and reminded herself that even though she was desperate to prevent another victim, she still owed it to the one on the scene to give the investigation everything she had.

Then she got back to work. She looked at the building whose address the desk sergeant had given her. It was six stories, pre-World War II construction, and made of dark beige brick that would require a vigorous power-washing before it returned to its original light beige. It had a Vietnamese restaurant named Pho Sure, with a facade of dark wood affixed to the brick, at the street level, and apartments above.

No surveillance cameras. At least none that Heat could see.

A uniformed officer was standing in front of the narrow alleyway next to the restaurant with his arms crossed. Heat nodded at him as she ducked under the Do Not Cross tape, then hurried down the alley.

When she reached the back of the building, she turned left and saw two more officers. One had a small notepad out and was talking to a white man with chest hair coming out of his shirt, who was standing on the back stoop. The other was kneeling next to a Hispanic man in a white apron, who was seated against the brick wall, hanging his head between his knees.

The Dumpster was snuggled up against a chain-link fence that separated this building's property from the building on 72nd Street. No one seemed to want to go near it.

The kneeling cop looked up as she walked closer. He pointed toward the Dumpster.

"Be careful, Captain," he called out. "Our friend here left his breakfast right over there."

Heat's eyes focused on the slick of vomit congealing in front of the Dumpster. A few feet away from that, a large white kitchen garbage bag, stuffed full, lay on its side. She continued on toward the cop with the notepad.

"Captain, this is Gus Kosmetatos," the cop said. "He owns Pho Sure. He's the one who made the call. That's his dishwasher. He's the one who discovered the body. His name is Jose. He wouldn't give us his last name. He doesn't *habla* a lot of *inglés.*"

"He's from Guatemala," the hairy-chested guy, Kosmetatos, said in an accent that was pure Flatbush Avenue. "He's only been with me a month. I don't think they trusts cops where he's from. Or here, if you know what I mean. But he checks out. I swear, I personally looked at his green card."

Which may have been a forgery. Not that Heat cared. If a Vietnamese restaurant with a Greek-American owner wanted to hire an illegal Guatemalan immigrant for a dish boy, that was business as usual, as far as the city of New York was concerned. If any authorities wanted to make an issue of it, they would have to be federal ones.

"We're not concerned about anyone's immigration status, Mr. Kosmetatos," Heat said. "Tell me about what happened here."

"We don't open till eleven. I was just in the office, getting some things done. Jose was cleaning up, getting things ready for the line chefs. They come in around ten. I guess he went out to empty the garbage. I wasn't even paying attention, when all of a sudden he starts yelling like crazy.

"I don't got a lot of Spanish, but I know enough to get by, you know? Seems like the Spanish are the only ones willing to work for me these days. So Jose keeps saying '*sin cabeza, sin cabeza,*' and I'm like 'What is he going on about?' So I go outside and I see him doubled over, puking his guts out, pointing at the Dumpster and—"

Kosmetatos looked toward the Dumpster and flinched involuntarily. "I used to work as a butcher at the A and P, back when I was a kid. I think that's the only reason I didn't ralph, too."

"So you went over and had a look?" Heat asked.

"Yeah. Awful stuff. I heard about it on TV this morning, what those ISIS sons-a-bitches did. But to see it . . ."

"Did you touch anything?" Heat asked.

"Nah, all I did was look. I probably didn't get closer than about ten feet."

He added: "I know the cops don't like you to mess with the body. I watch this show on TV. It's got this hot lady cop and her husband, this guy who writes books. It's clever, the solutions they come up with. The writer guy is pretty smart."

"You can't believe everything you see on TV, Mr. Kosmetatos," Heat said.

"Yeah, I guess you're right. Well, anyhow, point is, I know to keep my distance."

"Thank you. Do you by any chance have any security cameras installed on this building?"

"No. I don't. Sorry. The landlord doesn't like them. He lives in the building and he said he doesn't like the feeling that Big Brother is watching him."

"Okay. Thank you, Mr. Kosmetatos. We're going to have to ask you and the rest of your staff not to come out here for the next few hours while we gather evidence. I'm sorry for the inconvenience."

"Hey, once word gets out about what's back here, I don't think I'd be able to make 'em come out here."

Heat thanked him again, then moved over to the dishwasher, kneeling next to him. To the surprise of the uniform, who had assumed they would be calling a translator, Heat began speaking in fluent Spanish.

"Good morning, Jose. My name is Captain Nikki Heat. I'm with the New York Police Department and the only thing I'm concerned about this morning is solving this murder. Do we understand each other?"

Jose brought his chin up for the first time since Heat entered the alley. His face was still white.

"Yes, ma'am," he replied, also in Spanish.

"Can you tell me what happened?"

Jose told the same story as his boss had, looking all the while like he had not only lost his breakfast, but lunch wasn't going to much appeal to him, either. He finished with ". . . and then I opened the door to the Dumpster, and there she was."

"Did you touch her?"

"No, ma'am."

Heat looked toward the Dumpster for a moment, but did not yet walk over.

"Jose, were you working last night as well?" Heat asked.

"Yes, ma'am."

"Did you empty any garbage before you left last night?"

He thought about it for a moment and said yes.

"About what time?"

"Just before my shift ended. A little before eleven."

"Is it possible the body was in the Dumpster when you did it?"

He shook his head vigorously. "No. I would have seen it."

"It was dark. Are you sure?"

Now he was nodding. "Yes. I'm not tall enough to get the bag over the side. I have to use the door. I would have seen it."

"And would anyone else have emptied garbage after you? One of the chefs, maybe?"

"No. They leave it for me in the morning."

That told Heat the body had been deposited sometime between 11 P.M., when Jose had left work, and 9 A.M., when he arrived to begin preparing for the day.

"Jose, do you happen to know when your garbage company does its pickups?"

"Tuesday morning."

Of course. Which the killers may well have known.

Satisfied Jose had nothing more to add to her investigation for the moment, Heat approached the Dumpster.

The sliding metal door on the side was still open, as Jose had left it. Heat scanned the area immediately in front. But there were no footprints visible, bloody, muddy, or otherwise.

She peered inside. The body had been loaded in feetfirst, so the stump of the neck was facing her. Heat understood why Jose had gotten sick. Even with all the corpses she had seen in various states of defilement, this was tough on her stomach, too. She could see where the machete had cut through smoothly, but also the hack marks from where the assailant had to begin sawing.

The body was rolled up in a carpet, which told Heat how it had been transported there. Underneath, the Dumpster was about a quarter full with trash bags, making a kind of bed for the body and carpet to lie on. No additional trash bags had been dumped on top, which was a lucky break—less contamination, more of a chance the Evidence Collection Team might be able to get some useful information out of the scene.

The killers had obviously hoped the body would remain unseen in the carpet for a few hours until garbage pickup time, and then be transported to a landfill, where it would be unceremoniously entombed for all time.

"Call the precinct and tell them I want Benigno DeJesus pulled off whatever he's doing and to make this his first priority," she said to the uniform who was now standing near her. "I don't think there's going to be much here, but if there is, Benigno will find it. And if I'm not here when he gets here, tell him I want prints expedited. I don't know if our vic is in the system or not, but maybe we'll get a break and get an ID."

"Yes, sir."

"And tell the sergeant to let Dr. Parry know what's coming her way. I want this to be her top priority."

"Got it, Captain."

"And one more thing, if I'm not here when DeJesus gets here. Once they get the body out, I'm afraid someone is going to have to go looking through the rest of the Dumpster for the head."

The cop was wincing, but he said, "Yes, sir."

"And if we don't find it in this Dumpster, I want every Dumpster around here checked. Got it?"

"Yes, sir."

Heat shifted her gaze upward, looking at the corners of nearby buildings. None of them had any cameras, either. She wondered if the killers knew that this alley and the building in front of it were surveillance blind spots, and if they had selected this Dumpster for that reason.

She shifted her eyes back to the alley, trying to imagine the killers carrying the body in a rolled-up carpet sometime in the dark of night. Then she looked up again. There were no cameras. But there were apartments. She just hoped that New York, the city that supposedly never sleeps, lived up to its tagline. Or at least that this neighborhood had a few insomniacs.

Heat took out her phone to call Detective Feller. It rang once, twice, and then Heat realized she heard his rather distinctive ring tone—"The Final Countdown" by Europe—coming down the alley.

"You looking for me?" Feller asked as he came into view. Rhymer was two steps behind him.

"Sure was," Heat said. "According to the guy who found the body, the Dumpster didn't have a body in it as of eleven P.M. last night, and obviously it has one in it now. I want you and Opie knocking on doors in any apartments that have a view of the alley or the back of this building. Maybe someone heard or saw our killers without realizing it. They had the body rolled up in a carpet. I'm betting it took two of them to carry it."

"I got a better idea," Feller said.

"What's that?"

"You know there's a mosque right up the street, right?" Feller said, gesturing in that direction.

"Yeah? So?"

"What do you say we get a warrant and kick the door down? Dollars to donuts we'll find a couple of Jihad Johnnies hiding out with big-ass machetes under their skirts."

"And what, exactly, makes you think we have probable cause for a warrant?" Heat asked testily.

"Come on, Captain. You heard those guys. It was all 'Allah Allah bullshit bullshit.' Where else do you think they're hiding out?"

Heat stepped away from the Dumpster and approached Feller. She didn't want this conversation to be any louder than it needed to be.

"Let me ask you this, Feller. There's also a Lutheran church on this block. If they had said, 'Praise Jesus,' would you want us to go kicking that door in?"

"That's different."

"No. It's not. I don't want to turn this into a civics lesson, but you know we don't have a state religion here in America, right? That means Muslims get the same rights as Lutherans, Jews, atheists, and whatever other belief structure you care to name."

"Ah, come on. Don't get all PC on me."

"It's not political correctness, Feller. It's called the law. And we've been hired by the city of New York to enforce it, not create our own version of it based on our biases and prejudices. Are we clear?"

"You know they did it," Feller huffed.

"I only know what the evidence tells me, Detective," Heat said. "And until the evidence points me in that direction, I'm not going there. Because even if we could find a judge bigoted enough to give us a warrant, another judge would surely throw it out later. And then every piece of evidence we gathered at that mosque would be tossed out before trial. In the courts, they call that 'fruit of a poison tree,' and believe me, it would taste pretty nasty if our perps walked because we didn't take the time to do this the right way.

"Now," she said, glaring at him, "are you going to do this canvass? Or do you need two weeks on the bench without pay to think about why it's important to follow your captain's orders?"

"Jeez, okay, okay," Feller said, holding his hands in the air. "Come on, Opie. You heard our distinguished captain. Let's go knock on doors and ignore the fact that the killers are watching us do it from that mosque up the street, laughing their towel-headed asses off at us the whole time."

Feller turned and departed the alley. Rhymer gave Heat a sympathetic shrug before following his partner.

Heat watched them go, then walked back up the alleyway. She knew exactly where she was going, of course. Heat had worked the Twentieth Precinct her entire career. She didn't need Randy Feller or anyone else to tell her about its places of worship.

Without slowing, she turned right and walked halfway up the block until she was facing an austere, stoutly built concrete structure with stone steps leading up to its entrance.

To the left of the entrance was a sign. Half of it was in Arabic. The other half read MASJID AL-JANNAH in block letters.

Heat pulled out her phone and dialed a number.

"Raley," she heard.

"Hey, Rales. How's it coming with finding our crime scene?"

"Not good, Captain. This is like looking for a needle in a haystack, and the haystack is three hundred miles square."

"What if I were to make the stack a little smaller?"

"That would probably help."

"I don't want you to force this. If it doesn't shake out, it doesn't shake out. But write this down," Heat said, then read off the address for Masjid al-Jannah. "See if you can match our video to that location."

"You got it, Captain."

Heat stowed her phone back in her pocket. There was law enforcement, which involved understanding and respecting all statutes, from New York City regulations right on up to the Constitution of the United States. Then there was good police work, which involved developing logically sound hunches and finding the evidence to support them.

Captain Nikki Heat knew how to do both.

SIX

Once Benigno DeJesus and the rest of the Evidence Collection Team arrived—and Heat was sure they had all they needed to do their job—she excused herself from the scene.

It went against her instincts as a detective. She was still at the stage where she had to remind herself that she wasn't a detective anymore.

Delegate, The Hammer kept telling her, every time she blew off a CompStat meeting (to the ire of the brass downtown) or a meeting with a community leader (to the irritation of said leader) because she wanted to stay involved in an investigation. *Leadership means putting people in a position to do their job and letting them do it.*

So Heat got back in her pool car, with the intention of going back to the precinct. Except the car didn't seem to want to go there.

Almost involuntarily, she found herself driving south instead of north. Then east, across town.

She knew exactly where she was going, of course. And exactly what she was doing when she got there. Even if she couldn't quite admit it to herself or believe what she was about to do.

The morning rush had eased out and the midday gridlock hadn't started asserting itself yet, so she crossed town easily enough. She passed the United Nations, then followed signs toward the Queens Midtown Tunnel.

Then it was under the East River and out on 495, through the borough of Brooklyn. As far as a lot of Manhattanites were concerned, she had already entered the wilds of New York. But she didn't stop there. She kept going all the way out to Queens—the rural hinterlands of the city—where she was soon parking on an elm-lined street across from Mt. Olivet Cemetery.

Her first stop was the pool car's trunk. Thankfully, she found it had the items she needed: a screwdriver, which she discreetly tucked in her waistband, under her blouse; and a pair of blue nitrile gloves and an evidence collection bag, which she slid into the tiny half pocket of her slacks.

Why an expensive, nicely tailored pair of women's pants couldn't have full-size pockets was a gripe for another time.

Appropriately equipped, she walked with determined strides through a black wrought iron gate. Then it was up a concrete path toward a magnificent nineteenth-century limestone building that was perched atop a small hill.

The Fresh Pond Crematory-Columbarium was one of the oldest facilities of its kind in the city of New York. It had polished marble floors, high ceilings, Tiffany-style stained glass windows, and a peaceful, quiet dignity about its every detail.

It also housed the remains of Cynthia Heat.

Nikki hoped those remains would help her answer the question that had been haunting her ever since the half second earlier that morning that had challenged one of the most fundamental assumptions of her life.

Was her mother dead or not? She couldn't live anything resembling a settled, sane, balanced life until she knew for sure.

She pressed a buzzer next to the front door and waited for the lock to be released. When she entered, she found a smiling woman in gold-framed glasses there to greet her.

"Ms. Heat, yes?"

"That's right. Martha?"

"Yes. Very good. Here to visit your mother?"

"Yes," Nikki said.

The woman might have added, *It's been a while.* But at the Fresh Pond Crematory-Columbarium, they were far more decorous than that.

"You remember the way?" Martha asked.

"Of course."

"Very well. Let me know if you need anything."

Heat smiled thinly—just the right amount, she hoped—then started walking across the polished marble. Her heels echoed as she passed countless plaques, laid out in perfectly straight rows and columns. Each marked the spot where the ashes of a cremated New Yorker had been laid to rest.

The columbarium was designed with privacy in mind. There were nooks and turns and corners and alcoves, architectural features that assured mourning families could be more or less alone with the remains of their loved ones when they chose to visit.

It hadn't necessarily been designed for what Nikki was about to do. But it would suit her purpose all the same.

When she reached the small recess where her mother's ashes had been stored, she took a brief moment to look up and down the hallway where she stood. During weekends and holidays there were often other mourners. But on a Tuesday morning in October, she had the place to herself.

She stepped forward and found her mother's plaque, a handsome bronze piece that read:

CYNTHIA TROPE HEAT

B. JANUARY 5, 1950

D. NOVEMBER 24, 1999

LOVING MOTHER, MUSICIAN, PATRIOT

". . . THAT WHOEVER BELIEVES SHALL NOT PERISH,

BUT HAVE EVERLASTING LIFE."

Nikki had long ago noted that the words "in him"—which were in every other translation of John 3:16 she had ever seen—had been eliminated. She had dismissed it as Cynthia Heat striking one last blow against the patriarchy. But had her mother—who had left such explicit instructions in her will, including the language on the plaque—been trying to tell her daughter something?

Or was Nikki Heat about to desecrate her mother's final resting spot for no good reason?

"Sorry, Mom," she muttered.

Then she slipped the screwdriver out from under her blouse and got to work.

She knew she could have asked the staff to open the small vault for her. But she didn't want anyone at Fresh Pond Crematory-Columbarium knowing what she was up to. She was, more than likely, fully within her rights to do what she was about to do. Cynthia Heat was her mother. Nikki was her next of kin. Those ashes belonged to her.

But she didn't want any potential red tape to slow her down. Nor did she want to have to answer any questions.

As she unfastened the first screw, then the second, she couldn't help thinking back to November 24, 1999, the day that irrevocably changed the course of her life.

She was in her sophomore year at Northeastern and home for Thanksgiving break. She and her mother were making pies in the Gramercy Park apartment Nikki had called home since her parents brought her home from the hospital. The recipe called for fresh-ground cinnamon—not the pre-ground stuff—so Nikki had been dispatched to the Morton Williams grocery story up the block for cinnamon sticks.

She was in the spice aisle when her mother called her, which was why Nikki got to hear the harrowing sound of her mother being attacked. She even heard the voice of the attacker, who she later determined was Tyler Wynn. He was her mother's CIA handler and had employed Cynthia as a piano teacher/covert agent as part of what he called the Nanny Network, a group of domestic employees who spied on the rich families they worked for. It had been incredibly successful throughout the 70s and 80s. However, by 1999, Tyler Wynn had turned traitor, working for other governments, and he killed Cynthia before she could expose him.

Nikki didn't know any of that at the time, of course. All she knew was that someone was assaulting her mother. Nikki rushed home. By the time she arrived, she found her mother crumpled on the kitchen floor.

A knife—her own kitchen knife, a very real knife—was protruding from Cynthia Heat's back.

Blood—her own blood, also very real—had poured out on the floor.

Nikki had cradled her mother in her arms and felt her body going cold. Life was fading from her so quickly. Cynthia Heat was already beyond speech. Her breathing became slow and labored.

And then it had stopped. Hadn't it?

Same with her pulse. Nikki had held her hands against her mother's wrists and felt nothing.

Nikki now realized she had never seen the actual entry wound the knife had created. She had only seen the hole in Cynthia Heat's sweater set. It had never even occurred to Nikki that it mattered whether or not she saw the hole the knife had gouged in her mother, just as it had never occurred to Nikki until that morning that what she had witnessed all those years ago might have been a staged event.

From there, everything had happened so fast. A paramedic arrived, then a policewoman. She could still see them, coaxing her away from the body, telling her she had to let go. Then they had whisked her mother away.

The next time Nikki Heat saw her mother was after the cremation. Cynthia Heat's ashes were presented to Nikki in an urn—the urn she was about to pull out of the wall. Two screws down, two to go.

Nikki kept looking at the plaque as she worked. November 24, 1999, wasn't just the most tragic day of her life. It was also the dividing line in her life, the before and after in her personal biography.

Before that date, she had led a more or less unremarkable childhood and young adulthood. Yes, her parents had divorced when she was little. And, yes, her piano teacher mother was occasionally flighty, disappearing with little or no explanation and then reappearing without any clarification as to where she had been. But they had been happy when they were together. And Nikki, the beneficiary of more than a few of Cynthia Heat's many talents—not to mention her striking good looks—had been a promising theater student whose talent and charisma hinted at a boundless potential on the stage and in front of the camera.

After that date, everything changed. Her life became inextricably darker, tinged with a sadness that never seemed to fully leave her. Even when she was doing something that made her superficially happy—enjoying a workout, drinking a glass of wine, laughing with friends—there was a part of her brain pulsing with sorrow. It was like grief was a skin she couldn't shed. She dropped her theater major and took up criminal justice. She never again appeared onstage. She became obsessed with solving murders—first her mother's, then other people's. She became a cop, then a detective. She met a charmingly roguish magazine writer named Jameson Rook and became a captain.

All because of November 24, 1999.

She was working on the last screw, which finally came free. Carefully, quietly, she pulled the plaque away from the wall to reveal a small cubby.

The urn was inside. It was the same urn she remembered from seventeen years earlier, after the ceremony they had held for Cynthia. Nikki had personally placed it in the cubby. To the best of her knowledge, it hadn't been touched since.

Now she was hauling it back out. She grasped it firmly, with both hands. Once she had removed it, she cradled it in her arms for another moment.

Nikki looked down at the urn, still in disbelief about what she was doing.

Then she grasped the urn's lid. It had a tight seal, a ring of plastic that kept it snug against the rim. She tugged, working it back and forth until the seal broke.

As air that had not been disturbed in seventeen years escaped from the hole, Heat peered inside. She had wondered if perhaps the vessel would be empty. For as much as she wanted her mother to be alive, she was strangely dreading what she would see.

But, no, there were definitely ashes inside.

The question was: whose?

Was that mound of gray cinders all that was left of Cynthia Heat? Or was it . . . what? Another person? Just some other substance scraped off an empty funeral pyre? Floor sweepings from the crematory?

Nikki softly set the urn on the ground, then slid the nitrile gloves over her hands. She opened the evidence collection bag, then dipped her hand into the urn. A small fistful would be enough. More than enough.

"Remember that you are dust," she whispered. "And to dust you shall return."

She sealed the bag, then returned the urn to its rightful place. After restoring the plaque to its spot on the wall, she made her quiet escape from the Fresh Pond Crematory-Columbarium.

The evidence bag in her pocket didn't have more than a few ounces of material in it.

But it felt like it weighed a ton.

SEVEN

Heat tried Rook's phone several more times on the way back from her morbid errand in Queens, getting the same distressing non-response each time: straight to voice mail.

In a failed attempt not to be unnerved about it, she tried to think of all the perfectly benign reasons he might not be answering. He had a dead battery. He'd dropped his phone. He was deep in one of Kline Industries' mines.

All of it was possible. None of it reassured her in the slightest.

As she neared the precinct, she did her best to stuff her anxiety back in a box so she could concentrate on what she had to do next: pay a visit to room 23B.

It was ordinarily something she would have enjoyed—or at least not dreaded. Which, in itself, requires an explanation.

For most New Yorkers, a visit to room 23B at the Twentieth Precinct meant their lives had met one of two unfortunate ends: a lonely one, in the case of an unattended death, or a violent one, in the case of a murder.

In both instances, absent any religious restrictions, the law requires an autopsy. And for all citizens whose bodies were discovered north of 59th Street, south of 86th Street, west of Central Park, and east of the Hudson River, those autopsies were performed in room 23B. That made it a place where most people wouldn't want to end up.

Nikki had a different feeling toward it, mainly because of the woman who plied her trade there.

Medical Examiner Lauren Parry was Heat's best friend, the maid of honor at her wedding, and one of the very few people who was allowed a glimpse behind the walls Nikki erected to block out most of the rest of the world.

That's what made this particular visit to room 23B complicated. Heat always dealt straight with her friend. This time, because of what was in her pocket, she was going to have to come from the side.

Heat found Parry washing her hands, which meant she was either finishing up an autopsy or about to start one.

"Hey, I was just about to call you," Parry said.

"Oh, yeah?"

"Well, you said that Jane Doe was top priority, right?"

"Absolutely," Heat said, content to pretend like that was the reason she had come to 23B in the first place. "I was actually hoping she wouldn't be Jane anymore."

"No such luck. We already ran prints and got nothing. I'm sorry to say our Jane is a good girl who has never been in trouble with the five-oh. We're doing DNA as well, but of course that's going to take longer and I'm not real optimistic if we've already struck out on prints."

"Okay. What *can* you tell me?"

Parry dried her hands on a paper towel. "Not much, to be honest. Jane was a healthy Caucasian female in her early to mid-thirties. She was not pregnant, nor had she ever been pregnant. She had surgery on her left knee about ten years ago or so, but it was arthroscopic and I'm sorry to say it didn't involve any permanent medical devices for us to play Clue with. She wasn't a drug addict. She had no tattoos. She exercised regularly. She was a conscientious flosser."

"Sounds like a real party girl," Heat said.

"Yeah. If I was putting her on Match.com, pretty much the only thing you'd have to add to make her the most boring profile ever is that she likes taking long walks on the beach and watching romantic comedies."

"Tell me about her last date," Heat said. "You got any idea on time of death?"

"Well, there was no hint of rigor, so she had been dead for at least forty-eight hours when we got her."

"Forty-eight hours?" Heat repeated, feeling her brow crinkle.

"Lividity was a little tricky. She lost a lot of blood after the beheading. The heart stops beating once it no longer receives messages from the brain, but that took a little while in this case, on account of the difficulty that psycho had getting her head off. Plus, even once the heart stops, there's a lot of blood pressure built up. The carotid artery is like a busy highway at rush hour. Even if cars stop getting on at the entrance ramps, there's still plenty of traffic left on the road. It keeps spurting pretty good for at least thirty seconds. Have you found the scene yet?"

"No."

"Well, when you do, you're going to find a pretty big bloodstain, because this body didn't have a lot of fluid left in it. The better method for determining Jane's TOD was cell autolysis, also known as cell death. That turned out to be at a very early stage. Between that and the fact that skin discoloration had only just started, my best estimate is that she'd been dead for approximately fifty-four hours by the time I got her, but I'd have to put at least a four-hour margin for error on either side."

"Fifty-four hours?" Heat began. "But that's—"

"Sunday morning sometime. Conservatively, I'd put it sometime between midnight and eight A.M."

Heat stood there, her lower lip grasped between her teeth. As a detective, she had learned that establishing a timeline was a critical piece of any investigation.

This timeline had a definite gap in it.

"So, hang on a second, she's killed early Sunday morning sometime," Heat said. "But according to the dishwasher we interviewed, there was no body in the Dumpster on Monday night, and certainly a body there on Tuesday morning. So where was she from Sunday morning until Tuesday morning?"

"Beats me. That's what you fancy detectives are hired to figure out," Parry said.

"It's possible the killers were just waiting until garbage pickup day," Heat mused, even though that was also outside Parry's investigative scope.

"All I can tell you is that she was probably rolled up in the carpet the whole time. She was stuck to it pretty good."

"Please tell me it was a one-of-a-kind handmade Persian."

Parry shook her head. "Sorry. DuPont Stainmaster."

"Do you have *anything* good for me?"

"Depends. How good a nose do you have?"

"Pretty good, I think."

Parry walked over to a lab table. She grabbed a small plastic container with a piece of denim inside it. Then she walked toward Heat, pulling off the lid at the last second.

"Smell this. You get anything off that?"

Heat sniffed at it. "Yeah. Why do I suddenly feel like I'm on a camping trip?"

"Because you're smelling kerosene. Or at least that's my best guess until I have some tests run to confirm it. Her clothes reeked of it."

Parry put the lid back on the swab.

"ISIS has burned some of its captives alive," Heat said. "You think that was their plan with our victim, but then they decided to behead her instead?"

"That's one possibility. Though they were making it hard on themselves if that was their plan. Kerosene doesn't light nearly as easily as gasoline."

"Then they were going to burn the body but they couldn't get it to light?"

"I didn't find any marks on her clothes or her body to indicate they put a match to her," Parry said.

"Huh," Heat said.

"There's one other curious thing."

"Don't hold out on me, Laur."

"I'm not. I just don't know what it is yet."

Heat's head cocked to the side as Parry continued: "It came from the victim's shoes. She was wearing hiking boots. The treads had some good old-fashioned dust and dirt, but there was also a whitish powder that . . . Well, I don't know what it is."

"A whitish powder. Like coke? Heroin?"

"Could be. I didn't get a lot of it, and it was mixed in pretty good with the other dirt. The lab techs are going to have to find a way to separate it out before we can even start to pin down what it is."

"All right. Well, keep me looped in."

"You got it, Captain."

Heat made a big show of turning like she was going to leave, like what was about to come next was such an afterthought she had all but forgotten it. Parry had already sat down on a lab stool. She had turned her attention to a tablet, into which she was entering information about the autopsy.

"Oh, hey, Laur, one more thing," Heat said.

Parry looked up from her tablet without speaking.

Heat pulled the plastic evidence bag from her half pocket and briefly dangled it, then casually tossed it on the table. "Would you mind doing a little workup on this?"

Parry examined it from where she sat. The medical examiner had seen the human body in virtually every possible state of disintegration, including when it had been reduced to ashes. Now she was the one with the wrinkled forehead.

"Are those . . . cremation remains?" the medical examiner asked.

"Yeah," Heat said, trying to keep her tone breezy.

"Whose?"

"Don't know. That's part of the mystery."

Parry was shaking her head. "The covalent bonds of DNA start breaking apart at about eight hundred degrees Fahrenheit. Most crematories get up to eighteen hundred, two thousand. If they cooked it as long as they're supposed to, I won't be able to tell you who that was."

"I know. But I thought bones still told stories even after the DNA goes silent."

"They do. Sometimes," Parry said.

"Well, okay. So tell me whatever you can about this person."

"Is this for the ISIS case?"

"No. Something else."

"What's the case number?"

Heat tried to slide by this by saying, "Can you keep it off-books? It's . . . not really an official investigation yet. More something that might turn into an investigation depending on what you find."

But it didn't slide easily. Parry took a long moment to study her friend. Just as the Twentieth Precinct had been Heat's first station after graduating from the Police Academy, it had been Parry's first assignment after she completed the last of her medical examiner rotations.

Since that time, such a free and easy exchange of favors had passed between the women that they had honestly lost count of who owed what to whom. Heat probably would have said she was in Parry's debt. But Parry would have said the same thing.

Yet even within the bounds of that kind of relationship, this was an unusual request. It was explicitly against department policy. It could get Parry suspended or even fired. And, sure, Parry could play with case numbers in a way that not even the most stringent audit would turn it up, but . . .

At the very least, it begged a whole lot of questions that Heat wasn't ready to answer.

So, yeah, funniest thing, I was just walking along the street today and I happened to see my dead mother dressed like a homeless woman . . .

Heat was holding her breath. She could see Parry's eyes scanning her own in an attempt to divine what might be behind this ask. There was real wonder on Parry's face. And to Heat, her thoughts were easy to read.

What's Nikki not telling me? Why is she asking me to do this? What's really going on?

And then Parry suddenly returned her attention to her tablet.

"Yeah, no problem," Parry said.

"Thanks," Heat said.

Only then did she let the breath go.

EIGHT

As she returned to the bull pen, Heat was lost in her thoughts. About her mother. About the ISIS case. About where her husband might be and whether he was, at that moment, already himself doused in kerosene—for whatever reason the killers did that—and slated for an awful end.

Her distraction was to the point where she did not notice the man who had fallen into step behind her.

Nor was she aware of the lascivious look on his face.

Nor did she notice when his hands started reaching for her buttocks.

"Excuse me, miss," he growled in a lecherous voice. "But you have an extraordinary ass. Would you mind if I groped it?"

Heat turned to see the ruggedly handsome mug of Jameson Rook leering suggestively back at her.

"Rook! Oh, thank God," she gasped.

She immediately leapt into Rook's arms, pressing her entire body against his and grabbing him with both arms. Her near-tackle was so forceful it actually staggered Rook, but Heat wasn't letting go. If anything, she squeezed even harder, not caring that she was knocking the wind out of him. She buried her face in his neck, grateful for the feel of him, the smell of him, the sound of him, and the sight of him. The taste could come later.

"Well, this is certainly a nice how-ya-doin'," Rook said. "I should go away more often."

Then she released him, stepped back, and slapped him across the face.

"Or maybe I should just stay home," Rook said.

The journalist rubbed his jaw. "Was it the ass thing? Too crass?

For the record, I was going to call you 'callipygian' but I felt like that would—"

"Do you have any idea how worried I was about you?" Heat demanded. "Don't you *ever* check your phone?"

"We were in the air all morning," Rook said, hauling his phone, with its still-darkened screen, out of his pocket. "Huh. I must have forgotten to turn it back on. We were just having such an intense conversation."

"You *forgot*? And who is *we*?"

Heat now saw that Rook was being trailed by a blonde whom even statues would have referred to as statuesque. She was at least six feet tall, with gams that went on seemingly without end. Her A-line dress was hemmed just barely below scandal length, and its sleeveless bodice displayed arms with a perfect health-club tone to them. Atop that rather magnificent display of the female form was a set of perfect smiling teeth, framed by the kind of precisely symmetrical face that Bert Parks used to sing songs about.

Detective Ochoa had gotten up from his desk, where he was allegedly going through profiles of Muslim extremist groups with ties to New York City, with a smarmy grin plastered on his face.

"Oh, I'm sorry," Rook said. "Nikki, Miguel, I'd like you to meet Legs Kline's press secretary, Lana Kline."

"Hello, Ms. Kline," Ochoa said, extending his hand. "My name is Detective Miguel Ochoa. I'm the leader of the Twentieth Precinct detective squad—"

"Co-leader," Detective Raley piped up from behind his computer screen.

"—and I want you to know if there's anything you need during your visit to our fine city, you just ask me. The NYPD is here to protect and to serve."

Lana ignored Ochoa and beamed at Heat.

"Captain Nikki Heat," she purred with a gentle Texas twang. "I feel like I know you already! I know that's a silly thing to say, it's just that I've read all of Jamie's articles about you at least three times. And, as you know, Jamie writes so *well* and has such a knack for capturing the true essence of a person that I already feel this closeness to you. I never had a sister so I don't know what that's like. But I felt like you were the sister I would have had. I'm sorry, can I hug you?"

Before Heat could answer, Lana leaned in for a girl hug, the kind where no one's makeup gets smeared, no one's hair gets mussed, and no actual human warmth is exchanged.

"The only thing I don't understand is how you could resist marrying such an amazing man for so long," Lana continued, playfully patting Rook on the chest, letting her hand linger on his pectoral muscle in a way that flirted with passing chummy on its way to something more intimate. "He is such a remarkable talent and so scrumptious on top of it . . . If it had been me, I probably would have marched him down to the jewelry store after the third date and held him hostage there until he proposed."

Her eyes got a shine to them whose luminance was matched only by her lip gloss.

"Anyhow, I absolutely insisted Jamie bring me here so I could meet you in person," she continued. "I can't explain what a thrill this is for me. Daddy and I have such a deep respect for law enforcement. You really are the everyday heroes of our society and his administration will do everything it can to honor your bravery and sacrifice. We think Law Enforcement Appreciation Day ought to be its own national holiday."

She said it with a level of sincerity that made Heat think her next pronouncement would be about her abiding love for shelter pets and world peace.

"And, I'm sorry, you're Legs Kline's . . . press secretary?" Heat asked.

"Well, that and his daughter. I know I shouldn't talk about that too much. Professionally, I should stick with the more official title. But around Jamie I just seem to revert. He really is so good at breaking down the barriers between reporter and subject. It's like I forget he's even got a pen in his hand. Everything feels so cozy and personal with him."

Heat was already fighting the urge to allow her fist to get cozy and personal with Lana's face. Heat had made peace with Rook's old flings prancing in and out of his life, whether it was Department of Homeland Security Agent Yardley Bell or *New York Ledger* Senior Metro Reporter Tam Svejda.

To see a new contender for his affections was something else entirely. At least Heat knew what she'd be seeing the next time she worked the heavy bag at her gym.

Rook had this goofy grin on his face. Maybe it was because Heat was so glad to see him, but she was only slightly annoyed that he appeared to be eating out of Lana's hand. Rook was ultimately a prisoner to his gender. Men are helplessly susceptible to flattery and congenitally incapable of detecting when it's false.

"Oh, I'm sorry, where are my manners?" Rook said. Then he swept his hand toward a pair of tallish young men, dressed in nearly matching dark suits, their hair parted identically to the side. They looked like they were days away from the last meeting of their college chapter of the FYMA—the Future Yes Men of America.

These two were clearly fawning over Lana. But not in a sexual way. More in a her-daddy-might-make-them-assistant-to-the-undersecretary-to-the-ambassador-of-Peru kind of way. To Heat, something about them brought to mind a pair of palace eunuchs.

"These are two of the press office interns. This Justin and this is Preston," Rook said. "Or . . . wait. Is it Preston and Justin?"

"No, I'm Justin," said one.

"And I'm Preston!" the other said.

Justin continued, pointing to a spot on his suit jacket. "You can tell easily, because I have my American flag pin here, on my lapel—"

"While I have American flag cufflinks," Preston said, holding his wrists out for Heat to inspect.

Justin added, "People only get us confused—"

"Because we have the tendency to complete each other's sentences," Preston finished.

"All right, that's enough now, boys," Lana said, clapping her hands twice.

"Yes, Miss Kline," said Preston. Or was it Justin?

"Whatever you say, Miss Kline," said the other one.

Obediently, they stepped into the background.

"Aren't they just *adorable*?" Rook said, tenting his fingers over his mouth, shaking his head, and looking at them like they were puppies who were just days away from being paper-trained. "I'm thinking about getting two of them myself."

"What, as decorations?" Heat asked.

"No! As interns!"

"Rook, what does a journalist possibly need interns for?"

"Everyone in this world needs interns now and then," Rook said. "Anyhow, I'm sorry I've been out of touch. As I was saying, we were in the air."

"Daddy knows how important this *First Press* piece is," Lana added, "so he was letting us use one of his jets."

"The one with the king-sized bed in it?" Ochoa interjected.

"That's a big bed for an airplane," Raley added.

Heat glared at them.

"What?" Ochoa said. "I'm just asking."

Rook continued as if Roach hadn't interrupted. "We were coming back from Colorado. Did you know that Kline Industries has developed a new method of forest management that is actually good for the trees *and* for humans?"

"We use drones to identify trees that are at the end of their life cycle then carefully extract them," Lana explained. "So the forest only loses what the forest was going to lose anyway, which then leaves room for new growth."

"And they do it in a way that is both sustainable and actually makes the land less prone to forest fires, which in turn helps nearby communities that live under the constant threat of fire," Rook continued.

"Then we donate a portion of the profits to forest management research, ensuring that in the next generation, Kline Industries techniques will be even more refined and ecologically sound," Lana finished.

"Wait, wait," Heat said. "I thought you were fracking in North Dakota."

"No," Rook said. "Fracking was Sunday."

"That's when Jamie learned that the majority of our fracking proceeds are actually reinvested in Kline Industries' solar division," Lana said. "So the petroleum we still need today is not only fueling our cars and homes, it's also creating a future that is less reliant on fossil fuels."

"But I have to say," Rook volleyed back at her, "what I found even more impressive than that was your smelting operation on Lake Erie.

"Did you know," Rook continued, now aiming his lecture at Heat, "they have devised a technique that is not only completely pollution-free, but it actually collects all of the by-products from the smelting process and turns them into usable goods?"

"A zero-waste process is really to our advantage, of course, because we've developed markets for those by-products," Lana said. "The engineers are always telling me that humankind has been obtaining metal from ore for thousands of years. And this is, without exaggeration, the most efficient system ever devised."

"But that's not the cool part," Rook said.

Lana looked at him curiously. "It's not?"

"No, the cool part is that not only does your father have his own planes, he has his own *airports*."

"Well, to be accurate, I would really just call them runways," Lana clarified.

"*And* his own seaports and container ships," Rook added. "You should see the size of the cranes. The man has the biggest toys of anyone I've ever met."

"Well, yes," Lana said, and now she was the one who was lecturing Heat. "Daddy realized that Kline Industries could keep more of the money it made if it expanded vertically so that it controlled more aspects of getting its goods to our buyers. We save a lot of money by doing it ourselves, whether it's shipping by air, sea, rail, or ground."

"Rail? Ground?" Rook asked, almost like he was hurt.

"I'm sorry, Jamie. I know how much you were enjoying yourself. We just ran out of time before I could take you to the truck and train depots," Lana said, then turned back to Heat. "The point is Kline Industries has a profit potential far beyond any of our competitors. Or, when we feel like increasing market share, we can beat our competitors on price, knowing none of them can match our costs."

"Those trains . . . they have king-sized beds, too?" Ochoa asked from the sidelines.

"You could definitely fit a huge bed on a train," Raley said.

Heat glared at them some more.

Lana kept ignoring them. "And Kline Industries has never outsourced a single operation. One hundred percent of our business is run by Americans. Even when we extract resources in other countries, we do it with American workers. Every dollar we spend strengthens America, and every dollar we reinvest goes back into this country, too. That's why Daddy takes such a strong stance against immigration. He feels like the best workers in the world are already right here, in the United States of America."

She paused. Heat worried she was going to burst into a rendition of "God Bless America" right there, with Justin and Preston singing backup.

Instead, Lana continued: "What I've been trying to convince Jamie of is that when you look at the entirety of Kline Industries, it really represents the kind of independent thinking America needs in the White House—not the kind of failed policies that Lindsy Gardner or Caleb Brown will resort to. The Kline way is unconventional in some respects, but it's also very grounded in what some people would call old-fashioned values. My father believes in an America where the rags-to-riches story he experienced is still possible for any kid with a dream. I know it sounds corny sometimes. I tell him that myself. But my father really believes he can take what he's done for Kline Industries and do it for the rest of the country he loves."

"The boats, they *must* have king-sized beds," Ochoa said.

"More than one, I'm sure," Raley confirmed.

"Enough with the beds!" Heat screamed.

Then she turned toward Rook. "Do you have any idea that while you've been gallivanting around the country in Daddy's jet a terrorist group swearing loyalty to ISIS has released a video where they chopped off a journalist's head and then said that you're next?"

Rook immediately brought his hands to his throat.

"No," Rook said. "Though I'm glad you gave me a heads up."

Heat's nostrils flared.

"*Such* a bad choice of words," Rook said to the floor.

"Well," Lana said, brightly, "I think we should be going now. Daddy has a lunch event that I really should be at. Preston, do you have that press kit for Mr. Rook?"

"I'm Justin," said the one Lana was looking at. "Lapel pin, remember?"

"Right. Sorry."

"And, yes, here's the press kit," Preston said, producing a slick folder stuffed with paeans to Legs Kline and the company he created.

"Thank you," Lana said.

Then she turned to Rook. She folded his hands around the press kit, holding her own hands there far longer than she needed to.

"You'll call me as soon as Legs is free for a sit-down?" Rook asked.

"Absolutely," Lana said, still holding his hands, now bringing her face close to his and staring into his eyes. "And can I just say it has been *such* a privilege to get to spend this time with you and to get to know you so well. I've never come across a man of your ability. I can't tell you how much I admire your skills."

"As a reporter," Rook said, gently separating his hands and easing away with the press kit as he smiled at Heat. "She means as a reporter."

"Yes, of course," Lana said, breathily. Then she winked at him as she headed for the elevator. "Well, off we go. Come along, Justin, Preston."

The last thing they heard as the elevator doors closed was, "No, *I'm* Preston . . ."

Heat waited until she was sure Lana Kline and her entourage were gone to address Rook. Her voice was quieter than even she thought it would be.

"Your mother has been in a panic all morning," Heat said softly. "*I've* been in a panic all morning."

"Can I retroactively have been in a panic all morning?" Rook said. "Because, for the record, I'm quite fond of my head remaining attached to my body."

"Then, bro, can I give you some advice?" Ochoa said, clapping him on the shoulder. "You might want to stop hanging out with that blonde there."

"Don't you have something to do?" Rook said.

"Yeah, but watching you struggle is more fun," Raley called out.

"Roach, back to work," Heat ordered. "Rook, could you please join me in my office?"

Heat walked away without waiting for a reply.

"I actually feel bad for those ISIS guys," Ochoa said.

"And why is that?" Rook asked.

"They're going through a lot of trouble to grab you and chop your head off. But by the time she's done there isn't going to be anything left of it."

Rook followed Heat into her office, already bracing for the worst.

As soon as the door was shut, she quickly closed the blinds. By that point, Rook was actually flinching, in anticipation of another slap. Or worse.

Instead, Heat rushed up to him, cupped his face in both hands, and planted a deep, soul-searching kiss on his lips. Their mouths immediately became one, and Heat ground herself into him. Rook's body responded. Heat knew what Rook wanted. And she could tell from the way he was breathing that he thought he might finally achieve one of the dearest, longest-held ambitions he had held for their relationship; the thing he had hoped for almost from the moment he first walked into the Twentieth Precinct; the dream within a dream:

Office sex.

Heat finished the kiss and drew herself back slightly, a look of pure lust plastered on her face.

Then she released him and slapped him again.

"Okay," she said. "I think we're just about square now."

Rook was again rubbing his chin.

"That was for Lana, yes?"

"Oh, what, that thing? God, no. I give you more credit than that, Rook."

"You . . . you do? I mean, yes, of course you should. Thank you."

Rook paused. "But just so we're clear, what, exactly, have I done to earn this credit?"

"Because after eight years with you, I know your type pretty well. Physically she's it, sure. Physically *I'd* want to have sex with her. But emotionally? I bet she'd be delivering sound bites about your foreplay. It'd be like having sex with a talking blow-up doll."

"You're absolutely correct," Rook said, then hastily added, "Not that I'd know."

"I mean, really, I'd be more worried about you getting drunk and having sex with Flotsam and Jetsam."

"It's Justin and Preston . . . though extra points for the *Little Mermaid* reference."

Heat sagged into him, allowing herself to be enveloped in the comfort of his arms. She could actually breathe for what felt like the first time since she had seen that horrible video.

"Now," Rook said, "can we go back to the part about you wanting to have sex with Lana?"

When she didn't reply, he said, "Ha! Totally kidding! I'm such a jokester!" Then he added in a low voice, "I mean, unless you're considering it . . ."

Heat released him, then grabbed both of his hands. She locked her eyes on his.

"Rook, there's something I need to tell you," she said, and she said it in a way that even the perpetually clownish Rook got serious for a moment.

"And I don't want you to think I'm crazy," she continued. "Well, okay, maybe you should think I'm crazy. There are times when I feel like I must be crazy. But I need you to hear me out for a second."

"Okay."

She inhaled, held her breath for a moment, then exhaled and came out with it: "I think I saw my mother this morning."

Rook showed no immediate reaction beyond interested concern. In the all-time husband rankings, Rook easily placed in the top ten when it came to willingness to believe the absurd might actually be true.

All he asked was, "Where?"

"Just outside the precinct. She was sitting on a bench in a bus shelter, dressed like she was homeless. I only saw her for a fleeting instant, but . . . Rook, I know what I saw. And it was her. Almost twenty years older than the last time I saw her, sure, but certain things about a person's face don't change. It was Mom."

"Did you talk to her?"

"I tried. As soon as I registered who it was, I ran after her, but she—"

"Vanished into thin air? Like only the best spies can?" Rook suggested.

"Well, yes."

Rook released her hands and walked toward the window, which had a view out to 82nd Street. He peered out.

"That bus shelter? The one up near Columbus?"

"Yes."

"Then that would sure seem to point to it being your mother. Anyone else, you would have easily caught up to. How many aged homeless women could outrun someone in the shape you're in?"

"I know, but . . . Rook, how is that possible? She died in my arms. I felt her body going cold. I was *covered* in her blood."

Rook walked away from the window, then sat with one leg on her desk. This was Rook in his element, holding a new theory up to the light and rotating it around so he could look at it from all angles. Especially when it was a wild conspiracy theory.

It was a way in which his journalistic training and her police training melded quite nicely. Both involved assembling a narrative of events, and both taught you—often the hard way—what happens to those who don't continually reexamine and fact-check all the elements of the story they're trying to tell.

"Are you sure it was her blood?" Rook asked.

"Well, yes, I . . . I mean, I think it was. It was coming out of her body."

"Did you ever see the entry wound?"

"No," she admitted to him, as she had admitted to herself earlier. "Just the hole in the sweater."

"Did the police do any DNA testing on it?"

"Of course not. That was seventeen years ago. Those tests took weeks or even months back then and there would have been no reason to. There was never a doubt about what happened in the apartment."

"Of course not, thanks to Carter Damon," Rook said.

Damon was the cop assigned to the case. He turned out to have been paid off by Cynthia Heat's killers to thwart the investigation.

For years, Nikki had thought her mother's killer was just a random home-invader—because that's what Damon, a seemingly straight-up cop, had wanted her to think.

"Point taken," Heat said. "But that would still be standard operating procedure even now. We don't bother to run DNA on blood found at a scene unless we think the perp has spilled some. If it's just the victim, we don't waste our lab time."

"So, if we're going on what we can definitively prove, we have no idea whose blood that was leaking out of your mother. Yes, it could have been hers. But it also could have been stolen from the local blood bank. It might not even have been human."

Heat gave a resigned nod of her head. "Yeah. You're right."

They both stared at her desk for a moment.

"But there's still the matter of her vital signs," Heat said. "The drop in body temperature. The labored breathing. I mean, she was out of it. I don't care how good an actress we think she was—or is. How is it possible to fake that?"

"Oh, that's actually the easy part," Rook said.

"It is?"

"There are any number of drugs that mimic death when given at the right dosages. My personal go-to would be Baclofen. Ever heard of it?"

"No."

"It's most often prescribed as a muscle relaxer, particularly to people with spinal cord injuries," Rook said. "In low doses all it does is relax muscles. But at higher doses it actually sends the patient into either a coma—or, I should say, what appears to be a coma—or even death.

"There are cases of Baclofen overdose where the patients appeared to have lost all brain stem function and were actually declared medically dead. There was one hospital I read about that was about to begin harvesting the patient's organs until they realized the person was still alive. There are other stories of Baclofen overdose where the patient has woken up in a funeral home."

"But she felt *cold*, Rook. And I checked for her pulse. I remember that so clearly. She didn't have one."

"Hypothermia. Bradycardia. Those are common side effects of Baclofen overdose. Body functions slow down to almost nothing and the body goes into a kind of hibernation. It's difficult to detect a pulse when you're expecting a heart that beats sixty times a minute and it's actually only beating about ten."

"Still, I wasn't gone from the apartment for more than fifteen or twenty minutes. Surely a drug that powerful requires longer to reach full efficacy?"

Rook shook his head. "Baclofen absorbs rapidly in the bloodstream. It doesn't take more than a few minutes. If anything, it was probably one of the last things they did after they staged the rest of the scene. That's why she was even still breathing a little bit when you came home."

"Rook, I don't know . . ."

"You asked how it's possible. I'm telling you, that's how it's possible. To be honest, I'm surprised at myself I never thought about this before. Baclofen easily accounts for every symptom you've just described. The brilliant thing about it is your mother wouldn't have even needed to call on her acting skills. She would have actually felt like she was dying. She probably would have died if the dosage wasn't very, very precise. Baclofen is not to be toyed with."

Heat sat at her desk and buried her face in her hands. Rook was pacing now.

"You know, there's one thing I've always wondered about," he said. "It's something I never asked you because . . . well, because you fixated on your mother's death enough. You didn't need me bringing it up."

"What?"

"I never wanted to get into it, because it seemed like a small discrepancy," Rook said.

"Well, we're into it now. So spit it out."

"911."

"What about it?"

"Any time I've heard you recount the day of your mother's death—the trip to Morton Williams, all of it—I've never heard you say you called 911."

"That's because I didn't."

"And yet a paramedic and a police officer just showed up at your mother's apartment and whisked her body away."

"I always thought . . . I mean, I assumed my mother must have called them."

"Well, let's examine that for a moment, shall we? Let's just assume this wasn't all staged. Let's assume Tyler Wynn really did sneak into your mother's apartment, as he was certainly capable of doing, and then killed her with one blow—as he was also capable of doing."

"That's what he did to Nicole Bernardin," Heat said, referring to the woman who had been Cynthia Heat's best friend during her spy days.

"Exactly. So Tyler Wynn buries a butcher knife in your mother's back, while she's on the phone with you."

"Right."

"And yet she somehow manages to hang up with you, then dial 911 before losing consciousness?"

"Well, it's possible."

"Perhaps. Except," he said, now closing his eyes, "when I think back to photographs I've seen of the crime scene, I don't see any blood on the telephone. How is *that* possible? She had blood all over her when you found her. It was pouring out of her. But she managed to call 911 without getting so much as a drop on the phone?"

Heat was silent for a moment. Her head was starting to throb. She absentmindedly massaged her temples. Rook was clearly back in November of 1999, trying to reenvision the scene under every different scenario they were now creating.

"It's an easy thing to overlook," Rook said. "Whoever staged that scene was careful to get blood all over. But when you think about being stabbed in the back, wouldn't it be natural human instinct to reach around and feel the wound? Assuming she was aware enough to call 911, she'd certainly be aware enough to do that. That would put blood on her hands, which would put blood on the phone receiver. Except there wasn't any."

Heat was nodding. She had the same photographs imprinted in her mind.

"I hate to ask this, but have you thought about making a visit to Fresh Pond and—"

"Already did it."

"Of course you did. And?"

"There were ashes in the urn. I plucked out a sample and gave it to Lauren for testing."

Rook had stopped pacing and returned to his one-leg-sit on Heat's desk.

"Hang on," Heat said. "Tyler Wynn admitted to killing my mother."

"Only because that's what he wanted us to believe. Maybe that's what he wanted *everyone* to believe. But try this on for a moment: Do you think it's possible at the end that Wynn still cared for your mother?"

"I . . . I don't know."

"Think about when we saw him in the hospital in France," Rook said.

Heat closed her eyes and took herself back to that hospital room. They had watched Wynn "die"—or at least elaborately stage his own death, with fake doctors and a rigged EKG. But before he did, he had told Heat about the Nanny Network and the jobs Cynthia had done for him.

"Okay, I'm there," Heat said.

"Think about how he looked when he talked about her. They had a lot of good years together—a lot of great years, when they were both in the primes of their lives, before he had been twisted by money and betrayed his country. Tyler Wynn was your mother's 'Oncle Tyler.' It was clear to both of us he was incredibly fond of your mother. He admired her spy craft. He even loved her, in a platonic way."

"But that was all a fraud. He was just trying to trick us."

"Maybe he was and he wasn't," Rook said. "The best lies are the ones based on truth. Maybe it was easy for him to pretend he had affection for Cynthia because he really *did* have affection for Cynthia."

"Okay, so let's say, just for sake of argument, that Tyler Wynn loved my mother, in his own way."

"Right. And let's say he knew she had to die. Because of what she knew and what she was going to expose. But he couldn't bring himself to do it. For as twisted as he was, there was still good in him."

"What? Now he's Darth Vader?"

"Well, no. Because if he was, I definitely would have had him hook me up with a real lightsaber," Rook said. "But Vader *is* the perfect example of villainous complexity. In *Revenge of the Sith*, he only betrayed the Republic to save the life of Padme, the woman he loved. And in *Return of the Jedi*, he betrayed the Emperor to save the life of his son. Even for as evil as Vader was, he was always motivated by his devotion to others."

Heat stood up. Now she was the one pacing.

"So Wynn goes to my mother and says, 'I'm sorry. I have to pretend to kill you. It's the only way to save you from the people who will stop at nothing to see you dead.' And she goes along with it—"

"Because she knows he's right," Rook added.

"And then she stays dead for fifteen years. But then even after we expose Wynn and the entire plot he was involved in—the plot to infect New York City with smallpox—she stays quote-unquote 'dead.' Why would she do that? Why wouldn't she come back to life?"

"Because maybe we don't know everything yet," Rook said. "Maybe there's more to it we haven't uncovered."

"I don't know, Rook. That seems pretty far-fetched."

"I completely agree. But I'm not the one who saw her sitting in a bus shelter this morning."

Heat's head was legitimately spinning. For a journalist, Rook had a remarkable gift for fiction. He probably would have become a novelist if he weren't so busy doing something more important.

Did this actually happen? Did her mother fake her own death, with Tyler Wynn's help? Or was this just Rook's ability to spin any set of facts into a believable yarn?

Then she remembered the words of Tyler Wynn himself. He uttered them just after Heat and Rook discovered he hadn't really died in that French hospital after all.

At the time, she thought it was just the empty boasting of a criminal who couldn't resist a diabolical monologue. But now she wondered if, in fact, he had been trying to tell her something much more profound.

One thing you learn in the CIA, Wynn had said. *Nobody is ever really dead for certain.*

NINE

Another twenty minutes of supposition, speculation, and conjecture did not lead Heat and Rook any closer to a definitive conclusion beyond the fact that they couldn't really come to one. Based on the evidence at hand, it was every bit as possible that Cynthia Heat was alive as it was that she was dead.

Eventually, they reached a standstill, where Rook was staring at Heat and Heat was returning his gaze.

"So, can I ask a question?" Rook said.

"Shoot."

"Since we don't seem to be getting anywhere, and since the blinds are still closed, can we make out again? Because that was pretty hot."

"I know. But we probably both have other things to be doing."

"Drat."

"Though we certainly will tonight if you don't run out on me again," she added.

"Is a trip to Reykjavík a possibility?"

"A trip to Reykjavík is a near certainty."

"Then I'm not going anywhere," Rook said. "Now, at risk of being totally self-centered, did you say something about savage terrorists announcing to the world that they intended to decapitate me?"

"I did."

"Well, in that case—and with all due assurances that I will continue to train my journalistic powers on the open question of your mother's death—do you think maybe I can watch the video?"

"Yes. But call your mother first. She's worried sick and all she has for comfort is Jean Philippe."

"Eww," Rook said.

"I know. So call her."

Rook followed orders, withstanding a withering blast of maternal distress before being allowed to move on. By the time they returned to the bull pen, Roach was already hard at work.

"Hey, we hear anything from Rhymer and Feller yet?" Heat asked.

"They're still canvassing," Ochoa said. "So far, nothing."

"What about our search for the missing head?"

"ECT is going through the Dumpster where they found the rest of the body. They got uniforms going through other Dumpsters in the neighborhood. Hope the budget can handle some dry-cleaning bills."

"What about Aguinaldo? Anything from her on the scarf?"

"Negative."

"And your efforts?" Heat asked, gesturing toward the stack of files from the Counterterrorism Task Force arrayed in front of Ochoa.

"Also negative. I went through all of these quickly to see if anything popped out at me—maybe a group that was rapidly progressing toward more extreme rhetoric or more violent behavior. But nothing really hit on the first pass. I'm going through it slowly now, though I'm starting to think our beheaders might be a new element."

"Rales, you got anything yet?"

From the other side of the computer screen into which he was burying his attention, Raley just grunted.

"Okay, do we have the video cued up anywhere?" Heat asked. "Rook wants to see it."

Ochoa pointed at the computer sitting on Feller's desk. "Try that one."

Rook found his chair, the one with the wonky wheel, and pulled it up in front of the screen as Heat clicked play.

Heat watched Rook more than she did the video. Throughout the talking part, Rook viewed it with typical journalistic dispassion. Rook had been in the Arab world enough that the anti-Western rhetoric typical of the jihadist crowd did not faze him. He even knew aspects of it were justified. Rook had often remarked how the world was full of autocratic, backward-focused dictatorships that oppressed their citizenry, treated women like objects, and had policy aims counter to US interests . . . but the only ones America seemed keen to meddle with were the ones sitting atop the world's largest oil reserves.

Besides, it was just talk. And Rook could take in bombastic talk—then shrug it off—with the best of them. It's part of what a journalist learns to do.

But the moment the man with the machete flashed his steel, then sank it into the victim's flesh, Rook's expression changed. His face was awash in horror. One of the things that drives a reporter into his often hard and thankless line of work is a fundamental love for human beings and their stories. That made this kind of barbarism a total anathema to everything Rook stood for. Humanity—the thing Rook most connected with—was the thing ISIS lacked most.

And then, of course, on top of the repulsive conclusion came the shocking dénouement: Rook hearing his own name spoken by the abhorrent thugs. Even after the screen went black, Rook continued staring at it for a little while.

"Have we identified the victim yet?" Rook eventually asked in a hushed voice.

"No. Why?"

"I don't know. I just . . . I could be wrong, but I feel like I . . . know her. Like maybe I've worked with her somewhere or . . ."

"Do you want to watch it again?"

"No. I'm not sure I could if I wanted to. There was something familiar about her body language. I just . . . Maybe it'll come to me later."

Ochoa strolled over and put a consoling hand on Rook's shoulder. Then, showing the delicacy and tact for which the Twentieth Precinct's detective squad had become known, he grabbed a pen and pretended it was a microphone.

"Excuse me, Mr. Rook. M.T. Chatter with Channel 3 here. How does it feel knowing that a dude who sounds like Darth Vader wants to chop your head off?"

Rook sloughed off his funk and played along. "Well, M.T., I have to say I think you're mishearing it. To anyone who has seen *The Force Awakens* six times—no, sorry, seven—that sounds a lot more like Darth's grandson, Kylo Ren."

"Oh, you mean the dude who takes his lightsaber and—"

"Spoiler alert," Rook yelled. "Please. Think about the viewers at home, M.T. But, yes, that Kylo Ren. He's a much badder bad guy anyway. I mean, did you *see* the size of his Death Star? It was, like, a hundred times bigger than the other Death Star."

"I don't know," Ochoa said philosophically. "I thought he might have been compensating for something."

"Maybe. But being able to harness the power of a sun for your weapon? Admit it. That's cool. Much more badass than the first two Death Stars."

"Yeah, but how is it they can't manage to make a Death Star without a super-secret self-destruct button? I mean, first Death Star, okay, everyone makes mistakes. And the second Death Star, you're still working out the bugs. But the third Death Star? You'd think someone in the engineering department would have gathered everyone around and said, 'Okay, guys. Here's what we're *not* gonna do this time.'"

"True. But maybe it's like Preparation H," Rook suggested.

"What do you mean?"

"Haven't you ever wondered what happened to Preparations A through G?"

Ochoa just grimaced. Rook continued: "Besides, what fun would a *Star Wars* movie be without a Death Star that blows up? It'd be like Lucky Charms without the marshmallows."

"You mean Lucky Charms with only the icky oat bits?" Ochoa said, looking horrified.

"I do."

"Homes, that's just depraved. How are you even gonna go there?"

"Hey, you're the one talking about a *Star Wars* movie where the Death Star doesn't blow up. I'm just taking it to the next step in a logical progression."

"Uh, excuse me? Siskel and Ebert?" Heat said. "Can we put our eyes back on the prize?"

"Sorry," Rook said, chastened. "Anyhow, as I was saying, we have no line on who the victim is?"

"Sorry, not yet."

"And you've found the body but not the head?"

"That's right."

"Has Lauren had a crack at it yet?" Rook asked.

Heat gave Rook a rundown on Parry's findings, slim as they were, finishing with the discovery of the unknown whitish substance in the victim's shoes and the smell of kerosene on her body.

"Kerosene," Rook said, absentmindedly. "That's interesting."

"How so?" Heat asked.

Heat recognized the far-off look on Rook's face, the one that told her Rook was working on a theory. When they first began solving crimes together, Heat mostly dismissed Rook's hypotheses, many of which didn't merely come out of left field, but from the mailbox across the street from the bleachers that were behind left field.

But over the years, Heat had come to recognize that Rook's way of looking at things, while screwy, had its benefits. It turns out you can't build much of anything without screws.

And so she had learned to humor—and even respect—his remarkable, albeit sometimes off-the-wall, insight.

"Well, I'm not sure of the significance of this," Rook said. "But kerosene is very meaningful in Arab culture."

"How so?"

"Well, of course, because the first person to write about the distillation of kerosene was Muhammad al-Razi," Rook lectured. "He was an important figure in the Islamic Golden Age in the ninth and tenth centuries, a prolific author whose interests ranged from medicine to chemistry to philosophy. There are those who consider him to be the father of pediatrics. The Razi Institute in Karaj is named after him, as is Razi University."

"And so our killers used it . . . why, exactly?" Heat asked.

"Maybe they're trying to remind us that there was a time when Arab culture and science led the world," Rook said. "Eurocentric historians refer to this time as the Dark Ages. But from the Middle Eastern perspective, it really was a time of great light. As a matter of fact—"

"Uh, professor?" Raley said from behind his computer screen. "Do you mind if I intervene with something a little more relevant?"

"Since when do professors care about relevance?" Rook asked, offended.

"Well, cops do," Heat said. "What do you got, Rales?"

"I've been trying to run down the lead you gave me about Masjid al-Jannah," Raley said.

"Yeah? And?"

"I think I finally got something. Remember how I used the length of the light bulbs to extrapolate the victim's height?"

"Right."

"I used the same methodology to get a measurement of the dimensions of the room in which the video was shot. And I could be a lot more precise, because I didn't have to make guesses on the height of a kneeling victim."

Raley was clearly getting excited, bouncing in his seat. "Without that uncertainty, I was able to determine that the room in which the video was shot is exactly seventy-eight feet wide by one hundred and twenty-four feet long, with ten-foot ceilings. I then checked in with the Buildings Department in City Hall, where they keep construction plans and permits on file. It turns out there is only one building in the city of New York that has a room that is seventy-eight feet wide by one hundred and twenty-four feet long with ten-foot ceilings. And it's the main worship room at Masjid al-Jannah."

"Great work, Rales. Can you start typing that up for a warrant?"

"Already on it, Captain. I wrote it up while I was waiting for word from the Building Department. I can send it over to Judge Simpson's chambers right now."

"Thanks," she said.

Then Heat turned to see Rook had that far-off look again.

"What?" she asked.

"Nothing, it's just . . . Masjid al-Jannah," Rook said. "It's . . . It's so perfect, really."

"How so?"

"Well, you don't get as many assignments in the Middle East as I've had without picking up at least a little bit of Arabic," Rook said, already back in his professorial role. "*Jannah* is the Arabic word for heaven, but they don't think of heaven in quite the same way we do, with harp-bearing angels floating on clouds. The Quran describes heaven as a garden, but *jannah* comes from an Arabic word that means 'to cover' or 'to hide.' That's because, in Islam, heaven is not something that's meant to be seen by mortals. It's concealed, obscured from our view."

Rook paused for effect.

"So if you were to translate Masjid al-Jannah exactly, you might say it's the Mosque of the Hidden Garden."

"Yeah, well, it's not going to be hidden much longer," Heat said.

Raley volunteered, "The imam there is Muharib Qawi. He emigrated from Yemen in 2006. He has a prior for, get this, making terroristic threats. He was able to keep his green card by plea-bargaining it down. His mug shot is rolling off the printer right now."

Heat walked over to the printer and grabbed a photo of a man with his head wrapped in a turban. He had dark eyes, a narrow nose, and a long, scraggly salt-and-pepper beard that flowed down from his chin onto his chest.

"Muharib Qawi translates as 'strong warrior' in Arabic," Rook volunteered.

"Sounds like our guy," Ochoa said.

"Great, let's saddle up and go," Rook said, giddily. "I've got my bulletproof vest in the closet."

"Just hold your horses for a second there, cowboy," Heat said. "First things first: Oach, can you put together a team to execute this warrant? I want to have some muscle in case they're still holed up in there waiting for us. Pull some of the officers off the headhunt if you have to. Get the Bomb Squad to meet us there. The place might be booby-trapped. And call The Hammer and tell him I want to call in a chit to have the Aviation Unit get a chopper on standby in case we need air support. Also, tell ECT to be ready to move in once we've secured the building. This is our real crime scene. They're going to find a lot more evidence there than they will in the Dumpster where the body happened to end up."

"Got it," Ochoa said.

"Rook, can you come into my office for a second?"

"Of course."

The blinds were still closed. Heat clicked the lock on the door as she closed it behind herself. She turned off the lights.

"I'm sorry," she said in a husky voice. "But there's something I think we need to take care of."

Then she unfastened one of the buttons on her blouse.

"We have maybe twenty minutes right now," she said. "It'll take at least that long for Simpson to respond to the warrant request and for Oach to get a team assembled."

She undid another button. Rook's eyes went down to the lacy fringe of her bra and the curve of her breast.

"I know we said we'd do this tonight," she said, with a little bit of a moan. "But I'm not sure I can wait any longer."

One more button gone. Rook's eyes were wide.

"Office sex?" he said, his tone reverent.

She nodded.

"Come over here," she said, reclining on the floor on the far side of the room, by the wall. "I want you to take me right here. I'm afraid if we do it on the desk it'll make too much noise."

Rook practically dove on the floor next to her. She rolled on top of him.

"You have been an incredibly difficult suspect," she said, then she pulled out a pair of handcuffs from her belt. "And I'm afraid our interrogation is about to get rough."

"How rough?" Rook asked.

"I think it's safe to say this will be an act of police brutality you'll never forget," she said.

As she slipped one half of the cuff on Rook's right wrist, she began gnawing on his earlobe. Rook's breath was already ragged.

"I have been so bad," he panted. "Please, please punish me."

"Oh, I will," she said.

Then she quickly pulled his wrist to the side and fastened the other half of the cuffs to the leg of the radiator before rolling off of him.

Rook looked over, his comprehension growing as other parts of him were shrinking.

Heat was already hastily closing up her blouse.

"Sorry," she said. "But I can't have you running around out there while our suspects are still at large. I'll come unlock you later, once we have them in custody."

Rook just whimpered.

TEN

Forty minutes later, Heat was back on 73rd Street, behind Pho Sure.

She had decided on the restaurant as a staging area, reasoning that there had already been a police presence there most of the morning. If American ISIS was holed up inside Masjid al-Jannah, waiting to spring an ambush, they wouldn't be tipped off anything new was coming.

A warrant, freshly signed and e-mailed back from Judge Simpson's chambers, was tucked inside her bulletproof vest. There were twenty officers with her: twelve from the Twentieth Precinct, including four detectives, and eight from the Bomb Squad, along with a bomb-sniffing dog.

"Okay, we've checked the building plans and there are two main egress points: the front door and the back," Heat said. "In addition, there's a fire escape on the east side of the building, toward the back. Roach, I want you to take four officers and lead the team that covers both the back entrance and that fire escape. Rhymer, Feller, I want you and the rest of the uniforms with me up front."

"Now gentlemen," continued Heat, the only woman in the group. "Please remember, this is a house of worship, and we need to treat it with respect. I don't want to hear later that the NYPD acted like a bunch of jackbooted thugs. I am going to enter through the front door, which our surveillance indicates is not locked, and announce we have a warrant. We have to be on alert, of course. But it's more than likely these guys didn't stick around the mosque, okay?"

Heat nodded at a man who had already donned a blast suit, which looked like an armored astronaut's outfit.

"Once we determine there is no immediate armed response, Bomb

Squad goes in first," Heat said. "We're going to let them and their dog's nose do the work. McMains in Counterterrorism reminded me that these suspects probably wouldn't hesitate to blow themselves up in the hopes of taking of few of us with them, so let's not let our guard down until we're sure this place is clean. Got it?"

There was a general nodding of heads.

"Now, if any of the suspects attempt to flee, try to detain them peacefully, of course. But if you have no other choice, you are authorized to use force. Repeat: you are authorized to use force. These guys have already murdered one person, and they've threatened to do the same to Rook, so in my mind that satisfies the legal requirement that they pose a threat of serious physical harm. Shoot to maim, not to kill. But don't hesitate to shoot if you have to. Is everyone comfortable with that order?"

More heads nodded.

"Okay, Roach, you ready to move out?"

"You got it, Captain," Raley said.

Ochoa suddenly had his hands on his hips. "Uh, excuse me, but I'm leading today, remember?" he said. "It's the eighteenth."

Roach had decided they would split their co-leading duties by the day: Raley led the squad on odd-numbered days, while Ochoa handled the evens.

"So I'm not allowed to answer when she says 'Roach'?" Raley said indignantly.

"On the nineteenth, you answer," Ochoa said. "On the eighteenth, I answer. It's called sharing. Why is that so hard for you?"

"I don't know. Maybe because when you were introducing yourself to Lana Kline, you were acting like I didn't even exist."

"All I said was, 'Hello, Miss Kline, I'm the detective squad leader.' Which, on the eighteenth, is a statement of fact."

"You know, that's so like you to—"

"Guys, guys," Heat said, holding her hands up toward both of them. "Do you think you can sort this out later?"

"Sorry, Captain," Ochoa said.

"I'd say sorry, too," Raley sniffed. "But apparently I'm not allowed to talk today."

Heat sighed and shook her head. "Okay, let's just move out," she said. "Let me know when you're in position."

"I will," Ochoa said, narrowing his eyes at Raley, almost challenging him to disagree.

Ochoa led his team around the back of the building, while Heat took her group around the front and along 73rd Street. They walked quickly, sticking to the south side, the one the mosque was on, to limit their visual exposure.

Heat held up a hand, bringing her team to a halt just short of Masjid al-Jannah. She was waiting to hear Ochoa was in place.

Instead, she heard the distinctive pop of gunfire. It was coming from the back of the building.

"We got a runner," Ochoa called over the radio as more shots rang out. "He just jumped down from the fire escape and is heading east, toward Columbus. A guy in a white gown. I didn't get the best look at him, but I'm pretty sure it's Muharib Qawi. I'm in pursui—"

And then Ochoa's narrative was interrupted by an anguished yell, followed by more moaning that sounded almost animalistic until it suddenly cut out.

"Man down. We got a man down. It's Miguel! We got a ten-thirteen. Ten-thirteen!" Raley howled into his radio. The NYPD was moving toward plain talk in its communications. But in a crisis, Raley had fallen back on using the code for an officer in need of assistance.

Heat had her weapon drawn, but she was calm, in control. This was not her first firefight, and the NYPD spent countless hours training for these kinds of scenarios.

"Dispatch, you copy that?"

"Roger," crackled the voice of the dispatch officer, who was back at the precinct, ready to coordinate any other resources Heat might need to call on. "Sending assistance."

"Rales, you stay with your team and Ochoa," Heat ordered. "Repeat: stay in position. Send two men after Qawi. He might just be a decoy meant to lure us away from the mosque."

Or Qawi might have been the only one inside, and he ran the moment he saw cops approaching from the back alley. Either way, she had a warrant to execute and a crime scene to investigate, pursuit of a suspect notwithstanding.

"Dispatch," Heat said into her radio. "Call Aviation and tell them to get that bird in the air. I want some eyes in the sky."

"Roger that," the dispatcher said.

Heat clicked off her radio. "The rest of you, take positions around the front entrance. Nothing goes in or out, got it?"

Then she turned to Rhymer. Of the six officers on her side of the building, Heat had already determined that she and the slender Virginian were in the best condition for a footrace.

"Opie, come on, let's go run down a guy in a thobe."

Heat and Rhymer took off east, toward Columbus Avenue. As they reached the busy artery, a voice crackled on their radios. "Suspect turned left out of the alley, heading north on Columbus."

Sure enough, Heat saw a white flash as the imam crossed 73rd Street. She and Rhymer were perhaps a hundred yards behind.

"Dispatch," she said, talking as she was running. "I have visuals on a suspect running north on Columbus. I am in pursuit. I want all units in the area on alert."

"Roger that," the dispatcher said calmly. And Heat trusted that the BOLO was now being broadcast on the other UHF channels currently being used by the patrol officers of the Twentieth Precinct.

When they reached Columbus Avenue and turned left, Heat could see glimpses of Qawi, already a block ahead, weaving and dodging through Columbus Avenue foot traffic. She holstered her gun—there was no way she would have a clean shot with all the civilians around—and churned her legs.

She kept expecting Qawi would turn right, down one of the streets that would lead to Central Park, which was just a block to the east. There were more hiding places in the park than just about anywhere else in Manhattan. But Qawi kept charging north, covering two blocks, then three.

If Heat and Rhymer were gaining on him, it was only marginally. The other officers, the ones who had flushed him out from behind the building, were even farther back.

As Qawi continued his desperate dash, Heat finally heard the sound of rotor blades in the air. The NYPD Aviation Unit had recently upgraded its light choppers to Bell 429s, and it claimed it could be anywhere in the five boroughs within fifteen minutes from a standing start. With proper warning, it turned out they could be on the west side of Manhattan in a shade over four.

"Captain Heat, this is Police Two, we have eyes on the suspect," the pilot said. "He just crossed 76th Street and is continuing north."

"Roger that," Heat huffed into her radio as she streaked past, appropriately enough, the headquarters of the New York Road Runners, the organization that hosted the New York City Marathon.

"Two units now southbound on Columbus, at 82nd," the dispatcher advised.

Heat heard the sound of sirens underneath the whir of the rotors. At 77th Street, Qawi finally turned right, in the direction of Central Park, as Heat thought he would.

"Suspect now westbound on 77th," she said into her radio.

"Park Police have been notified," the dispatcher crackled back. "They have units on horseback coming from the 79th Street Transverse."

Which meant with Heat applying pressure from the southwest, two cars coming down Columbus from the northwest, and the Central Park Police coming from the east, they would soon have Qawi rather neatly surrounded. Heat hoped he'd go peacefully. In addition to her usual aspirations for regular justice—as opposed to the instant kind that came from the barrel of a police gun—dead suspects couldn't give up coconspirators. And Heat wanted the comfort of knowing the threat against Rook had been neutralized. Mostly because she didn't want to have to keep him chained to the radiator forever.

Heat felt her thighs burning and her speed flagging. She had to believe Qawi was just about out of gas as well—most clergy she knew didn't exactly have a lot of time for cardio.

Then she heard: "This is Police Two. The suspect is entering the natural history museum. Repeat: suspect has entered natural history museum."

It might have seemed like a mistake, in that Qawi was now trapped. Except a ripple of panic was coursing through Heat. Nearing midday on a Tuesday in October, the museum would be full of field-tripping schoolchildren and tourists. Both made for excellent hostages if Qawi was armed—or if, anticipating the police would eventually come after him, he had wired himself with explosives.

In addition, the American Museum of Natural History was a warren of rooms and corridors, many of which had no windows. Which meant a police sniper wouldn't have a shot. And it was filled with priceless and irreplaceable artifacts, which ruled out many of the other potential tactics that could be employed.

All in all, it was an excellent place for Qawi to stage a standoff, and a looming nightmare for the authorities.

"Okay. I want officers stationed at all the exits," Heat called into her radio. "Now that he's in there, let's make sure we hop on him if he tries to get out."

"Should we call the museum and tell them to initiate lockdown procedures?" the dispatcher asked.

"Negative. Repeat: negative," Heat said. "I want him to think he's gotten away, if at all possible. If he panics and grabs a hostage, we're all in for a long day."

Heat clicked off her radio. "You stay here," she called back to Rhymer, who had kept pace, just a few steps behind. "Cover this exit in case he doubles back."

She charged up the marble steps, past groups of students eating their bagged lunches and vacationers taking pictures.

As she entered the Grand Gallery, she was greeted by two sights: an enormous life-sized stuffed elephant and a security guard's desk.

The elephant didn't look like a talker, so Heat went toward the desk with her badge out. "Officer, thank goodness!" a guard said. "A man in a turban just ran past without paying."

"Which way?" Heat asked through heavy breath.

The guard pointed behind himself. "Glad to see you guys cracking down on these kinds of heinous quality of life crimes. You know—"

Heat was already out of earshot, dashing into the Hall of Northwest Coast Indians. There, dioramas of indigenous people hunting, trapping, and fishing became a blur as Heat ran through. From the far side of the hall, she saw Qawi turning right.

She continued following him through the Hall of Small Mammals, where it was now taxidermic minks, martens, squirrels, and badgers, staring at Heat with their fixed glassy eyes. But neither they, nor the short-tailed weasel, nor the red-backed vole, nor the collared peccary were any help in catching her suspect.

Qawi turned right again, into a hall where small mammals had given way to larger ones: moose, bison, bear, the glamour animals of the stuffed wild kingdom. Heat hoped a particularly rapt group of fifth graders or a burly museum visitor would do a better job of getting in Qawi's way. But Heat wasn't going to shout out for them to help. She'd sooner direct civilians into the path of a tornado.

Qawi exited the Hall of North American Mammals, and Heat thought he might be making a dash for the exit to Central Park West. She was about to make the radio call so the officers on horseback would be ready.

But no. He had turned right again and was going up a set of stairs. Heat was now more worried than ever. He was essentially trapping himself on the upper floors. His only play now was to snatch someone.

Unless he also had air support? Police Two was not a gunship. Was it possible he was heading for the roof, where a chopper would whisk him away?

Heat reached the bottom of the stairs as Qawi was at the top. She saw him disappear in the direction of the Hall of Asian Mammals. Heat continued her chase, ignoring the lactic acid that was now stinging her legs and the accompanying ache in her lungs.

She dashed into a room dominated by another elephant, this one no more talkative than the last. Heat again caught sight of Qawi just as he exited the other side. They were now in a part of the museum where, if Qawi wasn't careful, he'd run himself into a dead end.

Which wasn't necessarily a good thing. Heat worried that once trapped, he'd be every bit as dangerous as the Siberian tiger whose diorama she was now sprinting past.

Now out of the Asian Mammals room, there was only one way to go, toward the Hall of Asian Peoples. Heat bolted through it, past the Chinese Wedding Chair, the Yakut Shaman's Robe, and the plaster of paris model of Peking Man.

She had now lost sight of Qawi. Had he already cleared out the other side of the room? Had Heat slowed down without realizing it?

Heat cursed herself. She was nearly out of the room, heading toward the Birds of Asia, when her peripheral vision registered slight movement.

Something near the Traditional Clothing of the Persian/Arabian Gulf Area exhibit had moved. She stopped so fast she actually stumbled a little before sliding to a stop on the polished floor.

The exhibit consisted of two figures, dressed in a suitable fashion. One was inside the glass, perched in front of a landscape of camels, tents, and desert.

The other was outside the glass and sweating profusely.

Heat approached with her gun raised.

"Muharib Qawi," she said, through ragged breath. "You are under arrest."

The imam raised his hands slowly.

"I am unarmed," he said, his chest heaving. "Please don't shoot."

"Turn around. Hands on the wall."

Qawi complied.

"I must say," he said, as Heat patted him down for either weapons or explosives. "It is a great honor to be arrested by Nikki Heat. I have read all about you and your exploits."

"Muharib Qawi," Heat said, gritting her teeth, "you most definitely have the right to remain silent. And I suggest you begin exercising that right immediately."

ELEVEN

By the time Heat returned to the Twentieth Precinct, her first order of business was not justice, but mercy.

Rook had apparently started singing while she was gone. Everyone in the precinct with functioning eardrums was begging her to make him stop.

"Noboooooddddyy knows, the trouble I seen," Rook warbled in an unconvincing bass. "Noboooooddddyy knows my sorrow."

The previous hour of Heat's life had helped her learn three items of note.

One: Miguel Ochoa was going to be fine. He had suffered what the army referred to as a million-dollar wound, which meant his butt was plenty sore but the rest of him was fine. He was at the hospital but was expected to be treated shortly. They were unsure of the identity of the shooter. But since they had not found weapons at the mosque—and Qawi had been the only person inside—it was assumed to have been friendly fire. Heat didn't even want to think about the paperwork that was going to result in.

Two: Masjid al-Jannah had not been booby-trapped. Nor had the dogs found any evidence of explosives. What investigators did find, however, was a large square hole that had been cut out of the carpet, in the exact area where the video showed the victim had been kneeling. There had also been bleach applied to the subfloor underneath. Those efforts, however, had not been sufficient to eradicate all evidence. Using a blue light, ECT had been able to find a substantial blood spill, then had procured a sample.

Three: Jameson Rook couldn't carry a tune in a bucket.

Heat opened the door to her office just as Rook was raking his handcuffs along the spines of the radiator, like a convict in an old-time movie would run his tin cup along the bars of his jail cell.

"Warden! Warden!" Rook called when he saw her. "I want my lawyer!"

"Great, I'll call Helen Miksit," Heat said, dropping the name of a defense lawyer who was universally loathed by members of the NYPD.

"You will?" Rook said, legitimately surprised.

"No," Heat said.

Rook pouted.

"If I let you go, will you promise to be on your best behavior?" Heat said. "We've got Qawi but his coconspirators are still unaccounted for. That means you have to stay here, got it?"

Rook was already raising three fingers on his right hand.

"Don't even try and say 'Scout's honor,'" Heat warned. "I know you were never a Boy Scout."

"No, but when I was sixteen I almost got into a Girl Scout."

"You're not helping yourself."

"Fine," he said, changing his hand positioning to a split-fingered Vulcan salute. "Spock's honor."

"Is that even a thing?" Heat asked.

"If it's not, it should be. Vulcans are a very honorable people," Rook said. "But whatever you do, never trust a Vulcan who crosses his heart on the upper left side of his torso."

"And why is that?"

"Because, as everyone knows, a Vulcan's heart is on the right side of his torso, between the ribs and pelvis, about where the human liver is."

Heat studied him, then said, "Sometimes it astounds me you *ever* got laid."

"Tell me about it," Rook said.

"Okay, look, here's the deal: I'll let you watch my interrogation of Qawi, but you can't go anywhere, okay? I can't have you running off."

"Why would I want to?" Rook said. "Watching you break this guy will be better than the movies and I won't even have to overpay for popcorn."

Heat smiled, un-cuffed him, then listened to his griping about wrist chafing on the way to Interrogation One. Raley was already there, as were Rhymer and Feller.

Heat had instructed the detectives to leave Qawi for her. Forget delegating. This was one she had to do herself. There was too much at stake, starting with Rook's life and liberty.

Through the two-way glass, they could see Qawi seated in the chair, his cuffed hands folded in front of him, his chin resting on his chest, his scraggly beard flowing down the front of his thobe.

"He done anything or said anything I need to know about?" Heat asked.

"He prayed about ten minutes ago," Raley said. "But other than that, what you see is what you get."

"Has he been Mirandized?"

"Yes, sir."

"Okay, then here goes nothing."

When Heat entered the room, Qawi looked up and spoke his first words before Heat had taken three steps.

"Captain Heat, I am innocent," Qawi said.

"Innocent of what, Mr. Qawi?" Heat asked, choosing to remain standing.

"The video. I heard about it on the news this morning and immediately found it on the Web. And I speak for all peace-loving Muslims across America when I say I am horrified by it. But I swear to Allah, I had nothing to do with it."

"Which is why you ran the moment you saw my officers," Heat shot back.

"I ran because I am not a fool," Qawi said. "I have been in this country ten years. I know how it works here."

"And how is that, Mr. Qawi?"

"When something goes wrong, you blame the Muslim," he said, a mix of defiance and defeat in his tone. "America, it is a great country in so many ways. But it always needs someone to hate. Hate the German. Hate the Japanese. Hate the communist. Now, since 9/11, it is our turn. The Muslim is the boogeyman, the evil behind all evil. So now you hate us."

"Play the Islamophobia card somewhere else, Mr. Qawi," Heat said. "It won't work here."

"It is not a card to play. It is simply the truth. America has fallen into the trap of thinking that the religion defines the person. Really, it is the person who defines the religion. The Book of Joel instructs you to beat your plowshares into swords and let the weakling say he is strong. The Book of Isaiah instructs you to beat your swords into plowshares and let God be the judge. Yet they can both be found in the same Bible. The Quran is also filled with such contradictions. In some passages it instructs the faithful to kill infidels. In others, it teaches that if you kill a single individual, it is like killing all of humanity."

"Mr. Qawi, I'm not interested in a theology debate today. I'm interested in justice for a young woman who was butchered."

"Yes, I understand. And I had nothing to do with that."

"Of course you didn't. And yet there was a hole cut out of the carpet at your mosque and a bloodstain underneath. And I'm sure when we run the sample we'll find it matches the victim. Can you explain that?"

Qawi brought his gaze up to Heat. "Probably not to your satisfaction."

"Try me."

"Very well. After Friday prayers, I traveled to Boston to visit my brother, whose wife has just had a new baby. When I returned on Sunday, I found this stain. That is all I can tell you."

"So the stain just, what, magically appeared?" Heat asked, not bothering to hide her incredulity.

"Many people use that mosque. Not just the imam. It is open to the faithful twenty-four hours a day. I can't account for everything that happens there."

"But you tried to clean the stain," Heat said. It was a statement more than a question.

"Well, yes. I didn't know what it was. Not until this morning, when I saw the video. It was just this brown stain. So I asked our janitor to do something about it."

"Did you tell him to cut a hole in the carpet?"

"No," Qawi said. "He did that himself on Monday. He realized he was never going to be able to get the stain out. He said he had some leftover remnants from when the room was carpeted and that it would be better to graft a new piece in."

"How convenient," Heat said. "But then, of course, when you saw the video this morning and you realized it had been shot in your mosque, you immediately understood what the mystery stain was and, like a good law-abiding clergyman, you called the police."

Qawi bowed his head. "No, I did not."

"Which showed you had a guilty mind, Mr. Qawi, a detail that you surely know American juries love. Now, look, I know you didn't do this alone. And I also know you're too short to have been one of the men in the video who did the actual killing. Which makes you the guy behind the camera. So it's your lucky, lucky day, Mr. Qawi, that we caught you first. Because it means you can turn on your coconspirators before they turn on you.

"But you have to start dealing now. And I mean *right now*. If you identify the men in the video and help bring them to justice, that will be noted and weighed at sentencing. It will also probably keep the case away from the feds and in the hands of the NYPD, which, believe me, is in your best interests. New York State doesn't have a death penalty. The feds do."

Qawi was shaking his head. "But you don't understand. I can't turn over accomplices I don't have. And I can't confess to something I haven't done. I am a peaceful person. Ask any of my parishioners."

"So peaceful you had a charge for making terroristic threats?"

Qawi gestured excitedly. "This is exactly what I am talking about when I say the Muslim cannot get a fair shake! There was a man on our block. He insisted on putting his trash in front of the mosque. I told him this was offensive to Islam, that cleanliness was extremely important to our religion and to please put his trash in front of his own apartment. The next thing I know, this man files a report with the police, saying I had threatened to kill him!"

"And yet you admitted to it as part of your plea bargain," Heat said.

"Making terroristic threats is a class D felony in the state of New York, as I'm sure you know, Captain Heat. If it went to trial and a jury decided to hang the Muslim no matter what, I would have been deported. The prosecutor agreed to turn it into a misdemeanor disturbing the peace. I accepted the deal just to make it go away, rather than taking the risk."

"Right. Of course, Mr. Qawi. Just like you ran because you were innocent and the bloodstains in your mosque were left there by all the other people who use it."

Heat was now directly across the table from Qawi. She lowered herself until her face was close to Qawi's. "Who was she? The victim. Was she some weathergirl who you thought would be an easy mark? Was she a reporter who wrote something you didn't like? Or was she just some girl who wasn't even a journalist that you grabbed off the street? We're going to find the truth eventually. You left evidence all over that body. We know about the kerosene."

Heat studied Qawi's reaction as she said the word, thinking she might see a hint of fear, an involuntarily acknowledgement that his armor had another chink in it.

But Qawi's face betrayed nothing as he said, "I have no idea when you're talking about, Captain."

"Of course you don't," Heat said, getting even closer to him. "Our investigation is only just beginning, Mr. Qawi. We are going to crawl inside and outside of that mosque and your life. And when we're done, you won't have a single secret left in the world. We're going to put pressure like you can't believe on every single person in your life, and they're going to crack like fragile little eggshells, one by one. Because that's what they always do.

"Where did you hide the machete, Mr. Qawi? Is it back at your apartment? Because we're getting a search warrant for that right now, and we're going to find it. And when we do, I know you're going to try and say you use it for clearing cobwebs from your living room. I can tell you by that point, I won't be listening anymore. Because I won't need you anymore. *This* is your chance, right now, right here, to confess. You're already facing a long and difficult road. Your failure to cooperate will only make it worse."

She locked her brown eyes on his. Qawi couldn't hold eye contact.

For a minute, neither spoke.

Then there came a knock at the door.

"I'll be back, Mr. Qawi," Heat said, straightening herself. "Or maybe I won't be. It might already be too late."

Heat stalked toward the door with an ear still cocked in Qawi's direction, half expecting to hear a "wait"—or some similar admission of defeat.

But all Qawi did as she departed the room was return to his same position, chin on chest, hands in front, gaze cast deliberately down.

Heat returned to the small room on the other side of Interrogation One, where she found a group of detectives looking unusually grim-faced.

"What's the matter?" Heat asked. "Okay, so he's going to be a tough nut. That's not—"

"The only vehicle registered to his name has E-ZPass," Raley said, cutting her off. "It confirms his vehicle passed through the northbound toll plaza on the New England Thruway on Friday night. There's no southbound toll to confirm when he came back, but—"

"But he could have easily exited and doubled back, knowing he had created an electronic alibi for himself."

"Well, yeah, except I talked to the brother in Boston," Feller said. "The brother says not only can he confirm Muharib was there, he can produce fifty witnesses who were with him at a party on Saturday night. They had a celebration of the new baby. The brother pointed me to a video posted on one of the guests' Facebook accounts that shows Muharib very clearly. And, of course, it was time-stamped."

"That doesn't mean anything," Heat said. "Parry puts our TOD sometime between midnight and eight o'clock Sunday morning. Boston to New York is a four-hour drive. He could have easily—"

"The brother also says Muharib led morning prayers on Sunday," Feller continued. "Did the call and everything. There were at least another seventy-five witnesses to that one. And some of them would be people who aren't friends and family."

Heat frowned.

"You want, Opie and I can go up to Boston, start interviewing them, see if it checks out. But I don't know. That's a pretty big bluff for the brother to lay out there if it isn't true."

Heat put her hands on her hips, legitimately stymied. Solving murder was usually a straightforward exercise in identifying the most likely candidate. Cheating husband dead? It's the wife. The deceased had a big life insurance policy? Figure out the beneficiary. Someone runs from the cops? Catch him and you've found your killer.

More to the point, if you had a victim, *someone* had to be the killer. And, in this case, if Qawi wasn't involved, who was?

Heat was looking around the room for answers when her gaze fell on Rook, who was seated in a chair, staring intently at Qawi.

"Hello, you with us?" she said, waving a hand on front of his face.

"Huh? Yeah," Rook said. "It's just . . . I was thinking about what he said about America needing someone to hate."

"Oh, now you're starting on the theology lessons, too?"

"It's not theology. It's more sociology. Or even just history," Rook said. "You realize, everything now being said about Muslims in America—that they're not really American, that they can't be trusted, that their ideology is inherently dangerous and twisted, that they're here but their loyalties lie elsewhere—used to be said about Catholics? A hundred years ago, a Catholic couldn't even be hired as the principal of a local elementary school, because he would supposedly use his position to recruit followers for the pope. It took fifty years for America to realize how ridiculous it was. And even when we elected John F. Kennedy, there were lunatic conspiracy theorists who saw the hand of the Vatican in everything he did."

"Yeah, that's fascinating, Rook," Heat said. "But you want to tell me what John F. Kennedy has to do with the suspect in there?"

Rook turned his attention to Heat.

"Look, I didn't want to say anything, in case you really did break the guy. You know how much I love watching you work someone other than me over the coals. But—"

"Out with it, Rook."

"I just don't think this is the guy. While you had me locked up, I made some phone calls. I talked to Jeff Diamant, the *First Press* religion reporter. He did a big piece about the Muslim community in the New York area a few years back and knows all the players. He said Qawi is known as a progressive voice, pushing for not only a modern reading of the Quran, but also for Muslims in this country to take the lead in the fight against terrorism. He's been pretty consistent in saying that Muslims have to clean their own house if they're ever going to be viewed without suspicion."

"Which could be a cover," Heat said. "What better guy to start American ISIS than the one who pretends to be a reformer?"

"True. Although Diamant also hooked me up with a guy at Rikers. He said they had a problem a few years back with inmates preaching a very literal reading of the Quran, essentially trying to recruit young, impressionable men and indoctrinate them into an extremist mindset. They called Muharib Qawi to set the record straight. He gave a series of sermons about how the Quran calls on Muslims to do good. He kept coming back, leaving literature behind. He even talked to the guards about what to listen for that would indicate they had another bad seed."

"Great, we'll make sure we give Qawi a gold star on his way to life in prison," Heat said. "That doesn't change the evidence. There's no question where that video was shot and where that body was found."

"I'm not saying he doesn't know anything," Rook said. "I'm saying now that you've bad-copped him a little bit, let me good-cop him."

Heat made a face like someone had made her favorite drink—grande skim latte, two pumps of sugar-free vanilla—with two pumps of sugar-free sewer water.

But then a thought that had been buzzing around the back of her mind for the last hour finally worked its way to the front: If Muharib Qawi was really going to found American ISIS, then kidnap a journalist and provoke outrage with a gory decapitation video, then have the audacity to threaten a beloved Pulitzer Prize–winning writer . . . wouldn't he perhaps have a slightly better escape plan than trying to blend in to the Traditional Clothing of the Persian/Arabian Gulf Area exhibit at the American Museum of Natural History?

"You really think you can get something from this guy?" Heat said.

"I guarantee I can."

Heat forced a laugh. "Really?"

"What do you want to bet?"

"Your Star Trek posters," she said. "I want them out of the apartment."

"Okay," he said. "And I think you know what I want."

"The same thing you always want? You know I'm going to give that to you anyway."

"No, no," Rook said. "There's a catch. I'm looking for a little cosplay."

"It's about to get weird in here, isn't it?" Raley said.

"Every seven years," Rook said, ignoring him, "Vulcans lose the logical, rational way of thinking for which their people are famously known. When this happens, the only way for them to return to normal is to take a mate."

"Oh, Rook, you're not serious."

"Yes, I am. If I get something out of this suspect, you're going to make love to me dressed as a sex-crazed Vulcan."

Feller clapped his hand on Raley's shoulder. "I'm afraid we didn't even pause at weird before we went all the way to freakytown."

But Heat was reaching out her right hand.

"Okay," she said. "You're on."

TWELVE

With Heat watching from the other side of the glass, Rook walked into Interrogation One, wearing the kind of engaging smile that had won over guarded celebrities, reclusive geniuses, and wary politicians the world over.

"Mr. Qawi," he began. "I'm—"

"Jameson Rook!" Qawi supplied, standing up and returning Heat's smile, albeit in a more fawning fashion. "I can't believe it! Jameson Rook, here in front of me! Allah be praised! I am most honored to meet you, sir. Most honored."

Qawi had taken his cuffed hands and turned the palms against each other, in a prayerlike gesture, and was bowing slightly. Rook turned toward the glass of the one-way mirror and smirked.

Unseen by both of them, Heat was rolling her eyes.

"I am such a huge, huge fan," Qawi continued, gushing. "I have read all of your work, of course. Your reporting on the Middle East has been some of the most insightful work I have ever read on Islam. And I'm not just talking about American reporters. I praise your work above the Arab publications as well."

"Well, thank you—" Rook began, but was cut off again.

"Do you know my favorite thing you've ever written?" Qawi asked.

"No, please tell me," Rook said. He cast a glance in the direction of where he guessed Heat was standing and waggled his eyebrows. She rolled her eyes even more.

"It was just a small sidebar, no more than a few hundred words. Not one of your big investigations. Perhaps you don't even remember it? It was about the Hittites, a nation of people who vanished from the earth more than a thousand years ago."

"It . . . rings a bell," Rook said.

"Oh, it was brilliant. I can't tell you how many times I've referenced that piece, especially when talking to young people about the Quran. You quoted passages from both the Bible and the Quran that called on the faithful to smite the Hittites. They were, of course, a very significant threat during the times when both the Bible and the Quran were written. The Hittites came out of Asia Minor with their chariots and their advanced weaponry. But are they a threat today? Well, of course not. Because they no longer exist. My favorite line of the piece was, 'Hittite leaders could not be reached for comment.' "

Rook chuckled at his own long-ago joke. "Oh, right. Now I remember. The piece was making the point that passages in religious texts have to be understood as being a product of the time in which they were written, not taken out of that context and crammed into the modern world. The only way they should be read as a call to war is if you're prepared to do battle with the Hittites."

"Exactly," Qawi said. "Which is what I try to get young people to understand about some of the more violent passages of the Quran. Because, yes, there are some parts that call on believers to cut off the heads of infidels. But those who understand the Quran know that they were really only referring to a very specific time in history, when Muhammad, peace be upon him, was looking to recruit and rally warriors to his side. That time has passed. The enemies Muhammad was referring to are now just as dead as the Hittites, so we must treat those passages accordingly. It is a tragedy that the Quran has been twisted by those who act otherwise."

Rook was nodding his head. He finally took a seat across from Qawi.

"I must say," Qawi continued, "I was very distressed to hear your name spoken at the end of that video. Any true believer would understand Jameson Rook has been a friend to Islam. You have helped people in America understand our religion. Muslims everywhere should be in your debt, not making threats against you."

"Well, thank you," Rook said. "And, look, I want you to know, I've made some phone calls and . . . I know where you stand on these kinds of issues."

"You talked to Jeff Diamant, didn't you?" Qawi said.

Rook nodded.

"He is a good man, Jeff Diamant. We have had many fascinating conversations. There is a place in *Jannah* for him, to be sure."

"But I have to tell you—" Rook began.

Qawi finished the thought for him: "That none of this looks very good for me."

"Sure doesn't," Rook confirmed.

Qawi's turban bobbed up and down. "I know. I know. But what I told Captain Heat is true. I really can't explain how that bloodstain showed up in my mosque. I went up to Boston, it wasn't there. I came back, there it was."

"But you have some idea who might have been behind it, don't you," Rook said softly.

Qawi's attention went down toward the table.

"There are some young men in your congregation who have some very disturbing views about Islam, aren't there?"

The turban again bobbed, just a little. But it was detectable nevertheless.

Rook pressed on. "They have come to you with questions, and for as much as you have tried to convince them that Islam is a religion of peace, they've been reading some of those foul, virulent Internet sites that say otherwise. They're on Facebook, friending imams whose messages you disagree with."

"I keep telling them," Qawi said, his voice sounding distant, "that jihad is supposed to be an internal struggle. It is the fight between good and evil that takes place within a person. We do not take jihad outside ourselves. Those who do so misunderstand the entire concept."

"But those Internet sites can be so compelling," Rook said. "The voices they're listening to are louder and more persuasive. It's hard to out-shout a call to action when all you have to counter it with is a message of passivity. And these are young men who feel alienated from society. They're disaffected, angry."

"They keep applying for jobs dressed as I dress," Qawi said, gesturing down toward his clothes. "And they keep getting turned down. I . . . I actually suggested to them that perhaps they try to wear Western clothes for the interviews. They called me a traitor."

"And they kept getting more and more extreme in their viewpoints, coming to you with passages in the Quran that, read a certain way, would seem to urge them to violence against nonbelievers."

"I knew it was trouble when they quoted Wahhab," Qawi said.

Rook didn't need to be told that Muhammad ibn Abd al-Wahhab was an eighteenth-century religious figure who founded an Islamic sect that called for a return to a strict orthodox reading of the Quran, or that his ideology, Wahhabism, was followed by al-Qaeda and its successor in terror, ISIS.

"I tried to tell them that this was backward thinking, that they were turning toward a version of Islam that would have us ignore more than a millennium of human progress," Qawi said.

"But they were seduced," Rook said.

"Sadly. Yes."

"You even found out that they started posting things themselves on those Internet sites, not just lurking in the conversations but participating in them, adding to them."

Qawi nodded again.

"And now, even though I know you don't want to, even though you still think you can turn them back to your way of thinking, you're going to acknowledge they have gone too far. You're going to recognize they have done incredible damage to the religion you love. You're going to become a model of what you talk about when you say Muslims need to take the lead against terrorism. And you're going to tell me the names of those young men."

Rook had established such a mesmerizing rhythm Heat expected Qawi to blurt out the names. But the imam paused.

"If I . . . if I give you the names, your captain Heat, she will . . . She will continue to investigate, yes? There will not be a rush to judgment simply because they are Muslim. They will be treated with fairness?"

"I have had the pleasure of Captain Heat's company for many years now," Rook said. "The one thing I can assure you about her is that when it comes to her investigations, she is blind to race, ethnicity, creed, sexual orientation, or any other form of intolerance you might be able to think of. The only ethic that matters to Nikki Heat is the truth."

Qawi studied Rook. Heat could hear his chair creaking through the microphone as he shifted in his seat.

"Very well," he said. "Their names are Hassan El-Bashir and Tariq Al-Aman. I might be wrong. I certainly hope I am. But I think it might be them in that video."

With one hand, Rook reached toward Qawi. He grabbed the imam's shackled wrists, as if he was trying to inject human warmth into the cold steel of the handcuffs.

"You've done the right thing, Muharib," Rook said.

With the other hand, Rook reached behind his back and, in full view of detectives in the observation room, formed his fingers into the Vulcan salute.

Over the next half hour, Heat watched as Rook continued working Qawi for details about the new suspects.

Hassan El-Bashir had been born in Harlem; Tariq Al-Aman, in the Bronx. While not related, they shared similar stories. Each had a grandparent who started out Christian but renounced their "slave name"—Smith, Jones, whatever it had been—and had taken a new name when they joined the Nation of Islam.

That movement, founded in the crucible of the sixties, had lost steam. Their families' devotion to the religion did not. The next generation had been raised Muslim. That generation did the same with their children.

El-Bashir and Al-Aman were those children. Qawi said they first came to Masjid al-Jannah a few years earlier. Being of similar age and disposition, they gravitated toward each other, becoming friends first, then roommates who shared a cold-water flat in Harlem.

Qawi couldn't explain what led them to become radicalized, beyond what Rook had already theorized. It was a combination of disillusionment with an American Dream that didn't seem to include them and a series of Internet sites that presented a very different reading of the Quran than Qawi favored.

As Rook and Qawi talked, the detectives of the Twentieth Precinct were fleshing out other details of their new suspects' lives.

El-Bashir and Al-Aman were not unknown to the NYPD. El-Bashir had been caught with a few marijuana cigarettes during a stop-and-frisk a few years earlier, resulting in a misdemeanor possession charge. Al-Aman had several nebulous charges for loitering and disturbing the peace, though he sounded more like an annoyance to law enforcement than an actual threat. None of his priors were violent.

Rhymer had produced their mug shots for Heat. El-Bashir's was several years old. In it, he looked like any other scowling teenager, with a smooth face and short-cropped hair. He wore no headdress, nor any other clothing to indicate his religious affiliation.

Al-Aman's picture was more recent and more fitting for a young Muslim. His head was wrapped in a turban. His beard, which appeared to have been dyed red, was kept long.

But it was Raley, the king of all surveillance media, who got the big hit.

"Captain," he said as he entered the observation room, "I've got something you're going to want to see."

Heat glanced toward Rook and Qawi, who were now deep in conversation about the similarities between the messaging in the Bible and the Quran. Deciding she wasn't going to miss anything pertinent to her investigation, Heat followed Raley back into the bull pen.

"I finally got tapes from a camera across the street from Masjid al-Jannah," Raley said, sitting in front of the large screen. "This is a few minutes before eleven o'clock Saturday night."

He pressed play. Two young men in thobes and turbans were walking east, up 73rd Street. Taking the most direct path, they climbed the front steps and entered the mosque.

They moved with urgency, a pair of men with somewhere to be. One of them, the one on the right, gave a furtive glance up the street before entering.

"Awfully late at night to be going to mosque, wouldn't you say?" Heat said.

"My thought exactly."

"How long did they stay in there?" Heat asked.

"A little more than two hours. I got them coming out here. Actual time: 1:07 A.M."

Raley played the clip. It showed the same two young men exiting the front door. They walked back west, down 73rd Street, in the direction they had originally come from.

There was the same sense of urgency in their steps. If anything, they were in even more of a hurry.

"Anyone else go in or out during that time?" Heat asked.

"Nope. And not for several hours before or after, either."

"So we've just put two men who had become increasingly radicalized in their adherence to Islam at our crime scene during the window that Lauren gave us for time of death."

"If it's them, yeah. I've been looking at it for a while and . . . I can't really say for sure."

"Go back to the first video," Heat said, walking over to the murder board and grabbing El-Bashir's and Al-Aman's mug shots so she could bring them close to the screen and see if they were a match.

Raley did as he was told, and Heat watched the brief clip again.

"Can you give me a freeze-frame at a spot that shows their faces?" Heat asked.

Raley complied, halting the video during a moment when the men were passing directly under a streetlight.

"Okay, zoom in a little."

"I already tried," Raley said. "The resolution is pretty lousy. If you go too far, they just look like blobs."

"Can you sharpen it at all?"

"The light is pretty low. There's just not enough data for the computer to work with."

"Do your best."

Raley fumbled with it for a few minutes, slowly improving the image. But he was right. There were limits based on the raw material.

"Okay, that's probably as good as we're going to get," Raley said. "What do you think?"

It might have been their suspects. But it also might not have been. It wasn't easy comparing a mug shot—especially one several years old, as El-Bashir's was—to a piece of grainy surveillance footage.

"Give me a printout of that, along with a zoomed-out full-body picture of the two of them," Heat said.

"You got it."

"So two hours," Heat mused as she waited for the images to roll off the printer. "That's more than long enough to shoot a decapitation video, wouldn't you think?"

"Sure. Only thing is, we never see them hauling the victim in there."

"There is a back entrance," Heat said. "They could have brought her in that way. They probably did it earlier. The last prayer call of the day is at sundown. Mosques tend to be pretty empty after that. No different from a church, really."

"So they haul her in there sometime earlier in the evening, tie her up somehow, then come back in the dead of night to finish off the job?"

"That would be the theory."

"Any cameras on the back entrance?"

"Negative."

Heat stared at the screen, still frozen on the young men's faces.

"The only thing that doesn't really make sense is that, okay, let's say El-Bashir and Al-Aman killed our victim in the early hours of Sunday morning," Heat said. "But the body wasn't dumped until sometime after eleven Monday night, when the dishwasher at Pho Sure went home. That's twenty-four hours or more when that body is totally unaccounted for."

"Maybe they stashed it at the mosque somewhere?" Raley suggested. "They'd know the mosque well enough. It had to have a closet or a basement or someplace where they knew it was unlikely for the body to be found. Then they came back Monday night or early Tuesday morning to get rid of it."

"Possible," Heat conceded. "But why wait? You'd think they'd be eager to get rid of it."

"Well, hopefully we'll have a chance to ask El-Bashir and Al-Aman real soon."

"If it's them. Speaking of which," Heat said, grabbing the printouts from the printer and walking back to Interrogation One.

As she entered the room, Rook was in the midst of a sentence.

". . . so the guy goes to his local camel dealer, and he says—"

Rook stopped when he saw Heat's glare.

"Camel jokes? Really?" Heat said. "When I left you were talking about the commonalities of two of the world's great religions, and now you're telling camel jokes?"

"What's wrong with camel jokes?" Rook said. "Camels happen to be very important in Arabic culture. I realize here in America they're mostly seen as smelly, ill-tempered ungulates. But did you know that the word 'camel' comes from an Arabic word that means 'beauty'?"

Rook leaned toward Qawi and said, "I only know that because it was mentioned in a thriller I read. *Wild Storm* by this guy named Richard Castle. Ever heard of him?"

"He sounds like a total hack. I am surprised a man of your intellect reads such lowbrow, pulpy trash."

"I guess I just have a weakness for books that are actually entertaining," Rook said. "You do realize, of course, that many of the world's most enduring writers—like that Shakespeare fellow, to name just one—were actually considered the lowbrow pulp-style entertainment of their time?"

Heat cleared her throat.

"Another time," Rook said. "Sorry. You were saying?"

Heat shook her head, then placed the photos on the table in front of Qawi.

"I know these aren't the greatest quality," Heat said apologetically. "But I was hoping you could tell me if these men are Hassan El-Bashir and Tariq Al-Aman."

After just one glance, Qawi's hand flew to his mouth. The gesture told Heat all she needed to know, but Qawi still followed up with the words.

"Oh, Hassan. Oh, Tariq. What have you done?"

"So that's them."

"Oh, yes. I'm afraid so."

"This was taken from a surveillance camera at approximately eleven o'clock Saturday night. They stayed inside for about two hours, then left. Can you think of any reason they would have to be at the mosque during that time?"

"Well, the mosque is open at all hours because we believe spiritual needs can arise at any hour on the clock, but . . . but, no. Unless it was

Ramadan, there would be no reason I can think of for them to be there at that time."

The look on Qawi's face spoke to his misery at the confirmation that two members of the flock had strayed so far.

"You're doing the right thing," Rook reassured him.

"This is very hard, very hard," Qawi said. "But I know it is harder still for the family of this victim. Can you . . . Can you tell them that I would like to pray with them? It is important to me the family understands this killing is an abomination to Allah."

"I would if I knew who the victim was," Heat said. "We still don't have an ID."

At that moment, Randall Feller burst into Interrogation One, waving a photograph.

"We do now," he said triumphantly. "Uniforms found the head in a Dumpster two doors down from where they found the body."

"Yeah, and?"

"Sorry, Rook," Feller said. "I know you had some history with her."

"With whom?" Heat said. "Come on, out with it."

"Okay, okay," Feller said. "Meet the victim in the American ISIS beheading case."

Feller flipped a professional portrait on the table. There, looking confidently back at Heat, was the smiling face of *New York Ledger* Senior Metro Reporter Tam Svejda.

THIRTEEN

Rook's reaction was small at first: his mouth turning slightly down, his cheeks sinking a few centimeters, his chin giving a little quiver.

It is a strange thing for the heart, knowing that an ex-lover is gone. Because the heart thinks it has moved on from its one-time love. Until it learns that other heart is no longer beating.

Heat could see Rook was trying to keep up a brave front in front of Feller. Or perhaps he was attempting to seem disinterested for her sake. Possibly, he was maintaining a mask of impartiality in front of Qawi, who Rook was already prepping as a future source.

It just wasn't working. The human being in Rook far outweighed the tough guy, the loyal spouse, and the journalist.

Finally, he gave up.

"Oh, Tam," he said, reaching for the picture, tears welling in his eyes. "I'm so sorry."

"She was a friend of yours?" Qawi asked.

"Yes. Briefly. Long ago. It was . . . It was never going to work, two journalists who had to compete with each other for scoops, trying to be in a relationship. Especially when one of them reported for a place like the *Ledger*. So we broke it off. But we had some good times. Off the job, she really was a lovely person. She had this way of—"

Rook looked up and saw everyone was staring at him.

"Sorry," he said.

"No, it's okay," Heat said, walking over to him, bending down, and wrapping her arms around him from behind.

Rook grabbed her hand and took a deep breath. Even Feller seemed to be taking a moment of silence.

In life, Heat and the other detectives of the Twentieth Precinct had viewed Tam Svejda as lower than the stuff they scraped off their shoes after a careless walk in the dog park. She was some combination of the festering abscess that appeared on their faces on prom night, the neighbor who refused to turn down her stereo at 2 A.M., and the postnasal drip that wouldn't go away.

Cops had that kind of enmity for journalists. Ultimately, they were two groups whose goals and aims were often diametrically opposed. It was a cop's job to make sure nothing that would harm an investigation or tip off the bad guys became public. It was a journalist's job to make sure more or less everything—or at least everything they could reasonably source as true—became public.

But those kinds of workaday antagonisms were gone. She was now their victim. Their cause. And they would stop at nothing to make sure her killers were brought to justice.

"Mr. Qawi," Heat said. "Did either Hassan or Tariq know Tam Svejda at all?"

"I . . . I don't know."

"Did they read the *New York Ledger*?"

"If they would have read any paper, it would have been the *Ledger*. But I never saw them showing much interest in the news."

"Tam was out on the streets all the time," Rook said. "Especially when she was reporting on crimes. It's where she felt like the best information was. She might have just been a target of convenience for them."

"Or they might have singled her out for some reason," Heat said. "Or maybe they knew about her aggressive reputation as a reporter and found a way to—"

Heat dangled the thought out there, but cut it off, half finished. Even though she no longer suspected Qawi, she still didn't fully trust him. She didn't want to be trying out theories in front of him.

"Mr. Qawi, you're free to go," she said, removing his handcuffs. "We appreciate your help with our investigation. To show our goodwill, we're not going to press charges for evading arrest."

"Thank you."

"However, as a continued sign of your cooperation, can you please send us any evidence you can find of Hassan El-Bashir and Tariq Al-Aman radicalizing? Anything they might have posted on the Internet or any other signs they may have had ties to the extremist community?"

"I'll see what I can find."

"I'd also ask you to stay in New York and remain available to our investigators for further questioning. Is that fair?"

"Yes, Captain Heat, thank you," Qawi said. "And I want you to know, Masjid al-Jannah is going to be holding a prayer service for Miss Tam Svejda. Our congregation will join all of New York in mourning her loss."

"That's very thoughtful of you, Mr. Qawi," Heat said.

Qawi rose from his chair. Heat and Rook followed him out of Interrogation One, then saw him to the elevator, where they said their good-byes.

As Heat returned to the bull pen, with Rook still in tow, she was already thinking of next steps.

"Okay," Heat said. "Feller, grab Opie. I want you to put together a team to collar El-Bashir and Al-Aman. Start at their apartment. Bring the Bomb Squad and put caution first. They might be lying in wait for you and I don't want to take any chances."

"You got it," Feller said.

Heat turned to Rook. "Do you know where Tam's parents live?"

"Pennsylvania, I think. Somewhere outside Philly. Main Line, if I recall. Or near enough to the Main Line that the realtors call it Main Line. But beyond that . . ."

"Okay. I'm sure a name like Svejda won't be hard to track. Rales, can you figure out where her parents are, call the local PD and ask them if they'll do next-of-kin notification for us?"

"You got it."

"Also, get El-Bashir's and Al-Aman's heights off their driver's licenses or their mug shots and compare it to the men in the video. Let's see if we can get a match there. It's not exactly a fingerprint but it'll be better than nothing at trial."

"Will do."

"Speaking of matches, where the hell is Aguinaldo, anyway?" Heat asked. "Doesn't she have anything yet on that scarf?"

"She's still shopping, as far as I know," Raley said. "I'll check in with her."

"Please do. And have we heard anything about Ochoa?"

"Good news there," Raley assured her. "The wound was superficial. The doctors said the bullet ricocheted off something before it wedged in his ass. That's why it didn't go in more than an inch before it stopped."

"Do you think whoever shot him called backboard?" Feller asked.

"We'll find out soon enough," Heat said. "The docs know that slug has to be sent to ballistics for testing, right? One PP is going to want to know whose gun it came from."

"Already done," Raley said.

"Good work," Heat said, then turned her attention to Rook. "Now, as for you—"

Rook was already recoiling. "Not the radiator again. Anything but the radiator."

Heat laughed. "Well, that's one possibility. But I feel like if I keep you at arm's length, you'll be safe enough. Want to join me on a field trip?"

"Oh! Oh! How about the zoo? Can we go to the zoo?"

"In a manner of speaking, we will be," Heat said. "I want to talk to Tam's editor at the *Ledger*. It's possible these lunatics just grabbed the first journalist they found on the street. But if they found some way to lure her or if they had some specific reason for going after her, I want to know about it."

"Mmm," Rook said. "Walking into the belly of the beast, huh?"

Rook knew that for Heat, wading into the offices of the *New York Ledger* and asking for an audience was roughly akin to taking a dinner cruise down the River Styx and inquiring if the host had a minute to chat.

"That's why I'm bringing you along," Heat said. "I figure you know how to speak Journalist."

"So I'm being used."

"You can always spend more time with the radiator."

"In that case," Rook said, "use me like a rented donkey."

———

The newsroom of the *New York Ledger* occupied several floors of a large building on 6th Avenue in midtown, nearly thirty blocks south of the Twentieth Precinct. Heat thought about grabbing a pool car, but decided a cab would be quicker. The NYPD required paperwork. Cabbies didn't.

Rook settled in next to her. They took a right turn on Columbus and hadn't gone more than a block before Rook spoke.

"You're looking for your mother, aren't you?" he said. "Even as we were hailing the cab, I could see your eyes were looking elsewhere."

Heat took in a deep breath. "I know I'm supposed to be focused on the investigation. And I am."

"But?"

"But, yeah, I can't help it. Even when I was running after Muharib Qawi, I think I was keeping half an eye out for her."

"I keep finding myself doing the same thing. I spent half the time I was chained to that radiator looking out the window, studying everyone who walked by."

"Thank you," Heat said quietly, sliding her hand over his.

"We just have to be patient," Rook said, giving her hand a squeeze. "Lauren will get us answers soon enough."

"Maybe. Or maybe all she'll get us is a thousand more questions."

They didn't speak for the remainder of the ride. Heat took a moment to enjoy just being next to Rook. It continued to amaze her he could be so many things to her: not only her favorite sex toy and best friend, but also her comfort animal.

The cab let them out on the corner of 55th Street. As they gathered themselves, a slender dark-haired woman walked by them, engrossed in a conversation she was having on her cell phone.

"Look, you have to be willing to be a total slut here, okay?" she said. "That's our mantra, you know."

Heat waited until the woman passed by, then said, "High-end madam?"

"Literary agent," Rook said. "Though, admittedly, with the best ones, it can be hard to tell."

Heat looked up at the building they were about to enter. "Okay, so what's the scouting report on Tam's editor?"

"His name is Steve Liebman. I met him once or twice. He's the metro editor, if you know what I mean."

"No, actually, I don't."

"Metro editors are the stressed-out middle managers of the newspaper world. They are constantly being hounded by the editors above them in the food chain to produce sensational front-page news that will send copies of that day's paper flying off the newsstands and clicking all over the Web, whether or not anything sensational has actually happened. His job is to then take the misery of those impossible expectations and pass it on to his reporters tenfold, making their lives living hells if they don't deliver the exact story the higher-up editors think exists, even if the only place it exists is in their imaginations. It's a job that basically involves sucking dry every soul that wanders into your vicinity."

"Sounds charming."

"He's a pretty good guy, actually," Rook said, then added: "For an editor."

"Think he'll help us?"

"Under ordinary circumstances, if an NYPD captain stormed into the *Ledger* newsroom and demanded to know what one of his reporters was up to, Liebman would be professionally obligated to laugh you out of his office," Rook confirmed. "But, of course, these aren't ordinary circumstances."

"Well, then here goes nothing," Heat said. "Let me take the lead, okay? I want to have you around to make things right if I get off on the wrong foot and make a mess."

"I'll be your Mr. Clean," Rook said. Then he caught a glimpse of himself in some dark glass and ran a hand through his thick, stylishly cut mane. "With, you know, much better hair."

Heat led them into the building's lobby and announced herself to the rent-a-cops at the security desk.

Five minutes later, once they had been outfitted with paper badges bearing their names and pictures, Heat and Rook were met by a clerk. She was a frazzled-looking young woman who escorted them up fourteen floors to a large, open room with a sea of desks in the middle. Roughly half of them were occupied, with men and women in equal measure, most of them also young and harried. Newspaper economics had been so bad for so long, places like the *Ledger* were now chronically understaffed. Most of the employees were fresh-out-of-college rookies who would allow themselves to be scandalously underpaid in return for the "experience" of working at one of the country's largest dailies.

The clerk led Heat and Rook toward a glass-walled office on the far side of the room. Seated at the desk, behind mounds of old newspapers, was a rumpled, balding, and bespectacled middle-aged man with bad posture and a generally beaten-down-by-life air.

The clerk tapped on the door. Liebman didn't bother to look away from his screen when he said, "Hello, detectives, what can I—"

Then he looked up. "Jameson?" he said, almost like he was seeing a ghost. "Thank God you're okay, but . . . What are you doing here?"

Rook, following orders to let Heat go first, said nothing.

"Mr. Liebman, I'm Captain Nikki Heat with the Twentieth Precinct."

"I know who you are," Liebman said. "I read my own paper, you know. Are you here to give me a story?"

"Not exactly."

"Then I'm sure you'll have a good chat with our lawyer. Have a very nice day," he said, smiling for the first time.

"Mr. Liebman, it's about Tam Svejda."

The moment Heat said the name, Liebman's smile evaporated.

"Oh, no," was all he said, his shoulders slumping even farther than usual. "Oh, no . . . please . . . It was her in the video, wasn't it?"

"I'm sorry, Mr. Liebman."

The man's face went immediately into his hands. He didn't make a sound, but his body started shaking. When he lifted his head back up and took his hands away, there were tears in his eyes.

"I'm sorry," he said, trying to compose himself. "I think . . . I think I knew . . . Tam didn't exactly take a lot of days off. When I didn't hear from her on Sunday, I thought, 'Well, atta girl, finally giving yourself a little breather.' Then on Monday, no calls, no e-mails, which was . . . I mean, I don't think I've gone two days without hearing from Tam the whole time we've worked together. She always had some kind of story percolating. Then this morning, I saw the video and . . . Well, like I said, I think I knew. I mean, everything about the victim was . . . But I was still hoping it wasn't her. Oh, Tam."

He stood and turned away, walking toward the window behind his desk, not wanting to let Heat and Rook see him emotionally overcome.

"She was a helluva reporter," Rook said.

"She was more than just that," Liebman said to the window, his voice sounding hollow. "I know she had this image that she cultivated. She was this journalistic rock star. Sexy as hell. Relentless in her pursuit of a story. Every scoop she went after was a piece of raw meat, and she was a tiger. But that was more of a persona than anything. Underneath she was a total sweetheart. I had exactly one reporter who always remembered my birthday and my wedding anniversary, and it was Tam. When my mom died, she came to the funeral and cried right along with me. She was . . ."

Liebman was faltering, so Rook finished the thought: "One of a kind."

"Yeah. She was," Liebman said, now turning back toward them and offering Rook a sad smile. "But what am I telling you for? You know what I'm talking about. Back when you two were together, I always said if you had kids, they'd be the greatest reporters who ever lived. They would have had to make a permanent table for them at the Pulitzers, because one of them would have been winning every year."

He waved at the air, as if vanquishing the silly thought.

"Anyway, what's going on with the investigation?" Liebman said. "Have you caught the bastards yet?"

Rook was about to say something, but Heat grabbed his wrist.

"This is going to have to be off the record," she said.

Heat and Liebman eyed each other warily. The touchy-feely stuff now over, they had resumed their usual adversarial roles.

"So I'm supposed to help your investigation but then wait for the press conference to be able to report anything?" Liebman said. "You're joking. Tam was our reporter. She was also the public face of our metro staff. It's completely unacceptable for us not to be out in front of the competition on this. At the very, very least, you have to let us break the story that she was the American ISIS victim. It would be ridiculous for anyone else to have that first."

Heat took in a large breath, which she planned to use to give force to her argument until she caught Rook giving her a small nod.

She let the breath out. "Hang on," she said, taking out her phone and tapping at it a few times.

A voice came over the line: "Raley."

"Hey, Rales," Heat said. "Real quick: Have you done next-of-kin yet?"

"The Svejdas live in Media, PA," he said. "The Media Police told me they'll be sending a captain over to their house in the next fifteen minutes."

"Thanks," she said, then ended the call. She looked back at Liebman.

"Will you hold off for half an hour so Tam's parents don't have to learn about this from a reporter?" she asked.

He nodded.

"Then you got your scoop. You can source it from me. And I promise I'll keep you out ahead of the competition on the rest of the investigation when I can," she said. "But I need your cooperation. And I need your promise that if I tell you to hold something back, you'll hold it back."

"I won't do anything to jeopardize your investigation, Captain," he said. "I guarantee you I want to nail those scumbags just as badly as you do."

"Thank you," Heat said. "So had Tam been working on anything involving ISIS?"

"Well, sure, she did the Joanna Masters story for us."

"Tam did that?" Rook said. "Geez. I didn't even look at the byline."

"Sorry," Heat said. "The Joanna Masters story?"

"Joanna Masters is an aid worker who was shot by ISIS," Rook said. "She was Red Cross, right?"

Liebman nodded, then continued the story: "She was over in Syria, helping to distribute food and medicine to the crush of refugees there, when her convoy was set upon by a group of ISIS fighters. She was shot as they fled. Tam knew Joanna was from the city and was determined to get the first interview with her. Tam started working a source she had cultivated at the Red Cross to give her a heads up as soon as Joanna flew home. I think Tam was waiting outside Joanna's apartment in Greenwich Village when the cab pulled up from the airport. Everyone had already reported on what happened to Joanna Masters, but Tam was the first one to get the whole story."

Liebman chuckled. "The *Times* sent a reporter over the next day and Joanna Masters told them to beat it. As far as she was concerned, she had said all she had to say to the *Ledger*, and she was done. The *Times* ended up having to quote Tam's story, with credit, as opposed to what they usually do, which is pretend like they didn't get scooped by the down-and-dirty tabloid.

"Oh, Tam," he said again, shaking his head and sighing, his eyes getting misty.

"Okay, but that sounds like it was basically a human interest story," Heat said. "Why would ISIS care about something like that? It's not like they're worried about getting bad press. Heck, they seem to *want* bad press. Why would they be threatened by the Joanna Masters story?"

"Couldn't tell you," Liebman said. "I guess it's possible Joanna gave her some kind of lead. But that's just conjecture on my part. Tam certainly didn't say anything. You'd have to ask Joanna."

Heat made a mental note to pay a visit to Joanna Masters and do just that.

"Okay, so other than Joanna Masters, was Tam working on anything else that might have had an ISIS angle?" Heat asked.

Liebman cast his glance to the left. "Maybe," he said.

"What do you mean 'maybe'?"

"Tam and I had worked together for a lot of years," Liebman said. "I keep my younger reporters on a pretty tight leash. And you may have noticed I have a lot of them. But Tam was . . . Well, she was in a different category. She knew as soon as she told me about a story, I'd have to put it down on the story budget, and then everyone from the executive editor on down would start clamoring for it, whether it was ready to go or not. So there were a lot of times when she'd be working on something and tell me it wasn't fully baked yet. Frankly, I think she learned that approach from your husband."

"Editors have to be managed properly," Rook confirmed.

"I had learned to trust her to tell me when the time was right," Liebman said.

"So had she been working on something new that she hadn't told you anything about?" Heat asked.

"Yeah. She said it was big."

"How big?"

"Like supernova big. But she said she had to get it nailed down a little better before she let slip a single peep about it. She left town on Thursday to chase it down, but I honestly couldn't even tell you where she went. I usually only know where Tam has been after she submits her expense report."

"Do you think you could piece together what she was working on?" Heat said. "Does she have files we could look at?"

Liebman puffed out his cheeks as he exhaled. "Oh, geez. I have no idea. Her desk wasn't much cleaner than mine."

"Can we go have a look?"

"Sure," Liebman said. "Come on."

Liebman stood and walked out into the newsroom. Heat and Rook followed.

As she walked, Heat became aware she was being tracked by multiple sets of young, openly curious eyes. Then she realized the eyes weren't on her.

"Rook, why is everyone staring at you?" she asked.

Liebman answered: "You think you can take a two-time Pulitzer Prize winner and parade him around the city room of a major metro paper and people won't notice? Rook is like some combination of the pope and Elvis to these kids. Half of them probably have posters of him back home in their bedrooms."

"With all due respect to His Holiness," Rook said, "I have much better hair."

"Anyhow, here we are," Liebman said, stopping at a desk that occupied the corner closest to the vending machines, prime real estate befitting Senior Metro Reporter Tam Svejda.

Heat stared down at the surface of it, which was covered in old newspapers, takeout menus, reporters' steno pads, printouts of competitors' stories, and ketchup packets. The main organizing principle seemed to be entropy.

"Uhh, wow," Heat said. "Not sure where to start here."

"How about there," Rook said, pointing.

Heat followed his finger to the top of the computer. The *Ledger's* parent company hadn't sprung for new equipment since the Bush presidency—the first one, probably—so Tam's desktop computer was a big block of a thing that had plenty of room for knickknacks on top. Heat saw a preserved alligator head, a pair of miniature handcuffs, some fuzzy dice, a Rubik's Cube whose squares were pictures of male models, a tarantula under glass . . .

And a misshapen bullet slug.

"Don't touch it," Heat snapped as Rook reached toward it. She looked at Liebman. "Do you know anything about that?"

"Not much," Liebman said, adjusting his glasses, which had slid down his nose, so he could get a better look at it. "It showed up, I don't know, a week or two ago? I asked Tam about it and all she said was it was a souvenir."

"Strange souvenir," Heat said.

"Reporters are strange people, Captain Heat," Liebman said.

Heat was now looking at Rook, who, having been deprived of tactile feedback, was studying the slug from multiple angles. It had clearly struck something fairly hard, hence its crumpled form.

"Do you think maybe someone was trying to send a message?" Rook said. "If I was trying to scare a reporter off a story, sending them a bullet would be a nice old-school way of going about it, wouldn't it?"

"Tam didn't exactly scare easily," Liebman said.

"Yeah, but someone who was trying to threaten her wouldn't know that," Rook said. "And of course Tam took this quote-unquote 'threat' and stuck it on top of her computer like a trophy."

"Yeah, but wouldn't you send someone a new bullet?" Heat said. "One that's shiny and brassy and still in the jacket? That's more symbolic, isn't it? Why send an old busted-up slug?"

"Maybe that's part of the message: Not only do we have bullets, we know how to use them," Rook said.

The three of them stood around what had, in life, been Tam Svejda's desk. It was as if they were waiting for her ghost to visit them and whisper an alternative theory in their ears.

But wherever Tam's restless spirit had landed, it wasn't the *Ledger* newsroom. After thirty seconds of listening to would-be Jimmy Breslins type, overwriting their six-paragraph briefs, Heat snapped back to action.

"Can I bag that bullet for evidence?" she asked.

"Be my guest," Liebman said.

Heat produced a pair of blue nitrile gloves and an evidence bag and carefully dropped the bullet inside.

"What about these notebooks?" Heat asked.

Liebman looked at their front covers. "She usually kept the current stuff with her. These look like they're all for stories she's already put in the paper, so they're all old news. But our lawyer would probably have a fit if I turned them over without checking first. How about I go through them and see if there's anything that might be relevant, and I'll let you know if something stands out?"

Rook read Heat's indecision and spoke up: "That bullet was probably sent to her because of something not yet in the paper. There's no point in threatening someone once the story has already run."

"Okay," she said.

Heat then nodded toward the phone on Svejda's desk. "Did Tam use that or did she stick to her mobile?"

"No, she used both," Liebman said, then added a wry smile. "Sometimes simultaneously."

"Was her cell phone provided to her by the paper?"

"It was."

"So anything she would have been working on would have been reflected in phone records," Heat said.

"Probably," Liebman said. "Unless she was doing a lot of in-person interviewing."

"Who can I talk to about looking through your phone records?" Heat asked. "Ordinarily I'd just get a search warrant but I don't think any judge is going to let me paw through a newspaper's phone records when all I have is an investigational hunch that I'm looking to confirm."

"Well, if you're looking for phone records, you're out of my league, that's for sure. While it's our job to upend other people's privacy, we take our own pretty seriously. Since this is a criminal matter, you'll have to go through our outside counsel."

"Sure. Who do you guys use?"

"Helen Miksit," Liebman said.

Heat did not reply. She was too busy exerting the Herculean effort needed to block the sneer that was coming to her lips.

Which she did.

Barely.

FOURTEEN

Another twenty minutes of poking around the *New York Ledger* newsroom accomplished little beyond making Heat even more uncomfortable about being there.

Tam Svejda had clearly been up to something: perhaps something unrelated to her death, perhaps something that put her on a collision course with a terrorist's machete. Wherever the answers were, they weren't in Tam's desk. Or in the vending machines behind it. Or anywhere else in that newsroom filled with barely adult reporters.

Heat could also sense Liebman was getting eager to be rid of them so he could begin marshalling his resources to cover a big story. The reporters of the *New York Ledger* had a scoop to get online. They also had a colleague to mourn, which they would do concurrently with their work.

It was one of the small ways in which cops and newspapers actually did have a lot in common: neither was given much time to stop and grieve.

Heat and Rook were back out on 6th Avenue and had just hailed a cab when Rook's phone rang.

"Hello, this is Jameson Rook," he said, smoothly.

His face brightened. "Oh, hi, Lana!" he said, then cupped the phone. "It's Lana Kline. Legs's daughter?"

"Oh, I remember. Little Miss Sunshine herself," Heat said through a saccharine smile.

But Rook missed her passive-aggressiveness. He was already back to his call.

They had slid inside a cab. Heat told the driver to take them to the Church Street address downtown where she hoped to find Helen Miksit both in her office and in a good mood.

"Yes. Yes, that'd be great. How soon?" Rook was saying, then waited a moment.

"No, no problem whatsoever," he said.

Another pause.

"I keep a bag packed for just such emergencies," he said.

Then he laughed. "Yes, of course there's a bathing suit in there."

His face went mock-serious. "Rum? Miss Kline, that's rather naughty of you."

He waited for her reply, then responded with: "Oh, be*have* . . . But if you're looking for suggestions, I'd go with Pyrat Cask. They have an aged—"

Wait.

"Yeah, that's the one," he said. "Okay. Sounds good. Yep, see you soon . . . Okay. Ta-ta!"

He ended the call. The smile had morphed into more of a goofy grin.

Heat could feel her ears reddening. She wondered if there was actual steam coming out of them or if that was just her imagination.

"What?" he said innocently.

"Nothing."

"You look . . . angry all of sudden."

"Oh, I'm fine," she said, giving the not-fine smile.

"Oh, good," Rook said. "Anyhow, that was Lana Kline. Legs's daughter."

"You said that part already."

"Did I?"

"Yes. And?"

"Well, it seems Legs has an opening in his schedule for a one-on-one interview this afternoon, which is something I'm going to have to do before I write the profile. Because, you know, talking to a source is . . . Well, it's part of what you want to do when you're trying to capture someone in a . . . in a profile . . . Why are you looking at me like that?"

"Like what?"

"Like you are weighing whether disembowelment hurts more than dismemberment."

"No, I'm just . . . distracted, I guess."

"Because she's a blow-up doll, remember?" Rook said. "And no one wants to have sex with a blow-up doll. Except for, I mean, people who actually *do* have sex with blow-up dolls. Not that'd I'd know anything about that."

The taxi driver reached toward the small door in the bulletproof glass that separated his part of the cab from the back and slid it shut.

"Anyhow, my point is, you have nothing to worry about with Lana," Rook said. "That's just . . . professional cordialness."

"Okay," Heat said. "Anyhow, where does he want you to meet him? A hotel, or . . ."

"No, we're going to do the interview in the air on our way from New York to I-don't-know-where."

"In his 737."

"Yes.

"The one with the king-size bed in it," Heat said.

"This bed seems to be something of a fascination of yours. Am I to read into this that perhaps you haven't seen enough of my bed lately, Captain Heat?"

"I've seen plenty of it," she said. "It's just that your side has been empty the whole time."

"Which I will remedy as soon as I come back from . . . wherever it is we're going."

"I know," Heat said, her lip clenched between her teeth.

"What?"

"I just . . . Listen, I know we think we have the guys who did this. But until we have them in custody and know we've neutralized the threat, I'm nervous about you being out there without any protection."

"I'll be fine," Rook said. "Legs Kline is a leading presidential candidate. He's already under Secret Service protection, plus I'm sure he has his own security detail. And if *I* don't know where I'm going to be, how can these ISIS clowns? There's probably no safer place for me to be than . . . wherever it is I'm going."

He slid the glass divider back open.

"Excuse me, sir, but could you make a few more stops? Once you drop off my wife, I've got an address for you in Tribeca, then I'd need to head out to LaGuardia. It's a private hangar belonging to LokSat Aviation."

The driver mumbled his assent. Rook slid the door closed.

"LokSat Aviation," Heat said. "What an ominous-sounding name."

"Don't be ridiculous. You're making too much of everything," Rook said. "There's nothing ominous about the name LokSat."

He let that hang out there for a moment.

"In any event, I'll be safely returned before you know it," he said. "And then we'll both be more than ready for a very memorable return to Reykjavík."

"You promise?"

"It will be all I'm living for," he said.

Just as long as you keep living at all, Heat almost said, but she stopped herself. The thought was too morbid to be spoken out loud.

They settled into silence, watching the blocks fly by as the cab slalomed through small openings in traffic on 7th Avenue.

Heat pulled out her phone and checked her messages. "Feller texted to say El-Bashir and Al-Aman are definitely holed up inside their apartment. He says his team is moving on them shortly."

She clicked over to e-mail. "And Raley says he's got a preliminary height match on the video. El-Bashir and Al-Aman are both within an inch on either side of six feet, and so are the two men in the video."

"See? Everything is going to be fine," Rook said.

Heat just looked out the window as lower Manhattan continued to flash by. She knew what was bothering her, of course. It wasn't what was in the video, but what was just offscreen. The two men had clearly kept glancing at something just to the side of the camera. Something—like cue cards—or *someone*.

Someone who was really in charge.

Someone who would view El-Bashir and Al-Aman as expendable commodities and wouldn't register their arrests as anything more than a slight hiccup.

Someone who would see Jameson Rook's kidnapping and death as a vital part of a larger plan to instill terror.

The cab was slowing to a stop, having reached Helen Miksit's office, just around the corner from Tweed Courthouse. Rook's Tribeca loft was just a few blocks to the northwest. Heat could tell his attention was already on the bag he would quickly grab on his way to meeting Legs Kline's private jet at LaGuardia.

She kissed him, then grabbed his face with both hands.

"Be safe, not stupid," she said. "And come back home to me in one piece."

"Always," he said.

She slid out of the cab and watched it pull away, hoping it wouldn't be a moment forever imprinted in her mind as the last time she saw him.

Like a lot of criminal defense attorneys, Helen Miksit didn't tend to meet clients at her office.

Generally speaking, she had two kinds of clients: the rich and powerful, whom she went to see in their workplaces or mansions, and the poor (but high-profile), who she visited in their jail or holding cells or whatever government facilities they were incapable of getting themselves bonded out of.

It meant her headquarters were unadorned and utilitarian: a small suite of offices in a building whose lobby, elevator, and hallways were about thirty years overdue for an update. Not designed to impress. Just designed to keep Miksit and her team—which consisted of a secretary, a paralegal, an associate she kept around to do research, and an investigator—out of the rain.

It spoke to the nature of their relationship that Nikki Heat had known Helen Miksit the entire time she had been a defense attorney—ever since she had switched over from the prosecutor's office years earlier—but had never once been to her office. It was usually Miksit trying to get something from Heat (namely, a client out of police custody), not the other way around.

So this was a role reversal. And the surprise on Miksit's secretary's face when he saw Captain Heat of the Twentieth Precinct walking through the front doors of Helen Miksit & Associates spoke to that.

"Good afternoon, Captain," he said as he snuck surreptitious glances at the calendar on his computer screen. "I didn't realize you were coming in today. Do you have an—"

"No," Heat said. "Is Helen—"

"Is that Nikki Heat? In *my* office?" came a booming *alto-basso* from the next room. Hillary Clinton may have needed training to make her voice sound deep and commanding. Helen Miksit came by it naturally.

Miksit didn't just act like a bulldog in court; she sort of looked like one, too. Things that were round on most people were square on Helen Miksit.

If she was smiling as she appeared in her small reception area, it was only viciously. Miksit had been around the game long enough to know that NYPD captains didn't schlep themselves half the length of Manhattan just to make idle chat. They both knew: Heat was there to grovel for something she couldn't get through other means.

"Hello, Helen," Heat said, determined to use the get-more-flies-with-honey approach to the conversation. "It's so nice to see you again."

"Bullshit," Miksit spat. "The last time we saw each other you were trying to railroad my innocent client—"

"Who was so innocent you promptly sent him to Croatia," Heat said.

So much for honey.

"I didn't *send* him anywhere," Miksit informed her. "He may or may not have come across some information about which countries did and did not currently have extradition treaties with the United States. He then chose to act on that information. Surely I, as an officer of the court, would never have advised him to do anything that would impede the seeking of justice."

"Of course not," Heat volleyed back. "And it just so happens that my visit today will give you another opportunity to prove how, as an officer of the court, you will do whatever you can to aid a police investigation."

Miksit didn't bother to hide the rolling of her eyes. "Oh, my, it's getting deep in here. I hope you brought a shovel."

Heat took a deep breath, as much to calm herself down as to give the conversation a chance to de-escalate. She thought about Rook and how much he needed her to close this investigation—whether he acknowledged it or not. Maybe Tam Svejda's supernova-big story truly had nothing to do with her death.

Or maybe it had *everything* to do with it. Helen Miksit was right now the gatekeeper of the data that could give Heat clarity.

"Can we just talk for a moment?" Heat asked quietly. "I really need a favor."

Miksit frowned. Bluster aside, Helen Miksit was a member of the bar in good standing. As such, she could scarcely tell Heat, a sworn law enforcement officer, to stop back when she had more time. Miksit looked testily at her secretary. "Craig, hold my calls."

"Yes, Ms. Miksit," he said.

"Come on, Captain," Miksit said, turning back toward her office without really looking at Heat.

Helen Miksit's inner sanctum was just as unadorned and straightforward as her litigation style. There were no family photos, no quirky effects. The artwork was chain-hotel neutral and appeared to have been chosen without any attempt to match the taste or personality of the inhabitant.

For as strange as it sounded, Heat recognized in Miksit a kind of kindred spirit: a woman who didn't want to give away anything without a fight. Certainly not with something as cheap and easy as a memento of childhood left in the open. Miksit didn't even hang her undergraduate or law school diplomas. The details of Helen Miksit's personal life were on a need-to-know basis, and as far as Miksit was concerned, no one in her professional life had that need.

Miksit smoothed her St. John knit dress as she sat behind her desk. Heat perched herself on the edge of a chair set on the other side.

"So," Heat began. "I'm sure you've heard about this new ISIS-style beheading video?"

Miksit's face registered immediate disgust. "Yes, of course. But what does that have to do with me? I represent innocent victims of law enforcement overreach, not lunatic fringe-religious zealots."

"We've identified the victim," Heat said. "I'm sorry to say it's Tam Svejda from the *Ledger*. I assume you knew her?"

Miksit's nonverbal reaction told Heat the answer. The blocky lawyer went oval just for a moment as she digested the news.

"Knew her, loved her," Miksit said. "Unlike a lot of her colleagues, she didn't just lap up whatever slop the NYPD was spilling from its trough. She actually cared about the truth and didn't mind getting her hands dirty lifting up rocks to find it. The world would be a better place if there were a thousand more Tam Svejdas, not one less of her."

"You may or may not believe it, but I actually agree with you," Heat said. "That's why I'm hoping you'll help us catch her killers."

"Because of Tam or because of Jameson Rook?" Miksit asked. "I saw the video, Captain. I know they threatened to do your boyfriend next."

"Husband," Heat corrected. "But what does it matter? The end result is the same. We get some garbage off the street."

"Sure," the lawyer said, picking up a pen off her desk and giving it a twirl in her fingers. "But I don't see how I can possibly—"

"I'm told you represent the *New York Ledger* in criminal matters."

"I do."

Here goes nothing, Heat thought. "I'm also told Tam was working on something big when she was killed. Something her editor called 'supernova big.' And I think it might have gotten her killed."

"Might?"

"At this point, this is a lead I'm trying to track down. Someone recently sent her a bullet at the office. We think it might have been some kind of message, like maybe someone was trying to threaten her or scare her off a story."

"I see. And what are you looking for from the *Ledger*?"

"Phone records. Tam's mobile phone was company issued. She used her desk phone as well. I'd like to look through both."

Miksit pushed back in her chair, almost as if she was trying to appraise Heat from a wider angle.

"You're joking, right?" Miksit said. "Oh, no, wait, I get it: I'm being punked. Ashton Kutcher is hiding under Craig's desk and he's going to burst in here any second, right?"

"Helen, please . . ."

"No, no. You don't get to 'Helen, please' me with something like this. You said you needed a favor. A favor is like, 'Hey, I forgot my wallet today, can you buy me a sandwich?' A favor is 'Mind dropping off my dry-cleaning?' This is . . . This isn't a favor. This is asking me to commit a serious ethical breach. And all because you have a half-cocked hunch and some wild story about a bullet? Get real, Captain—"

"Listen, Helen—"

"No, *you* listen. You're a sharp cookie, Heat. So use that big brain of yours to think about it from our perspective for a second. You're asking for permission to go on a wide-open fishing expedition through the phone records of one of that paper's most high-profile and successful reporters, a woman who had more confidential sources than most people have Facebook friends. People talked to her because they trusted her, because they knew she was a *real* journalist who would never burn them, because they knew she would sooner go to jail than reveal her sources.

"Do you have any idea what kind of shit storm there would be if it came out at trial I just let the government sift through her phone calls? Do you have any conception of what that would do to the paper's reputation? People would stop talking to the *Ledger* overnight, and I wouldn't blame them. They might as well convert themselves to a Chamber of Commerce promotional piece because no one would ever take them seriously as a newspaper again."

Heat gritted her teeth. "You're willing to potentially let two brutal murderers get away so you can stand on principle?"

"Look, I'm sorry, Captain. I really am. I'm as big a fan of Tam as there ever was. I want to see you solve this case. But it can't be on this evidence. Some things are bigger than one case, and a free and vibrant press operating outside the purview of government meddling is one of them. You're just going to have to find another way to hang those bastards, because I just can't give you any string here."

Heat considered her possible options. She could go with threats . . .

Well, then I'll just have to hold a press conference and tell the world Helen Miksit sides with terrorists.

Or insults . . .

If you decide to change your mind and grow a conscience, let me know.

Or low blows . . .

I'm sure Tam's parents will appreciate your devotion to the First Amendment.

But ultimately Heat knew she had no leverage, and, in any event, Miksit would only get her back up higher the more Heat pushed. Heat decided on a graceful exit instead.

"Well, I'm sorry to hear that," Heat said. "I guess we're done here."

"I guess we are," Miksit said. "Sorry, Captain."

Heat took a business card and flipped it on the desk as she left.

"In case you have a change of heart," Heat said.

She left without another word.

FIFTEEN

Heat was still smarting from her defeat as she spilled back out onto Church Street.

She checked her phone to see if there was any word from Feller and company, who had probably already kicked in the door to the Harlem apartment of Hassan El-Bashir and Tariq Al-Aman and were right now hauling the men back to the precinct for questioning.

There were no updates. Heat considered her options: She could go back to the Two-Oh and wait for them, or she could take advantage of the fact that she was already downtown and see if Joanna Masters was still hanging around her Greenwich Village apartment, recuperating from her ISIS-inflicted injuries.

The second option won easily. Heat put her phone away and started walking toward the Canal Street subway stop, knowing it would be the quickest way to get there at this point in the afternoon.

But as she got underway, something flashed in the corner of her eye. It was such a small glimpse, it barely even qualified as fleeting. Except suddenly, those old neurons and synapses—the ones that had fired that morning when she saw her mother sitting on that bus shelter bench—were going off again.

What had she just seen? Heat frantically panned left, then right.

And yes. There. On the other side of the street, pushing a cart southbound: a stooped homeless woman.

Except Heat wasn't fooled this time. Nor was she going to allow her mother to get away again.

The afternoon traffic was pouring up Church Street as early birds tried to get a jump on the exodus at the Holland Tunnel. Heat was at the exact midpoint of the block. Running either up or down to the crosswalk would cost her time and wasn't the shortest distance. A straight line was.

Without hesitation and without a second look, Heat hauled out her badge, held it up, and stepped into traffic.

A minivan lay on its breaks and horn at the same time, skidding to a halt just inches from Heat. In the next lane over, the driver of a produce truck also barely came to a stop, flipping Heat a one-finger salute in the process. Then a man in the bicycle lane, his suit pants neatly clipped, had to go up on the sidewalk to avoid hitting her.

"Hey, lady!" he yelled.

Heat didn't pay them any attention. Nor did she notice a pair of pedestrians who were now standing with their backs to a nearby building, staring at Heat like she was a menace to their safety.

"Stop," Heat yelled. "Someone stop that woman!"

Her mother had rounded the corner, just under a banner that read NEW YORK LAW SCHOOL, and was now heading west on Worth Street, out of Nikki's sight.

Was Cynthia Heat going to pull another spy trick on her? Was she going to vanish into some crack in the sidewalk or some crevice in a building as if she had never existed?

No. Not again. Having now crossed the street, Nikki tore toward the corner. She barreled around it at top speed, just barely missing a woman in a pencil skirt who was carrying three cups of afternoon coffee in a cardboard caddy and swore at Heat when it was almost spilled.

Nikki was oblivious to it. All that mattered was that she again had her mother in sight. Cynthia Heat was continuing to scurry west, still stooped over her stolen shopping cart. But unless she had Harry Potter's invisibility cloak tucked under her layers of clothing, she wasn't going to get away this time. Nikki sprinted the final twenty-five yards and grabbed her mother by the shoulders, spinning her around.

"Hey, what's your problem?" the woman howled.

Nikki was now staring her full in the face. It was dirty, weather-lined, sunburned, and while the cheekbones were vaguely familiar, it was definitely not the face of Cynthia Heat.

"Get your hands off me, cop lady," the woman growled. "There ain't no law against being homeless. Not even in Man-freakin'-hattan."

Heat immediately released her grasp. Her face was already flushed with embarrassment. "I'm sorry, ma'am, I thought—"

"I know my rights. I'm gonna find one of these fancy lawyers around here and sue you for police brutality."

"Ma'am, I'm very sorry," Heat said, backing away.

"You damn cops. You're always hassling us. I got rights, you know. I think you hurt my back. I feel a—"

Heat quickly pulled out her wallet and grabbed a twenty-dollar bill. She planted it face up on top of the woman's shopping basket.

"My apologies, ma'am," she said, then began walking away.

"Thank you!" the woman hollered after her. "Bless you! God bless you!"

Heat waved without looking. *God bless me*, Heat thought. And then *Please, God, help me get a grip.*

Four subway stops and four blocks later, Heat had mostly shaken off the bizarre experience of seeing her long-dead mother—or, in this case, not seeing her.

Heat was now standing in front of a classic Greenwich Village brownstone that matched the address she had been able to find for Joanna Masters.

It was an early twentieth-century single-family home that probably cost its original occupants a few thousand dollars and was now worth a few million. That's if it ever went on the market. And homes like that one seldom did.

Heat rang the bell and waited, half wondering if a butler was going to come to the door. Instead, it was a middle-aged woman with shoulder-length brown hair who held herself in a way that made it pretty obvious she was not the help. She was also walking with a cane.

"Can I help you?" she asked.

"Joanna Masters?"

"Yes."

"I'm Nikki Heat. I'm a detective with the NYPD. May I come in, please?"

"What's this about?"

"It's about Tam Svejda."

"Oh, certainly," Masters said, stepping away from the door. "Why don't you join me in here?"

Masters pointed her toward a sitting room whose furnishings perfectly fit the dwelling in which it sat: they were a little old and a little dated, but they told you the person sitting in them had all the money she needed to replace them anytime she chose. And, to be clear, she chose not to.

The Queen Anne–style couch Masters had apparently set up as her sickbed had extra pillows and a blanket. On the coffee table in front of it were two prescription bottles, a glass of some gruesome green concoction that might have been wheatgrass, a box of tissues, and a Michael Connelly novel, half finished.

"A Harry Bosch fan, I take it?" Heat asked.

"That's actually a Mickey Haller. But yes," Masters said as she hobbled in behind Heat. The woman pointed to an antique chair whose wooden arms appeared to have been hand-carved long ago. "Take a seat, please. Can I get you anything to drink? I know you're on duty, but . . . water? Juice?"

Heat declined, then watched as Masters slowly lowered herself back onto the couch, going through an elaborate routine that she had clearly practiced more than once. It ended with Masters contorted into a half seated, half lying position with the cane propped next to her.

"How are you feeling?" Heat asked.

"Some days are better than others," Masters said. "My advice to you is if you're going to get shot, don't. But if you have a choice, try not to get shot in the back. You don't realize how much you use your back for everything until it stops working so well. Though they tell me I'm lucky. Had the bullet been two inches over I would have probably been paralyzed. Or dead."

Masters let that somber thought linger for a moment. "Anyhow, I doubt the NYPD is coming here for a medical update. What's this about Tam? Is she okay?"

Heat looked around the room. There was no television, no sign of a device with Internet connectivity. There were only old newspapers stacked a safe distance away from the fireplace—meaning Joanna Masters likely got her news the same way the brownstone's original inhabitants did.

"I'm sorry, Joanna," Heat said. "Tam has been murdered."

As Heat told Masters about the video, the woman gasped several times. Heat could sense a kind of post-traumatic stress reaction from the former Red Cross volunteer, who had clearly envisioned herself meeting a similar end more than once.

"Those . . . those *animals*," she said when Heat was through. "It's like life means nothing to them."

"I guess you've experienced that firsthand."

"You can only imagine," Masters said.

"Do you mind talking about what happened to you over there?"

"No, I . . . I guess not."

"You were there as a Red Cross volunteer, is that right?"

"Yes. I know to a lot my friends around here that makes me very strange. I've had a . . . a very comfortable life, Detective Heat. I don't say that to brag, I just . . . Well, it's the truth. It's not like I did anything to deserve being born into a wealthy family. And I'm certainly not complaining. It's just that, I don't know, I reached a point in my life where going to the latest benefit to help the next art museum, hospital, or pet shelter just didn't feel like enough. I needed . . . more of a sense of purpose than that."

"I understand," Heat said.

"I had been a donor to the Red Cross since, gosh, I can't even remember. My father had been on the board there, so I was on the board there. And I kept seeing these images their volunteers brought back of these people in Syria, who . . . who . . ."

"Had nothing?"

"No, that's just it," Masters said, propping herself up in her sickbed. "They actually weren't the prototype of the bedraggled, wretched, rag-wearing refugee, where you couldn't really see yourself in them. They were people who had been doctors and lawyers and shopkeepers. Just . . . ordinary people, the kind of people we pass every day on the streets of New York. Except, through absolutely no fault of their own, this civil war had turned their lives upside down and inside out. And here I was, living in my brownstone, scooting out to my cottage in the Hamptons like all my friends, and I couldn't do it anymore. I felt like I had been charged by this knowledge and I had to do more than write checks.

"So I signed up. All my society friends thought I was suffering from some kind of midlife crisis. It was like, 'Uh-oh, here comes Joanna's big crusade.' Even the people at the Red Cross tried to talk me out of it. But I was willing to pay my own way, and they really did need the help. So off I went."

Masters smiled and cocked her head. "This is usually the part where people start looking at me like what I really needed was a good shrink. Why aren't you, Detective Heat?"

"Because I understand that life sometimes presents you with situations where you feel you have no choice but to react in a certain way," Heat said. "Because if you don't, it turns out you're not the person you thought you were."

"Yes . . . Yes, I suppose that's it. Would you mind if I used that explanation with my friends?"

"Be my guest," Heat said.

Masters cleared her throat. "Anyway, I'll skip the travelogue part, because I sense that's not what you're interested in. Suffice it to say, I had been in the country for about a month, and was just outside a city called Deir ez-Zor. It's in the eastern part of the country and it sits along two fairly major roads—M-20 and Route 4—which made it a pass-through point for a lot of refugees. It's also probably the largest city close to the Iraq border, so it's been a battleground for several years now.

"ISIS was shooting at anything that tried to come into the city's airport. They weren't even allowing humanitarian aid to be flown in. Meanwhile, they literally had parts of the city under siege, not letting anything in or out. I think it was part of their strategy to starve civilians into submission. I was part of a truck convoy that was trying to break through with food, water, and medicine. We were in one of the northern suburbs when a detachment of ISIS fighters came upon us."

Masters's gaze was fixed on some indeterminable point in the distance. Heat could tell a part of her was no longer in a New York brownstone, but, rather, had been transported half a world away.

"The sad thing was, we were actually trying to give them some food," she continued. "They had been separated from their supply line and they were clearly hungry and we . . . Well, maybe it was partly a bribe for them to leave us alone, but there was a real humanitarian impulse there, too.

"I couldn't tell you what exactly was said. Our convoy leader was trying to convince them we were there as peaceful aid workers, working under the auspices of the Geneva Convention. But, of course, the Geneva Convention is . . . well, it's not even a joke to those people. It might as well have been negotiated by an alien species. These ISIS fighters are mostly young and illiterate. Half of them are fighting because they just don't know any better or because someone has promised them sex or food or money. They only know what their imams and their leaders tell them."

Masters paused and took a drink of her wheatgrass.

"Anyhow," she said as she put the glass back down, "things broke down pretty quickly, and the next thing I knew they were shooting at us. We started running toward the trucks, but a bullet caught me in the back first. Thank God one of my fellow volunteers was this big burly Turkish guy or else I probably would have ended up like Tam, with a starring role in some awful video. He scooped me up with one arm like I was a rag doll, stuck me in the back of the truck, and we outran them. From there it's been all hospitals and visits from Red Cross executives who are nervous they've lost a donor."

Heat smiled. Masters gave a polite chuckle.

"That's the short version," Masters said. "I could give you the long version, but . . . well, not that I mind the company—as you can see, it's just me here. But what does any of this have to do with Tam? Do you think they picked her because she wrote about me?"

"I'm not sure, to be honest," Heat said. "That's why I'm here. Had you been in touch with Tam recently?"

"No. Not really. Not since the story. I mean, she called me the next day, to see if I liked it, but that was it, really."

"Was she planning on doing any kind of follow-up?"

"I don't . . . I don't think so. Not that she told me. We were pretty much done as far as I was concerned. She told me she was going to give me my bullet back when she was through with it, but—"

"Wait. Your bullet?"

"Oh, yeah," Masters said. "I guess that's part of the long version. I eventually ended up in Istanbul. The bullet had lodged next to my spine. It was a pretty delicate surgery to get it out. When they were done, they gave it to me, like, I don't know, a present or something. When I showed it to Tam she got very interested. She asked if she could borrow it. I said, 'Sure, why not?' It felt kind of creepy to keep it around, to be honest. She said she was going to give it back. But, honestly, if she forgot, I wouldn't have made an issue out of it."

"Is this the bullet?" Heat asked, pulling the evidence bag containing the deformed slug out of her half pocket and dangling it in front of Masters.

"Yes, that's it. Where did you get it?"

"It was on her computer at work," Heat said. "We thought maybe someone had sent it to her as a threat or something."

"No, that's just my little old bullet, dug out of my little old back."

"But what was . . . What was Tam planning on doing with it? Was she working on some kind of story?" Heat asked, genuinely perplexed.

When the NYPD removed a slug out of a victim—like the one recently plucked from Ochoa's buttock—it was sent to ballistics for testing. But that was in an attempt to match it to the gun of the shooter. It's not like there was some great mystery as to who the shooter was in this case. And, in any event, there was no recourse even if they did figure out which illiterate ISIS teenager fired the shot. The boy was probably dead now himself.

"Search me," Masters said.

"Do you mind if I hang on to it for a while?" Heat asked.

"Suit yourself. Believe me, I don't need it."

Heat wasn't sure if she did, either. But her every instinct told her this bullet and Tam Svejda's death were two parts of one story. She just didn't have all the connective tissue to put it together yet.

Nikki Heat didn't believe in the occult. She left that to Rook and his active imagination. But she almost felt like Tam was trying to reach out to her through that bullet, to whisper the one secret that would help Heat make sense of everything.

She couldn't quite hear what Tam was saying. Not yet. But as she departed Joanna Masters's house, having pumped her dry of any further information and then refilled her glass of wheatgrass, Heat was determined to continue listening.

SIXTEEN

The shouting was loud enough that Heat could hear it even before the elevator doors to the Twentieth Precinct detective bull pen slid open.

"So you're trying to say you *weren't* aiming for me?" Ochoa was bellowing.

The doors parted. For the second time that afternoon, Heat was looking at a middle-aged person whose locomotion required the aid of a cane. Miguel Ochoa was standing stiffly next to a chair that already had a pillow placed on it. He was, rather pointedly, not sitting down.

"How could I have been aiming for you?" Raley yelled back. "I hit *asphalt* first! Did you miss that part of the report?"

"You hear that, right? You hear him dragging out the *s*, don't you?" Ochoa said to Rhymer, who seemed to be listening sympathetically. "He said *ass*-phalt. Is this fun for you, homes? Huh? You enjoying yourself?"

Heat sidled up to Feller, who looked like all he needed was a beer in front of him to turn this into an outing at the comedy club.

"Ballistics came back on the slug they pulled out of Ochoa's caboose," Feller said, then tilted his head toward Raley. "It seems this is another sad case of leprechaun on Mexican violence."

Raley turned toward Feller.

"I did *not* shoot him. I shot the asph—"

Raley saw Ochoa's eyes going wide. "The pavement," he corrected himself. "My bullet struck the ground first, then unfortunately and *accidentally* ricocheted into Ochoa."

"Accident, huh," Ochoa said. "And this 'accident' just 'accidentally' happened on the eighteenth."

"What are you talking about?" Raley asked.

"A day when I'm squad leader," Ochoa said.

"That is the most rid—"

"When you were clearly seething with jealousy because I—properly, I might add—introduced myself as detective squad leader to Lana Kline. That, homes, is motive. And I think it's pretty clear means and opportunity were not in question."

"Would you stop it, already? Did you miss the beginning of that ballistics report? It said the bullet skipped off the assss-phalt, you assh—"

"Okay," Heat broke in. "So not that this isn't charming, watching you two practice your act for Gorgeous Ladies of Wrestling, but can I ask for a status update on our ISIS case?"

As Raley and Ochoa continued staring each other down, Feller jumped in.

"We got Jihad Johnny and Taliban Timmy in Interrogation One right now," he said. "But so far they ain't said anything."

"You detained them peacefully?" Heat asked.

"If you consider getting called a motherfucker fifteen times 'peaceful.' Yeah. No incidents."

"And is ECT going through their apartment right now?"

"Affirmative," Feller said. "So far, all we can confirm is that the suspects are guilty of leaving their dishes in the sink. But our guys are going to turn the place inside out. I'm sure they'll get something."

"What about you? You got anything new?" Raley asked.

Heat told them about her dead end at Miksit's office, but also about the bullet she and Rook found on Tam's desk, its link to Joanna Masters, and its unclear significance.

"So I'm just not making much traction so far on what Tam was doing and whether it had anything to do with her abduction," Heat finished.

"Well, I'm not sure I can shed a ton of light on that," Raley said, ignoring Ochoa's continued glares. "But I did have a chance to pull Tam's financials. It's all pretty ordinary up until Wednesday, when she got herself a plane ticket to Cleveland for the next day."

"Cleveland?" Heat said. "What would possibly take a New York-based metro reporter to Cleveland?"

"Don't know. She rented a car at Cleveland Hopkins International Airport. The next charge is dinner at a restaurant called Jackalope Lakeside in Lorain, Ohio."

"Too bad Rook's not here," Feller interjected. "We'd learn all about the mythology of the great horned hare."

"You know, a mammal's horns are actually made of the same substance as human hair," Raley said.

"Aaaaand it's like he never left," Feller said.

"Anyhow, the next charge after that is the Motel 6 in Lorain. Then we're on to breakfast the next morning at a place called Mutt and Jeff's. Then . . . nothing."

"Nothing?"

"The last charge was processed at 7:54 A.M. Friday morning."

"So she was kidnapped from somewhere in Ohio?"

"Possibly. Or Lorain was just a convenient stopping point. Lorain is near the interstate. She could have driven anywhere from there."

Heat's expression as she pondered this looked as if she were sucking on a lemon.

"Was the rental car returned?" Heat asked.

"Negative."

"All right. Contact Ohio State Police and have them put a BOLO on the rental car."

"Already did it," Raley said. "Nothing so far."

"Well, since we're bothering our friends in flyover country already, why don't you e-mail a photo of Tam to Lorain PD?" Heat said. "Ask them to pass it around at Mutt and Jeff's and the Jacka-whatever and see if anyone talked to Tam or had an inkling what she was up to."

"Will do," Raley said.

"And do you still have those printouts from the surveillance video taken outside the mosque?"

"Yes, sir."

"Great. I'll take them off your hands."

Raley walked over to his desk and lifted a manila folder.

"There's a few other items of interest in there, Captain. Muharib Qawi sent us some of what El-Bashir and Al-Aman posted on the Web. It's . . . pretty startling."

He handed the folder to Heat.

"Thanks. Opie?" Heat said, looking at Detective Rhymer. "Can I give you a job?"

"Yes, Captain."

She nodded toward Roach. "Keep these two from killing each other while I'm gone. Feller?"

"Yes, sir," Feller said.

"Show me to your suspects."

Hassan El-Bashir and Tariq Al-Aman had been placed in separate inter- rogation rooms—all the better to expose inconsistencies in their stories and then play them against each other. Heat started with El-Bashir.

At least at one point, he had been less adherent to Islam. Maybe, Heat reasoned, that made him less radical now. And that, in turn, might make him easier to break.

This much was clear: the young man standing in the corner with his hands cuffed was very different from the one who had sneered at an NYPD camera as a teenager. His chin was now covered in a bushy beard that would have made any Brooklyn hipster proud. His head was wrapped in a turban.

There wasn't much recognizable about him, except for the scowl. That hadn't changed a bit.

"Man, this is bullshit, I ain't done nothing," El-Bashir announced as soon as she entered the room.

"Hello, Hassan, my name is Captain Nikki Heat. I'm the commander here at the Twentieth Precinct. Please have a seat. We need to talk."

"Fuck that," El-Bashir said, still standing, now crossing his arms.

"Look, Hassan, there are two ways this can go. One, you can have a seat and we can talk. Or, two, I can ship you right out to Rikers, where due to a paperwork slipup, we'll put you in with the white supremacists and accidentally mention that you're a terrorist who cut off a pretty white girl's head. Maybe we'll even show them the video, just to see if it gives them any ideas. Up to you."

"Fuck you."

"Okay. Next bus leaves for Rikers in about twenty minutes. Have a nice trip and pray all they do is pin you down and give you an Aryan Nations neck tattoo."

Heat stood up. El-Bashir sat down.

"Good choice," Heat said.

"Look, I told this to the other guy: I didn't do nothing. I don't know nothing about this girl, or no beheading, or nothing like that. Just because I'm Muslim don't make me a terrorist. Damn. I'm an American, just like you."

"No, you're right, Hassan. Being a Muslim doesn't make you a terrorist. This is what makes us think you're a terrorist."

Heat pulled a sheet out of the manila folder Raley handed her and began reading:

"'I will cast terror into the hearts of those who disbelieve. Therefore strike off their heads and strike off every fingertip of them. Quran 8:12,'" Heat said. "That was what you wrote on Facebook on September eleventh, Hassan."

El-Bashir didn't reply.

"I've got another one, too," Heat said, then read: "'Oh, Prophet! Strive hard against the unbelievers and the hypocrites and be unyielding to them; and their abode is hell, and evil is the destination. Quran 9:73.'"

Finally El-Bashir spat out: "That motherfucker."

"What are you talking about, Hassan?"

"Imam Qawi gave that to you, didn't he? He's like a motherfuckin' Muslim Uncle Tom."

"Maybe. But you're still the one who wrote it on Facebook."

"Whether I did or I didn't, that don't make it illegal. Damn, ain't you ever heard of freedom of speech?"

"I have. I've also heard of surveillance cameras. Tell me about this."

Heat slid a still photo of Hassan El-Bashir just as he was entering Masjid al-Jannah.

"That was taken around eleven o'clock Saturday night. We've got another one showing you leaving about two hours later."

"What, now it's illegal to go to mosque at night?" El-Bashir growled.

"No. But that just so happens to be the exact time that my medical examiner tells me our victim was killed. Care to explain that?"

El-Bashir sat in stony silence.

"Why Tam, anyway? Was it because of something she wrote? Something she was going to write?"

El-Bashir continued staring straight ahead.

"Hassan, none of this looks very good for you. We've got you at the crime scene at the time when the murder occurred. We've got our crime scene people crawling through your apartment right now. Maybe they'll find the murder weapon, maybe they won't. But there's something I can guarantee you they will find. Tam Svejda lost an awful lot of blood when you chopped her head off and I don't know if you know this about blood, but it gets *everywhere*. Even if you think you've cleaned it, it's still there. So we'll find some. And when we do, we'll match it to Tam, and that will be it."

This animated El-Bashir again.

"You ain't gonna find shit, because I ain't done shit," he said defiantly. "Look, your boy showed me that video. I don't know who those motherfuckers were, but it wasn't me and Tariq. That don't even sound like us."

"The voices were digitally disguised, Hassan."

"Yeah, but damn, we don't talk like that. All that 'imperial Yankee scum' stuff. Yo, I'm from here. I *root* for the Yankees, okay? I cried the day Derek Jeter retired."

"Look, Hassan," Heat said, folding her hands in front of her. "I'll be honest. You're in a world of trouble. And nothing is going to keep you out of prison for a long, long time at this point. But you really *can* make things better for yourself if you start cooperating. I've noticed something on that video, and it's something that I think is going to help us both out."

El-Bashir didn't reply. He was now looking at her with genuine curiosity.

"You and Tariq keep looking just to the left of the camera. You're looking at someone, aren't you?"

"Man, I keep telling you, that wasn't—"

"You're going to tell me who that someone is, and it's going to make both of our lives a lot easier. You tell me who was calling the shots and I'll make sure you're treated as well as possible. They have Muslim-only cell blocks. You'll be safer there. You just tell me who made you do this, sign a confession, and I'll make sure you're treated with dignity."

El-Bashir stood back up. "Oh, no. No, no. Don't you go talking about no confession. I read enough of those stories about black dudes who got put away for shit they didn't do, and it always starts with a bullshit confession that they got tricked into signing. Nuh-uh. I ain't playing that game. This is like some *Twilight Zone* shit here. Don't you come near me with no motherfucking confession. This *is* being taped, right?"

He started looking around wildly for a camera. "I didn't sign no fuckin' confession, okay? You hear that? I ain't confessing shit."

"Sit down, Hassan."

Just then, Feller broke into the room, half out of breath.

"Captain, Captain," he said. "We got a confession. Al-Aman confessed!"

"He *what*?" El-Bashir burst out.

"Shut up, shit bird, I ain't talking to you," Feller said, then turned back to Heat. "He admitted they had Tam at the mosque already on Saturday night, and that they were coming back to finish the job. He said he didn't want to do it, but shit bird here made him. He said his roommate brainwashed him with Muslim mumbo jumbo and got his head all turned around. He also said shit bird was the one who did the cutting."

"Oh, my God, no way. No way. He's lying. He's lying!" El-Bashir screamed. He was now clutching his turban with both hands.

"The only thing we haven't gotten from him yet is whoever the big boss is," Feller continued. "I guess whoever tells us first gets the best deal from the D.A., right?"

"Yep," Heat said. "That's how it usually works."

"No, no. That is *not* how this works, because this is some bullshit! This is . . . I don't know what y'all did to Tariq or what crazy pills you made him take, but he is lying! He is lying his fool head off. There's no way you can believe him."

El-Bashir sat back down and leaned across the table, his eyes wide and wild.

"Look, yes, we were in the mosque, okay?" he said. "We were

there for two hours, it's true. But all we were doing was Skyping. We don't have Internet access in our apartment, so we use the computer at Masjid al-Jannah. Eleven o'clock New York time is six A.M. in Riyadh. There's an imam there, he gets on the computer and talks with us after his morning prayers. But that's it. All we did was talk. If you go on the computer and load up Skype, you'll see he's one of the contacts. You can ask him if you want or . . . I don't know, can't you check the computer and see when it's been used to make calls or something? Please. I'm begging you."

"Sorry, shit bird. But even if you were Skyping, that doesn't prove squat," Feller said. "How do we know you didn't just pull up that imam so he could tell you the proper Islamic way to behead someone? Or so he could watch your progress and give you critiques?"

"Holy fucking shit," was all El-Bashir could say.

"Was that who you were looking at to the side of the camera, Hassan?" Heat asked. "Not an actual person but a computer monitor image of an imam in Saudi Arabia?"

"That's it," El-Bashir said, standing up again. "Y'all are straight trippin'. It's like everything I say, you just twist it like cops do. I want a lawyer. Right now. I want a motherfuckin' lawyer."

Heat stared at him for a long moment. She was now on shaky ground legally. The interrogation *was* being recorded. The moment the suspect invoked his right to counsel, she had to stop the interview. She was aware of trials where *everything*, even righteous confessions, said after the suspect asked for a lawyer were later ruled inadmissible.

"All right, Hassan," Heat said. "If that's what you want. Your lawyer will have to meet you at Rikers, of course. Because as far as I'm concerned this interview is over."

"Fuck yeah, it's over," he said. "I don't care if Tariq has gone cuckoo for Cocoa Puffs, you ain't getting no bullshit confession out of me."

Heat stood up and followed Feller out of the room.

"Good work on Tariq," Heat said as soon as the door closed. "Is he working on the confession right now or has he already signed something?"

"Are you kidding me? The only thing he's said the whole time is 'lawyer, lawyer, lawyer,'" Feller said. "I could tell Hassan was about to lawyer up, too. I figured the ol' false confession trick was worth a try."

Heat just shook her head. "For what it's worth, you even had me going for a second."

"I know," Feller said, then smiled broadly. "Maybe I ought to talk to Rook's mom about getting an agent. My talents are being wasted this far off Broadway."

Heat was about to make a joke about Feller's future in Actors' Equity when she heard a voice coming from the bull pen.

It was a voice she knew all too well.

SEVENTEEN

"Jamie's not here?" Yardley Bell was saying, sounding some combination of disappointed and put out. "Oh, that is *such* a pity. I really was looking forward to catching up with him."

Heat rounded the corner to see a slender, attractive brunette dressed in a sharply tailored pantsuit. Captain Heat and Department of Homeland Security Agent Bell were more alike than either woman would have wanted to admit. In addition to having the same coloring and build, they had the same professional ferocity and the same weakness for the substantial charms of Jameson Rook.

Despite that source of antagonism and the natural antipathy that came from representing different levels of government, the women had overcome a contentious start to their relationship and forged a detente. So, at least in theory, Heat should not have been displeased to see Bell.

Except Heat knew Bell hadn't simply shown up at the Twentieth Precinct to exchange pleasantries with her and the other detectives. Nor was Bell curious about whatever her ex-boyfriend was up to.

This had two possible endings. One went badly. The other went worse.

"Hello, Agent Bell," Heat said, feeling a sudden pressure in her sinuses as she spoke.

"Oh, really, after all this time, it's 'Agent Bell?' Honestly, 'Captain Heat,' I thought we were past that."

Bell was joined by two beefy agents who, between them, had perhaps half a neck. That confirmed for Heat everything she needed to know. There was only one reason why a Department of Homeland Security Agent would show up at the Twentieth Precinct with two agents—and probably an SUV parked outside.

"You're not taking my suspects, Yardley," Heat said, jamming her hands on her hips.

Bell, who had obviously been hoping to soft sell the purpose of her mission, looked down at the carpet for a moment, almost like she was embarrassed for Heat.

"Oh, Nikki, let's not make this difficult. I'm afraid they're not your suspects anymore."

"The hell they're not. This is a murder. Since when is murder not the purview of the local jurisdiction?"

"Sorry, but you're not the only one who subpoenaed Tam Svejda's credit card information, you know. We know she was in Ohio."

"You wouldn't have even known the identity of the victim if it weren't for us."

"You and the *New York Ledger*'s Web site," Bell said. "Be that as it may, there is clear evidence the victim was transported across state lines, which makes it our case. Kidnapping makes it our case, too. Plus, these men were already on the Terrorist Watch List—their Facebook posts had gotten our agents' attention. And this is an act of domestic terrorism, with potential ties to international terrorism. So that's at least five ways in which these are now our suspects. Plus there are . . . diplomatic considerations."

"What does that mean?" Heat asked.

"Let's just say there are things ISIS might be willing to give us in exchange for the right prisoners."

"But they're not even real ISIS," Ochoa said. "They're a couple of kids from New York."

"Yes, but ISIS hardly knows that, now do they?" Bell said. "Our operatives are already picking up chatter that the 'New York video'— that's what they're calling it—has been very popular over there. The stars of that video could be viewed as a very valuable commodity."

"So, what, a prisoner exchange?" Heat said. "Two of ours for two of theirs?"

"No, no," Bell said. "The United States does not negotiate with hostage-takers. That's a longstanding policy. If we broke that, it would be open season on Americans around the globe."

"What, then?" Heat asked. "What else could be worth not giving these two scumbags the punishment they deserve? Some American company that gives generously to its federally elected officials gets to keep tapping some oil well over there?"

Bell just smiled. "I've probably said too much already. All you need to know is that your government appreciates your cooperation. And your confidence."

"You're saying we're not only going to let two murderers go free, we're going to keep our mouths shut about it?" Ochoa said, making a face like the thought of it hurt him even more than the slug the doctors had recently dug out of his posterior.

"Welcome to the world of international relations, where you can have your morality in whatever color you like, so long as it's gray," Bell said.

"Unbelievable," Ochoa muttered.

"Oh, and I almost forgot reason number six these guys are ours now," Bell said, pulling two sheets of tri-folded paper out of the breast pocket of her suit coat. "We've got a judge's order. Habeas corpus. That's Latin for 'seize the body,' you know. In English, it means 'sorry, Nikki, you're going to have to turn them over.'"

Bell held the papers between two fingers. Heat stalked over and snatched them. Sure enough, it was an order issued by a federal judge from the Eastern District of New York.

Heat frowned at it, some combination of furious and impotent, knowing there was little she could do to fight it. No matter what a judge had to say about it, she had no intention of stopping work on this case. Not as long as Rook was still in danger. Not as long as she still suspected there was a greater threat out there, one that went beyond two New York kids who got some twisted ideas about Islam in their heads.

But if she even tried to escalate a local vs. federal turf war right now, it would result in a phone call from The Hammer, who would casually mention that he had just come from the commissioner's office, where everyone was pleased this was no longer the NYPD's problem. And, oh, by the way, how were her CompStat numbers looking?

"You should know, the Department of Homeland Security greatly appreciates the solid work of the NYPD," Bell said, as if the case were already wrapped up. "You really did a great job identifying the victim and the place where the crime was committed. We'll be sure to mention that when we announce the charges. We'll even let you stand in the background at the press conference if you'd like. It'd be nice to have someone from the NYPD near the podium anyway. The taxpayers do love to see interagency cooperation."

"Oh, yeah, that'd be great, Yards," Heat said, with acid sweetness. "Can I wear my police blues or would DHS rather skip the pretense and have me dress up like a monkey?"

Bell put on a pouty face. "Nikki, honestly, don't be like this. Did you seriously think this was going to stay your case? What did you think, that you'd transfer these two knuckleheads out to that zoo at Rikers Island? Because let me tell you what would happen out there. One, they'd radicalize the entire Muslim inmate population. And, two, the real ISIS would decide that it would be a marvelous plan to send some heavy-hitter jihadists over here to break them out. Can you imagine what a coup that would be for them? To make America look weak and incompetent on its own soil? You know it wouldn't be that difficult with that Swiss-cheese jail of yours."

Bell shook her head. "Sorry, Nikki. You know this isn't personal. We just have resources you don't. And needs you don't. This is bigger than your case clearance rate. You have to see that."

There was an uncomfortable silence. Ochoa shifted his weight, having already made his thoughts on the matter clear. Raley coughed needlessly. Feller crossed his arms. Rhymer was rocking back and forth between the balls of his feet and the heels.

But they were all looking at her. She could feel their eyes on her, and again, she knew she was being evaluated. What kind of leader was she? Would she stick up for her squad, for her department? Was she tough enough to tell the federal government to go and shove it, because this was the NYPD's case through and through?

She wanted them to know she'd battle for them; she'd battle for justice, tooth and nail and then some.

But, ultimately, there is a fine line between brave opposition and pointless resistance. And this was clearly an instance where trying to get in the Department of Homeland Security's way would put her on the wrong side of it. Heat reminded herself of an axiom her mother had taught her long ago: Sometimes a good run beats a bad stand.

"They're in the interrogation rooms," Heat said. "You should know they've both invoked their right to counsel. I don't think you're going to get anything more out of them."

"Thank you," Bell said. "We'll be sending a refrigerated truck over for the body tomorrow. I trust the victim can stay in your morgue overnight?"

"That's fine."

"Are there any investigative leads you've been working on that we can follow up on?" Bell asked.

"Other than what we got from her credit card company? Not a thing," Heat lied without skipping a beat. "And then there's whatever our Evidence Collection Team is getting from the suspects' apartment. But I suppose that's yours now, too. Otherwise, I trust you'll keep us apprised of the progress of your investigation?"

"Absolutely," Bell lied back. "I assume you've made contact with next of kin? You must have, since you notified the media."

"We did," Heat said. "Are you going to tell them that the brutal thugs who killed their daughter are going to be used as bargaining chips so gas can stay at two bucks a gallon?"

"No, of course not. And I don't even know if this has to do with oil. But just to ease your mind, yes, the family will be told that El-Bashir and Al-Aman have taken a plea deal to spare themselves the death penalty and are being sent to solitary confinement in a supermax prison for the rest of their lives. They'll be diverted at some point after that. The family will then be told each man attacked a guard and was killed during the altercation. That's if the deal goes through. But that's above my pay grade."

Bell read the incredulous looks around the room. "Look, guys, this is the way the world works, okay? I don't like it any more than you do sometimes. But there are considerations here that are bigger than any of us in this room can imagine. Sometimes we're all just extras who have to play our roles."

"This movie stinks," Raley muttered.

"Homes, if I had Jujyfruits, I'd be throwing them at the screen," Ochoa said, momentarily forgetting his feud with Raley. There was suddenly a bigger enemy in the room.

Bell ignored them. She clapped her hands together and smiled like they had been finalizing plans for a Labor Day picnic. "Well, I guess that just about covers everything."

"I guess it does," Heat said.

"It's been great seeing you again," Bell said. "And you'll tell Jamie I said hello?"

"Naturally," Heat said.

Which was just one more lie.

Heat could feel her detectives' energy sag as the no-neck guys from the Department of Homeland Security big-footed their way around, collecting El-Bashir and Al-Aman, then signing the appropriate paperwork.

Rather than witness the rapid demoralization of her squad, Heat retreated to her office and took a quick pass through the enormous list of unread e-mail that had piled up, only answering if she was sure ignoring it would get her fired.

Once Bell and her underlings were gone, Heat returned to the bull pen. Her detectives were all in various phases of shuffling meaningless paperwork around their desks, getting ready to go home for the day.

"Okay, guys," she said. "Back to work."

"What do you mean?" Feller huffed. "You just let the feds take our suspects so they can be part of something so big that us little people can't possibly understand."

"Yeah, but they didn't take what matters most."

"What's that?"

"Our information," Heat said.

"What are you talking about, Captain?" Ochoa said, rising from his throne of pillows and limping toward her.

"I can't believe I'm about to say this, but there is exactly one way we're going to ensure that Tariq Al-Aman and Hassan El-Bashir face justice in America."

"And how is that?"

"We're going to take everything we learn and leak it to the *New York Ledger.*"

Faces went slack. Jaws hung open. Heads tilted.

Dogs had just thrown their lot in with cats. Oil and water had just announced they were planning to have a nice mixer. Republicans had just decided they'd just go with whatever the Democrats said. Heat couldn't have shocked them more if she'd declared she was quitting her job to go work for a defense attorney.

Opie recovered first. Barely. "But . . . Captain," he stammered. "Can you . . . Can you do that? I mean, *goll-lleee!*"

"No. Of course not. Which is why we are all going to keep this quiet. If any of you don't want to be part of this, I totally understand. We'll just pretend this conversation never—"

"That's not even a question," Raley said. "We're in. Right, guys?"

"Yup," Rhymer said.

"Damn straight," Feller said.

"No doubt," Ochoa said.

Raley continued, "The only real question is: Do you think it'll work?"

"Spooks love to operate in the shadows," Heat said. "It's their world. So we're going to make sure there is so much light on this case they have nowhere to hide. We're going to cultivate evidence exactly the way we normally would, and then we're going to turn it over to the *Ledger.* Every leak is going to be a front page, and then you know other media outlets will follow. If we do it right, the fact that the *Ledger* is owning the story about its fallen colleague so thoroughly will become its own story.

"The Yardley Bells of the world rely on the fact that people eventually stop paying attention. They thrive on what they can do when everyone else's heads are turned. We have to make sure that no one forgets for half a second that Hassan El-Bashir and Tariq Al-Aman are in US custody, awaiting trial for their crimes. By the time we're done, they'll be celebrities wherever they go. They'll be too conspicuous to possibly slip out of the system unnoticed."

"Using the press like a pair of brass knuckles," Ochoa said, smiling. "I like it."

"And Tam would love it," Raley said, piggybacking on his partner's point. "I know you're all about honoring the victim, Captain. I do believe you've chosen the best way possible."

"I've developed a bit of a relationship with Tam's editor," Heat said. "I'll find a way to communicate with him in a way that won't come back to any of us. I'm sure he'll jump at the chance."

"Okay, so what do we do next?" Raley asked.

"We need to keep cultivating information so we can continue to feed the beast," Heat said. "One thing we need to get a better handle on is how they got Tam in there in the first place. We know they didn't bring her in the front entrance. So it had to be the back entrance."

"No cameras, I checked already," Raley said.

"I know. But someone had to see something back there. Opie and Randy, I know you guys were doing some canvassing around the alley where the Dumpster is. But can you shift a few doors up this time? I want us to talk to anyone whose apartment has a view of the back of the mosque."

"You got it," Feller said.

"I've also got a thought for something the king of all surveillance media could do."

"His Highness is at your service."

"We now have a pretty good sample of both El-Bashir and Al-Aman talking in the interrogation rooms. Can you see if you can start stripping away the filter on the original video and then see if you can match it to those new samples? Maybe if you can even restore some of the video, the computer will be able to find similarities our ears can't."

"Got it," Raley said.

"What about me?" Ochoa said.

"Go home. Take some painkillers. Lie on your belly. You've put in your pound of flesh for the day."

"No can do, Cap. If these guys are working, I have to be, too. That's how it works. I've always wanted to go to Cleveland, you know. Maybe this is my chance."

Heat shook her head. "No. A well-dressed limping Mexican-American with a cane would attract way too much attention no matter where he went. I can't have you playing secret cop on turf we don't control. Plus, I'm guessing Lorain, Ohio, is not exactly a throbbing metropolis. If the feds are there, too, they'll get wind of you in about six seconds."

Feller piped up: "We could use another pair of shoes to pound the pavement with us on the canvass."

"Good idea, Randy. Sound good, Oach?"

"You got it."

Heat looked down at her watch. It was after six o'clock.

"Okay, where *is* Aguinaldo, anyway?" Heat said. "Has anyone heard from her?"

From the far side of the bull pen, the elevator pinged. The doors slid open and, as if Heat had summoned her by rubbing the side of a magic lamp, Inez Aguinaldo appeared.

"Let's be very clear about one thing," she said. "I am *never* going shopping again."

EIGHTEEN

Her hair, whose ponytail normally remained neatly within its cage, had gone free range.

Her face, whose makeup needs were typically met by a biannual trip to her local drugstore, looked like ground zero for a Clinique Bonus Week bomb.

Her walk, ordinarily so straight and even, had a wobble to it brought on by the absence of the heel in her left shoe.

"Oh, my," Ochoa said. "Look at this."

Feller let out a low whistle.

"Gentlemen," Raley said, "I think it's pretty clear there's only one proper way for us to respond to this development."

"Insult-off?" Ochoa said, raising his eyebrows.

"Insult-off," Raley confirmed.

"What's that?" Opie asked.

"It's like a Bake-Off. But with insults," Raley explained. "Twenty bucks a head. Winner takes all."

Before Aguinaldo could even summon a protest, Ochoa, Feller, and Raley had whipped out their wallets and produced three twenty-dollar bills, which they threw on the desk in front of Feller.

"I want to go first," Ochoa said. "How about: 'Damn, girl, why didn't you tell me they were doing auditions for *The Walking Dead*?'"

Feller tried next. "See, that's good. But I was going to go with: 'I didn't realize the circus was in town. Does Mrs. Bozo the Clown know you've been sucking face with her husband?'"

Raley finished it off. "Naw, you guys are trying too hard. Be a little more subtle, like: 'Hey, I like your blush. I think I saw it on sale at Home Depot last weekend.'"

"Ohh, good one," Ochoa said. "Okay, Inez, you get to decide. Who's the winner?"

Aguinaldo watched them bat her hardship around without amusement. "You guys are super funny. I'm really laughing," she said in a perfectly flat tone.

Heat was trying not to show any reaction. But then, as Aguinaldo drew nearer, Heat wrinkled her nose, having detected a bouquet of aromas that could never exist together in nature—some combination of lavender, rose hips, vanilla, chamomile, and combat-strength insecticide.

"What . . . what is that smell?" Heat asked.

"Do you know how many times I've been sprayed today?" Aguinaldo said. "Those girls who work at the fragrance counters, they look all harmless. But they're really like perfume ninjas. All you do is walk through and they come up to you and start a conversation. And it's like, 'Hello'—squirt—'how'—squirt—'are'—squirt, 'you'—squirt, squirt—'today?' Squirt. And then, once they've stunned you, they hit you with another round. They are like walking quality-of-life crimes."

Heat involuntarily drew back.

"Look, tomorrow?" Aguinaldo continued. "If you need someone to canvass the housing projects? I'm in. Wake up sleeping bums and interview them? No problem. Go undercover as a drag queen? Just strap on a dick and an Adam's apple and I'm there. But whatever you do, do *not* ask me to do 5th Avenue again."

Heat tried to hide her smile but failed.

"So, dare I ask what happened?"

"What happened," Aguinaldo spat back, "is I had the misfortune of learning very early on that the scarf in the video is an original Laura Hopper."

"Laura who?" Heat asked.

"Laura Hopper. Apparently, when it comes to scarves, she is the one and only designer in the world. Beyoncé? Adele? Jennifer Lawrence? If they're going to wear a scarf, it's going to be a Laura Hopper. They're hand-painted silk and they retail for something like ten grand a pop. That's *if* you can get your hands on one. Laura only makes so many a year. There are fierce bidding wars if one ever comes up for auction. Any time one gets put on eBay it pretty much breaks the Internet."

"I don't get it," Rhymer said. "What could possibly be so special about a piece of fabric?"

"It's the sheer brilliance of Laura Hopper herself," Aguinaldo explained. "This is all new to me. But as I understand it, Laura Hopper is like . . . Well, if Louis Vuitton and Oscar de la Renta had a daughter, and then if that daughter got the best genes from both sides of the family, Laura Hopper would still put her to shame."

"Yeah, but ten grand for a scarf?"

"Her fans say a Laura Hopper is like a gift, not only to the wearer but to the world as a whole. Each one is unique and tells its own story. It's like a priceless piece of art you can wear around your neck. And Laura never repeats a design. She even throws out the colors once she's done and remixes a new batch for the next scarf. No two Laura Hoppers are alike in any way."

"Well, that's great news then, isn't it?" Heat said. "We can just call up Laura Hopper and ask her to see if she can remember who she sold this scarf to. If each scarf is so unusual, maybe she'll remember."

"Believe me, I tried that, like, eight hours and forty squirts ago. Laura is based in New York and I was able to get to her personal assistant. The problem is Laura Hopper is right now in Tahiti for her annual three-week totally unplugged vacation. Apparently, the only people who can reach her are the strapping cabana boys who are sent in to give her massages and make her daiquiris. But even they're sworn to secrecy on pain of death."

"But doesn't her assistant, I don't know, keep track of each scarf somehow? Do they catalogue it? Take a picture of it before they sell it?"

"Yes and no," Aguinaldo said. "They primarily sell to buyers in New York, because that's where most of the American fashion industry is anyway. The assistant had records of everywhere they've ever sold a scarf. But not *which* scarf was sold. It's not like they number them. Nor do they attempt to describe the piece—Laura Hopper feels that if you give a scarf a name, it diminishes it somehow.

"So," Aguinaldo said, making her aggravation clear, "I was left to go around to every name on that list, hoping someone might recognize this individual Laura Hopper as the one they sold."

"How many were there?"

"Hundreds. And the thing is Laura Hopper has these egalitarian leanings. So it's not just the super high-end places. Sometimes she'll give a scarf to, say, Macy's and ask them to quietly put it on the clearance rack for thirty bucks. That way even the non-rich get a chance to own a little piece of the glory that is a Laura Hopper, if they have a discerning-enough eye."

"Damn," Ochoa said. "So Laura Hopper is like Willy Wonka without the chocolate factory."

"And without the creepy thing for kids," Feller added.

"Yeah. The problem for us is, let's just say you're the lucky consumer who finds that singular Laura Hopper deep in the discount bin at Filene's Basement," Aguinaldo said. "The moment you realize that thirty-dollar scarf could get you upwards of ten grand, what do you do?"

"A happy dance that looks ridiculous on a white man?" Raley suggested.

"Well, yes, that," Aguinaldo said. "But then, chances are, you've got bills to pay and kids who need braces, and in any event, everyone at the big party you're going to is just going to think it's a knockoff Laura Hopper anyway. So you sell it."

"Is that what happened to this Laura Hopper?" Heat asked.

"I don't know," Aguinaldo said. "I kept hoping someone at one of these stores would recognize this particular Laura Hopper and give me some kind of trail to follow. But while a lot of people knew instantly it was a Laura Hopper, none of them knew *which* Laura Hopper it was. Which is why I currently look like I've been shopping Black Friday for three hundred straight days."

"Oh, that's a good one," Raley said, then looked at Feller and Ochoa. "How come you guys didn't come up with anything like that?"

Feller was about to respond, but quieted when he saw Aguinaldo still wasn't in the mood.

"So we don't know which Laura Hopper this was," Heat said. "But we do know it showed up at our crime scene. And that gets us back to our original question, which now only becomes that much more confounding. How is it a women's scarf—a one-of-a-kind, world-famous, absurdly expensive women's scarf at that—shows up in a New York City mosque as part of a beheading video shot by two kids who, if their apartment is any indication, don't have more than two nickels to rub together?"

"Could it have been Tam's?" Aguinaldo asked.

"Not on a journalist's salary," Heat said. "Besides, I've known her for years and I've never seen her wear any scarf, much less one like that."

It was one of the oddest odd socks of Heat's career, and she couldn't even begin to make sense of it. Not with the current evidence.

Neither could anyone else, apparently. The detectives of the Twentieth Precinct were holding an anti-staring contest: a game where no one could look at the other.

Eventually, Ochoa offered, "The real ISIS traffics in all kinds of stolen goods. They've stolen artwork, antiques, anything they can get their hands on they think has value. It's how they fund their empire. That and oil. Maybe these wannabe ISIS kids are just trying to act like the big boys?"

"Possible," Heat said. "Before you head out on canvass with Opie and Feller, why don't you check in with the Central Robbery Division and see if anyone has reported a Laura Hopper stolen, either from a store or an individual. I've got to think something this valuable would be insured, so a person who had it stolen from them would file a report. It might give us something to go on."

"Got it," Ochoa said.

"Okay, I think everyone knows what they're doing, except for you, Inez," Heat said. "But I've got a special assignment for you."

A look of pure horror was settling in on Aguinaldo's face.

Then Heat said, "Go home. Take a shower. You reek."

"And we have a winner of the insult-off," Feller said, scooping up the three twenties and shoving them at Heat.

She collected the money, then immediately handed it to Aguinaldo. "And get yourself some nice takeout, courtesy of your generous colleagues."

As the detectives dispatched themselves to their assignments and Heat returned to her office, she felt a buzz against her thigh.

She looked down to see a text message from Lauren Parry.

CAN YOU COME DOWN HERE?

Then, two seconds later, there came another one:

ALONE.

NINETEEN

For the second time that day, Nikki Heat was making the trip down to room 23B. And also for the second time, she realized she was nervous about it.

Lauren Parry didn't request a solo audience with Nikki for routine matters, especially not since Heat had been promoted to captain.

This had to be about her mother's ashes. For as much as Heat wanted to know the outcome, she also feared it in a way that was unexpectedly complicated.

Because, on the one hand, she had—despite her best efforts not to—allowed herself to entertain this fantasy that her mother was still alive. It was a fairy tale, yes. But doesn't everyone have an inner child who loves fairy tales? To think that she and her mother might someday cook dinner together again. Or that they might enjoy the symphony by each other's side. Or that Cynthia Heat might someday hold her grandchildren . . .

Grandchildren? Jesus, Nikki. Snap out of it.

Then there was the opposite result. Which was that Cynthia Heat was still as dead as she'd been for these seventeen years. And as much as Heat had tried to not let herself believe the fairy tale, she knew she would wind up mourning her mother's death all over again.

So if Heat's heart was pounding as she opened the door to room 23B, it wasn't because the walk down had been particularly strenuous.

"Oh, hey, Nik," Parry called out from the other side of the lab.

That told Heat they were alone. If there had been other people around, Parry would have called her Captain Heat.

"Hey, Laur," Heat responded.

Then she eyed the plastic evidence bag with her mother's remains, on the counter next to where Parry was standing. Heat quickly averted her eyes so it wouldn't seem like she had been staring at it.

"Thanks for coming down," Parry was saying. "I got the word from the feds that we're going to be deprived of Tam Svejda's company first thing tomorrow morning. What happened?"

"Yardley Bell happened."

"I thought you two were cool now . . ."

"We were," Heat said. "Until she stole my suspects."

"So do you still care about some results I got this afternoon?"

"Absolutely," Heat said. Then she put on a cat-that-ate-the-canary grin and added: "And not because I'm planning to continue looking into the case now that it's federal. This is only because I'm such an admirer of your work."

Parry didn't need Heat to draw a road map for her. "Well, I appreciate that," she said. "So now that we understand this is all strictly academic, you remember that whitish powder I found in the treads of Tam's shoes?"

"The stuff I thought might be cocaine or heroin?"

"Right. Except the mass spectrometer ended up with a far different take on it. Our mystery powder, once I separated it from the common dirt and grime that was also in her shoe, turns out to be zinc."

"Zinc?"

"Right. So not something you'd put up your nose. Though I guess lifeguards at the beach have been known to put it *on* their noses."

Heat crossed her arms. "What would *that* be doing on the bottoms of Tam's shoes?"

"How many times do I have to tell you that's why you get that fancy, flashy detective's badge of yours?" Parry said. "I'm just the girl who did well on her MCAT's, remember?"

"Yeah, but . . . I mean, where else is zinc found?"

"Where is it *not* found is a better question," Parry said. "You're taking me back to my organic chemistry days—which, believe me, I'm trying to forget—but if memory serves, zinc is the second most common trace metal in the body after iron. It's essential for the immune system, for healing cuts, all kinds of important things. That's when it's absorbed in the blood, of course. The stuff that's in metal form can be all over the place, too. You spray it on cars to deter rust. It's in gutters, fuses, you name it. It's probably in a lot of Americans' pockets right now."

"What are you talking about?"

"The penny. It's almost all zinc, with only a little thin coating of copper on the outside," Parry said. "Then if you're talking zinc oxide, which is the stuff the lifeguards use, it's found in a ton of cosmetics and pharmaceuticals. I mean, it's everywhere. I think it's even used in printing inks."

"Printing inks, like the kind the *New York Ledger* uses? Was she hanging around a printing press?"

"It's possible," Parry said. "It's also possible she went on a hiking trip three weekends ago and got some in her shoe. Zinc is naturally occurring and pretty common in the earth's crust. That's one of the reasons we've found so many ways to use it. It's cheap."

Heat tried to imagine how traces of zinc came to be in the treads of Tam Svejda's shoes. But she quickly recognized it as yet another piece that didn't want to be wedged into the puzzle just yet.

Or ever. Zinc might have been another odd sock. But it also could have been a red herring—something that had absolutely no significance.

"Well, okay, good to know," Heat said.

Her eyes drifted back to the evidence bag, then snapped back to Parry.

"Any . . . anything else?" Heat asked, her voice catching just a little.

"Yeah, remember that stuff on Tam's body that smelled like kerosene?"

"Uh-huh."

"Big surprise: It's kerosene. But don't start asking me questions about how it got there or what it might mean, because I'm just going to have to remind you about that badge of yours again."

"Okay, got it," Heat said, now rather pointedly looking at anywhere other than the counter.

"Now," Parry said. "About the stuff in this bag that you've been trying not to look at ever since you walked in."

Heat felt color rushing to her cheeks and stared down at her shoes instead.

"Yeah, what about it?"

"Where did you get it, anyway? From a crematory or . . ."

Heat's heart was pounding again. "It's . . . It's difficult to explain. Can you just . . . What is it? What did you find?"

Parry ignored Heat's faltering and went on. "Well, it's crematory remains, no doubt. All the organic matter is gone, of course. Including the DNA. When you bake something at that high a temperature, all you're left with is bones. But these bones . . ."

Heat had subtly grabbed on to the top of a lab table for stability. "What about them?" she asked.

"Well, one thing's for sure," Parry said, before uttering three words that changed Heat's life forever:

"They're not human."

Not human. As in, not her mother.

Heat sucked in a large gasp of air. Beyond that, she seemed to be outside her own body. She looked down and saw her knuckles whitening as she gripped the lab table extra hard, but she had no knowledge of telling her hands to do that. There was a throbbing in her ears, though she couldn't tell where it was coming from. She tried to form words but found her mouth had gone dry.

"You need to get it under a microscope to see it," Parry continued, seemingly unaware of the turmoil in which she had just plunged Nikki Heat's entire existence. "But once you do, it's pretty obvious. Some of it was definitely avian—you can tell, because bird bones are a lot less dense than human bones. There was also what might have been either squirrel or rat. Some kind of small rodent, though beyond that, I couldn't say. You'd need someone who knows animals a lot better than I do. There was also some larger mammal. Not dog, though. Maybe a deer."

"A deer?" Heat managed to choke out.

"When I was first looking at it, I thought it might have been from a pet crematory. Until I came across the deer. Then I started to think that maybe this was roadkill. You know the Department of Public Works takes all the critters it scrapes off the road and burns them up."

"Roadkill," Heat repeated.

She finally gave up on trying to stay standing—it was either find a chair or hit the floor. Luckily, there was a stool within easy grabbing distance. She slid it under herself just in time.

Roadkill. The ashes that Heat had lovingly placed behind that plaque in the most beautiful columbarium in New York, that she had faithfully visited for seventeen years, that she had communed with, that had made her feel closer to her mother's spirit . . . All along, they had been the remains of animals people had hit with their cars.

"Girlfriend, you okay?" Parry asked, her brow creased with concern. "You look like you're going to faint."

"Yeah, I . . . I just . . . I think I skipped lunch."

"And now your blood sugar is low. Hang on."

Parry disappeared into the next room. Heat leaned an elbow on the counter. Ever since that half second that morning, there had been a part of her that was absolutely convinced her mind must have been playing some elaborate trick on itself.

Now here was hard evidence it wasn't. And it had taken Heat's neatly ordered universe and given it a big-bang-style shake-up.

Her mother wasn't dead. Whatever had happened on November 24, 1999, had been little more than a clever piece of stagecraft by a woman who certainly had the sense of theater to pull it off.

The questions started pouring into Nikki Heat's head, unbidden: What had been so important or threatening or intimidating that it made Cynthia Heat feel she had to disappear from *everyone* in her life, her own daughter included? Where had she been all these years? What had she been up to? Why was she suddenly coming out of hiding now?

Nikki was just starting to wrestle with that and so much more when Parry returned with a small bottle of orange juice, which she opened for Heat.

"Here, drink some of this, and then hang out until you start to feel better," Parry said. "I can't have you falling over on me. I know most of my patients are a little late for the Hippocratic oath, but every once in a while I have to pretend to be a real doctor."

"Thanks, Laur," Heat said, grabbing the orange juice and taking a large swig of it for Parry's benefit. "But I think I'm actually already feeling better."

"You sure?"

"Absolutely," Heat said.

Which wasn't true. Not even a little bit. But there were now things she had to start getting straight. And she couldn't do it sitting in room 23B.

The only person in the bull pen when Heat returned was Raley, and he was deep in concentration, his eyes fixed on the pixels in front of him, a pair of earphones snug over his head. There was no point in bothering him.

The shadows were growing long outside. It was after seven o'clock. The Twentieth Precinct's day shift was long gone and the swing shift was already out on the streets, making New York safer.

No one would necessarily expect Captain Heat to still be there. She took advantage of that fact and made her exit. She was going home.

But not to the Tribeca loft she and Rook shared.

To her place. To the apartment in Gramercy Park, where she had known a happy childhood, where her parents had lived together until they split, where her mother had continued to reside after the divorce, where Nikki had returned during semester breaks in college, where she continued living by herself up until she met Rook.

And where her mother was murdered.

It had been a big step for Nikki when she listed the apartment for sale shortly before she and Rook had gotten married. They had already been living full-time in Rook's place for a while, of course. But somehow Heat had trouble letting go.

Her hesitation hadn't been because she somehow doubted that she and Rook would last. She already knew she was in love with him for better or worse and would never be whole without him.

It was what the apartment represented: her independence. Saying you'll be with one person for the rest of your life is one thing. Saying you're surrendering the ability to be on your own is quite another.

When Heat listed the place, she expected it to go quickly. Gramercy Park apartments often did.

Except, apparently, for hers. There had been one ridiculous lowball offer early on, then nothing. Was it because people still remembered what had happened there? Or because the kitchen was in need of updating? Or had she—subconsciously, perhaps—set the price too high, knowing she wasn't really ready to let go?

Whatever the case, the apartment still hadn't sold after a year on the market. The realtor kept making subtle hints about dropping the asking price, but Heat had put her off, always making an excuse about how she would think about it when she had a free moment—which, of course, she seldom did.

Rook had been a prince about the whole thing. From a strictly economic standpoint, it made no sense to continue paying the maintenance fees, taxes, and utilities for a place they never used. She should have simply cut the price, taken what she could get, and moved on. It wasn't like they needed to make top dollar.

But Rook recognized there were more than just financial considerations at stake. So, showing wisdom unusual for a hunky man-child such as himself, he had been careful never to suggest any course of action. He let Heat have her time when it came to her space.

Heat grabbed an unmarked car rather than dealing with the subway, then found street parking upon arrival. Bob Aaronson, the doorman, greeted her with the appropriate amount of noisy surprise—it had been a while—and when she stuck her key in the front door, she found the lock was a little sticky.

The air inside smelled stale. Not only had there not been offers, there hadn't even been many people viewing it of late. It was like the Multiple Listing Service entry had concluded with: UNMOTIVATED SELLER. DON'T WASTE YOUR TIME.

The place had been decluttered by the realtor to make it seem more appealing to the would-be buyers who were no longer showing up. But otherwise, it was exactly the same as when Nikki had lived there.

For that matter, it was pretty much unchanged from when Cynthia had lived there. The furniture was the same. The drapes were the same. Even the paint was the same. The most ambitious thing Nikki had done was get the kitchen tile replaced. But she had only done that because the blood wouldn't come out of the grout.

Nikki had never intended to maintain the place as some kind of shrine. She just liked it the way it was. It suited her. And, generally speaking, she had been too much of a workaholic to even entertain the concept of tackling major renovations or redecorations.

As she stepped in and closed the door behind her, she found herself back on November 24, 1999. She walked to the kitchen, remembering the exact spot on the floor where she'd found her mother, so prone, so dead-seeming, the knife protruding from her back. She remembered falling to her knees next to her mother, holding her mother, all of it. She saw the blood splatter, the gore everywhere.

Sometimes she wasn't sure whether other memories were real or whether they were the crime scene photos that she had stared at so many times.

Heat took a deep breath then left the kitchen. She wasn't there for a macabre nostalgia trip. Nikki Heat was many things. But she was, first and foremost, a cop.

A cop who realized the case she had spent more time on than any other in her life needed a new timeline, new evidence, new everything. How *had* her mother pulled it off?

Heat started with the moment her mother had left her possession. A paramedic—clearly an actress, or one of Cynthia's spy buddies—had separated Nikki from the body. Then a cop, another paid performer and/or friend, had taken Nikki into the next room while a crew of other pretenders secreted Cynthia Heat away.

A fraud. All of it. Perhaps aided by Baclofen, if Rook was right. Perhaps something else.

They had fooled Nikki thoroughly. But was that really so difficult? She was just nineteen then, so naive and trusting of anyone who looked like an authority figure.

But Cynthia would have needed to fool more than just a gullible teenager. Nikki had seen her mother's death certificate. It was as official as they came, issued by the city of New York. How had she managed *that*?

Heat walked over to the filing cabinet she kept in her small home office and thumbed it open. There were a number of files that pertained to her mother. But there was one, in particular, that Nikki was looking for.

She was glad the realtor hadn't decluttered that, too. Letting her fingers walk through the folders, she eventually found it:

A file labeled MOM'S ARRANGEMENTS.

This was a dead brain cell coming back to life. In the whirl of activity that immediately followed her mother's death—when Nikki had been far too stunned by what happened to cope with the more mundane details of death—it had seemed like a blessing: Cynthia Heat had made all of her own arrangements and even had them paid for.

She had picked out the funeral home. She had selected the crematory urn. And she had even selected, yes, the crematorium. It had all been neatly laid out in her will.

At the time, it had seemed like such a thoughtful thing for her mother to have done. And Nikki was relieved to have one less thing to worry about.

Now it struck her as utterly bizarre. Eighty-year-olds fretted over their funeral arrangements. Terminal cancer patients did, too. Cynthia Heat had been forty-nine and in perfect health. What kind of forty-nine-year-old picked out her own funeral urn?

Nikki opened the file. The services had been held at Gannon Funeral Home, which was clearly a very real, very legitimate place. It was just a few blocks away. She had been there not only for her mother's funeral, but to pay her respects to others in the years since, mainly neighbors who had passed. The people who ran it were very good at what they did, managing the details of a difficult time in their customers' lives with professionalism and caring.

Heat flipped through the paperwork. There was a brochure, a description of the funeral package being purchased. Cynthia Heat had even picked out the limo that would be used to take her remains out to the columbarium. The invoice had been typed on carbon paper—this was 1999, before everything had gone digital. It had been stamped PAID IN FULL at the top of the page. Nikki felt a little *flub-flub* in her stomach when she saw her mother's signature at the bottom.

Nikki kept pawing through the file. She next came to a similar grouping of papers from an establishment called Demming Crematorium. Again, a description of services to be rendered, all very official-looking. Again, an invoice, signed by Cynthia.

But this time Nikki had no knowledge of, nor experience with, the business. All she knew was that she had been handed the urn with her mother's alleged ashes in it at the funeral.

Curious, Nikki plugged "Demming Crematorium New York" into Google.

More than a thousand results flooded back at her. But even the top one, the one deemed most relevant by the all-knowing Google search algorithm, had "Missing: ~~Demming~~" in ghostly gray letters at the bottom of it.

The next one did, too. And everything else on the first page of results. Missing: ~~Demming~~, indeed.

She left off the "New York" and tried again.

This time, all that came up were obituaries of people named Demming that happened to be posted by funeral homes that also had "Crematorium" in their names. But there was no Demming Crematorium.

Heat leaned back, away from the keyboard. Was there such thing as a business that wasn't on the Internet in the year 2016?

Unlikely. But still possible. Especially if it was an old-world-business crematorium, which existed on referrals from other funeral homes, which were also old-world businesses.

Heat bounced over to the New York State Web page and, after the right series of clicks, checked business licenses. There was no license issued to Demming Crematorium in the "active" section. So she clicked on over to "all," which included licenses that had lapsed, back to 1984.

She tried all combinations, knowing how picky databases could be. But whatever she typed in, she got: NO BUSINESS ENTITIES WERE FOUND.

Which at least told Heat how the death certificate had been procured. The people at "Demming Crematorium" (really more actors, no doubt competent in their bearing) had delivered the ashen remains of "Cynthia Heat" (really incinerated Department of Public Works roadkill) to Gannon Funeral Home, which then went about applying for the death certificate, because that was part of the package Cynthia had purchased.

Which was how Cynthia Heat's death became official.

So that was one mystery solved.

Now if only Nikki Heat could begin to gain purchase on the many that remained.

TWENTY

The bottle of Bolla Valpolicella had cost Nikki Heat $13.95 and a sneer from the guy at the liquor store who knew it had only pulled an 81 from *Wine Observer*.

Heat didn't care. She wasn't drinking for taste. She was drinking for memory.

It was 1996. She was sixteen. First trip to Italy. Mom with her every nervous step of the way.

There was something about Europe that made Cynthia Heat come alive in ways she never did stateside. Her gestures became broader. Her face developed this permanent flush. Her voice became more enchanting, her stories more full of mischief. It was like her entire aura started glowing as soon as she cleared customs.

Nikki, then a teenager, just thought it was the excitement of foreign travel, the opportunity to use her languages—how *did* she know that many, anyway?—and the thrill of something different. She never understood, until much later, about Cynthia Heat's colorful history as an operative in the Nanny Network.

It was only in hindsight that Nikki recognized everywhere they went as a place her mother had been already been—likely in much more exciting circumstances than as a tour guide to her clueless daughter. Cynthia Heat wasn't just reveling in the present. She was reliving her thrilling past, with her daughter at her side.

What, then, had Cynthia been thinking when she'd selected their first destination after landing at Leonardo da Vinci Airport, jetlagged but exuberant? It wasn't the Colosseum, or St. Peter's, or the Forum, or any of the other of the must-see destinations Nikki had read about in her guidebooks. It was this unremarkable little piazza. Nikki was sure it had a name, though she couldn't remember it—if Cynthia had ever even told her in the first place.

Without explanation or deviation from her path, Cynthia led them to this unnoticed place and sat down on the marble steps. She uncorked a bottle of Bolla Valpolicella, took a long swig, then passed the bottle to her daughter.

Nikki had drunk alcohol before, of course. Her parents believed in letting their daughter have a sip of this or a half glass of that on the right occasion.

But she had never drunk alcohol like that before. She took the bottle, tilted it back just as her mother had, and took a gulp. Then she handed it back, only to have her mother give her this tilt of the head that said *drink some more*.

As the wine worked its way into her bloodstream, Nikki began to soak in what was around her. In the middle of the piazza was a marble sculpture of a Roman god whose face had been corroded by acid rain and whose left arm was only a stub, having fallen off centuries before. Had it been in America, it probably would have been one of the true centerpieces of the metropolis, an ancient wonder the Chamber of Commerce would have featured in every brochure. Here, it was just another chunk of rock in a city that really did have much better to offer.

Across the street was a simple stone church built in the eighth century AD, making its age unremarkable by Italian standards, but otherworldly to an American like Nikki, who had never seen anything so ancient. She stared at it in wonder, unable to fathom a length of time so out of context with her sixteen years. For more than half a millennium, the church had baptized, married, and buried generations of people, playing host to the drama of their lives. But the Romans just whizzed by it in their Fiats and Vespas without a second glance.

Just like they didn't pay attention to the two Americans sitting on the marble steps, guzzling straight from the bottle. Nikki's mom wasn't saying anything, wasn't narrating the scene like she sometimes did, wasn't doing anything but staring into the distance—or, as Nikki now surmised, into the past.

Nikki could remember only being in the present. Sixteen is a contentious time in the cycle of a mother-daughter relationship. The teenage wars, which actually begin around age twelve, have been raging for what feels like forever by that point. Both sides are exhausted from the endless cycle of battle—retraining new armies, sending them into the field, declaring victors, counting casualties, drawing new lines only to rip them up the moment the troops are ready to mobilize again.

That silent bottle of Bolla Valpolicella had been like a peace offering. They simply passed the bottle back and forth until the wine was gone and Nikki was half plastered. Then they ventured forth through the rest of the city.

Her mother never explained why that piazza had been their first stop. Nikki never told her mother how much she cherished the moment.

Now, all these years later, the sweet, fruity taste of Bolla Valpolicella took Nikki right back to the piazza, to that feeling of closeness with her mother.

And Nikki always drank it the same way: straight from the bottle.

By around nine o'clock, she was well into its contents. The Indian food she had ordered had yet to arrive so the wine was barely pausing at her empty stomach before going straight to her head. When her phone rang, she thought it would be the delivery guy needing to recheck the address, but it wasn't.

It was Rook.

"Hey, beautiful," he said in a warm, sexy voice that made Heat wish he was there to take advantage of her semi-drunken state, so she could then take advantage of him right back.

"Hey, you," Heat said, curling her legs underneath her on the couch. "How was the interview with our future president?"

"Good. Real good. We did half of it on the way to Pennsylvania and then the other half on the next flight. He's really something else. Especially when you get his guard down a bit. We talked about his business, about his family, about his politics. And not that I agreed with everything he said, but the man really is quite good one-on-one. Charming. Funny. Brilliant in a down-to-earth way. Articulate as hell. He's like Bill Clinton without the sleaze factor."

"Listen to you," Heat said. "You sound like a cub reporter who's just met his first rich celebrity."

"I know, right?" Rook said, laughing at himself. "Don't worry. I'll get ahold of myself before I sit down to the keyboard. I'll find some disgruntled ex-employee to rip him unfairly just so I can balance the thing out."

In the background, Nikki heard some giggling. And maybe the ocean.

"Where are you, anyway?" she asked.

"South Beach. Miami was the last stop of the day for the Kline campaign and all the flights out tonight are already overbooked. So I figured I'd scoot on over here for the night then head back to New York in the morning. Sorry, I know how much you were hoping to have me fill the other half of the bed. Believe me, I was, too."

"Actually both halves are empty right now."

"Oh? Working late?"

"Not exactly. I'm . . . I'm actually at my place right now."

There was a brief silence on the line. Heat heard a loud group of partygoers pass by somewhere nearby.

"Ah," Rook said at last. "What are you doing there?"

Heat told him about Parry's lab results and about the fictitious crematory.

When Heat finished, Rook's enthusiasm came bursting out of the phone.

"So, wow, she's . . . I mean, she's really alive? Not that I doubted what you saw, but . . . Wow! That's . . . that's great, isn't it?"

"Yeah, I . . . I guess so."

"You guess so?"

"It is, Rook, but . . . I don't mean to make this about me, but do you have any idea how much it hurt to lose her? It ripped my life apart for years. In some ways I'm still not over the trauma. I never will be. Couldn't she have found some way to spare me that? To let me know she was still alive and she would come back someday?"

"I'm sure she had a very good reason for doing what she did," Rook said. "If she just up and disappeared like that, it had to be a life or death situation. And I'm sure the death she was worried about was yours. She was protecting you. She couldn't take any risk that you knew. Your mourning had to be genuine."

"Rook, I was an actress," Heat shot back. "Don't you think I could have faked tears at a funeral? My mother had seen me cry onstage."

"But it wasn't just the funeral. It was everything. She probably knew people would be watching you. If you didn't act like she was dead every second of your life, it would have looked suspicious. She couldn't take the risk you'd cry perfectly at the funeral and then be seen laughing with your friends over a meal two days later."

"Yeah, but okay, where the hell has she been since then? Couldn't she have waited a month until things cooled down and then slipped me a note? She disappeared when I was nineteen years old, Rook. Nineteen! She missed my college graduation. She missed my wedding. She's missed close to half my life. What kind of mother does that?"

"A mother who was doing what she felt was best."

"Why are you sticking up for her? Whose side are you on, anyway?" Heat blurted, sounding childish even to herself. It was the wine talking. Or the old hurt talking.

"Hey, hey, I'm on your side," Rook cooed. "I'm always on your side. You know that. I'm just pointing out that your mom loved you and never would have hurt you if she could have avoided it."

"I know, I know. Sorry," Heat said. She put the cork back on the wine.

"So what's your plan now? Do you just wait for your mother to reach out to you? She's obviously in New York. Maybe she's just scoping you out, seeing if it's safe to reestablish contact?"

Heat reached for a blanket that was folded on the back of the couch and drew it up over her shoulders. "I don't know," she said. "I don't actually have a plan. I think that's part of what scares me. I have to do *something* proactive, Rook. I can't just sit here until my mother feels like appearing again. I mean, do you know what it's like? Walking down the street wondering if I'll see her around the next corner?"

"That has to be hard."

"And I keep thinking: if she's still in danger, what if she needs my help? I'm not some clueless nineteen-year-old anymore. I have resources now. I can do something."

Her voice was gaining steam now, like she was just realizing the power she had.

Rook began, "Careful, Nikki. You've been down this rabbit hole before. There's nothing—"

But Heat was beyond listening. Her brain was already going, her mouth just trying to keep up: "There are two people still alive who were connected with the events that led to my mother's death—or, I guess I should call it now, her disappearance. Carey Maggs and Bart Callan."

Maggs, Rook didn't need to be told, was the former brewery owner and pharmaceutical magnate who came up with the wicked scheme to dump smallpox on New York City because his business was the only one that made a vaccine. And Callan was the former operative in the Department of Homeland Security and FBI who helped him do it.

Both were now incarcerated. Everyone else connected with the plot was dead.

"Okay," Rook said. "And I'm not trying to play devil's advocate. I'm just trying to help you think things through. What is going to make Maggs and Callan willing to talk now?"

"Because time has passed," Heat said immediately. "They're no longer protected by a million dollars' worth of lawyers. They've been stripped of their dignity and their pride. Whatever money and influence they once wielded no longer matters. They're now just two more inmates in the federal system, facing a long and lousy incarceration that will only end when they leave prison feetfirst. If I can present myself as someone who can pull some strings to make a slightly more comfortable existence for them—even just a cell to themselves or a better work duty—I bet they'd be willing to trade just about anything."

Rook stayed quiet for a moment. Heat thought she heard music somewhere in the background.

"Well," he said at last. "I guess I can't think of any harm that will do as long as you don't whisper a word that you've seen your mother. You can't go blowing her cover. And just, look, be careful, okay? We don't know what made your mother feel like she had to do this, but whatever it was had to be big enough and dangerous enough that it was worth missing seventeen years of your life. So treat it with respect, all right?"

"I hear you," Heat said. And then she heard something else.

A singsongy voice was saying, "Jaaaammmmiiieeeee! Oh, Jamie! Are you coming? Justin and Preston have gotten us something naughty from the store!"

"Who is that?" Heat asked. "Is Lana still with you?"

"Yeah. And Flotsam and Jetsam. And Legs is going to join us once he's done meeting with some local powerbrokers. Once I told them I had a buddy who could get us into Versace's old place, one thing kind of led to another, and now I think it's going to happen."

"I'm sorry, *what* is going to happen?"

"Shots. On Versace's balcony. Overlooking Ocean Drive. How amazing would that be? Doing shots with the future president of the United States in the former home of an internationally known fashion designer who was brutally murdered by his lover? Heck, if I can figure out what that has to do with running the country, I might make that the lede to my article just because it's so cool."

"Rook—"

But now Rook was the one who wasn't listening. "Apparently, Legs never gets hangovers. He swears he can drink bourbon all night long and then wake up feeling like he spent the night at church. Talk about a superpower I wish I could borrow. No wonder he's poised on the brink of becoming the leader of the free world. Heck, I think I could become the leader of the free universe if I didn't get hangovers."

"Rook—"

"Legs told me about his first big deal. It was this oil well out in New Mexico. Half the mineral rights he needed were on federal land, which he had already secured. But half were on private land owned by this rancher who wasn't sure if he wanted to trust some kid who no one knew to run the operation. Well, Legs went out and they cracked open the Maker's Mark and started pounding it down. When I say Legs drank the guy under the table, I mean the man literally woke up staring at the underside of his kitchen table. But by the time he did, Legs was already outside, helping one of the ranch hands load an eighteen-hundred-pound Angus bull into a trailer. That's what made him decide Legs was a man who could handle any job sent his way. I'm telling you, the guy is—"

"Rook!" Heat said, loud enough to get his attention.

"Oh. Sorry."

"Look, just be careful, okay? Just because we have two of these ISIS guys in custody doesn't mean we've chopped the head off this snake. For all we know, we've only gotten the tail. So be careful, okay?"

"Yeah, I will. Don't worry. Between Legs's private security goons and the Secret Service guys with the squiggly things in their ears, I'm as safe as I can possibly be. Look, I gotta go. My Versace contact is here and if I don't look extra cool he might not let us in."

"Okay," Heat said. "Be safe."

But Rook was already gone. All she heard as she disconnected the call was more giggling.

Heat tossed the phone on the cushion next to her and let her head sag on the arm of the couch.

When she lifted it again, her eyes fell on the Steinway baby grand in the corner.

She swung one foot onto the floor, then the other. Before she even knew what she was doing, she was walking toward the piano. She always found comfort in the feel of her fingers gliding across its keys.

As the daughter of a piano teacher, Nikki was playing scales when she was eighteen months old. By age three, she was playing two-handed pieces. By age five, Mozart.

Nikki had never quite become the musician her mother was. Though, to be fair, Cynthia had world-class talent—even if she ultimately decided that spying on people at the Palais Garnier was more interesting than playing for them there. But Nikki could hold her own. She could play Chopin. Rachmaninoff. Bach. Or even just Billy Joel, when she felt like hacking around and belting out "New York State of Mind" at full voice.

She played right up until her mother's death. Then, to her surprise, she found she couldn't touch a single note. It was too painful, too much of a reminder of the person who was no longer there. Every part of the instrument, from the keys to the soundboard, whose integrity was the reason for the dehumidifier Cynthia Heat kept on at all times, was a reminder of her mother. So, for thirteen unlucky years, the baby grand in the corner of her apartment stayed silent.

That finally changed four years ago, when Nikki solved (or at least thought she solved) her mother's murder (or at least what she thought was her mother's murder). Ever since then, whenever she wanted to feel a connection to her mother, all she had to do was sit down and let her mother's spirit flow through her.

Which was exactly what she needed at that moment.

Thankfully, the realtor had insisted the Steinway stay in the apartment while it was on the market. Few things dress up a space better than a baby grand. And, of course, Nikki had kept it tuned at all times. One discordant note from those perfect strings would have been an affront to Cynthia's memory.

Nikki had reached the bench. She bent down and pulled out *Mozart for Young Hands*, with its dented cover and dog-eared pages. Then she turned to the page that was practically creased open anyway: Sonata no. 15.

She set the open book on the music holder, then walked around the side of the piano, letting her hand slide along the smooth black wood, admiring its glossy sheen. She lifted the top board and slid the prop in place, so the music could pour out of the piano and into her aching heart.

This was all so familiar now. She returned to the bench. She sat. She lifted the lid to expose the keyboard, all eighty-eight bone whites and ebony blacks. She took in air through her nose, being mindful of the feeling of her diaphragm expanding. She released the breath from her mouth. She reminded herself what her mother always told her about not rushing.

Like Mozart said, "The space between the notes is music, too." That had been one of her mother's favorite reminders.

She straightened her spine—Cynthia Heat did not tolerate slouching—and placed her fingers in position. She set a metronome going in her head, then began silently counting herself in.

One. She and her mother would play together again someday. Maybe they would finally master Mendelssohn's *Allegro Brillante*, the four-handed piece that Nikki had never gotten quite right.

Two. Except, of course, if Cynthia Heat never really intended to return. Maybe her self-exile was permanent. Maybe that one glimpse was all Nikki would get.

Three. What was more traumatic? Knowing someone was dead? Or knowing they were alive but refused to rejoin your life?

Four. Abandonment. The word sprang into her head. That's really what it was. And was there anything more powerfully painful in this life than being abandoned by your own mother?

Nikki stared at the staffs and lines in front of her. She was supposed to have begun playing by now. It was what the music demanded. It was what the piano wanted.

She tried counting herself in again. *One, two, three, four.*

Again, nothing happened.

Nikki Heat couldn't bring herself to strike a single note.

TWENTY-ONE

D awn. Or, wait, not dawn. That was always one of the problems with Manhattan. The city that never slept glowed no matter the hour. You could never be quite sure whether what you were seeing was sunrise or just light pollution.

Heat sat up in bed and looked at the clock: 3:23 A.M.

She lay back down, but only for a minute, until the pounding in her chest told her she was unlikely to find sleep again. Anxiety often hit her like this when she was wrestling with a big case or when something disruptive was happening in her personal life. And, right then, since she was dealing with both, it was like the stress was being dropped on her by a crane.

It left her with two choices: spend the next couple of hours tossing, turning, and tangling the sheets until it was time to get up, or face reality and get on with the day ahead.

Heat was soon on her feet and tugging up the bedspread. She might have ordinarily taken advantage of the early start by getting in a good workout, but the plan that had begun rising in her mind as she talked to Rook was now something like fully baked.

Bart Callan was at least somewhat out of reach. As a former federal agent, he had been placed in Florence ADX, a supermax facility out in Colorado—both for his own safety, so he wasn't incarcerated with convicts he had personally put behind bars, and because he was deemed to have all the skills necessary to be a significant escape risk. Reaching him would require a flight and, because of the nature of the facility, some pre-arrangement on Heat's part.

Carey Maggs was another story. He had been packed off to the United States Penitentiary at Allenwood, in Central Pennsylvania. It was still a high-security facility—a man who had been involved in the kind of mendacity that Maggs had would never qualify for medium security—but Heat could show up there and, as a sworn law enforcement officer, have a reasonable expectation of being able to see him immediately.

Heat worked out the rest of the details while she was in the shower. She could slip out there and be back before anyone at the Twentieth Precinct would miss her too much. Her detectives certainly had enough to keep them busy for the time being.

She left the apartment without taking time to tidy up. The realtor would throw a fit if she had to do a showing. Heat didn't care. She was suddenly less eager to be rid of the place.

Maybe she'd even take it off the market. Rook would understand.

Back out on the street, her last act before getting into her unmarked car was to stick the temporary gumball on top. The drive out to Allenwood was a shade under three hours at normal speed. But she could make it in closer to two if she kept the lights flashing and the pedal to the floor.

There was little traffic getting out of town at that hour, and she was soon crossing the George Washington Bridge, then heading west on Interstate 80. Once she cleared Bergen County, New Jersey, the highway straightened out and opened up, and she was able to make good time.

As she passed through the Delaware Water Gap, twisting through the small canyons carved long ago by that mighty river, dawn was still just a rumor. The first hint of daybreak didn't begin to appear in her rearview mirror until she was through the Poconos. Pennsylvania had flattened out somewhat by that point. It was rolling farmland, which Heat raced by in the dark, her flashing lights bouncing off hayfields and sleeping cows.

By the time she reached Allenwood, the first rays of Wednesday's light were just starting to make their way over the horizon to the east. She parked in a space that had been marked for law enforcement, then approached the main building, which looked more like a ski chalet than a prison. But, truly, most of the men inside were there because their lives had found a different kind of downhill slope.

The duty officer who greeted her from behind a thick slab of bulletproof glass seemed surprised to see Heat. Her visit was unannounced and, besides, he could do the math. It was a quarter after six in the morning. Anyone who had gotten there from New York City had woken early.

He seemed even more taken aback when, after he checked out her badge and driver's license, she said she was there to see Carey Maggs. Allenwood had its share of notorious inmates. But Maggs might have been their biggest celebrity at the moment. Attempting to wipe out New York City with smallpox is good for one's Q rating, if nothing else.

While she waited, Heat sat in the barebones lobby, whose furniture had been bolted to the floor—not because anyone would steal it, but because it couldn't be used as a weapon that way. The families who visited were sometimes every bit as violent as the men who were on the inside, and every bit as unhappy to be there.

With nothing else to do, Heat stared at a portrait of the president of the United States—now a lame duck, perhaps soon to be replaced by the man who had spent the night pounding shots with her husband.

Twenty minutes passed. Heat had expected this, of course. Nothing happened quickly at prisons. Everyone there—from the inmates to the guards who were just counting the days until retirement—had altogether too much time on their hands to even consider rushing.

Forty minutes passed. Heat had now inspected not only the portrait of the president, but also those of the vice president, attorney general, and director of the Bureau of Prisons. She wondered if, when the photos were snapped, those people knew that someday the image would find its way to such a desperate, forlorn place.

Heat was just about to raise a fuss with the duty officer—really, how long could it take to locate one inmate?—when the door to the side of the bulletproof glass box slid open.

A tall, handsome man in a crisply ironed uniform stepped out. Heat stood.

"Captain Heat," he said. "I'm sorry to keep you waiting. I'm Captain Wills. I'm the assistant director of security here."

"Good morning," Heat said, ready to have him begin reciting the protocol he expected for her trip back to see Maggs.

Instead, he said, "Can I ask why you're looking to talk with inmate Maggs?"

"He may have information about a cold case we're looking into," Heat said.

"A cold case," Wills repeated. "So this wasn't because of something that happened recently?"

"No. It's old news. Something from the nineties," Heat said, only half lying.

"Ah," he said, then looked down at his well-polished shoes for a moment before bringing his gaze back up. "I wish you had called first. I could have saved you the trip, Captain. Carey Maggs is dead. He was murdered yesterday."

Heat felt the words like a bucket of ice water that had been dumped on her head. It shocked her upon first contact and was now running down her spine in a chilling flow.

Wills had paused, like he expected Heat to say something. When she didn't, he continued: "It happened sometime between lunch and dinner, but that's about all we know. The guard who delivered lunch said Maggs bitched about how he was supposed to get a kosher meal. Maggs was pretending to be Jewish. Some of the inmates do that because they think we spend more money on the kosher meals. We don't, but . . . Anyway, the guard who delivered dinner found him dead. He had a deep gash across his throat, like someone got him with a garotte wire. We're currently investigating but at this point we don't have a lot to go on."

"Well, it had to be his cellmate, right?"

"That's the thing. Maggs was in the Special Housing Unit. He didn't have a cellmate. He was supposed to be in that room, by himself, twenty-three hours a day. He had already had his hour out for the day. He should not have had any interaction whatsoever with other inmates or guards between lunch and dinner."

"But if it's the SHU, you must have a camera or two on his cell, yes?"

Wills looked down at his shoes again. "Not in the cell, no. And the camera that covers that block of cells had a, uh, a malfunction yesterday."

"A *malfunction*?" Heat said. She could feel the blood draining from her face.

"When we went back to review the footage, it wasn't there. We don't know if the software had some kind of glitch or if it was erased. The computer stores footage in three-hour blocks. The block from yesterday afternoon was missing."

Missing. Of course it was. Heat felt her anger rising. She almost didn't need to hear more. But she felt compelled to continue asking questions anyway, just to be sure.

"Did you find the murder weapon?" she asked.

"No, ma'am. We're still looking."

"What about fingerprints? Stray hairs left by the killer? Any kind of physical evidence?"

"Sorry," he said. "The blood was smeared in a way that suggests the killer was wearing gloves. Beyond that, we've been having inmates in the SHU change cells a lot lately. It makes it harder for them to stash cell phones, weapons, and other contraband. Maggs had only been in that particular cell for about two days. And it's not like we have maids clean the rooms between inmates. There have been a lot of people in and out of that cell. Anything we could have found in the way of hair or fibers would have been inconclusive anyway."

Having already shifted into detective mode, Heat was now trying to rule out some trigger for Maggs's murder unrelated to her mother.

"What about motive?" Heat asked. "Had Maggs been having a dispute with anyone? Some kind of beef during yard time?"

"Not that we're aware of."

"Was he involved in any of the gangs here?"

"Maggs? Oh, Lord, no. He was in the SHU by his own request in part so he could get away from the gangs. It sounds funny to say, because I know what got him sent here, but he wasn't a criminal like most of the people in here."

"Is it possible he owed another inmate money, something like that?"

Wills shook his head. "He kept totally to himself. Even during his hour out, all he did was walk the perimeter of the fence. I asked each of our regular guards in the SHU on all three shifts, and they all said Maggs was a loner. None of them could recollect him having any meaningful interaction with another inmate. They couldn't begin to figure out why anyone here would want him dead."

"So what you're saying is you have no leads."

"No, ma'am," he said, adding another, "I'm sorry."

Heat wanted to rail at the man's incompetence, but she knew it wouldn't help. Someone had slipped into Carey Maggs's cell, ended his life, then slipped out without detection. Perhaps it was a crooked guard. Perhaps it was a cunning inmate.

Whatever the case, Heat knew the task, while a logistical challenge, wasn't impossible. For whatever security systems may be in place, prisons are ultimately large bureaucracies. And bureaucracies are made up of human beings, who make mistakes—or who can be bribed or threatened to look the other way.

"You were part of the team that took Maggs down and prevented that attack in New York City a few years back, were you not?" Wills asked.

"That's right."

"Well, then I suppose you should know one more thing. Maybe you can help us make sense out of it, because we're a little stumped by it to be honest. It's not something we were planning on releasing to the public. So I'd appreciate you treating this information with some discretion."

"Okay," Heat said.

Having given a full preamble, Wills just came out with it: "Carey Maggs had his tongue cut out."

"*Cut out?*" Heat asked.

"Yes, ma'am. The body did not have a tongue."

"But was the tongue . . . I mean, did you find it somewhere?"

"No, ma'am. It wasn't in the cell. And we did a surprise inspection last night. We literally tossed every other cell in the facility. We turned mattresses inside out. We flipped over tables. We performed cavity searches. We thought maybe the killer kept the tongue as some kind of trophy. We were also looking for the murder weapon. But we didn't find that or the tongue."

"So I take it you're operating under the theory the killer was a non-inmate who took the tongue and the garotte out of the prison with him."

"That's correct," Wills said.

"Which means your chances of solving this are slim."

For a third time, Wills was looking down at his shoes. "Also correct," he said.

Heat excused herself, assuring Captain Wills she would contact him if she learned anything in her own investigation that might help theirs.

But as she departed the prison's offices, two things were already becoming clear to her.

One, Maggs's death and her mother's reappearance occurred within hours of each other, which didn't feel like a coincidence. Anyone on the outside who had wanted Maggs dead for some other reason would have done it long ago. And Maggs didn't seem to have done anything to attract enough ire from anyone on the inside. This had to be related to Cynthia Heat somehow.

And, two, you didn't go through the trouble of severing someone's tongue and then carrying it out of a prison just because it sounded like fun.

The killer was trying to send a message about what happens to people who talk.

Heat stumbled back to her car, then sat heavily inside.

Bart Callan was now the only person on her mind. If Maggs was dead, had someone also gotten to Callan? Certainly, it would be more difficult for a perpetrator to reach Callan at a supermax facility. But Heat didn't dismiss the possibility.

It was seven o'clock her time, which was five o'clock Colorado time. That might have been a problem if Florence ADX had been the local bank, but the one good thing about prisons was that they always had someone staffing them.

She dialed the number for the prison. After passing through an automated menu, she punched the right sequence of numbers to reach a real live corrections officer. She introduced herself, explained her interest—going with the cold case angle again—and asked if she could arrange a conversation sometime that morning with Bart Callan.

"Callan? Hang on," the officer said. Heat heard keys clacking in the background, then: "Sorry, Mr. Callan is no longer with us."

"What do you mean?" Heat asked.

"It says here he was transferred to FCI-Cumberland three weeks ago."

Three weeks ago. Heat wanted to scream.

"Cumberland?" Heat asked. "I wasn't aware of a maximum security facility in Cumberland."

"That's because it's medium security."

"How is it possible a serial murderer like Bart Callan got transferred to medium security?" Heat asked, hearing her voice rising.

"Couldn't tell you. That's the B.O.P.'s call."

Heat somehow doubted she would find anyone at the Bureau of Prisons who would be able to give an adequate explanation. "Okay, thank you," Heat said, then ended the call.

She immediately dialed the number she found for FCI-Cumberland. She repeated the same number-punching procedure she had gone through for Florence until she found a guard who sounded almost identical to the last one she had spoken with. Again, she identified herself and her concern. She finished with, "What would I have to do to arrange a conversation with inmate Bart Callan?"

"Callan?" the man volleyed back. "Well, first, you'd have to find him."

For the second time that morning, Heat felt the ice-water sensation pouring over her.

"What are you talking about?" she asked.

"Bart Callan escaped from a work detail yesterday," the man said. "Don't you watch the news? It was all over the place out here."

"Apparently, that didn't make it to New York," Heat said.

"Yeah, well, he was part of a crew picking up litter on a highway not far from here. We had five CO's with his group, all of them seasoned men. None of them could explain where Callan had gone. As best we can figure, he got about a half-hour head start before they did a count and noticed he was missing. Since then, we've had everything from dogs to drones after him. We've done roadblocks, you name it. No Bart Callan. Not yet, anyway."

Or ever, Heat wanted to say.

"Our boys'll find him, though," the man continued. "You can be sure of that. But maybe you can tell your boys to be on the lookout in case he shows up in New York for some reason, huh? And if you find him, send him back our way."

Heat assured the man she would before she ended the call.

Except, of course, she knew Bart Callan all too well. She had been given a front-row seat to his treachery. He had not simply walked away from that work detail. He had likely been masterminding his flight plan for months. And he had not done it on his own. He'd had help. High-placed, highly capable help.

The authorities could search all they wanted to. They were never going to find him.

TWENTY-TWO

Heat didn't see any more of the countryside on her way back to New York than she had on her way out. Nor did her eyes linger on the mountains. Or the rivers.

This time, it wasn't because of darkness. It was because she was staring furiously ahead, using the windshield time to attempt to make sense of this chaotic series of events.

In rough order: her mother appeared, Carey Maggs was killed, and Bart Callan disappeared. All within hours of one another.

It was breathtaking. And, clearly, it was connected—coordinated, even?—in some manner. But what was the bigger picture? And who was behind it? And what did it mean?

Up until the previous morning, Heat had thought she understood the entirety of this twisted trail, having walked every step of it. Her mother was silenced because she was going to expose Tyler Wynn, who himself had gotten involved in the wicked smallpox plot of Carey Maggs, who was being aided by Bart Callan. It was . . . well, not neat. There was nothing neat about it.

But it was over. If nothing else, Heat thought the trail had ended.

Except now there was clearly something new happening. There had been some kind of precipitating incident.

Was it simply that her mother had come out of hiding? Had that been the trigger that led to Maggs's death and Callan's flight?

Or was her mother's appearance the result of something, not the cause of something?

Nikki was every bit as flummoxed at the end of the drive as she had been at the beginning. She parked the unmarked car behind the Twentieth Precinct, then, instead of marching through the back entrance, she walked around to the front. She could barely even admit it to herself, but, yes, she suddenly sensed her mother was there.

It was a hunch. Or maybe just a hope.

Heat scanned up and down 82nd Street. Her gaze lingered on the bus shelter, which was empty. She looked in alleys, behind parked cars, near tree trunks. She looked at every passerby, female or male—she had no doubt her mother could disguise herself as an old man as easily as she'd become an old woman.

But there was no one who raised Heat's suspicions. She leaned against the brick wall of the precinct, closed her eyes, and tried to put her most fervent wish out to the universe with all the force she could:

Mom, just come in. If you're in danger, I'll protect you. If you need something, I'll help you. Let's be together again. Like we were when I was a little girl. Like we were on the steps of that Roman piazza. Let's drink Bolla Valpolicella and solve all our problems together. There's nothing we can't conquer if we join forces.

She opened her eyes.

It was the same street it had been. With the same passersby, who were now just a little bit farther along in their journeys.

And Cynthia Heat was nowhere to be seen.

Just like she had been for all but a half second of the last seventeen years.

There were tears beginning to well in Nikki Heat's eyes. And that was the last thing a commander needed: to be seen weeping on the street outside her own precinct.

So Heat stood, stuffed her concerns about her mother into the most airtight compartment in her head she could find, and walked back inside. She would have to be a daughter later. Right then, it was closing in on ten o'clock in the morning and she needed to be a captain again.

Her first sight upon returning to the bull pen triggered a strong sense of déjà vu.

It was Raley, sitting exactly where he had been sitting when she'd left him the night before, wearing exactly the same clothes, still with the headphones clamped tight over his ears.

Heat went over to him. "Rales, did you go home last night?"

"No, thanks," he said. "I just had a cup."

His eyes never left the computer screen. Heat was next to him now. There was a bit of an odor wafting from him, a stench that told her his twenty-four-hour deodorant had passed the limits of its endurance.

"Hello? Earth to Raley? Please report to your captain. What are you doing?"

"That's okay, I'm not hungry," he said.

Heat reached for the front of the computer and pulled the headphone jack out of its port. Raley startled for a moment, then looked at her blankly.

"Hello. My name is Nikki Heat. Your name is Sean Raley. Are you with me?"

"Sorry, sorry," he said, removing his headphones and stretching out his arms, unleashing more stench.

Heat drew back, though he seemed not to notice.

"Did you sleep at all last night?" she asked.

"Yeah, I hit the couch in your office for a few hours. Don't worry, I feel like a million dollars."

"Yeah," Heat said. "Well, I'm sorry to tell you, but you smell like a buck fifty. And I think the money has been incubating in a homeless person's mouth all night."

Raley sniffed his right armpit, then his left. "Huh, I don't—"

Then he stopped himself. "Oh. Pungent."

"All right, I'm going to take two steps back now," Heat said. "But why don't you tell me what you've been up to."

"Yeah, sorry. I've been working the beheading tape like you asked. I focused in on one twenty-second bite where I felt like the audio was pretty clean. I isolated it, then started scrubbing it. How much technical detail do you want to be bored with about the de-filtering process?"

"Very, very little," Heat assured him.

"Okay, well then all you need to know is this is painstaking . . . but possible. The trick is you need to work with very narrow bands of frequencies. The best analogy I can come up with is that it's like making a copy of a painting while only being able to see one tiny little strip of it at a time. Which you can do, as long as you're very careful and very precise. One strip at a time, the painting comes together. Or, in this case, the recording. And eventually what you get is this."

Raley clicked the play button.

"*There is no greater symbol of your ignorance than your lying puppet media, which only exists to spread the distorted propaganda of your Zionist government. And there is no greater sin than the way your people allow your women to shamefully expose their bodies and flaunt that which ought to be seen only by their husbands.*"

Heat instantly recognized the words, but not the voice. It no longer sounded like Darth Vader or Kylo Ren. It sounded more like the deejay at the college radio station, nervous about his first on-air shift.

Just to be sure, Heat asked, "So what I'm hearing is . . ."

"The voice of American ISIS completely unfiltered," Raley finished. "To be clear, it's not the original any more than a copy of a Renoir is an actual Renoir. But it sounds exactly like the original—in the same way a good copy looks exactly like the original. All effects of the audio masking have been removed.

"Now," Raley continued, "listen to this."

Raley hit play again, and a familiar voice came out of the speakers.

"Look, I told this to the other guy. I didn't do nothing. I don't know nothing about this girl, or no beheading, or nothing like that. Just because I'm Muslim don't make me a terrorist. Damn. I'm an American, just like you."

It was Hassan El-Bashir, with his "New Yawk" accent and his baritone timbre—at least half an octave deeper than the one on the American ISIS video, and with completely different inflections.

"I ran those two samples against each other," Raley said. "It came back as a thirteen percent match. That's the lowest score I had ever seen for samples that were at least theoretically the same language. Or at least it was the lowest until I ran this one."

Raley hit play on another file.

"*Lawyer. Lawyer. Lawyer. That's all I'm gonna say, motherfucker, so you might as well get used to it. Lawyer. Lawyer. Lawyer.*"

The man pronounced the word "law-yuh," in true Bronx fashion. His pitch was even deeper than El-Bashir's.

"That was Tariq Al-Aman," Raley said. "And he scored an eleven percent."

"So, just to make sure I'm understanding this properly, there is just barely north of a ten percent chance the men in the video are Tariq Al-Aman and Hassan El-Bashir."

"No. It's actually something far worse than that. An eleven percent match means that, from the standpoint of vocal quality, there is only eleven percent of Al-Aman's voice that overlaps with the other sample. To even begin to consider two samples a match, you need to have at least a ninety percent overlap, if not more."

"So an eleven percent overlap is . . ."

"Absolutely, positively, and without a shadow of a doubt, not a match," Raley said. "I'd testify to it in court."

"Which means the two men currently in federal custody are . . ."

"Not our guys," Raley confirmed.

Heat closed her eyes for a moment. Their entire investigation had just been blown out of the water. Her seemingly ideal suspects—two young men, angry and radicalizing in their devotion to Islam—were nothing more than two foul-mouthed hotheads whose protestations of innocence had actually been real.

Worst of all, she was only minimally closer to figuring out who was behind American ISIS than she had been when she first laid eyes on the video. They had all been running as fast as they could, but unbeknownst to them, they had been doing so in quicksand. It had been an intense effort that had barely gotten them anywhere.

"I'm sorry," Raley said. "I know this isn't what you wanted."

Heat lifted her chin.

"All I ever want is the truth, Rales, you know that," she said. "But now if you'll excuse me, I think I have a phone call to make."

Heat went into her office, picked up her desk phone, and called Yardley Bell's mobile number. It rang once, twice. On the third ring, Heat heard:

"Nikki Heat. Don't tell me you've found some new excuse why this is your case. Because I can assure you—"

"Can it, Yardley," Heat said. "You have to cut El-Bashir and Al-Aman loose."

"And why would we possibly do that?"

"Because they're innocent."

"What . . . What are you talking about?"

"Innocent. That's a ninety-four cent word that means they didn't do it."

"Nikki, I don't have time for—"

Heat interrupted with a brief explanation of what Raley had uncovered. Bell seemed to be listening. But her response at the end nearly took Heat's breath away.

"I don't see how that changes anything from our perspective," Bell said.

"Yardley, what are you talking about? *They didn't do it.*"

"Yes, but ISIS doesn't know that. As far as they're concerned, they're getting the genuine item. The stars of the New York video. I've seen their Facebook posts and so has everyone else who matters. Those kids can talk the talk even if they didn't walk the walk. Hell, once we tell them what our plan is, they'll probably start taking credit for the video, just for the street cred it gives them with their ISIS homeboys. The point is, they're a valuable commodity, and we'll be getting what we need in return. That's what matters here."

"You couldn't possibly be that twisted," Heat said. "Those kids aren't bargaining chips. They're human beings."

"Nikki, don't go all 4-H club on me. We may be playing in a sandbox over there, but believe me, it's not kindergarten recess time. Obviously, this is over your head. You just worry about the jaywalkers on 7th Avenue and let us handle the grown-up stuff. Now, if you'll excuse me—"

"I'll go public," Heat said quickly.

Bell went silent for a moment. Heat filled the void with: "I've got a friend at the *Ledger*. He's Tam's boss, actually. If you don't cut those kids loose, I'll tell him the NYPD has developed credible exculpatory evidence showing the two lead suspects cannot possibly be responsible for the video, and that the Department of Homeland Security is holding them anyway. I'm sure that'll play great, DHS detaining two American citizens for no reason."

Bell's response came out in a growl. "You do that, and I'll have the US Attorney's Office on your ass faster than flies on shit."

"Go ahead and try, Yards. What are they going to charge me with? Administration of justice? Excessive kindness? Protecting the innocent? I'm trying to do the right thing here. Good luck finding a jury who would convict me for it."

"Doesn't matter. The US Attorney's Office can indict a ham sandwich. You know that. And once you're indicted? Well, the NYPD could hardly have someone under that kind of cloud running one of its precincts. You'd be placed on administrative leave and stripped of your command. And then, you know, the federal courts can be so slow sometimes. A couple of continuances. A change of venue. Then, right before trial, we'd have to switch prosecutors and delay things some more. We could keep you spinning through the system for a good four, five years. By the time you got cleared, you'd be such damaged goods the NYPD could never give you your precinct back. You'd be *that* Captain Heat. I bet they'd stick you in the quartermaster's office. Just think how satisfying your life would be, spending your day finding the lowest bidder for paperclips."

Heat wished she could see Bell's eyes right then. Because she was sure this was a bluff.

Well, mostly sure.

Somewhat sure.

Okay, a little sure.

Whatever the odds actually were, there was only one way to beat a bluffer in poker, whether it was a professional liar like James Patterson or an ethically ambivalent federal agent like Yardley Bell.

Call them on it.

"You know what, Yardley?" Heat said. "That sounds like a load of fun. And let's see how much resolve you have when every Muslim in New York is protesting outside your office."

"We can ruin you, Nikki. You know that."

"I'd like to see you go ahead and try," Heat said. "I'll make sure

DHS has so much egg on its face, your bosses are going to wonder if they should just quit and open an omelet shop.

"In the meantime, here's how this is going to go. You've got until noon today to release those boys. If you don't, I'm going to the *Ledger*, and then I guess we'll see who is going to ruin whom."

"You're throwing away your career, Heat. Don't do it."

"You want a fight, Yardley, you got it," Heat said. "I can't tell you how much I'm going to enjoy this."

She slammed down the phone, feeling rectitude in every part of her body.

Except for her hands. Those were shaking.

TWENTY-THREE

Half an hour later, Heat had her detectives assembled around her, having called them back into the bull pen.

Well, most of them. Raley was at home, taking a well-deserved nap—hopefully followed by a much-needed shower. In his absence, Heat took it upon herself to inform everyone about the results of his all-nighter and its significance.

The grim faces around her reflected the bleakness of their reality. Ochoa, Rhymer, and Feller had struck out on their canvass, both the previous night and that morning. And while they had only been able to leave business cards at some of the apartments that faced the alley, they knew that was the police equivalent of playing the lottery.

Aguinaldo, now rested from her shopping trip, had spent the morning trying to run down the scarf from other angles, surfing fashion Web sites and calling auction houses that had sold off Laura Hopper scarves. So far, she had no leads.

It was more than twenty-four hours since they had first become aware of this crime and more than seventy-two hours since it had been committed. Those were critical hours. And everyone assembled knew the statistics: most cases were solved within the first forty-eight hours or not at all.

But there they were, still without a single credible suspect. It was time to regroup. And fast.

"Okay, so here's the deal: We're basically starting over," Heat said. "But we're starting over with two significant advantages. We know who the victim is and we know where the killing happened. Miguel, do you still have that list of known Muslim extremists from McMains?"

"Yeah."

"Okay, we're going to divide and conquer. I want each of you to take a quarter of that list and start working through it. See if any of the people or groups on there have ties to Masjid al-Jannah. See if Muharib Qawi will come in and help us. We made the mistake of getting a little bit of tunnel vision on El-Bashir and Al-Aman. Let's try to broaden our scope now."

All around her, heads were bobbing.

"I'm going to work the Tam Svejda angle," Heat announced. "She was up to *something* out in Ohio. I'm going to try and figure out what."

"Sounds good, Captain," said Ochoa, whose heroic-but-pathetic act of limping toward his desk for the folder he had gotten from McMains had the effect of breaking up the meeting.

Heat followed him, then veered off to Raley's desk. He had been the one to contact the Lorain Police Department the day before. Heat could have woken him up to ask him who he talked with, but it seemed much more humane to search his desk for his notebook first. Ignoring the lingering smell of body odor, she moved aside printouts and manuals pertaining to audio de-filtering until she found a small wire-bound pad.

After a few page flips she came across *Lt. Jen Forbus, Lorain PD.* It was followed by a phone number.

Heat dialed it. As the line rang, Heat reminded herself she needed to recalibrate her manners. She wasn't going to be dealing with a brusque, impatient, perpetually ironic fellow New Yorker. The person on the other end of the phone would be polite, straightforward, and courteous.

And Heat would just have to bear it.

Moments later, Heat heard the kind of cheerful, middle-of-America accent she had been expecting.

"Lorain Police Department Detective Squad. This is Lieutenant Forbus. How can I help you today?"

"Lieutenant Forbus, this is Captain Nikki Heat of the NYPD," she said, then forced out, "How are you today?"

"Why, hello, Captain Heat. I'm doing just super, thank you for asking. How are you?"

"Very well, thank you."

"Gosh, that's just great," Forbus said. "So what can I do for you today?"

"Thank you for asking," Heat said, feeling pleased with herself that she had forged such an instant bond with this hinterland-dweller. But now, having established friendly relations, it was time to get on with it.

"Yesterday afternoon, I think you spoke with one of my detectives, Sean Raley?"

"Oh, yeah, he sure seemed like a nice fellow."

"He absolutely is. I was calling to see if you had a chance to circulate the picture he sent you?"

"We sure did," Forbus said. "Because, you know, we don't have any of our own cases. People out here are too simpleminded to even *think* about committing crimes. So we really have nothing better to do than ask 'how high' whenever a big-city detective tells us to jump."

Forbus continued, her tone every bit as friendly: "As a matter of fact, you know the only reason we in Ohio exist *at all* is to make New Yorkers feel superior to us. We *love* it when you refer to us as flyover country. It makes us feel so *special* that you sometimes consider waving to us as you pass above us in your fancy jet air-o-planes. Why, the little boys and girls in Lorain spend most of their time staring up into the sky, saying to themselves, 'Gee, I hope those fancy New Yorkers are looking down on us right now.'

"No, the fact is, Ohio isn't good for much. All we do here is beat the crap out of your sorry basketball team and pick your next president for you."

Heat still hadn't spoken. She couldn't get her mouth to work.

Forbus finally giggled. "Captain Heat, I hope you know I'm messing with you right now."

"Right! Right, of course," Heat stammered.

"Good. Now as for your victim. We took her picture around yesterday. There's no doubt she attracted a lot of notice, mostly from our male citizens. She started at the Jackalope, where she ate by herself at the bar. She was there for thirty-five minutes. She ordered a Caesar salad, a yellow Lake Erie perch, and a glass of white wine, which she only half finished. Then she paid her bill, tipped twenty percent, and left."

"Did she say anything about what she was doing out there?"

"Nope. The bartender admitted he gave her his very best service, on account of her being pretty much the most beautiful woman who had ever walked into the place. But it sounds like she shut him down pretty good. He said he couldn't get more than five words out of her at a time. She was just staring at her phone most of the time. It was the same story at Mutt and Jeff's the next morning. She came. She ordered. She ate. She kept her head down. She left."

"Oh. Well, I'm sorry to have troubled—"

"Oh, wait. There's more. After she left the Jackalope Thursday night, she hit East 28th Street, and everything changed."

"What's on East 28th Street?"

"Pretty much every dive bar in town. You've got City Bar, Three Star, the International Lounge, Grown and Sexy."

"Grown and Sexy?" Heat asked.

"The Grown and Sexy Lounge, 'Where the grown come out to play.' That's what its sign says, anyway," Forbus said. "These are steelworker hangouts. I don't want to say we're only in business because they're in business. But they do keep us busy. They stay open at all hours to accommodate the shifts at the mills, so no matter when you get off work, you can go pound a few. They're the kind of places that pretty much serve both beers."

"What does that mean?"

"Bud and Bud Light," Forbus said. "Anyhow, your victim apparently hit the row and hit it hard."

"She did?"

"Why do you sound so surprised?"

"I guess I'm not, it's just . . . She was traveling on business, yet no charges from any of those places showed up on her card."

"Oh, Captain Heat. Have you ever been to a steelworker's bar? You're looking at a male–female ratio of about ten to one. Do you think a woman like Tam Svejda had to buy herself a drink at *any* of those establishments? To me the only surprise is that we didn't have to send a car out there to break up fights between the guys who were lining up to get her next round."

"Fair point. Okay, so she goes to these bars, men start tripping over themselves, and . . . then what?"

"Well, it sounds like she was a lot more friendly to them than she was to the bartender at the Jackalope, that's for sure."

"Friendly how?"

"Just flirting a lot. Though she was pretty skillful about not letting anyone get too close. She'd kind of flirt with one, then move on and flirt with another, then move to the next bar and flirt some more. It was just a little chitchat, apparently. But you can't imagine what a stir she made around here."

"What was she chitchatting about?"

"Everything and nothing. Which is another way of saying I really don't know. These are blue-collar guys, Captain Heat. They're not exactly forthcoming with the police. They pretty much think of us as the people who are there to ruin their fun. And even the ones that will talk to us aren't providing us court transcripts of their conversations. From the best we could figure she was just asking them questions about where they lived, where they worked, what they did there, that sort of thing. Just your basic biographical stuff. The kind of stuff we ask all the time. It sounded like she was interviewing them, but they probably didn't know they were being interviewed."

"Mostly because they were too busy leering at her," Heat suggested.

"Well, exactly. I talked to some of the guys myself and most of them were just falling over themselves to tell me how hot she was. And let me tell you how much I enjoyed that."

"But did she go home with anyone?"

Forbus laughed. "In their dreams, yeah. No, the furthest any of them got was that a few of them gave her their phone numbers. At which point, they became instant legends with their buddies. But I talked to a bartender at Grown and Sexy, which was her last stop. He said she left alone. One of the guys walked her out to her car—we have nothing but gentlemen here in Lorain—but then he came right back in."

"Did you talk to any of the guys who handed out their digits?"

"Afraid not. People's memories tended to get real fuzzy at that point, on account of the drinking and the late hour."

"In other words, they worried they were going to get their friends in trouble."

"Bingo," Forbus said.

"Well, you can assure them we're not thinking this was some kind of sexual assault gone wrong. We know she left alone. We also know she was in one piece at breakfast the next morning. What I really want to figure out is if those steelworkers whose numbers she took had anything in common. I can't imagine it was their charm or the cleverness of their pickup lines. She was obviously after something specific."

"Oh, I'm not done with those guys," Forbus assured her. "I was talking to them in the bars, so they weren't going to give up anything there. Not in front of the other guys. But I'll get them at home sometime later. If they don't cooperate, I'll find a way to get some leverage on them. It shouldn't be hard. I'll get you those names, Captain Heat, it's just going to take me a little bit of time."

"Okay, I really appreciate that."

Forbus promised she'd be back in touch as soon as she knew more. The women swapped mobile numbers and e-mail addresses.

"By the way, I wasn't kidding about picking your president," Forbus said as they wrapped up the call. "You know Ohio has correctly predicted every presidential election since 1964."

"I know," Heat said.

"For the record, we're going to vote for Lindsy Gardner," Forbus said. "A librarian for president is exactly what this country needs."

After settling the phone back on the receiver, Heat wandered back out to the bull pen and to the murder board, which no longer contained the mug shots of two young New York Muslims.

It was, in truth, a depressingly empty board. Tam Svejda's professionally done portrait was there. The words *zinc* and *kerosene* were underneath her. A picture of Masjid al-Jannah hung nearby. So did a picture of the Laura Hopper scarf from the video.

Grabbing a dry-erase marker, she drew a line from Svejda's picture, then she drew three circles, also connected by lines. In the first she wrote *Joanna Masters's bullet*. In the second, *New York → Cleveland → Lorain, Ohio*. In the third, *Interviewing steelworkers*.

She paused for a moment, then drew another line and a fourth circle. In that one, she scrawled a question mark, signifying they didn't know where Svejda went next. It also neatly summed up what Heat could figure out about what this sequence of events meant. Maybe nothing. Maybe everything.

She wished Rook was there. He had a way of staring at the murder board, of looking at the exact same words she was, and yet forming them into a completely different story.

Heat was doing little more than staring at the board's white space, lost in concentration, when she heard a commotion coming from the far hallway.

"I said get your motherfuckin' hands off me. I ain't no suspect no more. I can walk without you grabbing my arm."

It was a "New Yawk" accent that, by now, she recognized. She just never thought that, of all the places fate and circumstance might have taken Hassan El-Bashir, he would again be treading the floors of the Twentieth Precinct. Certainly not voluntarily.

Her first reaction was relief. Yardley Bell had, improbably, done the right thing. Calling her bluff had been the correct decision, for all involved.

Her second reaction was curiosity. What was El-Bashir doing back there? He rounded the corner with the day-shift desk sergeant behind him.

"He showed up saying he wanted to talk to the 'lady captain,'" the sergeant said apologetically. "I tried to get a statement out of him, but—"

"But I ain't talking to no one but the lady captain," El-Bashir finished defiantly.

"Well, hello, Hassan," Heat said. "It's very nice to see you again. It's Captain Heat, by the way."

"Yeah, yeah, whatever. Look, can we talk? I spent the night getting anal probes from whatever *X-Files*, Area 51, black-ops bullshit place that fed lady put me in and I just want to get home."

"Okay," Heat said. "Would my office be okay?"

"Better than the one-way mirror room," he huffed.

"Right this way," Heat said, gesturing toward her office and holding open the door for him.

"You all right, Captain?" the sergeant asked.

"Yes. Thank you, Sergeant."

Heat closed the door behind El-Bashir, who had already taken a seat in front of her desk. She consciously chose the chair next him, rather than put the desk between them. It was a small gesture, a trick of psychology as much as anything, but it established a small measure of intimacy with a citizen who, understandably, had some trust issues regarding law enforcement at the moment.

"So what's up, Hassan?" she asked, angling her chair toward him.

Out of the presence of the desk sergeant—and anyone else in uniform—he now seemed more relaxed, no longer feeling the same need to show how tough he was.

"Yo, I just wanted to say thank you, Captain Heat," he said. "I don't know what those feds were going to do to me, but I think I was heading for some waterboarding at Guantanamo or some shit. But that fed lady, she told me you did me a real solid, with that audio stuff. She said you even stuck your neck out for me and kind of forced her to let me go."

"Just doing my job, Hassan," Heat said.

"Yeah, I know. I just . . . Well, let's just say I ain't been around a lot of cops who are decent like that, you know? I mean, some of them pretend to be your friend but you know it's bullshit, because they're just trying to get close to you so they can bust you or so you'll snitch on someone else. But you? Man, you for real. That fed lady said I owed you big time, and she's right."

"Well, you're welcome," Heat said, giving him a warm smile, hoping perhaps he would remember in his future interactions with the NYPD that the vast majority of cops really were motivated by the same good angels that she was.

El-Bashir shifted in his seat a little bit. Heat sensed he had something else on his mind, but she was going to let him come around to it in his own time.

Finally, he came out with: "So, I got something to tell you. I think . . . Well, I don't know if it matters or not. To be honest, I wasn't gonna say shit about this. In my neighborhood, snitches get stitches, you feel me? You don't go volunteering nothing to the cops. But I feel like . . . Well, I owe you one."

Heat nodded.

"So you remember how I told you we were at Masjid al-Jannah on Saturday night, Skyping with that imam in Saudi Arabia?"

"Of course."

"That wasn't bullshit. We really were Skyping—and just Skyping. But the thing is . . . well, I don't know what was about to happen, but something was going down right around the time we left."

Heat could practically feel the bolt of energy coming up from her chair, but she kept herself calm.

"What do you mean, Hassan?"

"So we were done with our Skype, and we were getting ready to leave, when we heard something behind the mosque. I went over to the window and looked out, and I seen these two big black SUVs pulling up. They had these tall antennas, like they were cop cars or something."

"Cop cars?" Heat asked. There was any number of divisions of the NYPD that might have black SUVs in its fleet. For that matter, the vehicles could have been state. Or federal. No branch of government had a monopoly on the ubiquitous black SUV.

"Did you manage to catch the make or model? Were they Fords? Chevys?"

El-Bashir was shaking his head. "They had white pinstriping on the side. That's . . . that's really the only other thing I saw."

"Okay, so then what?"

"Well, these guys got out. There were four of them. Two from each SUV. And they were huge. Like, I was looking down on them from the second floor and they were *still* taller than me, you feel me? They were dressed in all black. And they had muscles on their muscles, you know? They looked like they were mob guys or something."

"What makes you think that?"

"I don't know. I mean, for one, they were white."

"White? As in Caucasian? Are you sure?"

"Yeah, no doubt."

El-Bashir read the incredulity on Heat's face. "I ain't clowning you, Captain Heat. I know the Arab with the towel on his head is supposed to be your bad guy here. But I'm telling you, these dudes were white as you. And, I don't know, they just looked like bad news, you know? Who else has dudes like that but the mob?"

Heat could think of a lot of possibilities, but she didn't want to interrupt El-Bashir's flow. "Okay, what next?"

"I don't know. I mean, we weren't going to stick around to find out. Tariq was shutting down the computer and I was like, 'Yo, 'Riq, we gotta go, man.' I told him what I was seeing and he was like, 'Yeah. Let's get the hell out of here.' So we did."

"And what time did this all take place?"

"A little after one in the morning. Couldn't tell you the exact time. I wasn't exactly worried about looking at the clock. We just took off."

"Do you think you could describe any of the mob guys to a sketch artist?"

El-Bashir's face contorted. "Not really. I mean . . . I wasn't really looking at any of them real close. They were just big white guys. Sorry. It all happened so fast."

Big white guys. Black SUVs with white pinstripes and big antennas.

It signified a higher level of organization, of planning, of money. Of threat. Heat didn't know what was going on, but she'd actually liked it a lot better when she'd thought it was just two overzealous former juvenile delinquents.

"That's okay, Hassan," Heat said. She reached across to her desk, plucked a business card off it, and handed it to Hassan. "If you think of anything else, just give me a call, okay?"

"A'ight," he said. "And thanks again, Captain Heat."

"My pleasure," she said.

And she meant it.

TWENTY-FOUR

Having escorted El-Bashir out, Heat had settled back at her desk and was beginning to power through the mound of paperwork that had a way of breeding while her back was turned. And it seemed to get especially fecund when she was in the middle of a critical case.

She had lowered the mound by perhaps half an inch when she heard the welcome sound of Jameson Rook, entering the bull pen with his usual flourish.

"Luuuu-cy! I'm hoooo-oooome," he sang out.

Heat came out in time to see Rook toss his garment bag onto the wonky chair, then exchange fist bumps with the detectives.

"I came straight here," he announced. "Didn't even stop at home."

"Yeah, yeah, that's great," Ochoa said, barely able to contain himself. "You were on the plane, right?"

"What plane?" Rook asked, doing a poor job of looking innocent.

"Don't you play hard to get with me, Rook. I'll tase your ass. Come on. Give it up. You saw the bed, didn't you?"

"Bed? Was there a bed on that plane?"

"That's it. I'm charging the Taser."

"Okay, okay," Rook said. "Yes, there is a bed. Yes, it is king-sized. And, yes, I did sleep on it. Lana insisted."

Ochoa let out a little-girl-style shriek and brought his hands to his mouth in excitement.

Rook glanced quickly at Heat and added, "Alone, I assure you."

"What's it like?" Ochoa cooed. "Sprawling out all over the place at thirty-eight-thousand feet?"

"On thousand thread-count sheets? Atop the plushest, softest pillow-top mattress you've ever experienced? Pretty much the coolest thing since the air-conditioning of the American South."

Ochoa put his hand across his heart. *"Dios mío,"* he said reverently. "I mean, don't get me wrong, I'm still voting for Lindsy Gardner, because of her—"

Heat cleared her throat.

"—domestic policies," Ochoa said. "And she doesn't want to build a castle with a moat along our southern border. But it's still hard to beat Legs Kline for the overall cool factor."

"I don't know. The bed was pretty awesome, don't get me wrong. But if I was pimping out a flying vessel, I think I'd rather have smuggling compartments, like the *Millennium Falcon.* You just never know when you're going to be on the run from Jabba the Hutt."

"Nah," Ochoa said. "I think I'm going with the bed."

"Suit yourself. But I actually haven't even told you the coolest part," Rook said giddily. "So we were doing shots last night—"

"Wait, who's we?"

"Legs and me and some of his team."

"Including Lana?"

"Well, yes, if you're interested in that sort of thing."

Ochoa placed his hand back on his heart.

"Anyway," Rook continued, "we were doing shots, and one thing led to another, and we were, admittedly, getting a little sloppy. But we were having such a good time and getting along so well, he said that he was going to create a new cabinet position for me."

"What, Secretary of Stupid?" Feller asked.

"Is that a real thing?" Rhymer asked.

Rook ignored them both. "Legs promised that if he's elected, he's going to appoint me as the United States's first-ever"—he paused to give the moment its due gravitas—"minister of magic."

Heat couldn't stop her eyes from rolling.

"We hashed out my budget and everything. Admittedly, this was after about the sixth shot. Then we toasted Dumbledore with the seventh. So I'm a little fuzzy on some of the details this morning. But there's no question he's giving me broad latitude to run the ministry as I see fit."

Rook went over and clapped Rhymer on the shoulder. "You know, I'm going to need someone to head my Muggle Relations Office. I could use a good man for the job."

"Just as long as you don't want me to teach Defense Against the Dark Arts," Rhymer said.

"Oh, God, Opie," Heat muttered. "Not you, too."

"What?" Rhymer said. "That job is like a death sentence."

"So what's been going on here?" Rook asked. "You get those two ISIS wannabes to spill their guts? You know, once I'm appointed minister of magic, I *could* just send them to Azkaban."

Heat told him about how Raley's work with the video had exonerated the men, and that they were essentially back at square one. Rook's face changed as she was talking. She could tell he was doing what he did best: thinking through the investigation in his own peculiar way, trying to fit everything together, seeing what was left loose when he was done.

"What about the scarf?" Rook asked when Heat was through with her briefing. "Anything ever come of that?"

Aguinaldo volunteered, "Believe me, you don't want the long version of that story. The short version is that it's a Laura Hopper scarf."

"A Laura Hopper, really?" Rook said, excited.

"Why am I not surprised that would mean something to him," Ochoa said to Feller.

"I believe the word is 'metrosexual,'" Feller said.

Rook didn't let their attempt at ball-busting slow him down. "No, seriously, that's a great break. Every Laura Hopper is unique. That's part of what makes them so sought after. That, and Laura Hopper is just generally kick-ass awesome. Point is, all we have to do is figure out who owns this particular Laura Hopper and we'll have a major, major lead."

"Well, that's the problem," Aguinaldo said. "No one in the New York fashion world seems to know. Everyone recognizes it as an original Laura Hopper, but no one seems to be able to tell me a thing about this particular piece. And Laura herself is totally unreachable for the next three weeks."

Rook actually laughed.

"What's so funny?" Heat asked.

"What did her assistant tell you? Bora Bora or Seychelles?"

"Tahiti, actually," Aguinaldo said. "How did you—"

"And let me guess: the only people who have access to her are doting manservants who have signed nondisclosure agreements?"

"Actually, strapping cabana boys who have been sworn to secrecy on pain of death."

"Ah! That's even better! I love it when overprotective assistants up their game like that. Hang on," Rook said, whipping out his phone.

He jabbed at the screen perhaps four times then brought it up to his ear. "Don't feel bad she got you. She uses that story on all the undesirables. There was this one time she even had me going with it . . . Hold up."

Rook re-gripped the phone then boomed out: "Laura Hopper, you crazy redheaded bitch, it's Jameson Rook, how are you?"

He cupped the phone for a moment—"Don't worry. Private joke," he explained—then returned it to his ear.

"Oh, I'm just up to my usual, comforting the afflicted and afflicting the comfortable, like any good journalist should."

He listened for a moment then said, "Has it been that long? No, no, we saw each other at Bono's thing. Remember? The beach barbecue? We had that cute twenty-three-year-old English duke absolutely convinced you were an assassin who seduced men and then slit their throats, remember?"

Rook listened, then laughed. "You didn't," he said. "Oh, you are *so* bad."

He cupped the phone again. "She actually ended up taking the duke home. Which is pretty typical, actually. Men turn into Silly Putty around Laura Hopper."

Rook brought the phone back to his ear. "Well, *of course* he thought he was falling in love with you. I keep telling you, these guys aren't just toys for your amusement."

There was more talking on the other end. "I don't know," Rook said. "I think Duchess Laura Hopper has a nice ring to it, doesn't it?"

After another moment or two, Rook was nodding. "Yes, yes. I guess I get that. Can't tie yourself down, even to royalty."

He listened, then laughed again. "Too much, too much. Anyhow, listen, what are you doing for lunch today?"

There was a response, to which Rook replied, "Don't you play that game with me. I'll tell Brad about your duke."

Rook quickly put his hand over the mouthpiece and explained, "She's been seeing Bradley Cooper on the side . . . *Shhh!* The gossip rags have no idea."

He brought the phone back up, continuing the rapid-fire conversation, only one side of which Heat and the rest of them could hear.

"Great, that's more like it. How about twelve-thirty at Harlow . . . Are you kidding? I practically trained the chef there. Where do you think he learned how to do the world's greatest truffled egg sandwich? No, they took the mussels off the menu three weeks ago, but they now have Rappahannock River oysters from Virginia that are just *to die* for. But make sure you save room for the banana zapin. Best dessert *ever* . . . Okay if I bring a friend? She's a big fan and wants to ask a few questions about one of your scarves . . . Come on, you know me better than that. Okay, okay, you got a deal. Great. We'll see you in a bit, then . . . You too. Buh-bye."

He ended the call then looked around to see everyone staring at him.

"What?" Rook said.

"You know how weird it is that you can do that with, like, anyone on the planet?" Heat said.

"No. I'm sure there's someone living in a thatched hut in Micronesia who I could not get on the phone," Rook assured her. "Although, actually, now that I think about it, I do know this guy Tosiwo, who lives on Pohnpei, and he might—"

"Enough!" Heat said. "All right, people. Back to work. The Jameson Rook Show is over for the time being."

"Next performance in twenty minutes!" Rook said, but Heat shut him down with a glare.

"Never mind, it's just been cancelled," he said.

As the detectives went back to their respective desks, Heat tugged on Rook's sleeve. "Can I talk to you for a second?" she asked, jerking her head toward her office.

"Of course," Rook said. Then he turned to Aguinaldo. "You got the picture of that scarf?" he asked.

She patted the breast pocket of her suit jacket.

"Great," he said. "We'll probably want to take off in about ten minutes. Subway would be best if it's okay with you. The B will take us within a few blocks."

"Yeah, sure," Aguinaldo said.

"Great. Trust me, we do not want to be late. *No one* keeps Laura Hopper waiting."

Rook grabbed his garment bag off the wonky chair. Heat was holding the door to her office open for him. As she closed the door, he strolled to the other side of the room, then tossed his bag in the corner.

When he turned, Heat was there. She grabbed him by the back of his neck and used it as a lever to draw him toward her. As she locked her lips on his, she simultaneously brought their lower halves together for a full-body experience that instantly rated as the highlight of her day.

If her yearning for him in that moment could have been put on a scale, it would have outweighed Saturn. It was because she missed him. And because she had been through such haring turns of emotions that morning. But it was also because, at her very core, Nikki Heat found nearly everything about Jameson Rook arousing.

And the feeling was clearly quite mutual.

"Wow," he said, panting heavily as she broke away.

"This is just a little preview for later," she said, also a bit out of breath. "I figured it couldn't hurt."

"Let's see," Rook said, taking the opportunity to initiate another kiss. This one was deeper, slower, more soulful. And, if it was possible, even more electrifying.

"No," he said when they were done. "That didn't hurt a bit. As a matter of fact—"

"Sorry," Heat said, backing away. "If we do that one more time, I might make you late for Laura Hopper."

"Oh, to hell with Laura Hopper," he said, and tried to reengage. But she straight-armed him, Heisman Trophy–style. "Don't worry. We'll go to Reykjavík later, and it will be a better trip when I'm not having to worry about lunatics trying to kidnap you. Imagine how much more uninhibited I'll be."

"*More* uninhibited?" he asked, biting his knuckle.

Her only response was to mischievously plant a light kiss on the other side of his hand.

"Is that a promise?" he asked.

"Yes. But later."

"Fair enough," Rook said. "So how did things go with Maggs and Callan? Were you able to get anything out of them?"

Heat recounted her morning for him: the trip to Pennsylvania, the phone calls to various prisons. When she was through, he sat heavily in one of the chairs by her desk.

"So. Maggs dead, Callan escaped," he said, like he was still trying to absorb it. "Someone was very busy on Tuesday."

"Yes, but who?"

"That's the mystery, isn't it?" Rook said. "Stating the obvious, Maggs was clearly the loser in everything that went down. He was a loose end that someone finally felt the need to cut off."

"Yes, but why now?" Heat asked, wanting to know if Rook was thinking along the same lines she was. "Maggs had been in that prison for four years. It looks like whoever got to him could have gotten to him any time. There was obviously some kind of inciting event."

"Your mother's sudden reemergence," Rook said.

"It sure seems that way."

"Well, yes. Unless your mother resurfaced in response to something else. In which case *that* was the inciting event."

"I thought about that, too."

"Well, that's really a chicken-or-egg question," Rook said. "But just to talk it out, your mother's reemergence captured more than just your attention. While she was still 'dead,' Maggs's being alive wasn't particularly bothering anyone. The moment someone figured out she was back, Maggs became a threat again and had to be eliminated. And don't ask me why. Because I don't know."

Rook's left leg started bouncing up and down, his sudden surfeit of energy needing an outlet.

"I don't want to say Maggs doesn't matter," Rook said. "Because he does. But our chances of figuring out why he had to be silenced seem . . . remote."

"Dead men tell no tales," Heat said.

"Aye-aye, matey. That reminds me, do you want to be a pirate king and a pirate wench for Halloween? I made my publisher let me keep the corset from the cover shoot for my latest Victoria St. Clair novel. It would look *so* hot on you, especially if you—"

"Rook. Focus."

"Right. Sorry. By the way, is there a cold shower somewhere around here?" Rook said, taking a moment to physically shake himself.

"Okay, I think I'm good," he said. "Anyhow, as I was saying, I think Callan is the hot lead here. One, because he's still alive. Two, because someone clearly wanted him out of prison—and not dead—for some reason. That transfer to medium security six months ago was not some kind of random paperwork mix-up. He clearly had someone pulling strings for him."

"It had to be someone at the Bureau of Prisons, right?" Heat asked.

"Well, in the end, yes. But even if you find out who signed off on the transfer at the B.O.P., you haven't necessarily cracked anything. Our theoretical B.O.P. bureaucrat could have just been following orders from someone else, either in the B.O.P. or higher up in the Department of Justice."

"But Callan had to have help from someone who works for the government."

"Maybe. But maybe not."

"That's helpful."

"I'm just saying, yes, it could be some version of an inside job, where someone with the appropriate amount of juice within the federal government worked some levers. Callan was FBI before he was Homeland Security. When you start looking at the number of people he had contact with during his career who would still be around and could have helped him get that transfer . . . I mean, you're probably looking at hundreds of possible suspects.

"But," Rook continued, "we also can't rule out a bribe coming from the outside. I think history has shown that if you've got enough money, you can make the US government do just about anything for you. It makes our suspect list—"

"Enormous," Heat finished for him. "So it could be someone who needs Bart Callan's formidable mix of skills. Or someone who fears what he knows will get out, and was therefore pressured into helping him. Or . . ."

She let her voice trail off, then grunted in frustration. "There are too many possibilities. I wish my mother would just make contact somehow—for real, not as an apparition. We can sit here and spin theories for hours, but she could probably clear up everything in thirty seconds. Why won't she just let me help her?"

"We've been over this," Rook said. "It's because she knows it's too dangerous. We have to trust her. She knows more than we do right now, so she knows what's best."

Rook paused. Heat became aware he was studying her carefully. "You didn't sleep very well last night, did you?" he asked.

Heat shook her head. Rook stood, walked over to where Heat was leaning against her desk, and wrapped his strong arms around her. She allowed herself to be embraced.

"I've seen that look in your eyes before, Nikki," he said as she nestled her head in his shoulder. "That obsessed look. And I have to tell you, it scares me. It scares me to death. I know asking you to just stand down is impossible. But you can't let this consume you. Because it will. It will eat you up until there's nothing left of you."

She separated herself. "I'll be fine. Really," she said. "Anyway, I'm not the one being threatened by terrorists right now. I'm really not sure about you flitting all around town like this, having lunch, riding the subway."

"What are you worried about? Your typical New York subway car has at least three riders tougher than anything ISIS could throw at us. I'll be fine. Besides, I'll have an NYPD escort with me the whole time. We'll have lunch, then we'll come right back."

"I know, I just . . . I have a bad feeling about this. Every time you go out it's like we roll the dice again, and one of these times it's going to come up snake eyes. I want you where I can see you, where I can keep you safe."

"Once I get back from lunch, I promise I'll hunker down here," Rook said. "My Legs Kline feature is due by the end of the day tomorrow. I've got some written, but I really need to get going on it, if only because I need to get that minister of magic thing in print before he forgets.

"Now," Rook said, looking down at his watch, "speaking of deadlines . . ."

"Yeah, I know," Heat said. "Go. Just be careful."

They kissed one last time, then Rook walked out the door.

TWENTY-FIVE

Heat knew she should have plowed herself back into her paperwork immediately—and stayed at it until Rook and Aguinaldo returned with the lead that would give their investigation new legs.

But she couldn't help herself. She went to the window of her office, just to get one more glimpse of the man she loved before he disappeared from view.

She swiveled the blinds open as Rook and Aguinaldo descended the front steps of the Twentieth Precinct. Rook had a little-boyish bounce to his stride, as he tended to get whenever he was aiding an investigation. Aguinaldo moved with her usual compact efficiency.

Heat saw them turn right and walk up 82nd Street in the direction of the American Museum of Natural History subway stop.

Which was why she had such a clear view of what came next.

The first thing that caught her attention was the roaring of an engine followed by the accompanying squeal of tires coming from somewhere down the block.

She swiveled her head left to see a large black SUV with an extra-long antenna charging up the street at high speed, its pinstripe a white blur on its side.

Just as it whipped past the precinct, there was more sudden movement coming from the top of the block. Another large black SUV, identical to the first, screeched around the corner from Columbus Avenue and was roaring down the block—traveling west, against the direction of the one-way street.

The two vehicles were on a collision course until they came to a halt within twenty feet of each other, bracketing where Rook and Aguinaldo were standing.

"Run!" Heat shouted. Except, of course, they couldn't hear her from inside the building. And the window had been painted shut eons ago.

Rook and Aguinaldo had stopped in their tracks, more surprised about the sudden appearance of these two vehicles than threatened by it. That's when Heat realized neither one of them had been with her for Hassan El-Bashir's description of the strange late-night visitors to Masjid al-Jannah. And Heat hadn't yet put it on the murder board. Neither Rook nor Aguinaldo knew these SUVs were identical to the ones that had likely delivered Tam Svejda to her death; neither had any idea what danger they were in. Aguinaldo wasn't even reaching for her gun.

Heat was. There was no time for a phone call. She was already drawing her 9mm Smith & Wesson out of its holster.

But before she could take out the window—if she shot it then cleared away the remaining glass with her foot, she'd be able to lean out of it and perhaps take aim at the people who were about to pounce on Rook and Aguinaldo—she stopped herself. The bullet would take out the window, yes. The problem was what came after that. Heat had no idea where the projectile would go next. No angle of fire was safe. It would either go into the street, where there would be drivers or pedestrians, or into the building across the way, where there were apartments. It wasn't a clean shot.

In the time it took her to calculate this, the doors to the black SUVs had opened. Four men—large men with dark clothing and ski masks on their faces—had poured out. Their weapons were raised. They were shouting commands Heat couldn't make out.

Aguinaldo was, by now, reaching for her service weapon, which she kept in a shoulder holster under her jacket. But it was too late. Three of the dark-clothed men were on her, with one seizing her from behind and two closing in from the front. They had rightly determined that Aguinaldo—the armed police officer—was the greater danger, and therefore needed to be neutralized first. And they were doing so with ruthless efficiency. Aguinaldo was quickly overpowered. She never really had a chance.

Rook was trying to make a run for it, scrambling back in the direction of the precinct. But the assailants seemed to have anticipated this move. Coming from the back SUV, the fourth man, who had both the size and agility of an NFL linebacker, tackled Rook, driving him down to the sidewalk. Rook, no delicate flower, was nevertheless at a fifty-pound disadvantage, all of it muscle. Rook struggled gamely, but he hadn't learned a lot of wrestling moves in journalism school. The larger man had no trouble keeping Rook pinned down.

Heat was desperate now. She didn't bother yelling anymore. No one in the detective bull pen was going to be able to get there fast enough; no one downstairs would be able to hear her. She simply ripped the blinds off the window with her left hand. With her right, she gripped the Smith & Wesson by the barrel.

Then, using the handle of the gun like a hammer, she swung it at the center of the window.

It was thick decades-old safety glass, and it would not go easily. It merely spiderwebbed in response to the first blow. After the second, a small hole appeared in the middle. Finally, with the third strike, Heat shattered the middle portion, enough that she could use the gun as a claw to enlarge the hole. She ignored the dozens of small cuts she gained as pebbles of glass rained down on her exposed hand.

The scene outside was rapidly deteriorating. Aguinaldo had been disarmed, then carried to the farther of the two SUVs—thrashing frantically but also impotently. One of the men opened the back doors, while the other two tossed her inside. Whether there was another man inside the SUV, waiting to subdue her further, Heat couldn't tell.

The three men then turned their attention to Rook, who was still held down by their linebacker-sized colleague. Heat was now kicking away at the glass that stubbornly clung to the lower half of the windowpane, not slowing or crying out when one particularly stubborn shard sliced her pants leg and ripped into her flesh.

Rook was facedown on the concrete. One of the men had a firm hold of his top half. Another, a huge guy who looked like he hadn't seen two hundred pounds on the scale since grade school, was sitting on Rook's legs. The other two turned their attention to each of Rook's arms, which they bound together at the wrists using a zip tie.

As soon as they had Rook's hands secure, the man who had immobilized Rook's upper half produced a burlap bag. Even as she put all her effort into her work, Heat gasped. She could see the black stripe running down one side of the burlap. It was the same kind of bag—perhaps even the very same article—that Tam Svejda had worn at the time of her execution.

The man slid it over Rook's head. Then the four of them picked him up, one on each limb, and carried him toward the rear SUV.

Finally, Heat had enough of the glass cleared away that she could get the upper half of her torso out the window. Gripping the gun in her left hand, the only one that gave her any kind of angle at which to shoot, she leaned her body out.

If Heat had caught one break, it was that the street had cleared of pedestrians. They had all scattered when the guys in ski masks had drawn their guns. Still, Heat couldn't take aim at the men who had Rook. Maybe if she'd had a rifle. Maybe if she'd had a magnifying scope. Maybe if she'd had a firm shooting stance.

But not with her current setup. From that angle and that distance, with that inaccurate a weapon and that tenuous a position, there was too great a danger an errant shot would hit Rook.

Instead, she aimed for the tires of the SUV they were taking him toward, the one closest to her. She squeezed off one round, then two, then three. If she could disable the vehicle, strand it in the middle of 82nd Street, this could have a far happier ending than the one it seemed headed for.

"If" being the operative word. Heat had, on occasion, practiced shooting left-handed at the range. But it still felt foreign. She didn't have the control over the weapon she did when it was in her dominant hand. The well-practiced muscle memory, developed over the hours and years, simply wasn't there.

All three shots buried themselves harmlessly in the asphalt, short of the tire she was aiming for. In her effort not to miss high—the most common miss, especially with how untrained her left hand was—she had overcompensated and fired low instead.

The men had now wrangled Rook close enough to the SUV that she could no longer safely aim at it. She turned her attention to the SUV that contained Aguinaldo. It was the vehicle that was farther up the street, an even tougher shot. But at least—one more slight advantage for Heat—it was blocking the street. Shooting out this SUV's tires would slow the escape of the other.

Now, however, there was an additional danger: the man who had been carrying Rook's left leg had let go and drawn his weapon. He was soon returning fire.

Heat wasn't much of a target, with only her left arm, left shoulder, and head leaning out the window. But, if nothing else, facing live fire made it even harder to aim at her target, especially when one of the incoming bullets struck the side of the building only a few feet away from her. Small pieces of brick stung Heat's face.

She squeezed the trigger three more times. The bullets slammed into the SUV's bumper, creating three jagged holes in the chrome. She cursed herself for missing high.

In between trigger squeezes, Heat became aware the gunfire was attracting attention inside the building. She could hear the commotion of officers shouting orders. A response was coming, and soon. If Heat could at least slow the attackers down, the Twentieth Precinct would soon mobilize with overwhelming force. Four goons in tight T-shirts would be no match for the kind of manpower and firepower the NYPD could put on the street.

But the goons knew that, of course. They knew speed wasn't just desired. It was an absolute necessity. And their chain of action—so rapid, so coordinated from the start—was now reaching its end.

Rook had been tossed inside the back of the SUV. The three men were now scrambling toward the fronts of the vehicles. The fourth was laying a kind of cover fire for them, peppering Heat with shots that were coming increasingly close to hitting her, making it difficult for her to take aim at any of the men who were briefly exposed.

Another bullet pinged off the building, just above her, sending another shower of particles into her face. For Heat to keep her head outside the window was incredibly foolhardy. It was only a matter of time until the man's aim became true. For a moment, she kept her left hand and arm outside—if they got hit, so be it—and fired off two more rounds.

But she withdrew those, too, when she realized she was basically shooting blind. Not only were her odds of hitting the right thing now depressingly low, her odds of hitting the wrong thing—like Rook, Aguinaldo, or some civilian who was trying to crouch out of the way—had gone up astronomically.

The fourth man kept firing at her anyway, putting rounds into the side of the building, deterring her from even thinking about sticking her head back out. One bullet plowed into the windowsill, splintering the wood. Heat knew if she had stayed where she was, that bullet likely would have found her midsection.

Heat could hear the SUVs pulling out—away, she assumed, from the precinct. She had dashed over to her desk and was picking up the phone. She rang the desk sergeant.

As soon as he picked up, Heat began, "Shots fired on—"

"We know, Captain. We know. We're getting a response out the door right now. Give us thirty more seconds and we're there."

The sergeant hung up.

But they didn't have thirty more seconds. The gunfire from outside had stopped. As Heat scrambled back to the window, all she saw was the great black back end of the second SUV, making its escape.

TWENTY-SIX

There was blood oozing down her ankle from a gash in her calf. There was blood smeared on her right hand from countless glass abrasions. There was blood trickling down her forehead from where small bits of brick shrapnel had embedded themselves.

Nikki Heat didn't pay attention to any of it, didn't let it slow her for even a second. She just charged out of her office, past her detectives, who were scrambling to gather their weapons and their wits, and down the stairwell. She wasn't waiting for any elevator.

When she reached the lobby of the Twentieth Precinct, there were six officers assembled, very nearly ready to mobilize. The last of them was getting outfitted as the other five already had been: riot helmet, tactical vest, bulletproof shield.

Heat had nothing more than a bra and a blouse to protect her. She didn't care. Without hesitation, she led the charge out of the precinct, her 9mm pointing the way.

On the street, pedestrians were just starting to warily come out of their hiding places, having tentatively determined that since the vehicles were gone the threat had past. They immediately fled back to safety when they saw a bloodied Heat, followed by her pack of heavily armored officers.

When Heat reached the corner of Columbus Avenue, there was no sign of anything awry. Traffic, both foot and vehicular, were flowing normally. There were no more sounds of shrieking tires, roaring engines, or gunfire.

She turned to a hot dog vendor on the corner.

"There were two black SUVs," Heat said, panting. "Which way did they—"

The man stretched out his arm toward the light on the south corner of the intersection of 81st Street. "Almost took out a woman pushing a kid in a stroller. It was like this close."

The man brought up his hand to bring his thumb and forefinger together, but Heat didn't linger long enough to see just how closely a tragedy had been averted. Nor was she waiting for the officers behind her. They would either keep up or not. She was already dashing down Columbus Avenue, arms pumping, legs churning.

It was probably pointless, yes: a human powered only by the strength of her legs, trying to run down a pair of SUVs with eight cylinders of piston-pumping power under their hoods. But it was all Heat could do.

Maybe one of the SUVs would run into something—a light stanchion, a fire hydrant, a building. Maybe the desk sergeant, anticipating the SUVs would go down Columbus, would be able to get patrol units to form a blockade, meaning Heat would be providing critical support from behind.

Maybe doing something felt like a better option than doing nothing.

The light at 81st Street was red. Heat didn't bother going all the way down to the crosswalk. She took the straight line across the avenue, weaving through the cars waiting for the light.

On the other side was the natural history museum, its front steps covered with tourists, just as it had been the day before when she had been chasing Muharib Qawi. Heat didn't break stride as she rounded the corner. If anything, she accelerated.

And she didn't stop. Even as it became apparent she was running into a perfect mess.

The intersection of Central Park West and 81st Street was a tangle of cars, cabs, and trucks, some of which were pointed in the wrong direction, some of which had bashed-in bumpers, some of which had crushed hoods. Steam hissed from busted radiators. Chunks of plastic—which had until very recently been attached to vehicles—littered the street. Groups of tourists were gesturing with excitement.

The drivers were already gingerly climbing out of their cars and trucks to begin the process of assessing damage and assigning blame.

"Two SUVs," Heat blurted as she reached the intersection. It was all she could get out before she had to gasp for air.

"Yeah! I know!" the driver of a Ford Edge with a crumpled front end answered. "They ran the frickin' light like it wasn't even there, the bastards! I was just—"

"Which way?" Heat said with her next breath.

The driver jerked his thumb toward the 79th Street Transverse, which fed into the other side of the intersection—really, operating as a continuance of 81st Street, even though the street name changed.

It fed directly into Central Park. And it didn't have stoplights. It was just a long curved road with nothing to slow down a fleeing SUV, especially one that surely wouldn't mind swerving around slower cars or playing chicken with oncoming traffic.

Heat ran to the opposite side of the intersection, to where she had a view of where the transverse bent around and out of sight. There was no traffic going down it, of course. None had been able to get through the accident-clogged intersection.

Finally, Heat came to her senses and slowed. She bent forward, clutching her pants just above the knees, sucking in oxygen as fast as her lungs would allow.

There was no chance she was going to catch up. She brought her phone to her mouth and, in a series of short bursts, informed dispatch the SUVs were last seen heading east on the 79th Street Transverse.

She would have to rely on some of the other thirty-five thousand sworn officers of the New York Police Department to do the job she couldn't. And there was no question in her mind they would.

They would get Rook and Aguinaldo back, safe and in one piece.

SUVs didn't just disappear.

"What the fuck do you mean they just disappeared?" The Hammer yelled, and not for the first time.

It was an hour later. An hour during which the combined human and technological resources of the New York Police Department had not yielded one single clue as to where Rook and Aguinaldo had been taken.

It was time to regroup. But first there had to be recriminations. Zach Hamner had been dispatched from One Police Plaza to the Twentieth Precinct. Officially, he was providing "administrative support" to the search for a kidnapped NYPD detective and a high-profile member of the media.

Unofficially, he was there to ream everyone new assholes.

"That's not possible," Hamner continued. "Rabbits disappear from magicians' hats after they say abracadabra. Stains disappear from peoples' clothing after they harness the power of Tide. Enormous black SUVs do *not . . . just . . . disappear.*"

"Sir, we had boots on the ground within two minutes of when the first shots were fired," the desk sergeant said. "We had foot patrols in the area alerted even before that. We had every unit in the precinct on high alert and ready to respond. We had Police Two in the air and overhead within seven minutes . . ."

"And you had King Kong and Santa Claus manning sniper positions on the roof. I get all that. And I don't care. What I want to understand better—so I can explain it to the commissioner, so he can explain it to the mayor—is how the fuck four armed thugs kidnapped a police detective and a prominent journalist in broad fucking daylight when they were fifty fucking feet from the front door of a precinct. Can we run through that one more time? Because I'm still a little fuzzy on how the fuck that happens, and then even more fuzzy on how the fuck they vanish like a popcorn fart in a fifty-acre field."

They were in the detective bull pen: the detectives, the lieutenant who headed the patrol unit, the desk sergeant, and a few other uniformed officers who were deemed to have been vaguely responsible.

Heat was off to the side. Even The Hammer had the sensitivity to realize that someone whose husband had just been kidnapped—and who had risked her life trying to stop it—perhaps didn't need the pallid vampire face of the deputy commissioner of legal matters spewing spittle and profanity on her.

She was gazing ahead and down. Had anyone drawn a straight line from her eyes to where she seemed to be looking, it would appear she was staring at the side of a detective's desk. Really, she wasn't seeing anything. She was lost in thoughts that were going in a thousand directions.

She had to keep reminding herself that what she really felt like doing—collapsing into a heap of panic and self-pity—wouldn't help anyone, least of all Rook and Aguinaldo. She had to keep her focus on the case.

Who were these guys? Were they some of McMain's frequent fliers? Or were they, in fact, a direct offshoot of ISIS, able to contact the mother ship—in which case they ought to be harnessing federal intelligence assets? Or were they a new and previously unknown splinter cell of Islamic extremism, operating wholly independently?

More importantly, was there a way of figuring out where they were hiding?

Her detectives had redoubled their efforts to go through the Counterterrorism Task Force's list of known suspects. And they had the personnel—courtesy of The Hammer—to toss every apartment, housing project, and rickety single-family house they cared to toss. No effort was being spared.

But, likewise, no results had turned up.

Even the scarf lead was coming up empty. Once they realized Rook and Aguinaldo weren't going to meet Laura Hopper for lunch, Heat had arranged for two detectives from Midtown North to intercept Hopper at the restaurant and interview her.

She had remembered the scarf, right down to the particular tint of red she had used, and how the leaves turning on a tree near her brownstone had inspired it. The work had been commissioned. Unfortunately, it had been commissioned for a Saudi sheik who was well beyond the reach of the NYPD and the American justice system. The State Department was now making discreet inquiries. Heat had very low expectations about what they'd come up with.

Hamner had continued his rant while Heat had been lost in her thoughts. But she soon became aware he seemed to be finishing up.

"So what we're saying is, we're nowhere on this," Hamner said. "Nowhere. We've got every fucking unit in the city turning asphalt inside out looking for these two vehicles, but they have just vanished from the face of the earth. Jesus Henry Christmas on a street-meat stick."

He was met by a room full of ruefully hung heads and diverted eye contact.

"Okay, okay. We have to get out ahead of this thing with the media.

We're going to look like a bunch of jackasses no matter what we do. But maybe if we play the sympathy card they won't completely kill us. Heat!"

Heat looked up from the desk.

"You're the sympathy card," Hamner said. "You're going on TV asking for the public's help to find your husband. Then the media will have to play nice. Who knows? Maybe we'll even get a lead or two out of it. If we announce an emergency presser in front of the Two-Oh, can you handle that?"

"Yes, sir," Heat said.

"Good. Now get the blood cleaned off. You look like a goddamned extra from *Braveheart*."

Twenty-five minutes later, Heat was clutching the side of a podium that had been placed on the sidewalk in front of the entrance to the Twentieth Precinct.

She had cleaned up her face and, at the insistence of a nervous public information officer, applied a layer of cover-up. She had also changed into the uniform she kept hanging behind her office door. Better optics, she was told. Plus, the hat hid one of the cuts on her forehead.

There had been no time to set up lighting, so it was just Heat and the klieg lights from the cameras. And unlike the press conferences announcing high-profile arrests or big drug busts—where there are any number of cops jockeying for the refracted glory of a spot in the background—Heat was facing them alone. No one wanted a piece of this.

"Good afternoon," Heat began, trying to maintain a professional demeanor. "At approximately 12:03 this afternoon, there was a brazen kidnapping here on 82nd Street, outside the entrance to the Twentieth Precinct."

She ran through the narrative: the SUVs, the known escape route, the description of the suspects, the belief that the same men were responsible for the kidnapping and murder of Tam Svejda.

Then she reached the part the assembled media had been waiting for. "The victims are Inez Aguinaldo, a detective here at the Twentieth Precinct . . . and Jameson Rook, a reporter for—"

The reporters didn't wait for her to finish. There was a howling chorus of questions that came all at once. It took one of the PIOs to shout them down and regain order of the press conference.

"I'm sorry," Heat said when they had quieted. "I know you have a lot of questions, and we certainly do, too. But I will not be taking questions at this time. At this point, anything I said would likely be supposition.

"The main point of this event is to ask the public for its help. We are urging anyone who has seen anything suspicious to call our tips line. We have eight million pairs of eyeballs in this city, and we want every one of them on the lookout for those SUVs and for any clue that might help us find Detective Aguinaldo and Mr. Rook. The NYPD can't do this alone. We need your help and we need it now. On behalf of the New York Police Department, I thank you all for your help and cooperation."

As soon as she placed the period on the end of the sentence, the press corps lobbed a new hail of inquiries in her direction. But Heat had already turned away and disappeared inside the precinct.

The moment she was out of sight of the cameras, she felt her legs go wobbly. The strain of keeping it together had finally gotten to be too great. She could no longer muster the courageous front she had labored to maintain.

She sagged, finding a safe landing spot on one of the benches in the lobby, right beneath the MOST WANTED posters. And that's where she was still sitting, trying to concentrate on her breathing so the panic wouldn't completely overrun her, when The Hammer came into her view.

Hamner was a man whose only light exposure most days came from fluorescent bulbs. Yet as Heat lifted her chin to look at him, she saw a face that looked especially wan.

"What?" Heat said. "Was I that bad?"

"No. You were fine," Hamner said with uncharacteristic gentleness. "Can you come upstairs with me? There's something you have to see."

TWENTY-SEVEN

They were gathered around Raley's computer. The king of all surveillance media had returned from his siesta, though it looked like it hadn't done him much good.

The Hammer wasn't the only one who had lost color. As she approached, Heat noticed Ochoa's hand had gone to his throat. It was the same gesture of vulnerability she had subconsciously resorted to after she'd watched the first American ISIS video.

Suddenly Heat put it together. Those savages had not wasted time carrying out their threat. There had been another video. And this time Rook was the centerpiece.

"Oh, God," she said, bringing her hand to her mouth.

The world suddenly seemed to go on a slant. The blood flow to her brain had stopped. Her muscles stopped responding to her commands. She felt her body collapsing. She felt her world collapsing.

Rook was dead. Her always. Her everything.

Heat heard a moan. It was bestial, brutish, somehow elemental. It was a cry of ultimate grief, of boundless suffering; it was the kind of wailing heard at funerals, when mourners beat their breasts and tore at their hair. The sound of a heart breaking.

Then Heat realized, with surreal detachment, the sound was coming from her. Her lungs were pushing the air, her voice box was doing the rattling, her mouth was issuing this aberrant racket. And yet she was powerless to stop it.

The pain. It was searing, omnipresent. Her beautiful Rook. The face she loved. The arms that comforted her. The body that fit so perfectly with hers. How could that be gone?

Her eyes were open, but she wasn't really seeing anything. Just blackness. Or maybe just light. It was like her optic nerve had gone on strike and was now just issuing some neutral signal.

She felt someone else's arms on her. And hands. She seemed to know she was no longer standing. Her personal battle with gravity had ended in a loss. The only reason she was still upright was someone else—she couldn't even guess at who—was holding her up.

What had she been before Rook? She'd had a life, but she hadn't really been living. Rook had given her existence meaning. He had brought her joy. What would her life be without Rook? There would never again be joy.

The moaning stopped for a moment. And that was when her ears permitted another voice to enter them. It was insistent. And it kept saying the same thing.

"He's still alive," Ochoa was saying. "It's okay. We still have a chance. He's still alive. We're going to find him. He's still alive."

Heat's vision returned suddenly. She saw she was being held by Feller and Ochoa, both of whom had caught her when they realized she was about to faint. Raley and Rhymer were looking on with concern.

"Just take deep breaths, Captain," Raley said. "Deep breaths. Easy now."

She felt around, realized they weren't going to let her fall. Tentatively, she pushed herself away. She got her feet firmly on the ground, her legs underneath her. They had strength again.

"I'm sorry," Hamner said. "It should have been the first thing out of my mouth that Rook was still okay. I'm so sorry, Heat."

Heat just nodded her acknowledgement. She wasn't sure she could talk yet.

"Rhymer, go get the captain some coffee," Hamner said. "Or better, juice. When was the last time you ate, Heat? You can't let your blood sugar get low like that. Let's just take fifteen minutes to let everyone—"

The suggestion that they pause, that they do anything that wasn't immediately directed toward getting Rook and Aguinaldo back to them, was what brought Heat back to her full senses.

"No," she said hoarsely, her larynx still raw from her funereal keening. "We don't *have* fifteen minutes. What's going on? You guys were all looking at Raley's screen when I walked in and fainted on you. It's another video, isn't it?"

"Captain," Ochoa said. "Just give yourself a few minutes to—"

"Knock it off," she said sharply. "I'm fine. It's Rook and Aguinaldo who are in trouble. They're the only thing we need to be focused on right now."

She realized Ochoa was still holding on to her arm. She shook him off and walked over to Raley's computer.

"Play the video, Rales," she said. "That's an order."

Raley went over to his terminal and sat down. Moments later, a grainy video appeared in the middle of the screen. It looked to have been shot on the same camera as the first one.

The room was clearly different. Smaller. And the camera was zoomed in farther, making it more difficult to make out any surroundings. There was no natural light, just a dim bulb somewhere overhead. The back wall was shiny, unpainted corrugated steel. It could have been a storage unit, or a warehouse, or one of any number of industrial structures.

Rook was in the middle of the frame. He was kneeling, with his arms trussed behind him—and presumably his legs, too, though they were not in the frame. His position and posture were exactly the same as Tam Svejda's had been, though he didn't have a bag over his head. American ISIS wanted the world to know that it had captured its big prize, the two-time Pulitzer Prize–winning celebrity journalist.

On either side of Rook were what appeared to be the same men from the first video. Their masks, gloves, sunglasses, clothing, and headgear were also identical. As before, the one on the left did the talking.

"Greetings," he said again in the Darth Vader voice. "We again come to you in the name of Allah, the Supreme Being, the Living One, the Constant Forgiver. May Allah bless all believers who hear this message now."

"Allahu akbar," the one on the right interjected.

Rook was staring straight ahead, his face seemingly etched in stone, with only the occasional blink to signify he was not a statue. Whatever emotion Rook was feeling, Heat couldn't discern it. There *had* to be fear in him. But he was not allowing it to show. Not even the woman who knew him best could see any crack in his brave facade. He would not give his captors that satisfaction.

Still, Heat discovered after just a few seconds that she couldn't look at him anymore. It hurt too much to see him like that. She turned her attention back to his masked captor.

"Great is the power of those who follow in the path of Allah, who celebrate the Quran as the sacred word of Allah, who understand the revelations made by the Angel Gabriel to the Prophet Muhammad, peace be upon him, are the last and truest testimony of Allah gifted to man," the one on the left said. "Great also is the power of those who find inspiration in the supreme leader Abu Bakr al-Baghdadi and the caliphate he has founded. May the call to unite the world under the flag of Islam motivate all Muslims to declare jihad on our shared enemies."

"*Allahu akbar,*" said the man on the right.

Heat noticed, as she had with the first video, that the man's attention seemed to flick back and forth between the camera and something to the side of it. She was more sure than ever there was someone else in the room. It was the person who had been giving orders to the four thugs who pulled off the kidnapping and who was also clearly the boss of the men in front of the camera.

"As you can see, because Allah is great, He has led us to your imperialistic pig journalist king, Jameson Rook, who now cowers before us," the man on the left continued. "His efforts to run and hide like a scared cockroach were nothing compared to the might of Allah. Let it be known that all enemies of Allah will suffer a similar fate. Even now, when the infidels attack the Islamic State with their airplanes and their armies, it is as it was in the time of Hijrah, when Muhammad, peace be upon him, was forced to flee Mecca, only to again make his triumphant return. So will it be for ISIS. The righteous forces of Allah will always triumph."

"*Allahu akbar,*" the one on the right said.

"Now we make our next proclamation, and by the will of Allah, it will become just as true as our last," the one on the left said. "The infidel journalist Jameson Rook has committed many sins, and he will now be punished for his transgressions. May it please Allah, Jameson Rook will die at the edge of our swords tonight at midnight."

Upon seeing such a horrifying spectacle, there was any number of emotions that might have coursed through Nikki Heat—from rage to fear to despair.

Heat wasn't allowing any of them. That was what the terrorists wanted: for her to be incapacitated by the horror of what she was witnessing. She wasn't going to surrender to that impulse. As long as Rook was still alive—as long as there was some narrow chance they could rescue him—she would not allow any more time to be wasted on her feelings.

Especially when time was so precious. It was now 1:45 in the afternoon. Quarter of two had never felt so close to midnight.

So Heat did not hesitate. As soon as the video went black, she whirled around to face her detectives.

"When did this come in?" she asked.

"During the press conference," Raley said. "Ten minutes ago. It was sent to the main precinct e-mail address."

"And I assume it came from the same untraceable IP address?"

"Well, a different number, but they used the same process of covering their tracks," Raley said. "I could try to—"

"Don't bother," Hamner interrupted. "We've got some whiz kids in the Computer Crimes Squad down at One PP who can get on that. They whiffed on the first one, but maybe a second sample will help them untangle it. Hang on."

Hamner had already taken out his phone and was presumably making arrangements for Computer Crimes to drop everything and get to work on it.

"Okay, good," Heat said. "In that case, Rales, I want you working that video just like you did the last one. Go through the audio again and see if you can isolate any background noises that might give us a clue where this was shot."

"That won't take too long," Raley said.

"I know. So if you strike out there, I want you to check out the pattern on that corrugated steel. It looks pretty new to me. There's no sign of the grime that you expect to see on older steel. It's a long shot, but maybe we'll get lucky and you can match it to a particular brand or a particular product type. Then call the manufacturer and see if they can help us get to a local supplier who might know something."

"Got it."

"Oach, Opie, Feller, how are we coming with the McMains list?"

"We're going through it as fast as we can," Ochoa said.

"Did Qawi recognize any of the names?"

"Recognize? Yes," Ochoa said. "But he swore to us none of them were associated with Masjid al-Jannah. He said those kind of people would have probably found his messages of tolerance and peace unpalatable and sought religious guidance elsewhere."

"Okay. Well, keep up the pressure. Maybe something will break."

Just then, as if Heat's words had put out a wish that the universe felt compelled to immediately fulfill, Ochoa's desk phone rang.

"Ochoa," he said.

His face squeezed with concentration as the person on the other end spoke.

"Excellent, thank you," Ochoa said, then placed the phone back in its cradle.

"We might have a hit on the SUVs," he said. "They were found abandoned at a Central Park Conservancy maintenance yard. You want me to check it out?"

Heat was already moving. Ochoa was already following. The only words she uttered were, "I'll drive."

TWENTY-EIGHT

When Frederick Law Olmsted designed Central Park, he envisioned an 840-acre playground where New Yorkers could escape the pressures of city life and pretend they were in a sylvan sanctuary.

He did not envision the Central Park Conservancy maintenance yard.

As Heat and Ochoa pulled into the yard, having made a lights-and-sirens-blazing run from the Twentieth Precinct in something just under Mach speed, they saw what was essentially an overcrowded parking lot. It was surrounded by rusting chain-link fencing topped with razor wire, and it probably needed to be about four times larger in order to accommodate all the stuff that had been crammed into it.

There were trucks of varying sizes, double- and triple-parked. There were golf carts, ATVs, and small four-wheelers for hauling equipment. There were piles of dirt, piles of rock, and piles of who-knows-what hiding under tarps.

As if there wasn't enough stuffed in there already, there were two shiny black SUVs with tall antennas and pinstripes, jammed in the far side. Heat knew instantly they were the same vehicles she had seen on 82nd Street.

One had half its wheels over a curb on a thin stretch of grass, hard against the fence. The other was in the corner, blocking in a tractor, its bumper actually touching the tractor's front-end loader. Both were sufficiently covered by overhanging trees such that no helicopter would have been able to see them unless it had decided to land in the middle of the maintenance yard.

At the other end of the lot, outside an ancient brick garage with an open bay door, there was a man who looked like Danny DeVito—only a little taller and a lot less symmetrical—standing with a pair of Central Park police.

One of the officers stepped forward to greet Heat and Ochoa as they walked up.

"We were told to keep the witness here but not to ask any questions, so that's what we did. He's yours now."

Heat thanked the officer, then introduced herself to the witness. She went to shake the man's hand, but he held them up apologetically. They were covered in black grease. She moved on, taking down his name—not Danny DeVito, as it turned out—and job title, patiently withstanding a brief explanation of why it wasn't loftier.

Then she finally got around to: "So tell me about these two SUVs."

"Yeah, so probably around noon, maybe a little after, I got one of the F-150s up on the lift," Not Danny DeVito said, jerking his thumb back toward a Ford F-150 pickup truck that was, in fact, several feet in the air. "One of the bearings was damn near about to fall out. It had to have been grinding something bad for weeks. But did any of the guys who drove it say anything? Fuhgeddaboutit. These guys, they—"

"Sir," Heat said, with gentle firmness. "The SUVs?"

"Oh, yeah, yeah. So I'm working under the truck and I hear two cars driving in. Now, I know engines, right? And I know what our engines sound like. A lot of them are diesel or electric, anyway. And even the gas ones, well . . . you probably don't want me to get started on catalytic converters. Anyway, none of our engines sounded like what was rolling into the yard. So I'm like, 'Huh.' And I get out from under the truck.

"I walk out and I see those things," he said, pointing at the SUVs. "And I'm like, 'What the frig?' I thought maybe it was some kind of unannounced inspection from the city or . . . Well, I don't know. Anyhow, the next thing I know, these two huge guys in ski masks are getting out. And when I saw huge, I mean *huge*."

He pronounced the word *huge* as if it began with a *y*.

"Now, you'd think I'd seen enough movies to know that guys like that wearing ski masks like that are bad news. And I'm thinking . . . Well, I don't know what I'm thinking. But they were just walking away. And I'm like, 'Hey, you can't park there.' And they just kept walking, like they didn't give a frig. And I seriously don't know what I was thinking, because I looked at the bigger one and said, 'Hey, Muscles, I'm talking to you. You can't park here.'"

Not Danny DeVito shook his head. "I don't know what I woulda done if the guy came at me. He probably coulda rolled me up like a little ball and stuck me in his back pocket if he wanted to. But he didn't look at me. It's like I wasn't even there. So I'm like, 'Well, up yours, buddy. I'm calling Parking Enforcement and we're getting your ass towed. And you know those towing companies ding you extra for those big-ass SUVs. You'll be looking at a grand, easy.' And nothing. Nothing from either one of them. So I'm like, okay, whatever, and I called Parking Enforcement.

"Then I'm on my break, watching the little TV we got in back, and I see the captain here saying she wants to know about these two black SUVs, and I'm thinking, 'Hey, wait a sec.' And I just kinda put it together, you know? So. Is that them?"

There was no point in lying to Not Danny DeVito. "Yes, sir," Heat said. "We think so."

Not Danny DeVito made a profane observation about this revelation.

When he was done, Heat asked, "Did you touch the vehicles at all, sir? Either on the inside or the outside?"

"No, ma'am," he said earnestly.

"What about anyone else? Has anyone else been near them?"

"No, ma'am," he insisted.

"Okay, thank you," she said, then snapped on a pair of blue nitrile gloves. Ochoa, without needing to be told, was doing the same.

"Let's go have a look," she told him.

As Ochoa limped toward the SUV up on the curb, Heat went to the one parked by the tractor.

She did a near 360-degree walk around it, stopping only when the front-end loader wouldn't let her go any farther. She noted the lack of bullet holes in the bumper. That meant this was the one Rook had been taken in.

Up close, she could tell it was a Cadillac Escalade with an extended cab. The Cadillac insignia had been stripped off both the front and rear in an attempt to make it less recognizable. The owners had rightly figured the Cadillac crest was one most people would remember, even if they only saw it briefly.

She looked underneath—primarily to check if it had been booby-trapped, but also to see if there was anything else unusual about the undercarriage. But all seemed in order. Then she walked to the driver's side door, from which vantage point she could read the VIN number. She wrote it down in a small notepad.

Next she looked inside, peering through the tinted windows. The interior was all black, from the leather seats to the carpeting. She noted the way the chrome near the shifter gleamed, the absence of dust on top of the dashboard, the lack of smudging on the instrument panel. The entire inside of the vehicle had been wiped down, probably right before the kidnapping. The only prints they would likely find inside would belong to Rook.

With little hope of success, Heat tried all the door handles. But, of course, the Cadillac had been locked. There was no reason Muscles and his colleague would want to make things easier for law enforcement, even if it would take a well-practiced New York City cop less than a minute to jimmy the lock.

Satisfied she had seen all the nothing there was to see, Heat began making arrangements for the Evidence Collection Team to give both SUVs a thorough workup. She was not optimistic about their chances of finding anything.

Ochoa seemed to be coming to the same conclusions at the same time, because as Heat began to make her way toward the other vehicle, he was already limping toward her.

"Get anything?" Heat asked.

"Nah. I assume those bullet holes were your handiwork?"

Heat nodded.

"Other than that, this thing is clean as a baby's bottom. We could have the whole thing taken apart piece by piece and I doubt we'd find anything. Yours?"

"Same. You get the VIN number off yours?"

Ochoa's response was to pull a notepad out of his pocket and open it to the last page on which there was writing. Heat already had her phone out and was calling a number in her contact list: the NYPD had an officer with an open line to the New York State Department of Motor Vehicles.

"Hey, this is Captain Heat from the Twentieth Precinct," she said when an officer answered. "Can you run these VIN numbers for me, tell me who owns these vehicles?"

She waited, hearing the clatter of a keyboard, before the officer's answer came. "It's registered to a Mayo Nouns LLC."

"Mayo Nouns?" Heat said.

"Yes, Captain," the officer said, then spelled it for her.

Heat wrote the name in her pad. As soon as she did, her eyes solved the riddle for her.

Mayo Nouns was an anagram for Anonymous.

"It has an address in Albany," the officer said. "Would you like it?"

Heat said she would, even though she already had a sinking feeling about where this was heading. She had the officer check the registration on the other VIN number. It also came back as owned by Mayo Nouns, with the same address.

She thanked the officer, hung up, then Googled the address. Sure enough, the corporate address for Mayo Nouns LLC was a law firm near the state capital—a firm that had likely done the documentation for a limited liability corporation that did not exist on anything but paper. Mayo Nouns LLC was no doubt a wholly owned subsidiary of Nona Mousy Inc., or something similarly slippery, which would turn out to be a shell corporation in Delaware, which would lead nowhere at all.

When you have a nation whose laws were established by a bunch of wealthy landowners whose most vivid experience with authority was their dealings King George III—and who therefore trusted government about as far as they could throw their buckled shoes—this kind of legal evasiveness was remarkably easy to achieve.

"So what do we got?" Ochoa asked.

"A dead end as far as ownership goes," Heat said. "Other than that, I'd say what we have is two Cadillac Escalades that were ditched here very soon after the abduction so the kidnappers could switch to a vehicle or vehicles that the entire New York Police Department wasn't going to be looking for."

"Yeah, I was thinking the same thing."

"Which really means unless ECT has a miracle and actually finds something useful once they get inside those things, this has been a waste of time," Heat said, trying not to let the frustration overwhelm her.

She looked down at her watch, which told her it was quarter after two. Less than ten hours to go.

"And time," she added, "is one thing we are definitely running short on."

They waited until Benigno DeJesus and his crew showed up, then returned to the precinct, again with lights and sirens. Though, when they arrived, it quickly became clear they needn't have hurried.

There was a great blur of activity being coordinated out of the bull pen at the Twentieth Precinct, which Hamner had reorganized into a kind of situation room. Doors were being kicked. Skulls were being knocked. Wheels were being spun.

None of it was accomplishing anything. The New York Police Department was the largest municipal crime-fighting force in America, very nearly by a factor of two, and yet even its accumulated might was impotent. As an hour ticked by, Heat could feel the dread rising in her like an unstoppable tide.

The fact was they could spend all the time looking they wanted to. But if they didn't know what or who they were looking for—or where to look—they weren't going to get anywhere.

Heat had twice heard from Margaret Rook, who was sick with worry about her son. She was looking for assurances from Heat, but Nikki had none to offer. As she hung up, she heard Jean Philippe, already attempting the impossible task of trying to comfort a distraught mother.

There was certainly no shortage of media coverage. Already, all three presidential candidates—folksy Legs Kline, friendly Lindsy Gardner, and even heartless Caleb Brown—had made mention of it.

Another hour passed. Heat was in her office, reading a brief dispatch on yet another fruitless raid on a suspected terrorist haven, when her phone rang.

"Heat," she said, with more fatigue than she would have liked to admit. The words she heard next were among the last she expected.

"Hi. Nikki. It's Helen Miksit."

During their last interaction, Miksit had brushed her aside like so much dryer lint, in the process shutting the door on a major avenue of Heat's investigation into Tam Svejda's last story.

What is she doing now? Heat wondered. *Calling to gloat?*

"Counselor," Heat said guardedly.

"Are you recording this in any way?" Miksit asked.

"No."

"Good. Because this is an off-the-record phone call. It's either off the record or it ends right now. You absolutely cannot use what I'm about to tell you to get a warrant. I can't run the risk this ever gets into open court. Are we clear?"

Heat sat up a little straighter, getting herself ready for a fight. "No, we're not clear. I don't even know what you're calling about. How can I—"

"Damnit, Nikki, just shut up and listen for once," Miksit growled in the same tone she used to object to hearsay at trial. And Heat—probably because of the fatigue—acquiesced.

"I wasn't just blowing smoke when I said I wanted Tam's killer to come to justice. I loved that kid," Miksit continued. "So I went ahead and got the records from Tam's work phone and cell phone and I went through them myself. Most of it was pretty prosaic. Police flaks. Politicians. Chinese takeout. The staples of a reporter's life.

"There were a few numbers I couldn't figure out on my own. But Steve Liebman—Tam's editor, I believe you met him—was able to help me weed most of those out. By the time he was through, we were left with one number."

Heat realized she had started leaning forward in her chair as Miksit spoke.

"Okay," Heat said. "And who was that?"

"That's the thing. Neither Liebman nor I could figure it out. It's international, so the reverse look-up database Liebman had access to didn't give us anything. All we know is she tried it multiple times. The first three calls were short—long enough to leave a message, no more.

The fourth was five minutes fifty-eight seconds long, which didn't strike either of us as long enough to conduct an interview."

"But maybe it was long enough to set up a meeting?" Heat suggested.

"Or give a no comment," Miksit said. "The way to figure out would be to make contact with whoever it was and ask. But we thought . . . Well, actually, it was Liebman's idea. He said that was beyond the scope of what the newspaper should be doing in a murder investigation, and that we had reached the point where it really had become a potential police matter. He thought we ought to let you make the phone call."

Heat silently blessed Steve Liebman.

"Okay, great," Heat said. Then, before she forgot, she added: "Thank you."

"And just so we're clear, I also don't want you telling this person where you got the number. And you—"

"Can't use it to get a warrant. I got it. This conversation never occurred."

"Attagirl," Miksit said. "You always were a fast learner. Okay, here goes."

Miksit began reading off the number. Heat began recognizing it the moment Miksit reached the end of the country code. By the time she had given the whole thing, Heat was quite sure.

The number belonged to Fariq Kuzbari, the security attaché to the Syrian mission to the United Nations.

Long ago, Heat's mother had taught his children piano. More recently, he had helped Heat solve her mother's murder—back when Heat believed her mother had been murdered. And Heat knew he was involved in any number of undertakings, most of them on the hazier end of legal, all things he wouldn't have disclosed under the most intense torture.

"When did the five-minute phone call occur?" Heat asked.

"A week ago Tuesday."

"And nothing after that?"

"Nothing," Miksit said.

Heat couldn't begin to guess why a *New York Ledger* Metro reporter had felt the need to contact the Syrian mission's security chief.

But she was absolutely determined to find out.

TWENTY-NINE

Heat's first call, after she finished with Miksit, was to Fariq Kuzbari.

He didn't answer, naturally. He never did.

Heat tried another number she had for the man. Again, it rang through to voice mail. She left a message, if only to hear herself talk.

Then she tried the main number for the Syrian mission, where she eventually spoke with a gatekeeper, who assured her Mr. Kuzbari was out of the country and unreachable. Heat left another message, which she knew was heading for the bottom of a garbage can.

In her previous dealings with Kuzbari, the man had only been found when he felt like being found. As a rule, he was the initiator of contact, not the receiver of it. Even once he knew he was being sought, it was no guarantee he would engage.

That wasn't good enough. Not this time. Heat didn't have the twelve, twenty-four, or forty-eight hours it typically took for Kuzbari to suddenly materialize beside her on the street in his Range Rover HSE, as he had in the past.

Before she had a fully formed plan, she was on her way out of the office. She tossed an "I'll be back" in the direction of Hamner, whose questions and then protests were already becoming distant background noise as Heat walked away.

Heat knew there were thousands of places on the planet Kuzbari might be, but one place that was more likely than others. If nothing else, a visit there could hasten the process of flushing him out.

The Permanent Mission of the Syrian Arab Republic to the United Nations, which was getting a little less permanent every day in an increasingly fractured Middle East, was over on 2nd Avenue, a few blocks from the U.N. It was located in an office building that called itself Diplomat Centre—because Spy Centre would have been a little too honest for anyone's taste—in a neighborhood filled with other consulates and missions.

Heat was soon zipping across the 79th Street Transverse in a marked patrol car. There was no sense in using an unmarked. Subtlety didn't pay when trying to cut across town in 4:30 P.M. traffic.

With her siren going the whole way, forcing other travelers to the side, nudging through intersections no matter what color the light, she completed the trip in twenty high-intensity minutes.

Once on 2nd Avenue, she parked illegally and barged through the glass front doors of Diplomat Centre, flashing tin at a rent-a-cop on her way to the elevator.

That was fine in the lobby. Heat knew the Syrian mission itself was going to be a different matter. As the elevator doors opened, she was immediately confronting a pair of heavy wooden doors with a small buzzer next to them and a prominent security camera pointing down at her from the corner. She tried the doors, which were locked. Then she went for the buzzer.

She held her badge up for the security camera to see. Thirty seconds passed. She buzzed again. Still nothing. A minute this time. The people inside were either hoping she'd go away or drawing straws to see who had to answer. She buzzed again.

Finally, a slender man in a gray suit appeared at the door. He cracked it open just wide enough for half his body to show.

"May I help you?" he asked in accented English.

"I'm Captain Nikki Heat. I'm here to see Fariq Kuzbari."

"Yes, I believe we spoke on the phone before. As I informed you then, Mr. Kuzbari is out of the country. Now if you'll excuse—"

"You know what, friend? I'm not going to excuse you, and I don't have time to play this game your way. So we're going to play it like this."

In one swift movement, Heat stuck her foot in the door, removed her 9mm from its holster, and thrust its barrel under the man's chin. The man tried to slam the door on her arm, but Heat was too fast for him—and probably stronger than he expected a woman to be. She shoved him into the next room, which was really just a small ante-chamber with another set of heavy doors on the other side. The Syrian mission had been well-advised on security measures, most likely by Kuzbari.

She backed the man into a corner, the gun still digging into the soft flesh under where his tongue connected. Heat expected an armed response to emerge after perhaps a minute, perhaps less, and for some rather tense negotiations to follow that.

Instead, the door to the main lobby opened and just one man stood there. Fariq Kuzbari was fashionably dressed in a Western-style suit—Savile Row, if Heat wasn't mistaken—with a matching turban on his head.

"Nikki Heat," he said. "I was just getting ready to call you back, you know."

Heat promptly holstered her weapon. The man she had shoved uttered what sounded like an Arabic curse.

"Sorry," Heat said. "I'm on a bit of a deadline."

"So it seems," he said. "By all means, please come inside. Let's not delay."

Heat followed Kuzbari past four scowling security men, two of whom had AR-15s at their sides. He took her not to his office but to a conference room that overlooked both the United Nations and the East River beyond it. He gestured for her to take a seat, which she did.

"I have seen the most recent video, of course," Kuzbari said. "I am very, very sorry. As you know, I have great respect for Mr. Rook and even greater enmity for any group that claims to be ISIS. I don't believe I have to lecture you on the atrocities those barbarians are inflicting on my countrymen as we speak. How can I help you?"

"A week ago last Tuesday, you spoke to Tam Svejda from the *New York Ledger*," Heat said, stating it as fact so they wouldn't have to go through the dance of question and answer.

"I did."

"What about?"

"She was looking for my help with a story. But I'm afraid I couldn't give it to her."

"What story?"

"It was about bullets," Kuzbari said.

"Bullets?" Heat repeated. "What about them?"

"As you know, my country is fighting for its very existence against ISIS. We are carrying out that fight on every possible level. One of the things that has baffled us—and your government as well—is where ISIS is getting its stash of bullets from. We know some of it comes from enemy positions they have captured. The Iraqi Army had huge stockpiles of munitions, many of which it simply abandoned without a fight when ISIS first swept through the region.

"But that was by now more than two years ago. The guns would still be operating, of course. But the bullets? Even by the most liberal estimates of how many rounds the Iraqis possessed, ISIS should have long ago exhausted that cache. Whatever territory they gain now or positions of ours they overrun would result in little more than a trickle of new ammunition, certainly not enough to meet their demand. And we know they do not have their own arms factories. So they have to be buying bullets from somewhere. They have the money, of course, primarily from the oil they are stealing and from the tributary they collect from their citizens. And they have the supply lines to get the bullets in. But someone still has to be willing to sell them the bullets. Who is that? We do not know."

"And that's what you told Tam?" Heat said.

"Almost word-for-word, yes. She seemed rather disappointed."

"Why?"

"Because I wasn't telling her anything she didn't already know," Kuzbari said. "Everything I've just said has been reported in the media already. They've even done studies of spent ISIS ammunition. The two largest sources are arms manufacturers from China and the United States."

"So why haven't the authorities just gone after those manufacturers?"

"Because they have plausible deniability. Ammunition sales are not tracked internally. I can buy from a legitimate arms manufacturer and then sell to someone else, and it is perfectly legal. It is only when I sell to ISIS that it becomes illegal. Who is doing the selling to ISIS? The question has been posed many times. It's the answer that seems to be eluding everyone."

"Did she mention any theories to you?"

"She seemed to have one in mind, but she did not share it with me. If I was to guess, I would say it was only partly formed in her mind."

There was something partly forming in Heat's mind as well. She thought back to the bullet she and Rook had found on Svejda's desk. They had assumed someone was trying to threaten Tam, but she had told Liebman it was a souvenir.

Except, of course, it had turned out to be the slug that had been dug out of Joanna Masters's back. When Heat first learned that, she couldn't begin to fathom why Svejda had wanted to keep it. But now it was becoming clear.

It wasn't a souvenir. It was evidence. For Tam Svejda, that bullet had been the starting point for a story about where ISIS was getting its bullets from.

"Did she mention the name Joanna Masters to you?" Heat asked.

"She did not. Our conversation was rather brief. Just as this conversation has been brief. Perhaps five minutes? Certainly no more than ten. Once she learned that I did not have an answer for her, she was determined to move on to someone who did."

"And now," Kuzbari said, standing. "I'm afraid I must move on as well."

They said their good-byes, and Heat was soon back in the patrol car, battling back across town.

This time, she went with the flow of traffic. She wanted the time to assemble what she had learned into a new narrative.

Two weeks earlier, Tam Svejda had written a story about Joanna Masters, who had been shot by ISIS in Syria. Like good journalists do, Svejda had let that story lead her to another.

By the following Tuesday—just a week and a day ago—she had learned enough about the world of international arms dealing to know that Fariq Kuzbari was the kind of man who tended to have a great deal of information. Except Kuzbari did not have any easy answers. It seemed no one did.

But that hadn't stopped Svejda. By Wednesday, for reasons yet unclear, she had decided to book herself a plane ticket out to Cleveland the following day. By Thursday night, she was working the finer establishments of Lorain, Ohio, flirting with steelworkers.

That didn't make sense. Bullets weren't made of steel. And, in any event, what would steelworkers know about ISIS?

Was the Lorain visit for a completely different story? A side trip with no bearing on her ISIS investigation?

Possibly. But that didn't seem to fit. Svejda clearly had her teeth sunk deep into this story, and it appeared to have sent her out to Ohio.

All Heat knew for sure was that, after eating breakfast Friday morning, Svejda never again used her credit cards. It stood to reason she was kidnapped sometime that morning—before lunch, when she likely would have used her credit card again.

Had American ISIS followed her out to Ohio and chosen to kidnap her there? Was she simply more vulnerable out in a place where she was staying in motels, eating in strange places, and talking to strange people?

There were still parts of the story missing. And by the time Heat returned to the Two-Oh, she had not been able to fill them in.

While still sitting in her patrol car, Heat called the number for Jen Forbus, the Lorain Police Department lieutenant, hoping she might have found something by then. But the call went to voice mail.

Heat walked back into the bull pen, heading directly toward the murder board. She drew lines from Tam's picture and from the circles containing *Lorain* and *Joanna Masters's bullet*. She connected them to a new circle, in which she wrote, *Where did ISIS get its bullets?*

It was the last question Tam Svejda had been asking—and the one, it now seemed, that had gotten her killed. Perhaps because the real ISIS learned of her investigation and sent some of its emissaries to dispatch her.

Heat returned to her office, closing the door behind her, her head awash in new thoughts. As she turned toward her desk, she saw Rook's garment bag, still cluttering up the corner where he had tossed it that morning.

Suddenly, something inside her broke. All of those neat compartments in Heat's brain, the ones she imagined being made of the stoutest brick—the ones that kept the investigation from her feelings and vice versa—were instantly blown away. They weren't made of brick, after all, but of straw.

Before she even knew what hit her, Heat was on her knees in front of the bag, almost like she was praying in front of it. This lump of stuffed vinyl had, a few hours earlier, been like a piece of Rook, an object that had been almost melded with his body.

And now it was the only piece of him she had left. There were tears in her eyes, big enough that she couldn't see all that well. She reached for the bag and clutched it to her chest, which heaved in silent grief for the man she loved, a man who might now be in the final six and a half hours of his life.

Then, slowly, she rose, still holding the bag. She wobbled unsteadily to the chair in front of her desk and dumped herself roughly in it. At least this way, her diminished mind reasoned, she wouldn't look as ridiculous as she had when she was kneeling on the floor.

She looked down at the bag on her lap. The urge to be near him was as strong as she had ever felt it. Before she even knew what she was doing, she was unzipping the bag. She had to come to her senses soon, had to rebuild those compartments again—the part of her still corresponding with reality told her that—but first she wanted just one little reminder of him, even if it was just a small whiff of his clothes.

Ridiculous, maybe. But there it was.

She had reached the end of the zipper and was now opening the bag. She saw the suit that was neatly hung inside, the dopp kit that had sunk to the bottom, the shoes he had worn yesterday.

But then something grabbed her eye, demanding her attention. It was a flash of color from a piece of fabric that was instantly familiar, even if Heat didn't immediately know why.

She reached into the bag and drew it out, at which point she was glad to be sitting. She was quite sure that if she had been standing, she would have fallen over.

It was the Laura Hopper scarf. The one from the video. The handmade, totally one-of-a-kind item. There was no doubt in Heat's mind.

But what was it possibly doing in Rook's possession?

THIRTY

Nikki Heat had never suffered from carsickness. She was a nut for roller coasters. She didn't care how much a boat tossed in the high seas.

But in that moment, staring at the scarf that absolutely did not belong in her husband's garment bag, her ironclad stomach lurched.

She dropped to her knees. She crawled to the trash can under her desk, reaching it just in time. Then she vomited what little was in her guts until she was dry heaving.

It had just been so unequivocal from the earliest moments of this case. The scarf had been in the video, albeit in a part the kidnappers had perhaps not even noticed. The scarf was unique. Only one of them existed in the world. Therefore, whoever owned the scarf had been in the room when the video was shot.

Had Rook been there? *Rook?*

Even if he didn't participate in the plot, it would have meant he stood idly by as Svjeda was murdered, and then said nothing about it later—which, in the eyes of the law, made him just as culpable for her death as the person holding the machete.

It was not out of the question that Rook would have come into possession of the scarf. The item had been commissioned by a Saudi sheik, but Rook knew lots of those. His assignments had taken him to Saudi Arabia at least a dozen times, and Rook sometimes dined with members of the Saudi royal family when they made visits to the states. It was possible one of them had decided to give it to Rook as a gift.

But then, wait. If Rook was part of this, why had the terrorists announced they would seize Rook next? Especially when it wasn't an empty threat. She had watched him be kidnapped with her own eyes. She had seen him struggle against the men who did it. It made no sense. . . .

Unless, of course, that was some kind of elaborate cover-up. What better way to deflect suspicion than to make it seem you were the victim?

Heat found herself shaking her head. No way. There was just no way Rook was involved in this as anything but a victim. He had been mixed up in some cockeyed things through the years, yes. His actions had sometimes seemed questionable until all the facts had become apparent. He had hidden truths from her when he felt it was in her best interest, or when the ethics of his profession had demanded it.

But this would go far beyond anything like that. There was no misunderstanding that could explain Rook's participation in anything related to American ISIS. She could not square that idea with the man she knew and loved.

There had to be some explanation, something that would help this make sense. Heat had to believe that, as much for her sanity as anything.

In the meantime, she would have to stay quiet about what she had found. If she brought this out into the bull pen right now, it would only create confusion and take their investigation down a blind alley. She couldn't let the other detectives see this.

Because if she thought like a cop—rather than like a wife and a lover—she would have instantly shoved Jameson Rook to the top of her suspect list, even going so far as to issue a warrant for his arrest.

Heat dabbed her eyes on the sleeve of her blouse, sniffed back the mucus that was trying to run out her nose, and spit one more time in the trash can. She stood and walked over to where she had left the scarf.

Then, before she tossed the bag back in the corner, she took the scarf and stuffed it inside, knowing no one else would ever think to look for it there.

If anyone saw Nikki Heat sneaking off to the bathroom with a toothbrush, a tube of toothpaste, and a plastic garbage bag with vomit sloshing around in it, they didn't say anything.

Maybe they were too busy to notice. Or maybe they felt like vomiting themselves.

They had reason to. Six o'clock had passed—less than six hours until the terrorists' deadline—and they still didn't have a single credible lead.

The SWAT teams sent to survey—and possibly move in on—suspected terrorists had, by that point, come back empty. Raley was getting nowhere with the video. The Evidence Collection Team had culled a tremendous amount of nothing from the SUVs. The only fingerprints they found belonged to Rook and Aguinaldo.

The teams of detectives they had canvassing Central Park, in the hopes someone had seen the transfer from the black SUVs to the new "clean" vehicle or vehicles, had so far yielded nothing. The Computer Crimes Squad was also reporting a null result.

The tips line had continued fielding calls, with spikes in activity as the segment featuring Heat's press conference led the news at both five and six o'clock. Aguinaldo look-alikes had been spotted in all five boroughs, often sitting idly in pizzerias, window-shopping on the street, or walking a dog the real Aguinaldo did not have. There were fewer Jameson Rook sightings. He was well known enough that people tended not to get him confused with random civilians.

Desperation had settled in. New theories were thrown against the wall in hopes they might stick. None did. Muharib Qawi, the Masjid al-Jannah imam, had come in and was serving as a kind of on-call Islam expert. Yet nothing he said was helping.

There was plenty of door slamming, wall punching, and desk kicking. And while it may have momentarily relieved frustration, it was also not helpful in the long run.

It had reached the point that, at five minutes to eight, when Heat's phone rang, she snatched at it so violently she nearly dropped it.

"Heat," she said, barely even looking at the incoming number.

"Hello, Captain. This is Jen Forbus from Lorain. You called earlier?"

Forbus sounded more subdued than she had earlier. There was no hint of the cheerfulness that had been in her voice before.

"Yes. I was wondering if you had a chance to track down those men who Tam Svejda exchanged numbers with."

"I did and I didn't," Forbus said.

"What does that mean?"

Forbus took a moment, like she didn't know where to start. "Tam got the numbers of six guys," she eventually began. "I spoke with three of them, and they said she never called. One of them said she called but he never called back. He said he felt like she was up to something and he didn't want to be a part of it."

"Up to . . . what?"

"He wouldn't say. I think once he sobered up in the morning, he realized Tam wasn't interested in him for the same reason he was interested in her. And he thought Tam wanted him to do something . . . well, I'm not sure if it was illegal. But it sounded like, whatever it was, he didn't want to do it. I tried to press him for specifics but he didn't really have any. He just said he felt like she was trouble, and he didn't want any trouble."

"Okay," Heat said, "what about the other two?"

"One said Tam called and left a message and that he called her back. But then he never heard from her. And the final one . . ."

"What?"

Heat heard Forbus breathe deeply on the other end of the line.

"He's missing," she said.

"Missing? As of when?"

"No one is quite sure. His name is George Lichman. He's a single guy, no kids, lives by himself. His parents are in Elyria, which isn't far. He normally comes around for Sunday dinner and when he didn't do that, they called him and didn't get an answer. By Tuesday, his father went over to the apartment, which is in Vermilion, the next town over from us. The father said his son wasn't there, and neither was his car."

"Did they report him missing?"

"No. The dad said George hadn't been particularly happy and had been saving up money so he could leave his job and do something else—maybe go back to school so he could be a cop, if that's not ironic enough. The family figured he must have just taken off and was going to call when he was settled somewhere new. I think when I showed up and started asking questions was the first time they got really nervous."

"Were you able to go over to the apartment?"

"That's actually where I started," Forbus said. "I had the super let me in, and nothing looked out of place. But it also didn't look like he had left for any long trip. The closet and drawers were still full of clothing. I talked to some neighbors. They weren't exactly sure the last time they had seen him, just that it had been a few days. They were garden-style apartments, so everyone had their own entrance and kind of kept to themselves."

"Is it possible he disappeared on Friday, the same day as Tam?"

"That was the theory I was trying to nail down," Forbus said. "I can't say I confirmed it. But I also definitely haven't ruled it out. It seems pretty certain no one has seen him this week or over the weekend. As for when in the previous week they had last seen him, everyone's recollection was a little hazy. Sorry I can't be more precise."

"No, I understand," Heat said, having talked to her share of neighbors with imperfect recall.

"I've told the family I've added him to our Missing Persons database," Forbus said. "But between you and me, I'm operating as if we have another murder on our hands."

Heat took a moment to mark the memory of George Lichman. It wasn't quite her full ritual, being as it wasn't her case. But she still felt like she needed to honor him.

"There's one other thing I came across that might be of interest," Forbus said. "I tracked down the last guy to be with her at Grown and Sexy, which was the last place she visited during her bar crawl on Thursday night. This was the guy who walked her to her car and then walked back into the bar."

"Oh, right."

"He admitted right away he was hoping his act of chivalry might be rewarded in some way, even it was just a little hug or something. He got nothing, of course. But he said as he was walking away he saw something in the back of her car that caught his attention."

"Now," Forbus continued, "he admitted this was several drinks into the evening, but he was pretty adamant about what he saw. He said she had a self-contained breathing apparatus in the back of her car with a couple of extra air tanks."

"Like . . . scuba equipment?"

"No, scuba throws in the element of being underwater—that's what the u stands for. This is for when you're above water."

"And what was she doing with that?" Heat asked.

"Search me. The guy said he recognized it because he had used them before. OSHA is a lot tighter than it used to be about requiring workers to use a self-contained breathing apparatus for certain jobs."

"So was Tam planning on using it at the mill somehow? Or . . ."

"No clue. I just thought I'd mention it in case it makes sense with some other part of your investigation."

"I understand. Thank you," Heat said.

Except she didn't understand. She didn't understand at all.

They wrapped up the call with promises to keep in touch. Then Heat walked over to the murder board. She drew a line to Tam's name and then the words *self-contained breathing apparatus*.

Then she paused over the punctuation. Very deliberately—because it seemed to neatly sum up everything at the moment—she turned the period into a question mark.

THIRTY-ONE

Confucius once said, "It does not matter how slowly you go as long as you do not stop."

It was great wisdom—for a fortune cookie.

For the detectives of the Twentieth Precinct, who knew all too well what would happen at the stroke of midnight, it was little solace. Stopping was not an option in their thought process. Neither was slowing down.

And yet, as the hours until midnight grew smaller, they still had nothing to show for all the doors they'd knocked on (or down), all the empty leads they had followed, or all the energy they had expended.

Heat purposefully did not look at the clock on the bull pen wall. It felt too much like admitting defeat.

Instead, she had taken to doing two things, over and over again. She would go to a computer where the precinct's main e-mail in-box was up and hit refresh. When that yielded nothing, she returned to the murder board, sure that if she just looked at all those lines and circles, they would coalesce into a whole she had not seen before.

At ten o'clock, another news broadcast brought in a new flurry of "tips," none of which materialized into anything real. At eleven o'clock, the cycle repeated itself.

Hamner was, by that point, white as paper. He had made every conceivable threat he could think of to spur action, browbeating precinct commanders across the city. He had sent out random patrols, authorized overtime, dispatched K-9 Units and soundly berated every single officer who failed to deliver the results he expected.

None of it helped.

By 11:55, with their options as exhausted as they were, the detectives had settled into an eerie silence.

Ochoa was standing—his throbbing hindquarters made sitting untenable—going through half of the Counterterrorism Task Force list again. Rhymer was seated, going through the other half.

Raley had his earphones on. He had confirmed that the voices from the first video matched the ones from the second—if that mattered at all—and was now back to a painstaking review of any fringe background noise he could pick up. His efforts to determine the brand of the corrugated steel in the background had been a failure. Too many manufacturers used ostensibly the same mold.

Feller was pacing and perspiring, taking occasional glances at the murder board as he did so.

Heat was leaning against a desk by the murder board, but she was no longer looking at it. She had been attempting a form of meditation, trying to clear her conscious mind so her subconscious might be able to provide a new answer.

"Four minutes 'til midnight," Hamner said, breaking the quiet.

He walked over to Heat, put a gentle hand on her shoulder, and in a voice hoarse from screaming said, "I'm sorry, Captain. We did everything we could. Is there . . . someone you want to call, perhaps? Some place you want to go? It took them about an hour and a half to release the video last time. I can have an NYPD chaplain accompany you to your apartment, maybe? There's no need for you to be here."

He let that thought linger out there.

Heat shook him off. "No, I . . . I don't want to be thinking later I might have been able to do something if only I was at the precinct. I'm staying here until—"

Until the bitter end, she thought, but did not speak it out loud.

"Okay," Hamner said softly. "Your call. If you change your mind . . ."

Heat shook her head. Finally, because she could no longer help herself, her gaze fell on the bull pen's clock. Other precincts had replaced their old analog pieces with digital versions, preferring the precision of an LED screen to the comparative vagueness of the big hand and little hand.

Not the Two-Oh. They had the same time-worn timepiece that had been there since whenever the place was built. Its once-white background had turned yellow. Its glass facing had a permanently smoky look about it, even though the Twentieth Precinct had gone smoke-free more than twenty years earlier.

Heat watched as the second hand circumnavigated the numbers one through twelve. The minute hand was now on the last hash mark before the twelve. The hour hand was off the twelve by such an imperceptible amount that it appeared to be standing straight up.

The second hand began its next trip around. It swept by the two, the five, the eight. There was no stopping it.

There was no stopping any of this.

It hit the twelve. The second hand, minute hand, and hour hand were now one, standing at perfect attention. Midnight had come.

And, with one more tick of the clock, it was gone.

Somewhere, the unthinkable was happening.

For a while, no one moved. It was like the wake had already begun.

Five minutes passed. Then ten. It was now Thursday, technically. October 20 would take the place of November 24 as the most horrible square on Heat's calendar, an anniversary that would fill her with unspeakable heartache for as long as she lived.

Every once in a while, someone cleared his throat or wiped his brow. No one wanted to leave. That would have been an act of surrender, and also a kind of betrayal of their captain and friend. They all knew, without being told, that in some short amount of time, Nikki Heat was going to need them like never before.

It was perhaps a quarter after midnight, with Heat, Hamner, and the detectives still in a strange kind of suspended animation.

Then a loud noise came from downstairs.

Shouts. Applause. A tremendous and happy racket.

As if they were sharing one brain, everyone in the bull pen seemed to have the same reaction.

First, their chins lifted, as if they had been brought out of trances. Then their heads tilted, as if they couldn't figure out *what* they were hearing. Then their necks craned toward the source of the sound, as if they were trying to make sense of what was happening.

Hamner took two steps toward the commotion, then stopped himself. Feller ceased his pacing.

Ochoa muttered, "What the—"

Then the elevator doors opened. And there, standing completely unharmed, in the middle of crowd of police officers, with appropriately enormous grins on their faces, were Jameson Rook and Inez Aguinaldo.

Heat instantly felt a flood of warmth, relief, and joyful tears, all combining into one emotion that came gushing in. A cry escaped her lips, but unlike the anguished moan that had involuntarily come out of her when she had thought she'd lost him, this was more like the ecstatic, astounded yelp of a Powerball winner.

Rook had started walking out of the elevator and had just barely made it past the doors when Heat, who had broken into a run, leapt into his arms. If she hadn't driven him into the wall, she would have knocked him over.

"Oh, Rook," she said into his neck, and then she kept muttering the only words that came to her mind: "You have no idea. You have no idea."

"I can't . . ." he began, but he didn't seem to be able to form any more words himself.

Heat gripped him tighter. Her feet were barely touching the ground as she dangled on him. It was all coming out of her like a cathartic jet stream: the tears, the emotion, the mindless thankful babble. She was aware there were hands pounding Rook on the shoulder, that Aguinaldo, who had also just barely made it out of the elevator, had been surrounded by happy, hugging cops. Heat didn't let it distract her from her immediate goal, which was to deliver the greatest embrace of Rook's life.

"I can't . . ." he said, and then faltered again.

Heat was really enveloping him now. She was never letting go. Never, ever again.

And finally Rook completed his sentence.

"I can't breathe," he choked out.

"Oh, sorry," Heat said, relaxing her stranglehold just slightly.

She went down off her tiptoes. They both took a full breath— Rook's more urgent than Heat's.

In that moment of bliss, Heat was incapable of anything resembling rational thought. It was Hamner who was trying to make order out of the chaos, and he eventually corralled the attention of the mob that had pushed into the bull pen.

"Detective Aguinaldo, Mr. Rook, I think I speak for the commissioner and every man, woman, and transgender individual on the force when I say I am incredibly happy to see your safe return," he said as the officers congregated nearby beamed at this rare moment of humanity from The Hammer.

Then it ended and Hamner returned to form: "But I need to remind everyone there is still an active investigation, and that American ISIS is still a threat. So I need to know: how did you escape, and what can you tell us about this menace?"

Before Aguinaldo could respond, Rook took charge.

"I think it only appropriate we let the hero of the day explain," Rook said. "Lana?"

Heat was so shocked to hear the name that she was sure she did a double take as the tall, striking figure of Lana Kline emerged from the scrum. She was flanked, as always, by her aide-de-camp interns, Justin and Preston, who were grinning obediently. Her hair and clothing were perfect as ever, like she was prepared for a press conference to break out at any moment.

"Oh, believe me, I'm not the hero here," Kline said modestly.

Preston immediately jumped on this suggestion: "With all due respect, Ms. Kline—"

"You really are," Justin finished for him.

"Nonsense, boys. All I really did was tap into the capabilities of Kline Enterprises. I told my daddy what was happening and I told him I'd be just devastated if anything happened to Jamie. And Daddy sprang into action. Daddy is the real hero here."

"But how did he even locate Detective Aguinaldo and Mr. Rook in the first place?" Hamner asked. "We had every officer in New York City looking for them. We were monitoring a million surveillance cameras. We had choppers in the air."

"Well, I don't think I'm betraying any security clearances when I tell you Kline Industries has a fair number of contracts with various branches of the armed forces," she said. "There are enough generals and admirals who owe Daddy favors, and he called in a few of them. It really is remarkable what those military satellites can do and see. I've heard Daddy say they can read a newspaper over a terrorist's shoulder from twenty-two thousand miles in the air. But until they were able to locate Jamie and Inez, I didn't realize just how good they were."

"For the record, I believe they reviewed satellite footage to track us from the moment of the kidnapping, through the change of vehicles, all the way to the warehouse where they hid us," Rook interjected. "Then they used thermal imaging technology to confirm our positions within the warehouse."

"Thermal imaging. That was the picture with all those red blotches Daddy showed me?"

"Indeed," Rook said.

"Well, then, yes, thermal imaging," Lana said. "I just know that once Daddy was able to get a location, he didn't hesitate. He sent his best people right in."

Kline turned to Hamner, who she sensed was in charge. "I'm sorry. I know the proper thing to do would have just been to call y'all and let you do it. But Daddy was worried there wasn't time. And his private security is very, very good. Most of them are ex–Special Forces and he had already put them on alert that they might be needed. So they were geared up and ready to move. He just thought, given the circumstances, better to beg for forgiveness than ask permission."

"Well, officially, we can't condone vigilante behavior," Hamner said, pulling off what was, for him, a wry smile.

"But unofficially my neck has already written a long and eloquent thank-you note expressing its gratitude about not being sawed in two," Rook said.

"So where was this warehouse they took you to?" Heat asked.

"Along the East River, but on the Brooklyn side," Rook said. "I'll be honest, we really thought it was all over for us. They had both of us bound. We had those burlap hoods over our heads. Those are incredibly itchy, by the way."

Rook turned to Aguinaldo. "Did you find yours itchy? I think I might have a rash . . ."

"That was kind of the least of my worries," Aguinaldo assured him with a smile.

"Anyhow, it really was over astonishingly quickly," Rook said. "We couldn't see anything, of course. But the lights suddenly went out and then I'm guessing from the sound they used some flash-bang grenades—those things are *loud*, by the way. I could barely hear a thing after that. Even the gunfire that followed sounded muffled. By the time we even knew what was going on, someone had taken our hoods off and we were being helped up by these guys with night-vision goggles and gas masks on their faces. They were the very picture of efficiency. They had us back out on the street and in Lana's limousine before I even had the chance to thank them."

He thought for a moment. "Though hopefully my neck's thank-you note will get passed around."

"What about the assailants?" Hamner asked. "The four men who pulled off the abduction, the two men in the video, the leader. There had to be at least seven of them."

Everyone looked at Lana.

"Not anymore," was all she said.

The Hammer nodded grimly. Heat had worked with Hamner long enough to recognize the calculations he was already making. Hamner recognized there were circumstances where private enterprise could offer solutions not available to the government. And he realized, with the political instincts that had thrust him into his role as the NYPD's chief fixer, that this was one of those times when the less he knew, the better.

He would come up with some kind of story to pave things over with the press, the brass at One PP, and City Hall. He would do it because he was The Hammer, and sometimes hammers were used to countersink nails so they could then be covered over.

Towing Rook by the hand, Heat walked over to Lana Kline. Then Heat separated from Rook—if only briefly—so she could give Kline a hug.

A real hug this time. Not a girl hug.

"Thank you," she said, smothering her with an embrace that most certainly mussed both women's hair and makeup. "Thank you so, so much. To say I am forever in your debt seems . . . completely inadequate."

"Oh, pish," Kline said, smoothing her dress as Heat separated. "I'm just another opportunistic press agent trying to assure her candidate a nice profile in *First Press*."

She winked at Rook.

"I do believe," Rook said, "that Legs Kline has earned himself the most glowing profile in the history of *First Press*."

She nodded toward the murder board. "Well, then, my last quote for the article is that Legs Kline is proud of the NYPD for closing another case and for its continuing efforts to keep the citizens of New York safe."

"We appreciate that," Hamner said, clearly already thinking about how this would all play out on the morning news shows.

"Not a problem. And while we'd love to stick around and celebrate, I'm afraid we have to take our leave of you," Kline said. "They're holding the plane for us as we speak. Daddy is giving a big speech in Zagreb tomorrow . . . or, I guess, by now, today. He has to bolster his foreign policy credentials, you know."

Kline clapped her hands twice. "Justin, Preston!" she said. "Come along, boys!"

"Yes, Ms. Kline," Preston said.

"Yes, Ms. Kline," Justin said.

Or it may have been Justin, then Preston. Heat still wasn't sure as the elevator doors closed behind them.

Hamner still had a few questions, which Rook and Aguinaldo did their best to answer.

It wasn't a thorough debriefing, because that wasn't really what Hamner wanted. He just needed enough details so he could concoct a story that fit all the facts anyone on the outside would be able to uncover.

The detectives quickly began peeling away. Ochoa limped off with Raley. Facing a true life-or-death situation seemed to have put their squabble about the shooting incident into perspective. They had smoothed things over the way guys often do: not with words, but with a mutual silent arrival at the conclusion that what they had squabbled over was not really worth fighting about.

Feller and Rhymer followed them out not long after. Then Hamner and Aguinaldo departed, leaving just Heat and Rook, alone in the bull pen.

"So it's very late," Rook said.

"It is," Heat replied.

"And I'm beyond exhausted."

"As am I."

"And, of course, we've both been through a harrowing physical and emotional ordeal."

"The worst."

"The only thing we should be thinking about right now is getting home and collapsing into a deep sleep that lasts for at least a day."

"Or two."

"Because we just don't have a shred of energy left."

"None whatsoever."

They looked deeply into each other's eyes, and, at the exact same moment, said:

"Reykjavík?"

Heat said, "You're on," while Rook, in the midst of scrambling toward the door of Heat's office, simultaneously said, "I'll get my bag."

Rook's bag. The one with the inexplicable Laura Hopper scarf still stuffed inside.

It wasn't that Heat had forgotten about it. It had just slid out of the immediate forefront of her mind, what with Rook facing imminent decapitation. Should she make an issue out of it now?

No, she quickly decided. There were some mysteries that could be solved later. Or perhaps they could just stay mysteries.

Heat had her husband back, safe and sound. The men responsible for Tam Svejda's death had suffered the ultimate penalty. Their corpses were currently providing nourishment to aquatic life at the bottom of the East River—or wherever it was Kline's men had decided to dispose of them.

The point was they would never be able to terrorize anyone, ever again. For once in her life, Heat thought, she could attempt to ignore the legal implications and leave well enough alone.

Then Rook emerged from her office, dragging the scarf across his face like a gypsy dancer.

"I know it's not time for gift-giving," he said. "But this one is special. And I can't think of a better way to celebrate the end of this case."

He clumsily whirled around, took three long dancer's strides toward Heat, humming a made-up melody the whole way, then presented it to her with a high degree of ceremony.

"Your very own, one-of-a-kind, handmade Laura Hopper scarf," he said.

He bowed deeply.

Heat felt her mouth go dry as she accepted it. Her heart was suddenly pounding.

"Wow," she forced herself to say, as if she were pleased to be receiving it. "Where . . . Wherever did you get it from?"

"Oh," Rook said breezily. "Lana gave it to me."

THIRTY-TWO

ook didn't seem to notice that Heat's jaw had become unhinged. He just continued carrying on in very Rook-esque fashion.

"I know, I know, you're speechless!" Rook said. "I was, too. I mean, I think by now you know how rare these are. But we were down in Miami on Tuesday night and Lana had just changed outfits and she came out wearing it. And I said, 'Wow! A Laura Hopper?' And I think at first she was impressed I recognized it was a Laura Hopper—I daresay it takes a special kind of man with a special kind of eye. Then she asked if I liked it. And of course I said I did. And she said, 'Here, I want you to give it to Nikki.'

"At first I was like, 'No, no, no! I couldn't.' But then she insisted. She said some sheik or something like that had given it to her father just so he'd consider some kind of deal. I don't know the details. Anyhow, she said that it was a scarf that simply had to be shared, and she had enjoyed it for a while and had already worn it several times and she thinks so highly of you she liked the idea of you getting to enjoy it and why haven't you interrupted me yet? You generally always interrupt me when I'm babbling while we should be hurrying toward the bedroom."

Heat worked her tongue just to get enough saliva in her mouth to be able to talk.

"Rook," she said, her voice raspy. "That's the scarf from the first video."

She walked over to the murder board and pointed to its picture.

Now it was Rook's turn to stare with his mouth agape. "So, wait," he stammered. "That means . . . that means . . ."

"Lana Kline was in the room when the video was shot," Heat said.

Rook began, "But how is that—"

Then he stopped himself. Heat watched Rook's eyes greedily take in the murder board, which he hadn't really looked at since early in the investigation.

"What does this mean?" he asked, then started reading from the board. " 'Joanna Masters's bullet.' 'Where did ISIS get its bullets?' "

Heat told Rook about how the Joanna Masters interview had launched Svejda into a story about how ISIS was staying supplied with munitions.

"What about this?" Rook asked, pointing to the phrase *Interviewing steelworkers*.

Heat told him about Svejda's bar-hopping exploits, and how the steelworker she had managed to make contact with, George Lichman, had gone missing.

"And this?" Rook asked, jabbing at *zinc*.

"Traces of zinc were found on her shoes."

"And she was last seen in Lorain, Ohio?" Rook said.

"That's right."

"Then I can tell you exactly what she was doing there," Rook said. "And it wasn't interviewing steelworkers. Not exactly. To the cops in Lorain, I'd be willing to bet the word 'steelworker' is a kind of interchangeable term that they use to describe anyone who works in any of the factories down by the waterfront. But those aren't just steel mills. Remember how I told you my tour of Kline Industries took me to a smelting plant on the shores of Lake Erie?"

"Yes."

"That plant was in Lorain, Ohio. In addition to a smelting operation, that's also where the Kline Industries Munitions Division is located. That zinc on the bottom of her shoes? Zinc is what you add to copper to make brass. The brass they make is then moved right over to the armory, where it is turned into jackets for bullets."

"Which were then being sold to ISIS," Heat surmised.

"Tam must have figured it out. Or at least had a strong hunch. She was going around to those bars, looking for guys who worked for Kline Industries—guys who could sneak her in and then give her the kind of grand tour I got . . . just the sub rosa variety. And I bet I know where her tour ended. Because you know what else that arm of Kline Industries had in Lorain? Its own airstrip."

Rook pointed at *kerosene* on the board. "That's why she had this stuff on her. Kerosene may have been discovered long ago by al-Razi, but these days one of its major uses is in jet fuel. Maybe she was just skulking around the refueling area or got blasted with some jet exhaust. That's why her clothes reeked of the stuff. She was snooping around the planes, trying to confirm that the bullets coming from the armory were being loaded aboard.

"And then . . ." He was now pointing at the words *self-contained breathing apparatus* with his eyes aglow. "She was going for a long ride in the unpressurized cargo hold of an airplane. That's why she had all those extra tanks. One of the oldest rules of journalism is 'follow the money.' She was just doing a variation of that. She was going to follow the bullets. It was the only way she could confirm that Kline Industries was selling directly to ISIS and not some middleman."

Heat had her hands on her hips. It wasn't that she didn't believe Rook's version. It was that she wanted to test it.

"But why would Kline Industries sell to ISIS?" she asked.

"Because Legs isn't as wealthy as he lets on," Rook said. "Especially right now, with gas so cheap. His petroleum businesses are leaching money badly. And he's the modern version of land rich, cash poor. Except in his case it's stock rich, cash poor. All he ever does is reinvest, reinvest, reinvest. He never takes any capital out, and he's highly leveraged. That was going to be the one red flag in an otherwise glowing profile. I had one analyst tell me that if Kline Industries had one more bad quarter, there could be a margin call, and then the whole house of cards would fall in on itself.

"ISIS was probably willing to pay four or five times what the bullets were worth. So ISIS was doing the killing, but Kline Industries was *making* a killing. Legs knew he couldn't afford to pass up that kind of profit margin, and he was overconfident that no one would be able to track it back to him. He could always say, 'Well, yeah, you're finding our bullets over there. But you're finding everyone's bullets over there. It wasn't us selling them. It was a middleman.' One well-bribed pilot and copilot, and the scheme was, if you'll excuse the phrase, bulletproof."

"Until Tam Svejda came along," Heat said, picking up the narrative. "The timeline certainly works. She was last seen at breakfast on Friday morning. They could have easily gotten her to New York by Saturday night in time to shoot the video. She must have hooked up with George Lichman Friday morning and then gotten caught sometime later. Trying to sneak aboard with all those air tanks was probably what did her in."

"At which point Kline Industries had a major problem: a journalist who was onto their ISIS connection," Rook said. "You can't just let her go, because she'll continue asking questions, and sooner or later, things are going to unravel. So they had to get rid of Tam. And they had to do it in a way so that they didn't get caught."

Heat picked it up from there. "You couldn't just throw her in a smelter and forget about her. That's probably what they did to poor George Lichman. But no one was going to kick up a huge fuss about one missing millworker. Tam on the other hand? People were going to ask questions if she disappeared. They would have eventually followed her paper trail to Lorain and figured out what she was doing—unless someone came up with a huge ISIS-sized distraction, like that video."

"Blame the Middle Eastern terrorist," Rook crowed. "It works every time, because it fits so nicely into everyone's preconceived notions. It's like Muharib Qawi said. Ever since 9/11, the Muslim is America's favorite boogeyman."

Heat picked up where he left off. "And, as a bonus, it directly feeds the anti-immigration plank of Legs Kline's presidential platform. So not only was the video a great red herring, it was also the best campaign propaganda he could have hoped for. With a renewed wave of Islamophobia and xenophobia sweeping the nation, America would turn to the guy who was most vehement about keeping outsiders on the outside."

"What's more, quote unquote 'rescuing' Aguinaldo and me would give the Kline candidacy another big win in all of tomorrow's news cycles. And they knew it would further cast suspicion away from them.

Why would anyone think their hero and their suspect were the same entity?"

Having finally deciphered the mysteries of the murder board, Rook was now face-to-face with Heat.

"You know, you are so hot when you're solving crimes," he said lustily. "I want to go to Reykjavík with you so badly."

"Me too," Heat purred. "But we have this little issue."

"Legs and Lana Kline are getting away?"

"And not just getting away. They're going to Zagreb, which is in Croatia. Which as we all know . . ."

"Doesn't have an extradition treaty to the US," Rook said. "And there's no way we'll be able to keep the lid on this thing until he gets back. He'll go to Croatia and, when he figures out he's a wanted man, he'll cash out his stock for whatever it's worth and use it as bribe money. He'll be able to stay as Croatia's honored guest for as long as he likes. We have to stop him before he leaves US soil."

"Are we too late already?" Heat asked.

Rook said, "It's been thirty-five minutes since they left . . ."

"Which wouldn't be quite enough time to get out to LaGuardia *and* get a jet in the air. They'd still have to file a flight plan, get approval, then get themselves in the runway queue."

"By the way," Rook said, "you do realize we're starting to sound like Justin and Preston, completing each other's thoughts and sentences, right?"

"Speaking of which, I bet when we do voice-matching, it's those two in the video, pretending to be terrorists, knowing the Darth Vader filter—"

"Kylo Ren filter."

"—the whatever filter would throw it off. But when Raley stripped the filter away, it sounded like two kids who ran a college radio station—just like Justin and Preston. I bet one of them is left-handed, like the guy in the video who swung the machete. I *knew* that was strange for an Arab. It would also explain why they kept glancing just to the side of the camera. They were constantly looking to Lana for approval."

"Okay, but you know I'm not taking that bet," Rook said. "As you'll recall, you still have to make love to me dressed as a sex-crazed Vulcan. I haven't collected on that yet."

"You will. You will."

"But first?" Rook said.

"LaGuardia Airport," Heat said.

And Rook finished: "The LokSat Aviation terminal."

THIRTY-THREE

Rook drove. Heat worked the phones.

They probably should have done it the other way—Heat really was a better driver, even if Rook would have been loath to admit it—except they needed Heat's official status when it came to talking to Port Authority. Especially given the seemingly preposterous news she had to deliver: that Legs Kline was behind American ISIS, and that he and his plane had to be detained until she arrived.

Heat's next call was to Hamner, who promptly put out an APB on Kline's limousine, in case they had taken a detour or gotten slowed in traffic and were still en route.

Then she called Lorain Police Lieutenant Jen Forbus, who confirmed that George Lichman—who she was now referring to in the past tense—had worked for Kline Industries, a detail she hadn't realized was important before. All five of the other men whose phone numbers Svejda had collected also worked for Kline. ·

As Heat hung up, Forbus was making noise about search warrants and about declaring Lichman a homicide. Maybe they'd find Lichman's car somewhere. Both women knew it was more than likely far too late to find his body. A smelter can easily top two thousand degrees. There would be nothing left of him.

Heat soon heard back from Hamner, who said the limousine had been pulled over on Grand Central. The driver claimed to have dropped off the entire Kline party—Legs, Lana, and their security detail—at the LokSat Aviation terminal, then let the uniforms thoroughly search the limo, just to prove it.

All the while, Rook was living out a long-held vehicular fantasy. Google Maps would tell you the trip from 82nd Street to LaGuardia Airport takes twenty-one minutes. With Rook gleefully ignoring traffic laws and speed limits, driving with the impunity of an unmarked car and a flashing gumball, they made the trip in sixteen.

By the time Rook gunned the engine for the final time and pulled up in front of LokSat Aviation, a large warehouse-like building on the west side of the airport's acreage, it appeared half of the Port Authority Police had beaten them there. There was a tremendous show of force, half of it likely unnecessary—a fire truck, really?—but Heat knew enough about the incessant overtime padding at the Port Authority that she wasn't surprised.

Following the source of activity to its zenith, Heat and Rook worked their way around the building to the front of the hangar. There, a Boeing 737 NG was surrounded by Port Authority Police vehicles, looking like a rhinoceros beset by a pack of dachshunds.

"That's Kline's plane," Rook said.

The vessel had been painted like an American flag, with the stars on the tailfin and the red and white stripes on the fuselage. It was like a supersized version of Preston's—or was it Justin's?—American flag lapel pin.

"Yeah, I think I could have guessed that," Heat said, continuing her charge.

Flashing her badge to get past a variety of Port Authority cops who were working hard to justify their overtime, Heat eventually presented herself to the lanky dark-haired man who seemed to be running the show.

"Hi. Captain Nikki Heat. I'm the—"

"Reason I'm out of bed right now? Yeah, I know," he said, then offered a good-natured smile and stuck out his right hand. "Captain Ron Marsico."

Then Marsico turned to Rook. "Mr. Rook, I once thought about going into journalism before I came to my senses and joined the Port Authority. But I just want to say I'm a big fan."

"And I appreciate all you do to protect New York's bridges, tunnels, and ports," Rook said. "And I know there are hundreds of thousands of New Yorkers who feel the same way every day."

He was laying it on a bit thick, but Marsico seemed to be lapping it up.

Or at least he was until he turned back to Heat. "I guess you're responsible for there being a mess, but I'm responsible for the mess itself. So please tell me you have a very, very good reason for me detaining the plane belonging to the future president of the United States. Because I like my job and prefer to stay unfired."

"Don't worry about that," Heat said. "Where's Legs Kline?"

"You tell me. He wasn't on that thing, if that's what you're thinking," Marsico said, pointing at the plane.

"What?" Heat said.

"We intercepted this vessel just as it was starting to taxi out toward the runway. We instructed the pilot to come to a full stop, saying it was a police matter and that we had to board the plane to apprehend a suspect. The pilot complied, but when we boarded the plane, there were no passengers, just crew."

Heat scowled at the plane with consternation. "That's not possible. We talked to a limo driver who said he dropped off Legs and his people here."

"Tell that to the pissed-off pilot I interviewed," Marsico said. "He swore up and down that his orders were to fly an empty plane over to Europe somewhere to pick up some Kline Industries VIPs and then bring them back to the states. He was cursing me out for making him late, going on and on about how he'd have to file a new flight plan, yada yada. For what it's worth, we interviewed the co-pilot and the flight attendant separately. They both backed up the pilot's story. They're all still in the interrogation room back at our place if you want to talk to them."

Heat crossed her arms. Rook pouted silently.

"I also talked to the entire LokSat Aviation graveyard shift, which consisted of one kid who, admittedly, might have been stoned," Marsico said. "For what it's worth, he said he didn't see any passengers boarding the plane."

"Probably because he couldn't see beyond the end of his blunt," Rook said.

"That may be true. And, look, I'm all for striking blows against terrorism. Anyone who has been with the Port Authority as long as I have lost friends on 9/11. But I can't just impound a plane for no reason. If you don't have some kind of probable cause that this particular vessel or its crew was involved in the commission of a crime, I'm going to have to let it go. I shouldn't have even held on to it this long, but I watch the news. I know what you and your husband have been through today."

"Thanks," Heat said.

She turned to Rook. "Okay. I'm too tired to figure this out. How did they slip the hook? How did they even know we were onto them?"

Then Heat snapped her fingers. "The murder board! Lana was looking at it while she was at the precinct. She must have looked at everything on there and figured it was only a matter of time until we put it together. They must have known we were coming and then switched planes. Damn it. They were just using this thing as a decoy. I should have asked them to halt *all* private air traffic."

Marsico volunteered, "For what it's worth, I don't think it would have made a difference. He didn't escape from here. This was LokSat Aviation's only scheduled departure for tonight. And we've had units at the other private aviation terminals asking about him, just to be sure. Legs Kline isn't exactly a guy who can just tiptoe in and out of places unnoticed. No one has seen him."

Heat groaned. She was too tired to have come this far and fallen this short. She uttered a rare swear.

The entire time, Rook had just been looking up at the red, white, and blue monstrosity before them with a distracted smile on his face.

"Captain," Rook asked, "do you mind if I board the plane for a moment?"

"What for?"

"Nostalgia," he said.

"Excuse me?"

Rook steadied his gaze at Marsico. "Legs Kline has a king-sized bed on that thing. I was allowed to sleep on it once for forty-five minutes. It was a very special, very magical experience and I'd . . . I'd just like to say good-bye."

"Rook, seriously?" Heat began. "We don't have time to—"

But Marsico was already shrugging. "For Jameson Rook? Sure. Why not. I need a little time to announce that this party is over and clear my people out of here. You got five minutes while we make ourselves scarce. After that, I have to let this thing go on its way."

"You got it," Rook said. "And thank you."

Rook was already taking long strides toward the portable stairs still attached to the side of the plane. Heat had to scramble to keep up.

"Rook, I know you loved that bed, but isn't this a little much?"

He didn't answer. He was already climbing the stairs.

"Rook, come on. We're wasting time. Legs Kline is probably finding some other way to flee the country as we speak. He obviously knows we're after him. He's probably on board a boat or a submarine or God knows what."

Rook, ignoring her completely, was now inside the plane. Heat continued giving chase. She finished climbing the stairs, took a right turn at the cockpit, and passed through the first cabin, which contained a dozen extra-wide leather chairs that were bolted to the floor. Each of them had enough space around them that they could have reclined completely and still had room to spare.

The cabins were separated not by a curtain, like a commercial airliner would be, but by a door. It was solid-looking, perhaps steel-reinforced, probably soundproof. Extra privacy, she thought, for any Mile High extracurricular activities that might be happening on the other side.

She opened the door and walked into the second cabin, which contained the bed. Rook was jumping on it. Then he dropped and sprawled out on it.

Actually, the word "sprawled" didn't do him justice. He was rolling around, almost like a dog trying to itch its back on the grass.

"Okay, Rook," Heat said. "You've had your fun. And I'll tell Ochoa all about it so he can be more jealous than he already is. But can we go now?"

Rook paid her no heed. He had already moved on to a set of buttons on the side of the bed, which was apparently adjustable. Rook was pressing the buttons in random order, almost like a toddler who had discovered a new toy. The bed responded to this conflicting set of commands spasmodically, with various parts of it reclining, then flattening, then reclining again. Overhead lights went on and off. Music played then cut out. The flight attendant call button dinged several times.

Heat slapped her forehead. This was a new low, even for her husband. Rook may have sometimes acted like the only child in the world to have won two Pulitzer Prizes. But, underneath, she now realized there was something far less mature.

"Okay, Jameson," Heat said, hoping she sounded enough like Margaret Rook that Rook would snap to. "Playtime is over. Now let's—"

She was interrupted by the humming of a motor kicking into action. Then the bed started to move. Not up or down, like when Rook had been working those controls.

The bed was moving to the side.

"I *knew* it," Rook said. "It really *is* the *Millennium Falcon*!"

Rook was wearing an enormous self-impressed grin. Sure enough, the bed was sliding over to reveal a secret compartment underneath.

Heat watched in amazement as the gap between the bed and the side of the compartment grew to be about a foot wide.

Then a black rectangular object, about the length of a candy bar and maybe twice as thick, flew out of the opening.

Rook shouted, "Flash bang!"

And the world went white.

The noise hit them a split-second later, a deafening wall of sound.

It was even more stunning than the light. And between the shock wave and the way it threw off the equilibrium of their inner ears, Heat and Rook had been knocked off their feet.

A human being has five senses, but they get the majority of their input from either sight or hearing. If you disable one, most people can still find a way to function, albeit in diminished fashion. Without both, Heat and Rook were totally incapacitated.

Heat felt a hand touching her holster. She tried to grab it, but she was so off-kilter she had a difficult time even knowing where her holster was. Whoever wanted her gun, probably one of Kline's thugs, now had it as easily as if he had been disarming a baby.

She braced herself for a shot. Was there a greater ignominy for a cop than being killed with her own gun?

Her head throbbed. She kept blinking, hoping it would restore her sight. But there was still nothing but blinding lightness. It was like she had stared at the sun too long.

If there was one saving grace, it had been Rook's warning. In that split second between Rook's shout and the object's detonation, Heat was able to close her eyes and bring her hands to her ears. It spared her from the grenade's full force. She was recovering ever so slightly faster than if she had been caught completely unawares.

Heat got to her hands and knees and crawled around until she found the bed. It steadied her somewhat, just having something she could hold on to. She kept blinking. Her eyes still throbbed, but she felt like she was starting to be able to distinguish between light and dark again.

Then she felt a lurch.

Was it just her disturbed sense of balance playing tricks on her, or . . .

No. There was no question about it. The plane was moving.

With the small amount of hearing that had returned to her, she could distinguish that the engines had been turned on. The whine of the turbines was unmistakable.

Legs Kline was trying to escape the United States in a plane painted like an enormous American flag.

Surely, Heat thought, someone on the ground would notice this grandiose display of overblown patriotism on the move. And they would stop it.

But who? And how? When they had left Captain Marsico, he'd seemed more concerned about clearing his forces out of the private aviation area. His people were traveling in the wrong direction. And once a big plane like this got moving, there would be no stopping it.

That was why Kline's goons hadn't shot them yet. They were trying to make their getaway first. Either that, or they knew a police captain and famous writer would make for valuable hostages if things went sideways.

"Rook! Rook can you hear me?" Heat yelled.

"I'm still on the bed," he yelled back.

"Is Legs Kline crazy enough to think he'll be able to fly this plane out of here?"

"Legs Kline probably thinks he can do anything," Rook shouted. "He used to fly crop dusters in college. And I bet at least one of those ex–Special Forces guys he employs knows something about how to work an airplane. Between them, they could probably get this thing in the air. And if you know anything about how to engage the auto-pilot, these planes will fly themselves. It could make it all the way to Croatian airspace without anyone so much as touching the controls."

Heat was still blinking. She could now see shapes. Using the bed for leverage, she hoisted herself up. She found she could stand again, if unsteadily. She staggered a few steps until she found the side of the fuselage, which she used to help keep herself vertical.

The plane was picking up momentum. It wasn't to takeoff speed, not yet. But it was definitely now at a fast taxi. A plane that size would need a real runway in order to gain the velocity needed to achieve lift-off. But whoever was at the controls seemed determined to get to a runway in a hurry.

Heat groped along the walls, working her way to the front of the cabin. Between her limited—but quickly returning—sight and her hands, she was able to find the door to the cabin.

She tried to open it, but it was locked. Naturally. She felt along until she located the handle. She squinted at the spot, then delivered a devastating back kick.

The handle didn't move. This was a door built to last. She stomped it again. Nothing happened. It was steel reinforced, no question. She could kick it all day. Her foot would break before the door did.

"Don't waste your energy," Rook said. "You'll never get that thing open. And even if you do, there are a couple of beefy security goons waiting for you on the other side. Beyond that, you've got Legs and a flying buddy in the cockpit. And all cockpit doors these days are designed to be completely impenetrable. You'll never get through."

"So what's our plan?" Heat said, realizing she no longer needed to shout as much to be heard.

"We have to keep the plane from taking off somehow," Rook said. "Once it gets in the air, the only thing that's going to get it back down on the ground is the US Air Force."

"You really think they'd shoot us down?"

"An unauthorized plane being flown by confirmed terrorists in New York airspace? In a heartbeat," Rook said. "And I don't mean to point out the obvious, but I don't think the F-18s who take us down are going to be real concerned about our soft landing. They'll probably wait until we're over water so we don't fall on any civilians below us and then enjoy the target practice."

So that was it. They were locked in a rear cabin, behind an impregnable door, on an aircraft that would essentially become a huge flying coffin the moment it got into the air. They had no firearms nor any weaponry more powerful than the pillows on Legs's king-sized bed. And they could only dimly see and hear.

The plane made a sharp right turn, throwing Heat off balance again. Then, as soon as the vessel straightened, Heat was tossed backward by the sudden g-force. The pilot had just demanded full power from the twin CFM56-7B engines, which were now kicking out close to 27,000 pounds of thrust.

Heat slammed into the rear wall of the cabin, then slumped to the floor, momentarily stunned.

They were on one of the main runways now, accelerating rapidly. This was no cumbersome commercial airliner, weighted down with passengers and their elephantine luggage. This was a basically empty private plane. How long until it gained the necessary speed to get airborne? Twenty seconds? Less?

Heat willed herself back up, fighting against the plane's continued surge. She glanced at Rook, who was little more than a blob-like human shape in the distance. He seemed to have worked his way to a sitting position at the end of the bed and was trying to find the wherewithal to stand.

Their semi-useless eyes scanned around the cabin, looking for something they could use to keep the plane on the ground.

A fire. They could find a way to start a fire. No. That would kill them long before it would disable the rest of the aircraft.

The plane's electrical systems. Could they bust through the ceiling and rip out some wires that controlled the tail section?

No time. There was no time to do anything. The engines were really pouring out the power now. The plane had that feeling planes get right before takeoff, when gravity makes its futile last stand before finally giving in to the incredible upward forces being exerted on the wings.

They had ten seconds left, if that.

"If only there was an emergency brake or something," Rook bellowed, now teetering unsteadily with his butt off the bed and his legs spread wide.

"Emergency! Rook, that's it!"

Simultaneously, their limited eyesight fell on the emergency exit door in the rear of the cabin. "The evacuation slide!" they exclaimed together.

Rook got there first, scrambling over to the door and depressing the handle, which was like cocking a revolver. The slide mechanism was now armed.

Having once freelanced for an airline magazine, Rook could have told Heat that FAA regulations require all aircraft doors come with evacuation slides that deploy in six seconds or less. This would be a test of that capability, one where failure had dire consequences.

Rook pulled the handle up, which was like pulling the trigger. From somewhere just below his feet, there was a thundering *crack* of highly pressurized gas exploding. The slide shot out the side of the fuselage. Rook grasped the door with both hands and tossed it out of the way.

The plane swerved as the slide, now fully unfurled, started skipping along the ground. It was a bulky thing, wide enough to accommodate several adults sliding down it at the same time. It was made of tough vinyl and anchored to the side of the plane in a way that was meant to stay.

Between the flapping slide and the open door, the vessel's aerodynamics had been thrown off. There was enough drag to prevent the plane from getting into the air.

But Legs Kline, or whoever was at the controls, either didn't know it or wouldn't admit it. The engines kept screaming, their throttles still jammed against the stop. They were traveling at least eighty miles an hour. The ground beneath Rook and Heat was a blur in the night.

Heat was trying to summon the courage to leap down the slide when Rook grasped her arm. "Don't jump," he said. "We're going too fast. If the head trauma doesn't kill you, the road rash will make you wish you were dead."

"Okay, so what now?" she said.

The wind was rushing furiously past the open door. She again had to shout to be heard.

"Now we crash," Rook yelled.

"So let's prepare for a crash," Heat said.

"The mattress," Rook said. "It's extra plush *and* pillow-top. It'll give us enough cushion if we get it against the bulkhead."

Heat scrambled toward the far side of the mattress. They each grabbed half of it and wrestled it until it was essentially acting as padding against the front wall of the cabin.

Then they wedged themselves against it and braced for the worst.

As anyone who has ever flown in or out of LaGuardia knows, the airport's main runways are essentially peninsular, bounded by water on three sides. It treats millions of passengers a year to the specter of a very unwelcome swim if their aircraft veers off course during takeoff or landing.

And an aborted takeoff was what Rook and Heat had now assured for themselves as the plane hurtled toward the murky darkness of Flushing Bay.

Still traveling at eighty miles an hour, the 737 plowed through the fence at the end of the runway, bending its concrete-reinforced iron poles like they were pipe cleaners.

It skidded across a concrete pad and over a thin strip of grass. Then it reached the shoreline, which was buttressed by a thick riprap wall, to protect it from erosion.

From there, it was a fifteen-foot drop into the drink. The plane seemed to hang over the precipice, floating in midair. It was as if, having gone through a period of ambivalence, the aircraft was now finally contemplating fulfilling the purpose for which it had been so masterfully designed.

A long time ago, a man named Bernoulli came up with a principle of fluid dynamics that neatly describes how the miracle of flight is possible. An even longer time ago, a man named Newton came up with a law for how two larger-than-atom-sized objects will interact with each other in space.

For a brief moment, Newton's universal law of gravitation and Bernoulli's principle seemed to be having a disagreement. Mr. Newton explained how two bodies attract each other with a force that is directly proportional to the product of their masses and inversely proportional to the square of the distance between them. Mr. Bernoulli asserted that because the pressure in a stream of fluid is reduced as the speed of the flow is increased, air flowing over the curved top half of an airplane wing will have less pressure than the flat bottom half, creating an upward thrust.

But, really, it wasn't much of a fight. In this case, Newton kicked Bernoulli's ass.

The plane dropped, its nose splashing into the water at a roughly ten-degree angle, shallow enough that the plane skipped a little bit, its momentum carrying it across the water like a flat rock tossed out into a calm lake.

But even a skimming stone eventually finds the bottom. As soon as water began flooding the plane's turbines, the engines came to a halt. Once the forward momentum they had been supplying was no longer available, the plane slowed until it stopped.

The deceleration was gradual enough that the mattress was more than sufficient to cushion Heat and Rook. When the plane came to a halt, there in the middle of Flushing Bay, they stood up.

"Feel like going for a swim?" Rook asked.

"That sounds delightful," Heat answered.

They righted themselves and headed for the door. The plane had enough air in its cargo hold and cabin that it would float for at least another minute or so. But not much more. This vessel was not designed for the high seas. Water was already leaking through the bolts and seams of its decidedly non-waterproof underside.

Heat could hear sirens heading their way. The Port Authority Police, along with every fire and rescue vehicle they could summon, were now racing toward the end of the runway. Farther off, Heat could hear a helicopter and a Coast Guard cutter, closing in from air and sea respectively.

Heat was about to step onto the slide when another noise, this one much closer, sounded.

It was the thunderclap of a gunshot.

Heat and Rook braced themselves. Was this about to become an armed standoff? Were Kline and his men really going to defend a doomed plane even as it sank to the bottom of Flushing Bay?

But no. Only one bullet had been fired. And Heat could already guess the target.

"I think Legs Kline just permanently suspended his presidential campaign," Rook said, reading Heat's mind.

"Probably just as well," Heat said. "I was going to vote for Lindsy Gardner anyway."

THIRTY-FOUR

The next several hours passed in a blur of exhaustion and exhilaration.

Kline's security people were falling over themselves to see who could rat out whom faster as soon as they were pulled into interrogation, each trying to outdo the others with how much information they could provide, in hopes of getting the best deal.

But they were tight-lipped compared to Justin and Preston, who started giving it up the moment they were hauled aboard the Coast Guard ship.

Lana Kline was apparently not going gentle into that good plea bargain. The only thing to which she had confessed was that she was eager to invoke her right to counsel.

But the general outlines of what had happened were emerging quickly enough. It was just as Rook and Heat had thought. Tam Svejda had sunk her teeth into Kline Industries as one of the major sources of ISIS munitions. With George Lichman's help, she had been secreting herself aboard a plane bound for Turkey when she was discovered by Kline Industries security. Lichman had been tortured into confessing everything before he had been killed.

That still left the problem of what to do with the nosy reporter. The video was, naturally, Lana's idea, one that Legs had embraced immediately. Politically, there was just nothing better for him than a good terrorist scare three weeks before voters went to the polls. They had chosen to film and distribute the video in New York because they knew it was the media capital of the world. Nothing would assure them more attention.

The scarf appearing in the video had been Lana and company's biggest mistake, one made out of the desire to be too perfect. They had wanted to make the video appear low-budget and poor quality, like real ISIS videos. To that end, they had edited it on old equipment that had a monitor with a narrower aspect ratio. They hadn't even realized the scarf would be in the frame of more modern screens.

All of this earnest confession had taken place at the Twentieth Precinct, with Ochoa, Raley, Rhymer, Feller, and Aguinaldo tag-teaming on the interviewing.

Rook had disappeared before first light. He was nearing the deadline for his *First Press* profile of Legs Kline. The art department balked at having to redesign the cover on such short notice, a difficulty they solved with a small change in punctuation.

WHO IS LEGS KLINE, REALLY? was changed to WHO IS LEGS KLINE? REALLY?

At one point mid-morning, Heat snuck a nap. She had already changed out of her uniform and back into civilian clothes. They were the same clothes she had worn the previous day, but at least they didn't smell like fish and motor oil.

By six o'clock Thursday evening, Heat had half the precinct—and, more importantly, most of the brass down at One PP—telling her it was time to go home and get some sleep. When she got a text from Rook, saying he had filed his story and would be waiting for her at home, she decided it was time. She texted him back saying she'd be right there.

She walked out into the sinking sunlight on 82nd Street to look for a cab. She was so bone-weary she didn't trust herself to drive home or even to navigate the subway. Other than that nap, she had been awake for thirty-nine hours straight, ever since her Wednesday morning had begun just after three o'clock, when she woke up worrying about . . .

Her mother.

Without even meaning to, Heat took a glance toward the bus stop where Cynthia Heat had appeared on Tuesday morning. The pounding in her chest that had made sleep so impossible at 3:23 A.M. was back.

Her mother was not dead, but Maggs was; and Callan, clearly with help from someone on the outside, had escaped.

As she hailed a cab and began traveling south, toward the Tribeca loft she and Rook shared, she tried to force thoughts about her mother from her mind.

But they just wouldn't leave. Her mother was out there, somewhere. That fact changed every other assumption in Nikki's existence. And by the time Nikki reached Rook's place—she was, she realized, back to thinking of it as Rook's place—she knew resistance to her new reality was totally futile.

She wouldn't be able to truly rest until her mother was safe. To pretend otherwise was an act of self-delusion that Nikki simply couldn't pull off. Finding her mother, saving her mother. That was now the main focus of her life.

And she had to do it alone. There had been too many bodies dropped already. Whatever was happening, she couldn't entangle Rook in it. The risk was too great. She was eighteen hours removed from thinking she had lost him forever. She simply couldn't go through anything like that again.

The only way to keep him alive was to keep him at a distance.

As the cab sped away, she knew what she needed to do, even though she already hated it. She pulled out her phone and punched the number for her realtor. Heat got the woman's voice mail, which was just as well. It would be easier this way.

"Yeah, hi, it's Nikki Heat," she said after the tone. "Look, I know this may seem sudden, but can we take my mother's apartment off the market? I'm going to need it for a while. Call me if you have any questions. Thanks."

She stowed her phone and then, before she could lose her courage, rode the lift up to Rook's loft.

As she inserted her key in the lock, she could already hear the sound of Barry White coming through the door. She pushed through it to find Rook, sitting on the couch, wearing a silk bathrobe and a come-hither smile.

On the table in front of him, there was champagne on ice, a pair of crystal flutes, a silver tray with oysters on it, and chocolate-dipped strawberries.

"Sorry if I went a little overboard," he said, pouring a glass for her. "I just thought we had a lot to celebrate. Now come and let me help you unburden your—"

"Rook," was all she said.

"Uh-oh," was his reply.

He stopped pouring the champagne, sinking the butt of the bottle back in the ice bucket.

"What's wrong?" he said.

Heat could feel the tears trying to form, but she willed them away. She needed to stay strong for this. She didn't know if she'd be able to convince Rook or not, but she knew this was the right thing to do.

She knew it in the deepest part of her heart.

"As long as my mother is out there, I can't . . . I can't be with you."

"What does that even mean?" Rook said.

"I have to go," Heat said. "I have to get my head right so we can have a happily ever after."

"Where is this coming from? Why are you giving up on your marriage?"

"I'm trying to save it," Heat insisted.

"By leaving me?" Rook said, and the pain on his face almost shattered something inside of Heat.

Rook rose from the couch. He walked up to her slowly, cautiously. It reminded Heat of the way he had wooed her in the first place, all those years before: cautiously, with tender patience and the recognition that a too-direct approach with someone so damaged would only scare her off.

"Look, if you have a problem, we have a problem," he said. "That's how this works."

"No, Rook," she said. "Not this time."

She whirled around and left the apartment before she could see just how much agony she had plunged him into. As she disappeared back down the elevator, she plugged her ears so she wouldn't hear his tortured voice calling after her.

She was on a bench, outside the loft. A strategically positioned tree guaranteed he couldn't look down and see her. But she could still look up at the warmth of the lights pouring from Rook's place. The tears wouldn't stop now. She had held them off as long as she could.

She didn't know how long she had been there, only that the sun was now down. She had turned off her phone. She knew Rook would be calling, texting, making his pleas and entreaties; he would try logical appeals, emotional appeals, whatever he could attempt. She wasn't sure she was strong enough to fend them off yet.

At least three times, she'd nearly changed her mind and walked back up to the loft. She imagined throwing herself in Rook's arms. They would cry together, make love, eat strawberries, then cry some more, then make love again.

It would be the easy thing to do. It would be the comfortable thing to do. It would be the selfish thing to do.

But Nikki Heat had never been about any of those things. And as soon as she'd thought about what she had to do—taking on an opponent whose dimensions were unknown but likely enormous—she realized she didn't have a choice.

Finding her mother had to be her only mission, her only purpose. She would be no kind of daughter until she did. And she would be no kind of wife while she was doing it.

Finally, when the tears would no longer come, she caught a cab uptown to her mother's place in Gramercy Park.

Or, Heat thought, she might as well start calling it what it was again: her place.

This had been her home, and her home alone, for more than a decade. It would serve as her sanctuary again—or, rather, as her base of operations.

Bob Aaronson was on doorman duty again.

"Good to see you, Miss Heat," he said. "Just checking on the old place again?"

"Actually, I'm going to be staying here for a while."

"That's wonderful," he said. "For how long?"

"I don't know," she admitted. "I just don't know."

She rode the elevator up to her floor, thinking of all the nights she had done this before Rook came into her life. She had been alone once and survived. She could be alone again . . . for a time.

And then? Then she'd have everything. Her mother. Her husband. It was the greatest happiness she could imagine, a perfect life she had never even allowed herself to consider before.

All she needed to make it happen was total discipline and focus.

The door wasn't sticky this time. It had, after all, just been used. And the air inside wasn't musty either. She had been there two nights before. The place remained untidy, just as she had left it.

But as soon as she took a second step inside the darkened space, there was something going off in her mind, some primitive part of her brain sounding an alarm. Whether it was a smell, or a disturbance in the air, or a sixth sense, Heat couldn't say.

She just suddenly knew she wasn't alone in the apartment.

Heat reached for her gun, drawing it from its holster as silently as she could. She took another step, listening intently for the sound of breathing, or for the creak of a floorboard, or for any small noise that would indicate where the intruder was.

Then she heard: "You can put your weapon away, Captain."

It was a man's voice, a familiar one. But Heat couldn't quite place it. With her weapon still raised she eased her free hand over toward a light switch and flicked it on.

Sitting there calmly in her mother's favorite chair was a ruggedly handsome man with dark hair, dark eyes, a square jaw, and an impressive build.

Heat recognized him immediately. He had, very briefly, been a suspect in a case she had caught a few years earlier, about a currency trader who had been brutally murdered. She had since come to learn that he was considered one of the greatest assets of the US government, a man who had saved the world many times over.

"Derrick Storm?" she said in disbelief.

"Hello, Nikki," he said. "We need to talk about your mother."